PHOBOS
MAYAN FEAR

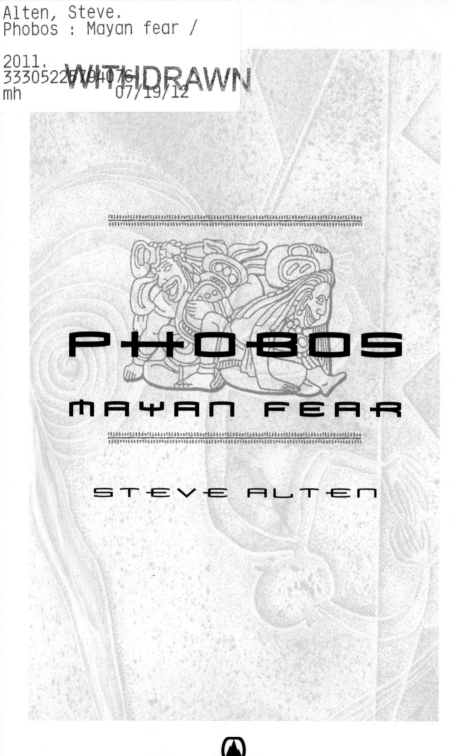

PHOBOS
MAYAN FEAR

STEVE ALTEN

TOR®

A TOM DOHERTY ASSOCIATES BOOK
NEW YORK

PHOBOS: MAYAN FEAR

A Tor Book
Published by Tom Doherty Associates, LLC
175 Fifth Avenue
New York, NY 10010

www.tor-forge.com

Tor® is a registered trademark of Tom Doherty Associates, LLC.

Library of Congress Cataloging-in-Publication Data

Alten, Steve.
    Phobos : Mayan fear / Steve Alten. — 1st ed.
        p. cm.
    "A Tom Doherty Associates book."
    ISBN 978-0-7653-3033-8
    1. End of the world—Fiction.   I. Title.
    PS3551.L764P47 2011
    813'.54—dc22   2011021554

First Edition: October 2011

Printed in the United States of America

0 9 8 7 6 5 4 3 2 1

For my father
Lawrence Alten
in loving memory

And for my friend and literary manager
Danny Baror
with love and respect

Acknowledgments

It is with great pride and appreciation that I acknowledge those who contributed to the completion of *Phobos: Mayan Fear* and the continued success of the entire Domain 2012 series.

First and foremost, to the great people at Tor/Forge, with special thanks to Tom Doherty and his family—my editor, Eric Raab, and his assistant (now editor) Whitney Ross. Thank you to my copy editor, M. Longbrake. My gratitude and appreciation to my personal editor, Lou Aronica at the Fiction Studio (laronica@fictionstudio.com), whose advice remains invaluable, and to my literary agent, Danny Baror of Baror International, for his friendship and dedication. Thanks as well to his assistant, Heather Baror-Shapiro.

A very special thanks to Dr. Steven Greer, former chairman of the Department of Emergency Medicine at Caldwell Memorial Hospital in North Carolina, and the founder and director of CSETI and the Disclosure Project, who generously allowed me to use quotes from his incredible press conference held on May 9, 2001, at the National Press Club in Washington, D.C. I encourage everyone to visit his website at www.DisclosurePro ject.org and to watch the entire news conference. As always, my gratitude to my cover artist, Erik Hollander (www.HollanderDesignLab.com), for his amazing cover art, and to forensic artist William McDonald (www.alien UFOart.com) for the original artwork found within these pages.

A heartfelt thanks to the brilliant Jack Harbach O'Sullivan, who offered me his scientific advice; my friend and webmaster, Leisa Coffman, for her continued dedication; and editor Barbara Becker, who also works tirelessly in the Adopt-An-Author program.

To my wife, Kim, and my kids, Kelsey and Branden, for their love and tolerance of the long hours involved in my writing career, and last, to my readers and fans, who have given this series continued life beyond 2012 . . . mere words cannot express my gratitude.

8

Author's Note

Phobos is the third book in the Mayan Doomsday Prophecy series that began with the release of *Domain* in 1999 and continued with *Resurrection* in 2004. Back in 1999, few people knew about the 2012 prophecy, and fewer still probably cared. Nevertheless, over the years I have often been asked, "Do you think humanity will really end on the winter solstice of 2012?" My answer is always to explain that either a natural disaster (asteroid strikes, Yellowstone caldera erupts) or man-made threats (biological weapons—see Fort Detrick and Battelle Labs) could do the job. As the 2012 date approached and man's ego gave us runaway greed, corruption, and new lows in human morality, I often wondered if we'd even make it to 2012.

    Phobos simply scares me. Had I known about this very real threat when I penned *Domain* I would have written the book you now hold in your hands back then. But this threat didn't exist back then, and ultimately the series is better for it. Still, *Phobos* gives me nightmares, just as its conclusions scare a small minority of scientists attempting to use legal action to shut down a ten-billion-dollar science experiment. Sadly, unless the silent majority gets behind their gallant effort, far worse than the Mayan prophecy may come true. Theoretically, it may already be under way.

    Whenever possible, I seek out the advice of experts whose opinions can improve key parts of the story. Upon reading the original conclusions I put forth in *Phobos*, a quantum physicist far smarter than this former Penn State physical education major rendered the following comment:

> Steve, I'm "wowed." Aside from the story line à la CERN Hadron: if {IF!} your scenario were a naturally occurring phenomenon (and I perceive that very well might be fact) then the posit that your description makes is indeed the very process of planetary expansion with the "monster" rather becoming a quasi-white-hole aka balanced gray hole---->core-star---->making the very planet a version of a plasma-breach transdimensional bleed-through reactor---->AND these reactors DO EXIST and the SUPERCOLLIDERS are "inadvertently" COPIES of the "general" ELECTROMAGNETIC RING that these plasma-breach hyper-gravity-lobe bleed-through reactors actually are . . .

Let me make two points abundantly clear: I have no idea what the hell that means, and my brain hurts when I read it. What I do know is that, as a writer of science-based "faction," I take pride in researching my topic to exhaustion before penning digestible conclusions designed to entertain my readers while standing up to the scrutiny of experts. And that's why *Phobos* scares me: first because I know the scenario is plausible; and second because anytime you combine man's ego with atom splitting or colliding, bad things are apt to happen.

As you read this passage they are happening right now.

In Geneva.

All should leave Geneva; Saturn turns from gold to iron.
The contrary positive ray will exterminate everything.
There will be signs in the sky before this.

—NOSTRADAMUS, CENTURY 9, QUATRAIN 44

The LHC [Large Hadron Collider in Geneva] is certainly,
by far, the biggest jump into the unknown.

—BRIAN COX, CERN PHYSICIST

PHOBOS
MAYAN FEAR

WARNING:

Unauthorized access or viewing of the following document without the appropriate authorizations will result in permanent incarceration or sanction by authorized use of deadly force.

TOP SECRET / MAJESTIC-12

PROJECT GOLDEN FLEECE
EXTRATERRESTRIAL HUMAN SUBSPECIES (HUNAHPU)
&
ACCESS TO ZERO-POINT ENERGY

6 NOVEMBER 2042

The following report summarizes GOLDEN FLEECE, an UMBRA-LEVEL NASA program initiated outside of MJ-12 jurisdiction in January of 2013 by President Ennis Chaney following the discovery of an extraterrestrial starship (*Balam*) buried beneath the Kukulcan Pyramid (Mayan, circa AD 900) in the Yucatan Peninsula (Chichen Itza). Subsequent investigation of subjects involved in discovery and activation of spacecraft led to the confirmation of a new subspecies of *Homo sapiens*—classification: <u>Hunahpu</u>. DNA origins trace insemination into humanoid gene pool 10,000 years ago (est.). Hunahpu subspecies has (potential) access to zero-point energy. Based on pressure by President Chaney, all atom-smashing experiments were banned in 2013, and the Large Hadron Collider (LHC) at CERN (Geneva) was shut down. This report seeks to reverse that moratorium.

<u>BACKGROUND:</u>
On 14 December 2012, at approximately 14:30 hours EST, an electromagnetic force field equivalent to several billion amperes activated across the ionosphere, destroying more than 1,200 inbound nuclear ICBMs and SLBMs fired from US, Russian, and Chinese launch platforms. NORAD traced the EM array to nodes and relay junctures within and/or below the ancient structures of Angkor Wat (Cambodia), the Great Pyramid of Giza (Egypt), Stonehenge (Britain), the Pyramid of the Sun at Teotihuacan (Mexico), and under the fortress of Sacsayhuaman (Peru). Triangulation of the EM relay junctures pinpointed the origin of the pulse to the Kukulcan Pyramid in Chichen Itza, specifically to a vessel buried <u>beneath</u> the structure. Discovery/access of the starship and subsequent activation of the EM array was credited to MICHAEL GABRIEL and DOMINIQUE VAZQUEZ.

MICHAEL GABRIEL – bio:
American male, Caucasian, age 37 at time of event. Only child of archaeologists Julius Gabriel and Maria Rosen-Gabriel. Mother died of pancreatic cancer (1990); father died of heart failure in 2001 while speaking at a Harvard lecture hosted by PIERRE BORGIA (secretary of state 2008–2012). Gabriel and Borgia had been colleagues investigating extraterrestrial insemination into ancient cultures until a personal rift severed the relationship. According to eyewitnesses, Borgia's verbal attacks during the lecture preceded Professor Gabriel's cardiac arrest and the subsequent physical retaliation upon Borgia by Gabriel's son, Michael. Pierre Borgia lost his right eye during the attack. Judge sentenced Michael Gabriel to fifteen years in a mental asylum. Gabriel spent most of the next eleven years in solitary confinement before he escaped with the assistance of his intern, DOMINIQUE VAZQUEZ.

DOMINIQUE VAZQUEZ – bio:
Guatemalan female, Mesoamerican, age 31 at time of event. No information available on biological parents. Immigrated to America at age nine following reported death of her mother. Lived with a cousin in Tampa, Florida, until school officials filed sexual abuse charges against the relative. Adopted by foster parents (Edith and Isadore Axler) in 1998. Graduated from Florida State University with a degree in psychology. Attended FSU for her master's degree. Interned at South Florida Evaluation and Treatment Center in Miami in September 2012, assigned to patient Michael Gabriel. Vazquez aided Gabriel's escape in December 2012.

SUBJECTS' ASSOCIATION WITH MAYAN DOOMSDAY EVENT:
On 21 December 2012, a "transdimensional" extraterrestrial biological was released from a vessel located beneath the Chicxulub impact crater (Gulf of Mexico). The biological immediately targeted the EM pulse originating from Chichen Itza. Mexican and US Armed Forces failed to stop the entity. Michael Gabriel was able to deactivate the biological using an energy beam originating from the buried starship. Gabriel then entered the orifice of the terminated entity. Upon his entry, a wormhole appeared in the ionosphere and retracted both the entity and Michael Gabriel into its opening. Michael Gabriel's status remains unknown.

POST MAYAN DOOMSDAY EVENT:
Starship *Balam* (GOLDEN FLEECE) was secretly excavated and relocated to a top-secret facility at Cape Canaveral. Dr. DAVID MOHR (NASA/MAJ-12) was appointed director of GOLDEN FLEECE in 2013. On 22 September 2013, DOMINIQUE VAZQUEZ gave birth to twin boys (MICHAEL GABRIEL, father).

GABRIEL TWINS

JACOB GABRIEL – bio:
White hair, Mayan-blue (turquoise) eyes. Superior intellect, bordering on schizophrenic. Advanced physical attributes (see HUNAHPU gene). Following a staged public "death" in 2027, subject was sequestered at his request (age 14 through 20) at GOLDEN FLEECE facility where he advised Dr. Mohr on extraterrestrial vessel's technologies while "training" for what he claimed was the twins' prophesied journey to Xibalba (Mayan underworld, pronounced *She-bal-ba;* see Hunahpu mythology). On 23 November 2033, *Balam* activated for the first time and flew into Earth-space with Jacob and (GOLDEN FLEECE DIRECTOR) Mohr aboard. Two days later, on 25 November 2033, the *Balam* landed on the field of the University of Miami football stadium. Mohr exited the craft, which departed moments later with Jacob Gabriel and his mother, Dominique Vazquez, on board. Eyewitnesses to the event included Dr. DAVID MOHR, EVELYN MOHR (wife), RYAN BECK (bodyguard), MITCHELL KURTZ (former CIA assassin), ENNIS CHENEY (former president), LAUREN BECKMEYER (fiancée of Immanuel Gabriel), and IMMANUEL GABRIEL (Jacob's twin brother).

IMMANUEL GABRIEL – bio:
Dark hair, black eyes. Though subject graded out top one percent of population both intellectually and physically, Hunahpu gene remained dormant in this twin. Following his public "death" in 2027, subject was given a new identity as SAMUEL AGLER. Attended University of Miami as two-sport scholarship athlete. Engaged to LAUREN BECKMEYER, also a student-athlete. On 25 November 2033, subject refused to board *Balam* with his twin. Moments after *Balam* departed, Lauren Beckmeyer was terminated by biocide cartridge. Assassin most

likely worked for LILITH AURELIA MABUS (see Hunahpu bio). Current whereabouts of Immanuel Gabriel: UNKNOWN.

SUMMARY OF RESEARCH ON SUBSPECIES: HUNAHPU

<u>EXTRATERRESTRIAL ORIGIN:</u>
Unknown.

<u>EARTH ORIGIN:</u>
Lineage traces back to three ancient "teachers." KUKULCAN (Mayan), QUETZALCOATL (Aztec), and VIRACOCHA (Inca). All three males were described as tall Caucasians with white hair, matching facial hair, Mayan-blue (turquoise) eyes, and elongated skull. Kukulcan is credited with construction of his pyramid and with the astronomy that factored into the Mayan calendar. Quetzalcoatl is credited with Sun Pyramid used in EM relay. Viracocha is credited with Nazca drawings and lines.

<u>HUNAHPU MYTHOLOGY:</u>
Mayan Popol Vuh's creation story describes ONE HUNAHPU (First Father) as an Adam-like figure who was decapitated by the Lords of the Underworld (Xibalba). Genesis 6 (Old Testament) describes similar figures as "Sons of God" (Nephilim) who cross-bred with human women. MJ-12 classifies these extraterrestrials as "NORDICS."

<u>HUNAHPU DNA – CHARACTERISTICS:</u>
- Superior intellect
- Superior strength and senses
- Subjects possessing dominant Hunahpu genetics are able to access a higher dimension (corridor) of physical consciousness, referred to as "the Nexus." Subjects who enter the corridor experience a 57 percent reduction of time/space, correlating with a 33 percent increase in gravity (see DAVID MOHR research studies on subject JACOB GABRIEL).
- Hunahpu DNA is associated with <u>Rh negative blood types.</u>

Excerpted from DAVID MOHR studies:

The Rh factor is a protein found in human blood that links Homo sapiens *DNA to primates, specifically the Rhesus monkey. Eighty-five percent of the world's population is Rh positive. Conversely, 15 percent of the Earth's human population is Rh negative, meaning the evolutionary link to primates DOES NOT EXIST. Rh negative factor has been confirmed in subjects MARIA ROSEN-GABRIEL (exhumed), MICHAEL GABRIEL, DOMINIQUE VAZQUEZ, and JACOB AND IMMANUEL GABRIEL. Extensive historical research into the Rosen maternal lineage reveals a family tree that traces back to the Inca civilization and possibly Viracocha himself. While the Vazquez family tree (the Gabriel twins' mother) remains unknown, DNA and circumstantial evidence involving Dominique Vazquez's heritage correlates highly with a Kukulcan/Mayan lineage. The "Hunahpu wildcard" is LILITH AURELIA (MABUS), Jacob's Nexus "playmate" during his childhood years. The exhumed bodies of MADELINA AURELIA and CECILIA AURELIA (Lilith's biological mother and maternal grandmother) confirm a maternal heritage that dates back to the Aztec culture.*

LILITH AURELIA MABUS – bio:
Born on same day as Gabriel twins. Half Mesoamerican (mother), half African American (father). Dark hair, Mayan-blue (turquoise) eyes. Mother (MADELINA AURELIA) murdered by father (VIRGIL ROBINSON) shortly after birth. Aurelia clan traces back to early Aztecs, possibly Quetzalcoatl. Subject fits Hunahpu profile, with extreme psychotic tendencies exacerbated during an abusive childhood and adolescence. At age 18, Lilith married LUCIEN MABUS, CEO of Mabus Tech Industries. Lilith took over as CEO of PROJECT H.O.P.E. (space tourism organization) two years later following Lucien's death (relatives accuse Lilith of poisoning her husband, no charges were filed). In 2034, Lilith gave birth to DEVLIN AUGUSTUS MABUS, believed to have been sired by JACOB GABRIEL. While medical examinations of both Lilith and her son are strictly prohibited, MJ-12 genetic scientists have formulated the following Hunahpu genetic family history:

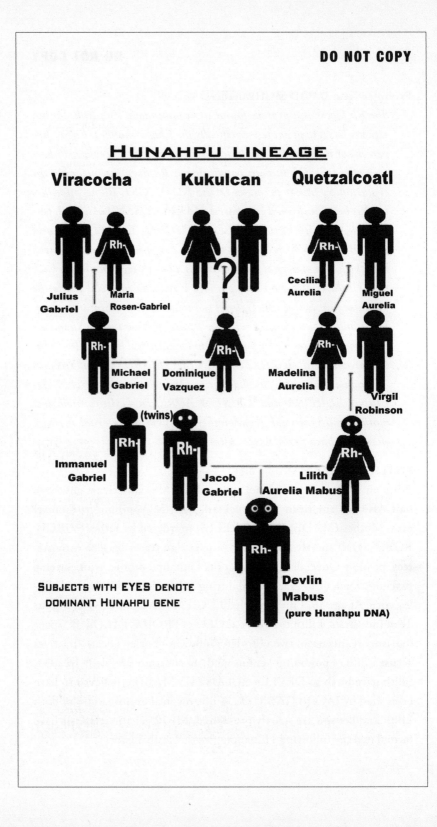

HUNAHPU LINEAGE

Viracocha **Kukulcan** **Quetzalcoatl**

Julius Gabriel — Maria Rosen-Gabriel (Rh-)

Cecilia Aurelia (Rh-) — Miguel Aurelia

Michael Gabriel (Rh-) — Dominique Vazquez (Rh-)

Madelina Aurelia (Rh-)

Virgil Robinson

(twins)

Immanuel Gabriel (Rh-)

Jacob Gabriel (Rh-) — Lilith Aurelia Mabus (Rh-)

Devlin Mabus (pure Hunahpu DNA) (Rh-)

SUBJECTS WITH EYES DENOTE DOMINANT HUNAHPU GENE

RECOMMENDATIONS

The *Balam* possessed zero-point energy, the means to achieve trans-galactic travel beyond light speed. This information is vital to MAJESTIC-12 and US interests as it can be used to provide limitless clean power to a world population (10.2 billion) now experiencing major food and fuel shortages. It is highly likely that subjects IMMANUEL GABRIEL and DAVID MOHR possess at least a limited knowledge of zero-point energy. Both subjects are fugitives and remain at large. While all efforts to apprehend subjects and their associates should be maximized, MJ-12 is recommending that all suspensions on the LARGE HADRON COLLIDER *be lifted at this time* and that the CERN atom smasher experiments in Geneva be restarted as soon as possible to allow MJ-12 physicists access to zero-point energy.

W. Louis McDonald (ret.)
GOLDEN FLEECE

Balam *starship: Excavated September 2013*
MJ-12 photo 13-GF-71

Existence and extermination have one thing in common—they are both subject to the law of cause and effect.

—PROFESSOR JULIUS GABRIEL,

AUGUST 24, 2001

PART 2

THE EFFECT

The countdown to "D-day" has started. Our group has been preparing for LHC [Large Hadron Collider] data for many years now and we are all truly excited about the prospect of finally getting a glimpse of whatever surprises Nature has in store for us.

—DR. PEDRO TEIXEIRA-DIAS,
LEADER OF THE ATLAS GROUP
AT ROYAL HOLLOWAY,
UNIVERSITY OF LONDON

The Final Papers of
Julius Gabriel, PhD

Cambridge University archives

AUGUST 23, 2001

*P*hobos: *a Greek term, translated as "morbid fear."*
    Fear: a state of mind, inducing anxiety. The trepidation preceding an unwanted outcome. Fear is the mind-killer that disrupts the higher aspects of brain activity, overruling common sense.
    It has been argued that modern man suffers from six basic phobias: Fear of poverty. Fear of old age. Loss of love. Criticism. Poor health. And, of course, our most overwhelming fear—fear of death.

My name is Julius Gabriel. I am an archaeologist, a scientist who investigates humanity's past in search of the truth. Truth is the light that eliminates the darkness induced by fear. Conversely, lies are the weapons of darkness, designed to spread fear.
    What you are about to read is the culmination of more than half a century of research that reveals startling truths about man's existence, our intended purpose, and our prophesied demise. The evidence that follows has never been made public, for to do so would

have violated a dozen nondisclosure agreements that would have resulted in my incarceration and very likely a quiet execution made to look like a suicide—ramifications rendered moot following a recent visit to my cardiologist.

In truth, my decision to finally go public with these papers was based more on anger than my own intended exit strategy. I am sickened by an illegal and unconstitutional black ops program that exists solely to empower and enrich members of the military industrial complex and the fossil fuel industry. These pseudo-emperors have committed high treason against our entire species. They have lied to Congress and continue to operate outside the bounds of the Constitution of the United States, thereby voiding the previously mentioned nondisclosure agreements. Worse, they have murdered one president, disrupted the administration of another, and have refused to be held accountable by any office, though they are funded with an annual budget that exceeds $100 billion. In order to preserve their secrets, they have killed people of fame and fortune and innocent bystanders alike, and have orchestrated false flag events that have led to wars. Of most importance to mankind's future, they covet and have bottlenecked advanced technologies in the field of energy and propulsion that would not only provide free endless power for all but avert a looming global catastrophe.

To ensure the survival of their "Ivory Towers of Power" they are prepared to unleash a final false flag event that will lead to planetary fear and eventually the weaponization of space. Before that happens, or perhaps as a result, every living being on this planet shall die.

Am I being overly dramatic? Keep reading and you too will know what real fear is.

Within these pages I am going to reveal everything to you, the good, the bad, and the mind-boggling truth—from the very secrets of existence that predate the Big Bang to the big bang that shall eradicate our species. In the process, you will come to understand that the universe is not what it seems, nor is human existence, and that this ticking clock of physicality that begins at conception and terminates with our final breath is neither the end nor the beginning, but an elaborate ruse constructed by our Creator . . . as a test.

And we are failing miserably.

Judgment Day is coming, and we have reaped this destruction upon ourselves. Greed, corruption, hatred, selfishness . . . most of all sheer ignorance—all brought about by the one human weakness that continues to define and poison our species even as it lures us toward the precipice of our very demise: our ego.

The pages you are about to read will unveil forty years of lies and deception, but do not covet the truth: enlightenment comes with a price. Seed the information to the four winds, be the cause of your own hard-won salvation. For what hangs in the balance is nothing less than a fate prophesied by every ancient civilization and every major religion . . . the End of Days.

Phobos: fear.

Fear is the elephant in the living room. To overcome the mind paralysis of fear, you must master it, you must, in a sense, consume it. But how can one consume something as large as an elephant?

The answer, of course, is one digestible bite at a time.

To digest the Doomsday Event requires that I not only deliver the facts but that I do so in their proper context lest you dismiss this document as merely a work of fiction—a source of entertainment. It is neither! Question the author; take nothing within these pages for granted. Research every fact. Cross-reference any statement and every conclusion that draws your ire. Only then will your mind begin to accept the truth; only then will you realize that there are evil entities lurking in the shadows playing with matches, and unless you open your eyes and act they will incinerate the world.

Like it or not, accept it or not, a Doomsday Event is coming. How can I be so sure? Because, dear reader, the event has already happened! Even more bizarre—some of you reading these very words were there to witness the end.

Confused? So was I, until I stopped thinking like a third-dimensional creature trapped by my own perception of linear time and unraveled the truth.

Before you render a verdict, allow me to present my case.

As previously stated, I am an archaeologist. In 1969, having earned my doctorate degree from Cambridge University, I set out on a journey of discovery, motivated more by curiosity than fear. My inspiration was the Mayan calendar, a two-thousand-year-old instrument of time and space that predicted humanity's reign to end on December 21, 2012.

Doomsday.

Let us pause a quick moment and make that forkful of elephant meat more digestible. A calendar, by definition, is a device used to measure time, in this case the amount of time it takes for our planet to revolve once around the sun. Somehow a society of jungle-dwelling Indians managed to create an instrument of time and space that, despite being 1,500 years older than our modern-day Gregorian calendar, remains one ten-thousandth of a day more accurate.

The Mayan calendar is a device composed of three cogged wheels operating in a fashion similar to the gears of a clock, plus a fourth calendar—the Long Count—which details twenty-year epochs, called katuns. Each katun is a prophecy in its own right, detailing happenings on Earth in accordance with the astrological ebb and flow of the cosmos.

The Doomsday Event is aligned with precession. Precession is the slow wobble of our planet on its axis. It takes the Earth 25,800 years to complete one cycle of precession—the exact amount of time that defines the Mayan calendar's five great cycles, the current and last one terminating on the day of 4 Ahau, 3 Kankin—the winter solstice of 2012.

How were the Maya, a race of Indians who never mastered the wheel, able to create such an advanced scientific instrument that prophesied events over thousands, perhaps millions of katuns? How were they able to plot our precise position in the cosmos, comprehend concepts like dark matter, or fathom the existence of the black hole at the center of our galaxy? Most important: how were the ancient Maya able to describe events that had yet to happen?

The simplistic answer is they couldn't. In reality, it was their two mysterious leaders who possessed the knowledge.

The first was the great Mayan teacher, Kukulcan, who came to the Yucatan Peninsula a thousand years ago. Described as a tall Caucasian man with silky white hair, a matching beard, and intense azure-blue eyes, this "messenger of love" who preached against the blood sacrifice remains a paradox of existence, for not only does his knowledge of science and astronomy dwarf our own, but his presence in Mesoamerica predates the arrival of the first white explorers (invaders) to the Americas by five hundred years.

Still convinced you are reading fiction? Travel to the Yucatan and visit Chichen Itza. Harbored within this long-lost Mayan city is the Kukulcan Pyramid, a perfect ziggurat of stone, stained with the blood of ten thousand human sacrifices intended to stave off doomsday in the wake of the great teacher's passing. Ninety-one steps adorn each of the temple's four sides; add the summit platform and you have three hundred sixty-five, as in the days of the year. Arrive on the fall or spring equinox and you'll witness the appearance of a serpent's shadow on the northern balustrade, a thousand-year-old special effect constructed to warn modern man of the cataclysm to come.

The second mysterious Mayan was Chilam Balam, the greatest prophet in Mesoamerican history. Chilam is the title bestowed upon a priest who gives prophecies, Balam translates as jaguar. The Jaguar Prophet was born in the Yucatan in the late 1400s and is known for his nine books of prophecies—one of which foretold the coming of strangers from the east who would "establish a new religion."

In 1519, Cortés and his invading Spanish armada arrived in the Yucatan, armed with guns, priests, and Bibles, just as Chilam Balam had prophesied.

Though he is not credited for it, I strongly suspect Chilam Balam to be the author of the Mayan Popol Vuh, the Mesoamerican equivalent of the Bible, at the heart of which is the Mayan creation story. Much like the Old Testament, the Popol Vuh's stories contain historical mythology that strains the boundaries of credibility. Like our own Judeo-Christian Bible, the Mayan creation story was never intended to be taken literally (more on that later). Instead, it was encrypted with an ancient knowledge that unveils the truth about mankind's future and past.

Following decades of work, I managed to decode the Mayan creation story. And therein lies yet another paradox, for the deciphered text reveals incredible details regarding Homo sapiens's mysterious ascension as an intelligent force of nature—only the evolutionary events described in the Popol Vuh took place millions of years ago!

In archaeology, we call this a paradox. In layman's terms, one might call it a déjà *vu. By definition, déjà vu is the uneasy feeling that one has witnessed or experienced a new situation previously—as if the event has already happened.*

It has.

As incredible as it sounds, I have discovered that our physical universe is caught within a temporal time loop that begins and ends with our destruction on the winter solstice of 2012, and the very instrument that once more shall be responsible for the Doomsday Event has been constructed on our watch—

—funded by our tax dollars.

—JG

Note:

Professor Gabriel's final papers were subsequently banned from publication or public review as per ruling of the Massachusetts superior court (Borgia v. Gabriel estate; Hon. Judge Thomas Cubit presiding). The Cambridge University archaeology department petitioned and received the papers following Professor Gabriel's death on August 24, 2001, and his son Michael's incarceration at the Bridgewater State mental facility for the criminally insane. The Pentagon successfully appealed the ruling to the British courts, who ordered the papers sealed and not to be reviewed. They remained archived until 2032.

33

1

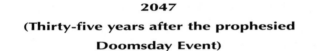

2047
(Thirty-five years after the prophesied
Doomsday Event)

ATLANTIC OCEAN

107 NAUTICAL MILES SOUTHWEST OF BERMUDA

(BERMUDA TRIANGLE)

APRIL 16, 2047

Displacing 130,000 tons, the cruise ship *Paradise Lost* knifes through the deep blue waters of the Atlantic, its twin propellers churning a quarter-mile-long foamy trail. A thousand feet long, with a 120-foot beam that supports thirteen guest decks, the ocean liner is powered by the latest in NiCE (Nonpolluting i-Combustion Engineering) system design. Replacing the old steam-driven turbines (a gallon of fuel for every fifty feet of propulsion), the ship's turbines draw power from the primary phase of the NiCE system—a five-megawatt solar plant. Occupying an acre of upper deck space in the stern is a water tower, surrounded by seventeen hundred rotating solar mirrors. As sunlight strikes the mirrors, the magnified heat is redirected to the tower and its built-in boiler, raising internal temperatures to a superhot 875 degrees Fahrenheit. The generated steam is used to turn twin turbines located in the engine room, driving the ship's propellers.

Phase two of the NiCE system kicks in once the boat is under way. Smokestacks that once belched toxic plumes of carbon dioxide have been replaced by wind turbines. As the ocean liner moves forward, these towering lightbulb-shaped blades capture the steady supply of wind, converting the kinetic energy into enough electricity to power every device on the floating hotel.

Like all cruise ships, *Paradise Lost* is first and foremost a pleasure boat. Inside the massive craft, virtual reality suites augment the boat's five-star restaurants, Broadway-caliber shows, and casinos. Outside, the six open-air decks are dominated by "hydro-leisure activities," at the center of which are two cascading waterfalls that churn a lazy river, rapids, and pit stops at open buffets.

For guests preferring something a bit more sedentary, "smart chairs" are situated around the lagoon and adult-only privacy areas. Designed to levitate eight inches above a grated deck that generates a maglev (magnetic levitation) cushion, these lounge chairs not only are luxurious but also eliminate seasickness. Rollers and robotic fingers housed within the chairs' microfiber cushions deliver everything from a soothing massage to deep-tissue shiatsu. Dial up the chair's "body spritzer" and one can cool off with a pure water mist or, for an additional fee, apply a vitamin-rich emollient (dermal dips having eliminated the need for SPF lotion applications a decade earlier).

For the 2,400 passengers aboard the *Paradise Lost*, the eight-day round-trip cruise from Fort Lauderdale to Bermuda is paradise found.

The privacy decks surrounding Dolphin Lagoon are filled to capacity—five hundred passengers stretch out on lounge chairs, drifting in and out of consciousness while they await the next cattle call for first dinner.

Jennifer Ventrice lies on her back facing the late afternoon sun, her assigned recliner situated between the starboard rail and the lazy river. The seventy-three-year-old Brooklyn native is awake, watching an opti-vision movie projected inside her wraparound i-glasses. Despite her sensory comforts, Jennifer is nervous. It has been fourteen years since she and her husband were forced to flee the United States, and though her passport and embedded smart chip reflect her new identity, she knows her spouse's enemies have long tentacles and other "less conventional" means of tracking them down.

Relax, Eve. You already made it through international checkpoints in London and Miami without any problem, security in Bermuda should be—

No! She clenches her eyes shut, the self-scolding inflection causing the movie to pause. *It's Jennifer, not Eve. Jennifer . . . Jennifer!*

She powers off the movie, momentarily blinded by the sunlight reflecting off the ocean until the smart lenses adjust their tint. *This was all Dave's fault. Why couldn't he have allowed me to use my real first name as an alias? Didn't he realize how hard it was to think of myself as anything but Eve?*

For the thousandth time she thinks back to the date—November 25, 2033—the day Evelyn Mohr ceased to exist, the day Lilith Mabus forced Evelyn's husband and the rest of their entourage into exile. Only twenty years old at the time, the unleashed widow of the late billionaire Lucien Mabus had firmly entrenched herself as CEO of Mabus Tech Industries and its space tourism company, Project H.O.P.E. Within months, Lilith had used her newfound influence in Washington to coerce President John Zwawa into allowing MTI to take control of Golden Fleece, a covert NASA project overseen by Evelyn's husband, Dave.

What Lilith Mabus sought was access to zero-point energy, a warp-drive propulsion system that powered the extraterrestrial starship excavated back in 2013, which she hoped to use on her Mars Colony shuttles.

What she found instead was her long-lost soul mate, Jacob Gabriel.

Jacob and his twin brother, Immanuel, had faked their deaths years ago. Intoxicated by Lilith's pheromones, Jacob submitted to the one act his father had expressly warned him about—copulating with his schizophrenic Hunahpu cousin.

Jacob and his mother had left the Earth aboard the extraterrestrial starship on November 25, 2033, leaving behind Immanuel Gabriel, his two bodyguards, and the Mohrs as fugitives from Majestic-12 and Lilith Mabus. Identity changes accompanied relocations in Canada, Mexico, Honduras, and Peru, Evelyn Mohr playing the dutiful role of supportive wife while her husband continued to advise and tutor Jacob's still-evolving dark-haired Hunahpu twin.

Six years ago Evelyn declared she had had enough. While she understood Manny was "special," she yearned to stay rooted and establish a life, something the earthbound twin, still filled with anger and angst, was loath to do. Dave finally relented, agreeing to leave his protégé with the two bodyguards so that he and Eve could live out their days in peace.

Sigerfjord was a barrier island, one of hundreds surrounding the coast of Norway. Isolated from the mainland, with a population that rarely exceeded eight hundred, the remote location seemed beyond even Lilith Mabus's long reach. Dave quickly endeared himself to the local community after repairing a malfunctioning turbine at Sigerfjord's geothermal plant, while "Jennifer" used her legal experience to find gainful employment at a law firm.

Peeking beneath her smart glasses, Evelyn Mohr steals a glance at the young woman lying topless in the lounge chair on her right. May Foss is her employer's daughter, a daddy's girl from the neighboring island of Gjaesingen. As a present for graduating law school, May's father had promised his daughter and her best friend, Anna Reedy, an all-expenses-paid, two-week vacation anywhere in the world, and the twenty-four-year-olds chose Miami.

The entrepreneur had agreed, with one stipulation: Foss's American assistant, Jennifer, would serve as escort.

Dave had naturally protested, but to deny her boss's request would have sent up red flags. The job was good, and relocating again was risky, so the former Mrs. Evelyn Mohr packed her bags, assuring her husband she'd be safe.

After six years living in Norway, the South Florida heat was heaven.

"May? May, where are you?"

May sits up, waving to her friend. "Over here."

Anna Reedy hurries up the aisle, the dark-haired Italian beauty flush from running. "May, I'm in love!"

"Again?"

Evelyn smiles to herself, eavesdropping on the girls' conversation.

"His name is Julian. He's tall, six feet six, with long brown hair and the physique of a Greek god. And those eyes—"

"How old is he?"

"Twenty-nine and single. And he's traveling with a friend."

"Have you seen the friend?"

"No, but so what? They want to meet you. You too, Jen."

Evelyn's skin tingles. "Me? Why me?"

"I don't know. I showed him our photo, the one of the three of us in South Beach, and he asked me to introduce you."

May nudges her. "Maybe the Greek god likes older women."

Fubitch! Lilith has our images streaming everywhere, along with offers of a sizeable reward. What if . . .

"Wait here, I'll go get him."

"Anna, wait!" Evelyn is about to go after her when the buzz of the i-glasses' phone reverberates in her ears. She taps the control by her right temple, accepting the call.

David Mohr's liver-spotted face replaces the eastern horizon of the Atlantic. "Jen, where the hell are you? According to my GPS, you're somewhere in the *fukabitching* Bermuda Triangle."

Her husband's attempt to use streaming slang profanity elicits a smile. "Calm down, *Erik*. The girls wanted to take a cruise. It was either Bermuda or Cuba."

"Oh, geez. No, you made the right choice. Cuba, gee whiz. If you have so much as a traffic violation, island security demands an anal probe."

"I won't ask you how you know about that. Miss me?"

"Intensely."

"Know what I miss?"

"Jennifer—"

"I can't help it. Being back in Florida . . . the warm weather . . . the palm trees—"

Without warning, the ship shudders violently, as if its keel has run aground. May screams as she's tossed from her feet, along with hundreds of other passengers, everyone looking around, confused and fearful.

"Did we hit something?"

"Are we sinking?"

Dave Mohr yells to regain his wife's attention. "Jen, what is it? What's wrong?"

"I don't know. It felt like the engines seized. Maybe we hit . . . whoa!"

Without warning, the ocean liner rolls hard to port. Passengers scream, the listing deck causing hundreds of levitating lounge chairs to flip like concentric circles of stacked dominoes.

Evelyn tumbles forward, landing hard against the starboard rail. Passengers are flung haphazardly across the shifting deck as the ship executes a radical course change.

After a long terrifying moment, the cruise ship levels out, continuing on its new heading—due west.

May helps Eve to her feet. "Jennifer, what's happening?"

"I don't know. Find Anna."

The girl fumbles with her bikini top as she runs off.

Eve turns her attention back to her husband. Dave appears in her right eye lens, the physicist frantically operating his projection screen computer, the free-floating images of the ocean liner appearing via satellite feed.

"Dave, what happened? Why have we changed course? Was it a tsunami? A rogue wave?"

"No seismic activity. No telltale ripples. No other ships in the area. I don't—" The scientist pauses, his already pale complexion losing color. "What in God's name is that?"

Robert Gibbons, Jr., rushes into the bridge, the disheveled captain demanding answers. "Mr. Swartz, report!"

First Officer Bradly T. Swartz hovers over his navigation board, clearly baffled. "Sir, it wasn't us. The ship appears to be caught in some sort of rogue current."

Captain Gibbons focuses his binoculars on the surface of the Atlantic, now rippling like a swiftly moving river.

"Captain, ship's compass has gone haywire. Zero degrees is now pointing . . . due west."

"What?"

"Sir, lookout has spotted something! Requesting your immediate presence."

Gibbons rushes out of the bridge, ascending a narrow flight of steel steps to the lookout post. An ensign steadies the deck-mounted scope, his eyes filled with fear. "It's a mile straight off our bow, sir. Never saw anything like it."

The captain presses his right eye to the spyglass's rubber eye guard. "Good God . . ."

Neither whirlpool nor maelstrom, it appears simply as a hole in the ocean, its dark circumference several miles in diameter. The Atlantic Ocean drains down its throat like a 360-degree Niagara Falls, its vortex inhaling the surrounding sea—along with the *Paradise Lost*.

The captain grabs the internal phone. "Change course! Forty degrees on the starboard rudder!" Without waiting for a reply, he races down the circular stairwell to the bridge. "Mr. Swartz?"

"Executing course change now, sir."

Gibbons stares at the ship's bow. *Come on . . . turn!*

The cruise ship sways to the right, meeting resistance. The boat shudders but is unable to escape the gravitational forces in play.

"No change, sir."

"Stop engines. Full reverse!"

"Full reverse, aye."

The propellers shut down, the bow veering back to port. Gibbons focuses his binoculars on the massive anomaly, now looming seven hundred yards away, its edge spanning the entire horizon, *dropping off . . . to where?*

The *Paradise Lost* shudders as its twin screws reverse and fight to catch hold of the sea. The ship's forward speed slows, but still they cannot break free.

The captain's heart pounds in his chest. "Mr. Halley, send an SOS. Inform the Coast Guard we need emergency airlift choppers. Warn all sea-faring vessels to stay clear of this area."

The stunned radioman manages a raspy, "Aye sir."

Deck officers line up by the bay windows, staring in fear and disbelief. A few attempt to call their loved ones—unable to get a signal.

A chorus of screams builds to a crescendo as passengers catch sight of what lies ahead.

Light-headed, his limbs shaking, Captain Gibbons finds his way to the command chair, a sickening feeling invading his gut as the 130,000-ton cruise ship slowly topples over the edge of the fourth dimensional vortex . . . into oblivion.

Screams of protest mute in Evelyn Mohr's consciousness, the sudden silence accompanied by the strangely familiar angular face of a dark-haired man, his azure-blue eyes radiating intensely behind his sunglasses, his powerful arms lifting her away from the listing deck to somehow carry her inside the ship, his muscular physique moving in defiance of the laws of physics. She experiences a quantum second of weightlessness before gravity's unleashed forces take over, simultaneously fragmenting and dispersing every cell in her body.

If we go on the way we are, we may not get through the next century at all. When there is a clear danger in the headlights, common sense says hit the brakes, but scientists often want to keep the foot hard down on the accelerator pedal.

—MARVIN MINSKY, PHD

The palatial mansion of Lilith Mabus, widow of the late billionaire Lucien Mabus, stretches along a private ocean lot in Manalapan, a small island town just north of Boynton Beach, Florida. The thirty-one room, three-story home features a seaside swimming pool complete with waterfall and swim-up bar, two tennis courts, a fitness center, a 1,200-square-foot grand salon illuminated by a six-thousand-pound crystal chandelier imported from a nineteenth-century French chateau, an observatory dome, and an eight-car garage, its floors paved in Saturnia marble. Each of the six bedroom suites has its own balcony facing the Atlantic, the mansion's windows self-cleaning, made with a thin metal oxide coating electrified to help rainwater to wash away loose particles. A small NiCE electrical station is located on the northern grounds, harnessing power from the sun and wind.

The newest addition to the oceanside luxury home is a configuration of satellite dishes situated in a concrete bunker on the south lawn. The receivers allow Lilith Mabus and her intel team to pirate a network of Pentagon surveillance satellites from the convenience of her home office, though "officially" they merely provide MTI's CEO the means of communicating with a fleet of space planes owned and operated by her subsidiary company, Project H.O.P.E.

The origins of America's space program can be traced back to the first Cold War, when the conflicting ideologies of the United States and the Soviet Union blossomed into a full-fledged race into space. President John F. Kennedy raised the bar in 1961 by setting a goal to land an American astronaut safely on the moon—a goal that was accomplished on July 20, 1969.

For the four decades that followed, space exploration floundered.

Part of the problem was a lack of clearly defined goals, exacerbated by President Nixon's decision to hinge NASA's future on the space shuttle—a nonexploratory Earth-orbiting vehicle hampered with design flaws that would lead to the fatal *Challenger* and *Columbia* disasters. With the rest of the outdated fleet reserved for "shuttle duty" to and from the International Space Station (yet another Earth-orbiting tortoise), the public's interest in the space program waned.

What NASA officials never knew was that all lunar missions had been permanently scrubbed as part of a top-secret directive that dated back to the Lyndon Johnson era. It was not until 2029 that a private company would break the military industrial complex's stranglehold on space exploration, the revolt led by a billionaire's son hell-bent on his own self destruction.

Lucien Mabus was born with a platinum spoon in his mouth. The only child of defense contractor Peter Mabus and his late wife, Carolyn, Lucien was raised by private tutors and athletic trainers for much of his childhood while his father mounted a political campaign to challenge the incumbent President Ennis Chaney for the White House. Bitter over losing the 2016 election, Mabus sought other avenues to rid the country of its leader. He was eventually "sanctioned" by the Gabriel twins' bodyguards after hiring an assassin to kill Jacob and Immanuel.

In shock over his father's murder, Lucien Mabus spent what remained of his teen years under the watchful eye of an uncle, who preferred to keep his defiant nephew confined to rehab centers rather than deal with the boy's ongoing drug and alcohol addictions. Lucien celebrated his emancipation on his eighteenth birthday by leaving his halfway house and tossing his court-appointed guardian out of his father's home. The family fortune now his, Lucien would pacify his angst with the self-abuse that comes from a lifestyle dependent on immediate gratification.

Six years, two bad marriages, and a four-month jail sentence later, Lucien found himself in the company of Lilith Aurelia. The mocha-skinned dominatrix became his obsession, her ruthless ambition sweeping him along like a raging river. Born into poverty, Lilith sought the kind of power enjoyed by society's new elite—pathological globalists who were slowly and steadfastly manipulating the international powers into a one world government.

To be a player in the New World Order required a niche, and Lilith would find it in Project H.O.P.E.

Humans for One Planet Earth was a space program conceived in 2016 by a group of former astronauts, design engineers, and rocket scientists who had left NASA because of the agency's "good ol' boy" policies. Unlike other private space companies who were in the business of launching satellites, H.O.P.E. wanted to pioneer the space tourism industry, their team having completed designs for a new passenger vehicle that could take off horizontally like a jet, rise to its maximum turbojet altitude, then use boosters to rocket the plane into space. Once in orbit, the paying public would enjoy twelve hours of zero gravity and a lifetime of memories.

All H.O.P.E. needed was a major investor.

At the urging of his fiancée, Lucien Mabus struck a partnership with H.O.P.E.'s directors, taking over the company as majority shareholder. On December 15, 2029, the world's first "space bus" took off down its new fifteen-thousand-foot runway at the Kennedy Space Center. Onboard were 120 VIPs, including key stockholders, political dignitaries, members of the media, Lucien and Lilith, and a crew of twelve. Nothing real or imagined could have prepared these civilians for the magic of space. The flight was smooth, the accommodations first-class, and the views both humbling and inspirational. Midway through the trip, Lucien and Lilith were married, the couple consummating their wedding vows in their honeymoon berth in zero gravity, becoming the first official members of the 22,000-mile-high club.

They would not be the last. Within a few months, H.O.P.E. was shuttling four space buses a week at a cost of $100,000 per ticket. Even with its high price tag, there was still a fourteen-month waiting list. Three more planes were quickly added to the fleet, with plans announced for Space Port 1, the first space hotel designed to accommodate the paying public. When a lunar shuttle was included in the brochure, the Defense Department stepped in, declaring the moon off-limits.

Lucien was furious. Maybe the New World Order could control his freedoms on Earth, but nobody owned the moon. A high-priced law firm was engaged, lawsuits threatened.

Lilith charted her own course around the gauntlet, rendezvousing in secrecy with President John Zwawa.

A week before his twenty-sixth birthday, Lucien Mabus died of heart failure, an ailment his physician blamed on a decade of alcohol and drug abuse. Weeks after the funeral, Mabus Tech's new female CEO was granted access to Golden Fleece, a top-secret space program overseen by NASA's Dave Mohr.

Three months later, reports began to circulate that Lilith was pregnant. Devlin Mabus was born eleven months after Lucien's death, confirming suspicions that the boy's mother had been having an affair. Popular consensus around the District of Columbia was that President Zwawa had been the man who had sired the white-haired, blue-eyed infant.

They were wrong.

The black limousine follows its police escort north along scenic State Road, A1A, turning into the gated drive of the Mabus estate.

President Heather Stuart exits the vehicle, the auburn-haired Democrat escorted by her chief of staff, Ken Mulder, and National Security Advisor Donald Engle. Ignoring the bell and intercom, the 280-pound Engle bangs his fist several times against the double oak doors. Waits. Then knocks again.

Mulder casts a perturbed look at the president. "Is this some kind of game they're playing?"

The second female president of the United States and the first homosexual ever to reach the executive branch nods. "It's poker, Ken. Make no mistake, they're watching and evaluating our responses."

Mulder glances up at the surveillance camera. "Poker's a game of chance. I prefer chess."

The door opens, revealing a putty-complexioned man in his late sixties. His short-cropped hair is mouse gray and curly, his matching piggish eyes heavy behind rose-colored spectacles. Barefoot, he is dressed in a paisley Hawaiian shirt and matching Bermuda shorts, his narrow lips sucking on a pacifier bong.

Donald Engle casts a wide shadow over the doorway. "Lilith Mabus?"

A buzzed smile creases into a giggle behind the portable cannabis device, freed by manicured fingers. "No, big man, I'm Lilith's personal assistant. Benjamin Merchant, at your service. Y'all come in, we've been expecting you." The accent is a southern Alabama drawl, laced with saccharine.

Merchant leads them through the grand entrance, the floors polished onyx marble, the bay windows at the rear of the house revealing the pool, its invisible lines melding perfectly into the azure shades of the Atlantic Ocean.

"May I say, Madam President, that finally meeting you is quite an honor. I'm a flamer myself. Probably stems from my upbringing. Did your Catholic priest fondle you, too?"

Heather Stuart's face flushes pink. "No, he most certainly did not."

"Yeah, I suppose they restrict themselves to little boys. What about the nuns?" Moving past a sweeping oak staircase in a drug-induced saunter, he leads them to a matching set of interior doors. "The lady of the house is inside. Go on in while I fetch us something to drink."

Ken Mulder waits for the annoying man to leave before opening the door.

The study is a thousand-square-foot pentagon-shaped chamber, its walls paneled in rich mahogany, its high arched ceiling crisscrossed by teakwood beams. A matching desk houses a wraparound computer station featuring a 270-degree plasma screen. On the other side of the room is a sitting area—three leather sofas and two bamboo chairs forming a square.

Seated on the middle sofa is Lilith Mabus. Brilliant turquoise eyes gaze up to greet them, the Hunahpu-blue radiance exuding the luminescence of a cat's nocturnal eyes. Wavy raven hair flows like ivy down her black kimono, the sheer fabric pressed against her breasts.

More startling—the mocha-skinned thirty-four-year-old goddess's lower body is nude beneath the hip-length kimono. With her bare feet propped on the coffee table, Lilith is clearly flaunting her sex, daring her guests to look.

Mulder's and Engle's eyes widen. President Stuart merely shakes her head.

The man-eater smiles. "Welcome to the oral office, Madam President."

"Cute. But my last name's not Zwawa and this isn't a social call, so if you don't mind."

"Oh, I don't mind a bit. You're the one who requested a face to face, and I find formal wear too conforming. You can have a seat, or stand there gawking, it's up to you."

Heather Stuart motions to her two cabinet members. The two men share the sofa catty-corner to Lilith's, the president selecting a bamboo chair directly in front of their host.

Lilith leans over to the wide-bodied national security advisor and winks. "What's wrong, Donald? Don't trust yourself? You never averted your eyes when I used to visit John in the West Wing."

"You weren't naked, Lilith."

"Ah, but you were imagining me naked, weren't you, Donald? The way you used to ogle my cleavage . . . the way you inspected my ass every time I crossed the room. Tell me, was I good in bed?"

"What?"

"When you masturbated later that night . . . was I good in bed?"

"That's enough!" The president turns to her national security advisor. "Brief her."

Donald Engle positions his attaché case on the coffee table next to Lilith's bare feet and opens it, revealing a holographic projector. "The report you're about to see has been classified UMBRA, beyond top secret. Reveal its contents and you will be subjected to arrest."

"How exciting."

Engle activates the device, causing a 360-degree aerial video of Yellowstone National Park to bloom above the sitting area. "While Yellowstone National Park is known for its geysers and hot springs, to scientists it represents a ticking time bomb of Mother Nature, packing the explosive force of ten thousand Mount St. Helenses. Buried five miles beneath the surface, fueling those geysers and hot springs, is a coneless supervolcano, more commonly referred to as a caldera."

The image changes, converting to an animated color-coded thermal display revealing a massive subterranean magma pocket. "There are actually three calderas buried beneath Yellowstone. The largest and most lethal of these triplets is 112 miles across and 48 miles wide, encompassing nearly the entire park.

"Yellowstone has erupted three times in Earth's history, the first event occurring 2.1 million years ago, the second 1.2 million years ago, the last

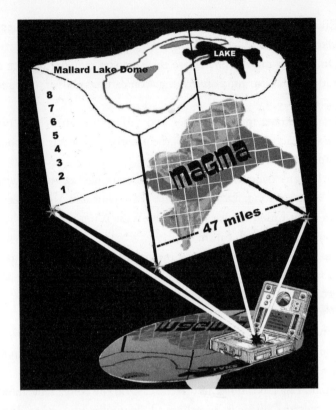

630,000 years ago. The eruptions unleashed a combined six thousand cubic miles of debris, the ejection of lava causing the tops of the volcanoes to collapse, forming these three massive depressions."

The animated eruptions change to a real-time aerial view of a flooded forest.

"Our scientists have known for decades that Yellowstone's calderas are overdue to erupt. What you are looking at is Yellowstone Lake. Situated aboveground along the northern section of the park and directly beneath the pocket of magma is a mammoth, hill-size bulge. The bulge has been rising since the first geological survey of the park was taken in the late 1920s. Scientists became alarmed back in the 1990s when the bulge actually began lifting the northern end of Yellowstone Lake, causing its waters to spill into the forest along its southern shoreline."

"A rising bulge, spilling into the forest?" Lilith winks at Engle.

The national security advisor ignores her. "When the caldera erupts again, the explosion will yield a detonation compatible with an asteroid strike. The pyroclastic blast will instantly kill tens of thousands of people living in the area. The resultant ash cloud that rises into the stratosphere will cover most of the United States, primarily affecting the Great Plains—America's breadbasket. Harvests will be obliterated overnight. The ash plume will eventually span the entire globe, blanketing the atmosphere and blotting out the sun's rays, condemning our planet to a hundred-thousand-year ice age."

"Brrrr."

"I'm so glad you're amused."

"Donald, darling, everyone with a sixth-grade education knows about Yellowstone's caldera. The Army Corps of Engineers have been focused on the problem for a decade. Your own administration siphoned a billion dollars from the Midwest farm subsidies program to vent the magma pocket."

"For some unknown reason, the vents failed. The caldera's volcanic chambers collapsed four weeks ago, creating one massive magma pocket. Pressure within the pocket continues to rise. Our geologists now predict the caldera will erupt within the next four to six months. Maybe sooner."

"Of course, you already knew that," the president states, staring hard into Lilith's unnerving turquoise eyes. "We know you've had contacts feeding you information directly from the US Geological Survey long before you married your deceased billionaire and long after you began humping John Zwawa in the Oval Office. You must have been one helluva lay; either that, or you really put the fear of God into the former president. A hundred billion a year since 2032, secretly diverted from the bottomless money pit over at the Pentagon into H.O.P.E.'s Mars Colony project. Sweetheart leasing deals at Cape Canaveral and Houston . . . even access to Golden Fleece. All that support and you still fell behind."

Mulder jumps in, as rehearsed. "The problem, Madam President, is that Lilith was relying on Golden Fleece to equip her shuttles with zero-point energy." The chief of staff shakes his head. "It was a risky gamble, Lilith. The geeks over at Majestic-12 have been vying for the same breakthrough for a century now; in fact, it was at their insistence that the moratorium on the Large Hadron Collider was lifted during President Stuart's first term in office."

Lilith remains silent, her internal thoughts whirring at light speed.

"Face the facts," Mulder continues. "Engineering mistakes delayed the first Mars supply shuttles by three full years. Four weeks ago, only days after the caldera collapse, H.O.P.E. took on new investment partners in Moscow and Beijing. Coincidence? Maybe. More likely another cash shortage, caused by the sudden escalation in raw materials and astro-engineers. After fifteen years you've only managed to complete two bio-dorms on Mars and three agricultural pods, reducing your capacity to sustain a populace from nine thousand to just over fifteen hundred. Compounding the problem is that you only have a dozen operational shuttles, each one capped out at fifty-two passengers."

"Twelve shuttles," reiterates the president. "It takes a minimum of six months to get to Mars, another six months to return. That's a full year to transport the first eight hundred or so prepaid VIPs while you finish the fleet, only Yellowstone's temperamental volcanic residents have determined there won't be any more shuttles to launch. That means, from the roughly nine thousand investors who coughed up more than a trillion dollars, less than ten percent actually get to make the trip off our doomed planet."

"If word leaked out . . ." Mulder raises an eyebrow. "You're messing with some very powerful people, Lilith—world leaders and bankers who could shut you down long before those twelve shuttles are set to take off down H.O.P.E.'s runway in twenty-eight days."

"Of course, we could do that, too," Engle chimes in. "Health inspections, safety code violations. It could cause some unfortunate delays."

"Now, Donald, everything's negotiable." President Stuart sits back, propping her flat-heeled shoes on the coffee table, mimicking her host.

Lilith smiles coldly. "Is that what this is, a negotiation?"

"More like a partnership guaranteeing our mutual survival. My terms are simple: I want passage and accommodations for two hundred of my top aides and their families. Do that, and you'll have no worries come the twenty-ninth."

Lilith's grin conflicts with the malice in her eyes. Standing, she saunters barefoot around the sitting area until she's standing behind the president. Leaning over, she whispers into the commander-in-chief's ear. "Darling Heather, you really have no idea who or *what* I am, do you?"

President Stuart is about to respond when something moves across her peripheral vision, a white blur that leaves her with a sense of vertigo and something more bizarre—a sensation that feels as if the aura in the room has suddenly changed.

Devlin Mabus gazes at the president and her entourage from across the chamber. The fair-skinned fourteen-year-old's hair is silky white and shoulder-length, drawn into a tight ponytail. His high cheekbones and thick lips match his mother's features, but the adolescent's Hunahpu eyes are far different. Each sclera features a jagged patchwork of thick choroid blood vessels, turning the normal white of the eye bloodred. Devlin's irises are pitch-black, making his matching ebony pupils appear like two barrel holes of a gun. Over six feet tall, he is dressed in a skin-tight white sensory training

STEVE ALTEN

suit that accentuates his overly developed two-hundred-pound muscular physique.

Lilith kisses the teen on his neck. "Madam President, have you met my son, Devlin? Dev, this is Heather Stuart, the most powerful leader on the planet."

The man-child's eyes stare coldly through the president. "Leaders do not extort their citizens."

"Corrupt leaders do."

"Who wants lemonade?" Ben Merchant bursts into the study, wheeling a cart of drinks and a serving dish piled high with cakes and sweets. He serves the beverages, then places a chocolate square on a plate. "Madame President, you simply must try one of my brownies, they're to die for."

Stuart drains half her glass, pushing aside the offered sweets. "*Corruption* is a relative term, coming from a woman who poisoned her own husband to take over his company." She glances at the white-haired adolescent. "What happened to his eyes?"

"Devlin's biological father was Jacob Gabriel. My son is the first full-bred post-human of our era, the next evolutionary step above *Homo sapiens*. His eyes are normal for his species. The enhanced blood vessels feed his sight organs with a far greater supply of oxygen, enabling him to see in ways you could never comprehend."

"Is that right? And such an appropriate name—Devlin. Why not just call him Lucifer or Satan and get it over with?" The president leans forward in her bamboo chair. "So then, *Mom*, are you interested in playing ball, or should we—"

Her throat constricts, the room spinning until it is completely enshrouded by a white fog. Sinister red pricks of light move through the dense mist toward her, distorted voices echoing in her drugged brain.

We discussed this, Dev. It's dangerous. Your course of action leaves too many loose ends.

And yours resolves nothing.

Nevertheless, this was my decision to make.

I did what was necessary. You, on the other hand, have grown far too tolerant of these human leeches. President Zwawa feared you, which is why his people maintained the caldera's secret for so long. You've grown weak and careless, Mother. It concerns me.

You would be wise to know your place.

And you would be wise not to underestimate me.

A sickening feeling of vertigo forces the president awake. She expels the remains of her lunch until the retching becomes a whimper, then opens her tear-filled eyes.

She is strapped to the bamboo chair, her vision blinded by purple spots. Through the haze of annoying lights she sees Mulder and Engle. They stand bound beneath one of the ceiling's teak beams. The nooses tightened around their throats offer no slack, forcing both men up on their toes.

Ben Merchant circles them slowly, as if the homosexual were inspecting a pair of horses being readied for the glue factory. "Dev, I think you gave Mr. Engle too much phenobarbital. He just pissed all over himself."

Now fully awake, President Stuart twists in her bonds. "This is insane. Release us!"

"Releasing you would be insane," Lilith coos. "And please don't think for a moment the reason you're still alive has anything to do with your elected office or the Secret Service agents posted outside my gate. My son could dispose of them as easily as taking out the trash."

Lilith kneels before the president, resting her chin between the older female's trembling knees. "Now, as to your generous offer of extortion, I'm afraid I'm going to have to pass. You are quite right, of course—Mars Colony remains vulnerable, at least until we leave orbit. Now, had your terms of self-preservation merely asked for accommodations for the three of you, I would have probably relented, just to keep things running smoothly. Had you wanted an additional spot for a significant other, I would have at least considered the request, commitment to a loved one being a desirable trait when hoping to extend the reign of a threatened species. Instead, you demanded passage and living accommodations for two hundred people, the majority of whom have nothing to offer the colony. Perhaps that was your opening bid, a means to negotiate a hundred spots, or even fifty; perhaps it was simply greed. Either way, you once again demonstrated the difference between a politician and a leader, the latter putting the needs of the people first, the former always ready to trade the needs of the many for the privileges of the few."

"Who are you to judge me? You cheated your financial backers. You murdered your own husband to take over his company!"

"My financial backers lived their lives of splendor off the toil of the lower classes. By taking their money to preserve our species, I help cleanse their souls. As for my dearly departed husband, he too paid the price of a life stained by selfishness. What I gave him was a legacy to be proud of. Sadly, all I can offer you is a drug that simulates a massive stroke."

Removing the president's left sandal, she injects a clear elixir between Heather Stuart's fourth and fifth toes.

The elder woman's face twitches for several moments, until her head flops across her still-convulsing chest.

Satisfied, Lilith crosses the room to deal with the two terrified men. "I need a witness who will testify to the president's unfortunate demise. Any volunteers?"

"We've known each other fifteen years," Donald Engle pleads. "Whatever you need, you know you can trust me to do it!"

Ken Mulder locks eyes with Lilith. "We have Dave Mohr."

For the briefest of moments, the female Hunahpu's eyes radiate a burnt orange.

Ben Merchant, reclining on one of the sofas, sits up. "Dave Mohr? Now there's a name I haven't heard for quite some time. Wasn't he the head of that defunct MJ-12 project?"

"Golden Fleece." Mulder strains to remain on his toes. "His wife was aboard the cruise ship that sank last week. We intercepted their communication just before the vessel went down with all hands aboard. Dr. Mohr's in custody, off the grid. He's been . . . talkative."

Lilith circles behind the chief of staff. "I'm listening."

"Mohr told us all about this Hunahpu gene. The Gabriel twins had it, you have it, too. And your son."

"Tell me something I don't know."

"Jacob's long gone, off to rescue his father. Turns out his twin never made the trip."

"Liar!" The Hunahpu seductress yanks Mulder's rope tighter from behind. "The Popol Vuh foretold of the twins' journey. The sons of Gabriel now inhabit Xibalba!"

Mulder rasps, his body swaying beneath the noose. "Manny refused to go. Mohr says his powers manifested the day Jacob left. He told us Manny is Jake's genetic equal . . . that he's growing stronger."

Lilith turns toward her son, her thoughts telepathic. *How could you have allowed Immanuel to remain undetected all these years?*

The only way for me to track another Hunahpu is when they enter the Nexus. Immanuel never engaged the Upper Worlds. At least, not during my life span.

Your blade. Give it to me.

In one rapid motion, Devlin withdraws an eight-inch obsidian knife from his belt, throwing it at his mother—

—who plucks it out of midair by its hilt, and in one motion jams its lethal end into Donald Engle's heart. The stunned national security advisor slumps forward, hanging himself in the process.

"Ben, Mr. Engle has decided to remain with us on an extended stay."

"I'll prepare a guest room right after I clean up his remains. What about our purple-faced friend?"

Lilith withdraws the blade from Engle's chest, using it to slash Mulder's rope.

The chief of staff collapses to his kness, each gasped breath restoring color to his face. He stares at his dead companions, his body trembling. "You really think you can get away with this?"

"That depends upon you. Secrecy and Dr. Mohr buy you passage for two; if I were you, I would choose carefully between your wife and Italian mistress."

She wipes the blade clean on Donald Engle's corpse, then whips it at Devlin, who snags it, his limb moving so fast it is undetected by Mulder's eyes.

"Find Immanuel Gabriel and bring him to me, and you can add your two children to the voyage. Those are my terms, Mr. Mulder. Accept it, or join Mr. Engle on his unscheduled three-week holiday."

The Final Papers of
Julius Gabriel, PhD

Cambridge University archives

AUGUST 23, 2001

If you believe in the existence of a supreme being, then I pose to you that the End of Days, though instigated by man, must surely be a supernal event to come, for how could any power in this physical universe be greater than God? This conclusion naturally raises the follow up question: why would God allow man to destroy what He created?

In order to understand and therefore prevent a Doomsday Event, we need to ask an even more important question: why were we created in the first place?

For the moment, let us eliminate God from the creation equation. From a purely scientific perspective, we now know that the Big Bang begat the physical universe, that the physical universe birthed galaxies and solar systems and planets—one of which was our own superhot volcanic world. The Earth cooled and developed an atmosphere through asteroid bombardment over millions of years, each space rock containing molecules of life-giving H_2O. Gradually the planet cooled and the oceans and atmosphere formed, and then, some three-and-a-half billion years later, life took hold in the sea through a combination of chemical reactions and perhaps a random stroke of lightning. Another billion years of trial and error birthed more complex organisms, evolving into oxygen-producing coral, trilobites, and fish. Amphibians charted the land, becoming reptiles and dinosaurs . . . and a fragile new class of life form evolved: mammals.

And then, sixty-five million years ago, another seemingly random sequence of cause and effect unfolded with the arrival of a seven-mile-in-diameter asteroid, which struck our planet in the Gulf of Mexico near the future Yucatan Peninsula. The cosmic collision enveloped the Earth's atmosphere in dust, blotting out the sunlight and warmth. Photosynthesis ceased, the ensuing ice age wiping out the dinosaurs. When the sun returned, the planet had reshuffled its deck, allowing our surviving mouselike mammal ancestors to evolve into primates: a missing link away from primordial man, which eventually became Homo sapiens sapiens—modern man.

While this reverse-engineered scientific method offers us a convenient hook upon which to hang our hat, it does little to help us understand who made the hat or why He needed a hat in the first place. And so man invented religion, and religion gave us a "Big Guy in the Sky," along with war and hatred and all the other wonderful things our egos demanded as we set out to force others into believing which "Big Guy" was the right Big Guy to believe in. And yes, since religion required organizations and establishments from which to pray, money was required. Not just tithing to help the poor, but endowments and donations to seed seats of great power and political influence, along with inquisitions and crusades. Because there's nothing more spiritually uplifting than torturing and robbing and massacring your fellow human beings in the name of God and patriotism—those annoying ten commandments be damned.

But again, we have no concept of why our Big Guy created us, or why we're here, or why our species is so prone to doing everything counter to what formalized religion tells us we're supposed to do—namely, love one another.

Raised a Christian, I questioned religious dogma, but was more than willing to sprinkle a "supreme being" over my theories of evolution, mostly because my donors felt more comfortable signing their checks to a "God-fearing scientist." Logically, I saw no reason to exclude a Creator from the evolutionary process—provided, of course, the evidence could be found.

Maria Rosen was a friend and fellow student at Cambridge, majoring in religious studies. The future Mrs. Julius Gabriel was born in London to a British father and Spanish mother, she and her two sisters were raised as Reform Jews. While on summer break, Maria traveled to Israel, to pursue her archaeological interests.

By fate or chance, she met Rabbi Yehuda Tzvi Brandwein.

Brandwein was an Orthodox rabbi living in Tel Aviv. In clear defiance of the ultraconservatives, Brandwein was openly teaching a secret ancient wisdom that, for the last two thousand years, had been rigorously restricted to devout Orthodox Jewish males over the age of forty. Rabbi Brandwein believed the time had come for all people, regardless of their particular faith, to have an opportunity at spiritual fulfillment. At his own peril he began offering this long-hidden knowledge to the masses.

The secret ancient wisdom: kabbalah.

The word kabbalah translates as "to receive," a reference to receiving fulfillment from the Creator's light. While some may define kabbalah as "Jewish mysticism," it is in fact a nondenominational primer of spirituality that predates organized religion. Four thousand years ago, God passed this wisdom down to Abraham, the unintended patriarch of Judaism, Christianity, and Islam. Abraham encoded the knowledge into the Book of Formation, where it was secretly passed down through the ages, its information far too "mystical" for ancient man to comprehend.

Moses was handed the wisdom on Mount Sinai. Fourteen centuries later, about the time the Maya were developing their calendar, a kabbalist by the name of Rabbi Akiva began openly teaching the ancient wisdom to a new generation of Jews in the Holy Land, among them one Rabbi Joshua ben Joseph, more commonly known as Jesus. Akiva was skinned to death by the Romans, Jesus crucified. Another disciple, Rabbi Shimon bar Yochai, managed to escape into the mountains of Galilee with his son, Rabbi Elazar. The pair spent the next thirteen years living in a cave studying the Torat HaSod, the hidden wisdom encrypted within the Aramaic passages of the Old Testament.

The fruit of Rabbi Shimon's labor produced the Zohar, the main text of kabbalah.

The Zohar firmly placed God behind evolution, revealing the very secrets of existence, providing answers as to how and why man was created along with the "cause and effect" that actually led to the Big Bang and the creation of the physical universe.

In retrospect, it is no wonder why the wisdom had been kept hidden from the masses for so long, for it contains advanced concepts that deal with everything from atomic structure to the quantum physics of black holes. Over the next twenty centuries the Zohar's wisdom would be tapped by some of our species's greatest thinkers, including Galileo, Copernicus, Albert Einstein, and Sir Isaac Newton, whose personal copy of the Zohar remains on display at Cambridge.

Included within the Zohar is a passage that refers to the End of Days. According to the ancient wisdom, when the scales of humanity are finally swayed toward the Light, fulfillment and immortality shall be had by all. But when negativity outweighs the positive forces, then the End of Days shall be upon us. As transcribed in the Zohar, this epoch of human existence shall begin in our present era—the Age of Aquarius on the twenty-third day of Elul in the Hebrew year of 5760. It shall be ushered in by an event, described as "a great tall city, its many towers collapsed by flames, the sound of which shall awaken the entire world."

The Hebrew date translates to September eleventh in the year 2001... nineteen days from today.

How this date ties in to the Doomsday Event forecast for December 21, 2012, may be revealed to me in three weeks' time. In anticipation of things to come, Michael and I have returned to the States, accepting an invitation from my rival and former colleague, Pierre Borgia, to debate the Doomsday prophecy at a Harvard symposium.

What Pierre does not know is that my real purpose in accepting his invitation is to use the symposium to expose the illegal and heinous acts taking place on a remote Air Force base located in the Nevada desert. These acts and the covert operations illegally funded through our tax dollars have but one purpose—to further empower the elite while indenturing the rest of us to servitude. Armed with startling videotaped evidence, I shall once and for all prove to the world that we are not alone in the universe, and that the advances we used forceful means to render from our cosmic cousins were, in fact, a gift intended to benefit all of humanity... while preventing our own self-inflicted demise.

Tomorrow is but an opening shot. In the weeks to come, more than three hundred additional eyewitnesses shall come forth to join a courageous physician hosting a symposium in Washington, D.C., that will forever change the world as we know it.

The odds are long and the enemies of truth legion, with vast resources and influence in the halls of government. Our own vice president feeds this machine as he monopolizes energy policies with the very entities that continue to reap personal fortunes by shunting off our future. I fear for my family, yet I also have a responsibility to my Maker to do what is right. And so I steel myself for the battle ahead, knowing failure is not an option.

As Rabbi Brandwein wrote, "What is a life worth living without enemies?"

—JG

Note:
Professor Gabriel suffered a fatal heart attack moments after delivering his speech at Harvard on August 24, 2001. All grants supporting archaeological investigations into the Mayan calendar were suspended three weeks later following the terrorist attacks of September 11, 2001.

When asked: "What did God do before He created the universe?" Augustine didn't reply: "He was preparing Hell for people who asked such questions." Instead, he said that time was a property of the universe that God created, and that time did not exist before the beginning of the universe.

—STEPHEN HAWKING,
A BRIEF HISTORY OF TIME

Earth News & Media

May 2, 2047: The US Geological Survey registered a magnitude 7.9 seaquake at 11:40 p.m. (local time Indonesia). The epicenter was located in the Banda Sea, 140 miles NNW of Saumlaki (Tanimbar Islands, Indonesia). Coastal towns in the Tanimbar Islands, Ambon, Jakarta, and the Northern Territory in Australia were struck by seven- to twelve-foot tsunamis.

Government officials had evacuated the areas, keeping casualties to a minimum.

The western Galilee town of Peki'in is one of the most ancient villages in Israel. The population of twelve thousand is dominated by the Druze—Greek Orthodox Arabs who live in peace (usually) with their Christian, Muslim, and Jewish neighbors. Peki'in is old stone houses and olive trees, with grapevines as thick as your waist that wrap around windows and doorways. The town's synagogue contains carvings that date back to the Second Jerusalem Temple after the Roman destruction.

Peki'in is also the site of an ancient cave used by a great sage to channel energy from the Upper World two thousand years ago.

Orthodox Jews, dressed in their traditional long black suits, matching hats, and white shirts, bob and pray in groups by the barricades. Tourists, dressed in shirtsleeves and sunglasses, mingle along the roadside, having just arrived by tour bus. The groups are wary of each other, though both are here for the same reason—to connect with the light of the soul of Rabbi Shimon bar Yochai.

Tonight at midnight marks the beginning of the festival of Lag b'Omer, a holiday occurring thirty-three days after the last night of Passover. Many worshipers have arrived early, hoping to camp out by the cave of the holy man who blessed the site with his presence more than two thousand years ago.

This year, they will have to wait.

As sundown approaches, orange security signs appear, indicating the holy site will be shut down at 5 p.m. The roads leading up the mountain are closed, with police posted along the foot trails. Skirmishes break out between local security forces and disappointed visitors. The mayor of Peki'in assures the masses the holy site will reopen tomorrow morning at seven in time for the Lag b'Omer holiday. When pressed for an explanation he mumbles something about a security threat.

Having received 75,000 US dollars to seal off access to the cave from sunset to sunrise, the Arab mayor has no qualm in dealing with a few hundred disgruntled Jews.

* * *

The forty-nine days of the Omer that immediately follow Passover correspond to the period of time 3,400 years ago that followed the Israelites' physical emancipation from Egypt and Moses's descent from Mount Sinai. The seven weeks of Omer are considered dark days, a time when the Israelites' uncertainty about God had cost them the gift of immortality, condemning an entire generation to wander the desert for forty years.

The thirty-third day of Omer commemorates two important historical events, both involving great spiritual sages that lived fourteen centuries after Sinai, when the Holy Land was ruled by Rome and harsh laws were enacted that strictly forbid the study of the Torah.

Akiva ben Yosef held no interest in studying the Torah. Born the son of a Jewish convert, Akiva was a poor shepherd who fell in love with the daughter of one of the wealthiest men in Israel. Faced with being disinherited should she marry the shepherd, Rachel rebuked her father and accepted Akiva's proposal, but only if he agreed to learn the Torah—no easy feat for an illiterate forty-year-old man.

Keeping his word, Akiva left his bride to study outside Roman jurisdiction. When he returned twelve years later, he was an ordained rabbi with a large following. With Rachel's blessing he would continue his studies for another twelve years, becoming a great sage whose students numbered twenty-four thousand.

In 132 CE, a Jewish leader by the name of Shimon bar Kokhba led a revolt against the Holy Land's Roman oppressors, the movement supported by Kokhba's spiritual advisor, Rabbi Akiva. When the dark judgment days of the Omer came, they arrived with a plague that killed all but five of Rabbi Akiva's students. Sages interpreted this epidemic to be a result of the students' growing egos and lack of respect for one another while studying the Torah.

The devastation from the plague finally ended on the thirty-third day of Omer.

Despite the horror of his losses and in direct violation of Roman law, Rabbi Akiva continued to teach his surviving students. The Bar Kokhba revolt would fail: 580,000 Jews massacred. Three years later Rabbi Akiva was captured and skinned alive in front of his people, dying a martyr's death. Before he perished, he revealed to his favorite student, Rabbi Shimon bar Yochai, that the Torah was encrypted with a hidden wisdom that was, in essence, the instruction manual of our existence.

Fleeing Roman persecution, Rabbi Shimon and his son, Rabbi Elazar, escaped to a cave in the mountains of Peki'in. Sustained by the fruit of a carob tree and water from a spring, the two holy men devoted themselves to unraveling the Torat HaSod, an ancient wisdom that Rabbi Akiva claimed had been secretly encrypted in the arrangement of the Aramaic letters in the Torah. Each morning the two men would remove their clothing to preserve the cloth, then bury themselves neck-deep in the sand, channeling the prophet Elijah to aid them in their quest.

For thirteen years father and son remained hidden, until they learned of the Roman governor's death. When they returned to civilization, they carried with them a secret knowledge they would later transcribe into the book of splendor—the Zohar. Knowing the world was not ready for its knowledge, the Rabbi and his disciples hid the sacred text.

The Zohar would not surface again until the thirteenth century.

Rabbi Shimon bar Yochai passed away on the thirty-third day of Omer.

The three Americans hike up the steep mountain trail in single file. The imposing black man takes the lead, followed by the older Caucasian, who arrived in Peki'in two days earlier with a suitcase filled with cash. Both men carry backpacks.

The third man is far younger—a white man in his early thirties, his dark hair long and ponytailed, his eyes hidden behind tinted sunglasses. Unlike his two older companions, he climbs with an athlete's grace.

Mitchell Kurtz feels his sixty-two years as he limps up the path after Ryan Beck. The former CIA assassin's black beard and mustache have grayed over the last decade, matching his short-cropped hair. At five feet, eight inches and 160 pounds, Kurtz looks anything but dangerous, yet what he lacks in physical stature he more than makes up for in advanced gadgetry and a ruthlessness in using it. Concealed beneath the man's right sleeve, strapped to his forearm and powered by a waist-worn battery pack, is a pain cannon. Designed for riot control, the weapon fires pulses of millimeter-waves at its target, heating the victim's flesh as if the subject had just touched a hot lightbulb. The device can scatter every living being within a half-mile radius or deliver a death blow to a specific target a mile away. Kurtz stays in practice by "cooking alley rats."

Kurtz's partner in crime is Ryan Beck, a former star football player whose six-foot, six-inch frame still carries 280 pounds. Though the clean-shaven Beck has lost his edge due to bad knees and his advancing age, his size and martial arts training still render him a formidable opponent.

Affectionately known as Salt and Pepper, the duo have spent the last fourteen years guarding one client, not for money but out of loyalty, love, and a devout understanding that the younger man they have known since his birth thirty-four years ago may represent their species's last shot at salvation.

It is dark by the time they reach the cave of Rabbi Shimon bar Yochai. The mountain air is a chilly fifty-two degrees, the wind howling through the jagged stone opening. Kurtz ducks his head and enters, using the night vision setting in his smart glasses to verify the cave is empty. Beck scans the summit and surrounding hillside with a thermal imager.

Both men concur they are alone.

The younger man with the chiseled physique kneels in the coarse sand and closes his azure-blue eyes. Moving into a transcendental state of meditation, he slows his heart and alters the rhythm of his brain, dropping from the faster Beta waves at forty cycles per second into the lower thirteen-hertz Alpha frequency. Descending farther still, he slides into a Theta trance, the electrical signals transmitting between his nerve cells aligning with the electromagnetic waves present in Earth's atmosphere, which pulsate at a steady 7.8 hertz.

Registering the electrostatic deviations around the cave, he opens his eyes and points to a "hot spot" located just outside the cavern entrance. "There."

The two bodyguards remove telescopic shovels from their backpacks and set to work, digging through the hard-packed sand.

The younger man peels off his clothing.

Immanuel Gabriel was born into a maelstrom of chaos. His father, Michael, who "disappeared" days after his conception, had been branded everything from a Mayan messiah to a paranoid schizophrenic. His mother, Dominique Vazquez, became the Mesoamerican Eve to Mick Gabriel's Adam, her soul mate's departure leaving her alone to raise Manny and his white-haired, turquoise-eyed twin, Jacob.

Jacob and Immanuel: the Mayan hero twins.

One boy fair-haired and empowered with an active post-human gene that rendered him Superman—further convincing him he and his brother were the warriors written about in the Mayan Popol Vuh; the other boy dark-haired and troubled, a hybrid who simply wanted to lead a normal life.

Jake and Manny: yin and yang.

Polar opposites, sharing a symbiotic relationship. Jacob was a spiritual being trapped in a physical form, his dedication to his "perceived" life's mission often voiding out his human emotions. Immanuel was the human condition with all its flaws—emotion driven by ego. A blue-collar athlete, Manny had found dynamite in his developing adolescence—a harbor of tranquility where everything slowed down, a state of existence where fulfillment came in abundance and peak performance was ensured.

Athletes called it the zone.

Jacob called it the Nexus.

The Nexus was a higher dimension, an unveiled channel to the Creator's light. As his alter ego, Samuel "the Mule" Agler, Manny had used the Nexus to score touchdowns and hit tape-measure home runs seemingly at will. The big man on campus at the University of Miami, he had quickly become the most coveted amateur athlete in modern history and a cult hero who could have anything he desired. Fame and fortune rested at his feet, and his ego basked in its glory—

—his fall from grace all but guaranteed.

Like every soul intoxicated by power, the Mule fell hard. In the span of a few weeks leading up to his twentieth birthday, the dark-haired Gabriel twin lost his athletic career, his future, his identity, his family . . . and his fiancée.

Lauren Beckmeyer was an innocent bystander. A scholar athlete motivated by altruism, she was a young woman with a bright future who had loved "Sam" since their second year together in junior high school. On the fateful early morning of her fiancé's twentieth birthday she would discover his true identity. Then, only moments after Immanuel Gabriel refused to join his twin brother aboard the starship *Balam*, Lauren was felled by a sniper's bullet intended for him.

Though the killer had been contracted by Lilith Mabus, Manny blamed Lauren's death on Jacob.

Suddenly forced into exile, unable to cope with the loss of the only woman he had ever loved, Manny fell into a deep depression that kept Beck and Kurtz on an around-the-clock suicide watch. While Dave Mohr and his wife, Eve, had become surrogate parents to Jacob, they hardly knew Manny, and neither they nor the two bodyguards felt qualified to deal with the despondent twin's grief. Desperate, they arranged a clandestine reunion between Manny and his foster father, the man who had raised him since his orchestrated death seven years earlier.

The fugitive twin spent two weeks hiding out with Gene Agler in a motel room in the Pocono Mountains, vocalizing his hatred and contempt for his missing brother, whose insistence upon following the "hero twin legacy" had left his own life shattered.

Agler consoled his foster son by comparing the Gabriel boys to another famous set of twins. "Sam, I know you're not religious, but do you remember the story of Abraham, Isaac, and Jacob? If you recall, Jacob also had a twin brother, Esau."

"Esau was like some hairy hunter who wanted to kill his brother after Jacob tricked their father into giving him his birthright."

"Basically, yes. But that's just the simplistic Bible story. There's a far deeper meaning hidden in the passage. Jacob was attuned to the light of the Creator. Esau, a man of enormous ego, represented the negative side of existence. Esau's hatred for his twin grew out of jealousy and anger, his internal fire fanned by a voice in his head that cried out, 'Why isn't my life perfect? Why must I suffer? Why don't I have money or wealth or good health?' It's a voice attuned to darkness."

"Okay, Dad, what are you saying? That I'm the negative twin? That I'm Esau?"

"Son, the metaphor of Jacob and Esau applies to everyone. Light and darkness cannot coexist in the physical world; enter a dark room with a candle and the light overcomes the darkness relative to its intensity. The darker the room, the more intense the light.

"On a metaphysical level, the light is love, the darkness—hatred. Love is the only weapon that can overcome one's enemy. When Jacob stole his twin's birthright, Esau wanted to kill him, forcing Jacob's mother to send him away in exile. When Jacob returned, Esau had grown in power, commanding an army. But the moment the twins confronted one another, Jacob's love removed Esau's hatred and drew him back into the light, and Esau forgave his brother. You see, deep down Esau still felt love for Jacob, which means there was light in Esau.

"Now let's look at you and *your* twin. Jake has overshadowed you since birth. He pushed you to train hard since the day you started walking. No doubt he drove you crazy with this Mayan prophecy nonsense, but he also warned you about using the Nexus for selfish reasons, and he was right. Your ego got the better of you, and you became intoxicated by the light, in your case the limelight that came with fame. Things changed when the moment of truth finally arrived: Jacob insisted you accompany him to the Mayan underworld, only you refused. We have no way of knowing the ramifications of that decision, but I suspect something positive may come from it."

"How do you know that?"

"Think about it, Samuel. Jacob overstepped his boundaries, he tried to use his physical superiority to forcibly drag you aboard the *Balam*; in doing so, he robbed you of your free will. And what happened? Your genetics suddenly kicked in—you became his physical equal and stopped him."

"You think that was intended to happen?"

"There are no accidents, Son. We may not understand it, but God has a reason for everything."

Manny snapped. "Does that include Lauren's death?"

"Lauren's death was a pebble tossed into a pond. We have no idea where the ripples may go or what outcome they were meant to affect, just as your decision not to follow the hero twin's legacy has no doubt sent ripples across the fabric of space and time. What's important here is that, like Esau, you lose your hatred and negativity and complete your transformation by moving toward the light."

"How do I do that?"

"By living a selfless life. By using the powers God gave you for the greater good. You know, I remember how things were, leading up to the events of 2012. Greed and corruption ruled Wall Street and Washington. While people lost their jobs and homes, the two political parties were more focused on waging war against each other, everyone vying for control. The media poured gasoline on the flames, dividing the country in half. Two wars raged on, fostered by hatred and corporate greed, while the stepping stone to World War III loomed in Iran. Fear ruled the day when the tinderbox finally burst into flames. Only a miracle, precipitated by your father, prevented the end of our species. But from that darkness—from that overwhelming negativity and divisiveness that pushed society toward the brink of annihilation—came a new doctrine. Alternative clean energy replaced fossil fuels, forging new industries while helping to heal the environment. The people rallied to change the political process, removing the variable of money from the equation. With lobbyists and big businesses strictly forbidden from the halls of government, Washington began working for the betterment of society instead of for its own self-interests. Once people started working to help one another, the darkness that veiled the light was lifted."

"Dad, I'm not Jake. I mean, look at me! I'm lost physically . . . emotionally—"

"Focus on the spiritual side, Samuel. The rest will come."

Completely naked, Immanuel Gabriel jumps down into the five-foot-deep, freshly excavated hole.

The two bodyguards look at one another. "You sure about this, kid?"

"I'll be fine. Go on. Bury me up to my neck."

The sand is cold and coarse, each shovelful stinging his skin. Manny focuses his gaze upon the dark silhouette of the carob tree, its leaves dangling pods of edible seeds. In Roman times, the purity of a gold coin was weighed against the weight of the seeds: twenty-four carats or seeds equaling a pure gold coin, twelve carats being half gold, half alloy. Rabbi Shimon bar Yochai and his son had subsisted on the seeds for thirteen years.

Like the famous sage, Immanuel Gabriel's intent is to channel the spirit of a righteous man, hoping to discover his own path to fulfillment.

The sand reaches his neckline. Beck hides the shovels beneath a bush while Kurtz collects the backpacks, offering Manny a sip of bottled water. "Pep will be stationed below, I'll guard the trail from above."

"I'll be all right."

"You'll be in a transcendental state, which means you'll be vulnerable." Kurtz removes a small matchbox-size transmitter from his backpack, the device attached to a three-pronged spike. He counts off five paces from the Gabriel twin's head, then pushes the object into the ground. "On the quarter of every hour I'm going to do perimeter sweeps with my pain cannon. The transmitter will seal you off from the microwaves, anything outside this perimeter gets lit up like a Christmas tree. So if you have to pee, pee in the hole."

Manny smiles. "You're like a protective Jewish mother."

"Somebody has to watch your ass. I mean, what would I do without you?"

"Have a life."

"I have a life. And I get laid a helluva lot more than you do."

"The Israeli waitress from Carmel?"

"Actually, she's an American, Arlene Lieb. She teaches English in the West Bank. Forty-two and divorced, with a set of hooters that could feed a starving African nation. Speaking of which—"

Beck rejoins them. "Perimeter's secure. Salt talkin' about his new woman again?"

"You're so jealous."

"Know what he told her? He told her he was a film producer, scouting locations for the next Zach Bachman movie. You should see the posters he made up."

Kurtz's frat house laugh is infectious. "I said I couldn't get her a speaking part, but if she could play sexy I might be able to use her as an extra in the opening brothel scene."

"You never change. I remember you pulling the same crap when Jake and I lived at the compound."

"What can I say? I'm a dirty old man."

Beck smirks. "You're definitely old."

"You're only as old as your penis. Remember your penis, Pep? It's that thing hidden somewhere beneath your belly."

"All right, you two, go. I'll see you at sunrise."

Manny waits until they're gone before closing his eyes, shifting his brain's biorhythm back into Theta waves—awaiting the midnight hour and the channels that will open, allowing him to communicate with the higher dimensions.

68

CAPE CANAVERAL, FLORIDA

MAY 2, 2047

4:56 P.M. (EASTERN STANDARD TIME)

The facility lies on 140,000 acres of wildlife refuge, located on two barrier islands situated to the northeast of Cocoa Beach, Florida. The smaller landmass wedged between the Banana River and the Atlantic Ocean is Cape Canaveral. Just west of the Cape is Merritt Island, a much larger domain harbored between the Banana and Indian rivers. Two decades ago, Merritt Island was home to the Kennedy Space Center and her sister organization, NASA. Now, both islands are the property of Project H.O.P.E.

The privately owned site is protected by a small militia and an electrically charged, forty-foot-high perimeter fence. Gun towers are positioned along each corner, two by the adjacent beach, one more along the shoreline of the Banana River. Aerial drones patrol 24/7. No one gets in or out of H.O.P.E. without permission.

The completed Mars shuttles are located in twelve of the twenty-two steel and concrete structures situated on the southernmost tip of Cape Canaveral. As wide as a football field and three times as long, each of these

STEVE ALTEN

seven-story buildings contains two monstrous bay doors that lead onto one of two launch tarmacs. Unlike the antiquated STS shuttles employed by NASA, the Mars fleet are space planes, designed for horizontal takeoffs and landings.

The private office of Lilith Mabus is located on the fifth floor in Building 1. Bay windows look down upon one of the twelve completed Mars passenger shuttles, the transport vehicle four times larger than those designed seventy years ago by NASA's engineers and more than twice the girth of H.O.P.E.'s original Earth-orbiting space plane. The CEO works at her computer, carefully finalizing the list of 875 passengers and twenty-four pilots who will be granted salvation on Mars Colony.

The remaining eight thousand elitists who were guaranteed passage, along with the world's other 9 billion people, will remain behind on Earth to die.

Selecting the survivors had been a tricky process. To design and build the Mars Colony and the fleet of space planes and supply shuttles necessary to complete the venture had required fifteen years, two trillion dollars, and a small city of skilled laborers, engineers, and rocket scientists. Acquiring the talent and money while safeguarding Yellowstone's rapidly changing timetable had required cunning. Lilith knew how to play the game, offering passage for favors, the threat of cancellation ensuring secrecy. It never bothered her that her financial partners in the New World Order would be left behind. In truth, Lilith had no use for the vermin on Mars; her priority was to amass the most qualified experts in the fields of science, engineering, agriculture, and medicine, then scrutinize the gene pool. Variety was as essential to ensuring the colony's survival and future expansion as the tens of thousands of frozen plant seeds already en route to the Red Planet. Just as important was compatibility. Democracy was a luxury reserved for large populations—a useful tool that provided the masses with the illusion of freedom.

Mars Colony would function best under autocratic rule. No one perceived as a potential future threat to the Mabus clan's leadership would be permitted on board.

Lilith is reviewing the medical histories of three hundred electrical engineers when the video communication blinks to life on one of her monitors, establishing a connection with Mars.

Alexei Lundgard's face appears, the bearded Russian engineer's expression grim. "The supply ferries arrived. We're still short seven hundred metric tons of steel."

"Two more supply ships will launch on the tenth."

"This does me little good now."

"What about mining operations on the two moons?"

"Deimos is yielding water and organic compounds. Phobos appears to be a hollow mass of iron, we've destroyed three drills attempting to excavate its surface. There is some potential good news. One of our tomography satellites detected a vein of metallic ore approximately 220 meters below the surface of the Vastitas Borealis basin. If usable, there should be more than enough to complete the third biodome."

Lilith accesses a map of Mars on her monitor, quickly locating the basin. "The area's not volcanic, it used to be a primordial sea. How could—"

Devlin bursts into her office, the teen's pale cheeks flushed, his blood vessel–laced eyes wide with excitement. "Did you feel it? There's a disturbance in the higher realms."

"What sort of disturbance? Has Immanuel finally entered the Nexus?"

"It's not Immanuel, it's Jacob. His light is filtering down from the Upper Worlds."

Dreams that you gather, until the day that you are taken from the Earth. Dreams are the substance of the heavenly juice, the heavenly dew; the yellow flower from heaven is dream. Perchance have I taken from you your time, have I taken from you your sustenance?

—CHILAM BALAM,
THE BOOK OF THE ENIGMAS

MIDNIGHT

Waiting for Lag b'Omer to arrive, Immanuel had dozed off. Now, as a wave of energy zaps his brain like a neurological tuning fork, he opens his eyes to an ebony sky seasoned with a billion stars: a tapestry of glittering perfection—spoiled by a cosmic fissure. Dividing the heavens like a celestial spinal cord, the dark zigzagging rift bulges with sporadic cloudlike clusters, each cosmic vortex representing a million suns.

So bewitched is Immanuel Gabriel by the Milky Way's galactic womb that several moments pass before he realizes he is no longer buried. He looks around, baffled.

There is no hole. No cave. He is lying on the ground, his groin covered by a breechcloth made of cotton. Sitting up, he discovers that his chest hurts and his right shoulder burns and his hands are covered in blood.

"Beck? Kurtz?"

He stands in the clearing surrounded by a dense forest and hears heavy breathing. In the darkness revealed by a waxing moon rising above the jungle canopy, he sees the jaguar. A big male, it is on its side panting blood, the hilt of an obsidian dagger protruding from its heaving chest. One of its front paws is cleaved with blood, its sharp claws matching the four dripping track marks oozing from Manny's wounded shoulder.

The forest rustles.

He drops to his knees by the dying beast and yanks the blade free, releasing a tortured growl and a reflexive upward twist of the wounded predator's head.

The big cat's heart ceases beating before gravity returns its skull to the hard limestone earth.

Weak, Manny staggers into a defensive crouch and waits.

The Spanish conquistadors seep out of the jungle. White men and facial hair and fire sticks that spit out hot insects. The blood drains from his face. The heavens spin and the forest swoons and his body folds beneath him, his glazing eyes staring up at the dark canyon splitting the midnight sky.

Daylight burns red behind his closed eyelids. He opens them to morning streaming in from a rectangular hole set high in the straw and mud hut.

"Balam?"

The female native lying on his chest looks up at him through dark brown pools, her raven hair wild and unkempt. She is naked, her warm brown skin sepia . . . like his.

"Another vision?" She speaks in the Nahuatl language of the Toltec and somehow he can understand her—his brainwaves tracking his shifting consciousness, completing the transformation of his altered identity.

He is Chilam Balam.

He is the Jaguar Prophet.

Communicating in her native tongue, he responds to his soul mate's question. "I saw the bearded white man."

"The great teacher returns?"

"No, Blood Woman." He slides out from beneath her, his body void of the wounds from his dream. "The bearded white ones are invaders. On one Imix they shall arrive by sea from the east bearing a symbol of their god. By violence and death they shall introduce their new religion."

He kneels by the long parchment lying on the bare floor and begins painting new images, translating his last vision into Mayan glyphs. "Go to the Council. Advise them that I shall seek the assistance of the great teacher in his sacred temple tonight."

It is nearly sunset by the time Chilam Balam leaves his dwelling.

He follows the *sacbe*, the raised dirt road cutting through the dense Yucatan jungle. Farmers work the fields, growing maize and other crops. Laborers clear brush for new trails. Faces turn, heads bow. Chilam Balam is revered.

He heads south in the direction of the blood-red pyramid, the Kukulcan rising in the distance like a giant ant colony to tower a hundred feet over the vast ceremonial center. Thousands crowd the esplanade, bartering their wares. Potters display vases and plates, growers their food, weavers their breechcloths and dyed skirts—the fabric provided by the ceiba, a pentandra tree whose fruit is a six-inch pod containing seeds surrounded by a fluffy, cottonlike yellowish fiber.

Thirty thousand Maya: drawn together to discourage enemy raids, bound by their affiliation with the Itza clan, tasked with servicing their gods and their community.

Chilam Balam makes his way past craftsmen and healers until he arrives at the pyramid's northern balustrade. The prophet remains the most important advisor to the J-Men, Ix-Men, and Mayan priests who rule the Council. He is the architect of the katuns, each twenty-year epoch of existence foretelling a vision of the future . . . visions that come to the Jaguar Priest in dreams. He has seen the bearded white men arriving in wooden ships. He has witnessed their fire sticks spitting death among his people. He has envisioned the Itza warriors suspended from wooden crosses, tortured by the white men's god.

What confused Balam was that the great teacher, Kukulcan, had been a bearded white man. His arrival had raised the Itza, his wisdom had ensured food during times of famine. Most important, his knowledge of the heavens had provided them with the sacred device wheels that served to organize and prepare the Itza for things to come. Before he departed, the Pale Prophet had promised the Itza-Maya that one day he would return.

That Chilam Balam is able to channel the great teacher's spirit is what renders him such a powerful seer. But the great teacher had been a man of peace. These bearded white men clearly were not.

Seeking answers, Chilam Balam climbs the narrow steps of the pyramid's northern face and enters the sacred temple. A fire burns on the charred stone floor. Bowls are filled with fruit and cacao leaves.

The Jaguar Priest closes his eyes and mumbles an ancient chant, waiting for the arrival of Kukulcan.

The night sky reveals the dark road to Xibalba, the galactic womb only a day away from converging with the horizon. The fire is gone, reduced to smoldering embers.

"Balam."

Kukulcan appears before him, the pale Caucasian dressed in a white ceremonial robe that matches his long flowing silky hair and beard. His azure eyes share the luminescence of the jaguar.

Chilam Balam bows in reverence, his forehead kissing the warm stone. "Great teacher, I ask your help in interpreting these latest visions. Does the arrival of the bearded white men portend your return or our demise?"

"Both. For I am here with you now, and I offer salvation."

"Instruct me, teacher."

"Amass the Itza-Maya tomorrow evening at the sacred cenote. Instruct the farmers to bring with them enough seed to ensure bountiful harvests for at least three tuns. Instruct the healers to do the same with the seedlings that sustain their medicines. Instruct the laborers to bring their tools. Instruct the people to bring only the belongings they can carry on their backs. Leave everything else, including your books. The invaders shall conquer the Azteca, whose lust for blood rivals their own. When they enter Chichen Itza, they shall find a city of ghosts."

"Teacher, where shall we go? Do you wish us to hide in the jungle?"

"At midnight the dark road to Xibalba shall arrive. All who venture down its path shall henceforth be known as Hunahpu. The Hunahpu shall seed the sixth great cycle of man. A thousand times a thousand katuns shall pass before the Hunahpu return. When the race of white men slips into the darkness of ignorance, oblivion, and despair, the wisdom of the cosmic light shall again return, offering mankind a means of salvation at the end of the fifth cycle."

The fire suddenly returns, crackling with energy.

The great teacher is gone.

The Council convenes at midday atop the platform of the Temple of the Warriors. Chilam Balam recounts the great teacher's words, only to be openly challenged by a rival priest, Napuctun.

"The arrival of the bearded ones from the lands of the sun must be met by the sons of the Itza. They are bringers of a sign from our Father God. They bring blessings in abundance!"

Balam puffs out his chest. "Who are you to defy the words of Kukulcan? The raised wooden standard shall come. It shall be displayed to the world, that the world may be enlightened. There has been a beginning of strife, there has been a beginning of rivalry, when the priestly man shall come to bring the sign of God in the time to come. A quarter of a league, a league away he comes. You see the mut-bird surmounting the raised wooden standard. A new day shall dawn in the north, in the west. The bearded ones shall bring bloodshed and death to the sons of Itza, shattering the pottery jars into dust. I am Chilam Balam, the Jaguar Priest. I speak the divine truth."

The Council huddle together with Napuctun.

After a few minutes, Balam's archrival addresses the prophet. "Assemble the sons of Itza as the great teacher instructed."

The Jaguar Priest bows. "Napuctun is wise. It shall be done."

Dusk arrives in Chichen Itza, summoning tens of thousands of men, women, and children to the grand esplanade. They organize by status, filing in long procession lines before hundreds of clay pots filled with blue dye. The striking turquoise pigment is a combination of indigo and palygorskite, the ingredients heated at high temperatures. The color, known as Mayan blue, matches the intense color of the great teacher's eyes.

Now blue-skinned, Indians follow the *sacbe* north through the dense jungle. Torchbearers light the way, directing the masses to the sacred cenote—one of thousands of freshwater sinkholes created 65 million years ago when an asteroid struck the shallow sea that would eventually become the northern tip of the Yucatan Peninsula.

Lunar light from a blood-orange moon illuminates layers of geological grooves sculpted along the interior of the chalky-white limestone pit.

Vegetation has turned the cenote's placid waters a pea-soup green. Four centuries earlier, desperate after the sudden departure of Kukulcan and in direct violation of their great teacher's law, the Maya had turned to human sacrifice, hoping their acts would force the return of the Pale Prophet. Thousands of men, women, and children had been killed on the pyramid's summit, their hearts torn from their chests by zealous priests, their lifeless bodies kicked down the temple steps.

The cenote had been reserved for sacrificial virgins.

Unblemished females were locked in a stone steam bath for purification, then led out to its rooftop platform by ceremonial priests. Stripping the young maidens naked, the death merchants would stretch them out upon the stone structure, then use obsidian blades to cut out their hearts or slice their throats. The virgin's body, laden with jewelry, would then be ceremoniously tossed into the sacred well.

Only at the urging of the Jaguar Priest had the rituals finally ceased.

In the circular clearing that defines the sacred cenote, Chilam Balam stands atop the stone bath house and gazes upon the blue tide of humanity. The crowd occupies every square foot of surrounding jungle for as far as the eye can see.

And they are grumbling.

"Who is the great teacher to demand that we leave our homeland for the underworld?"

"Why should we listen to a man who deserted our people more than twenty katuns ago?"

"What if Chilam Balam is wrong? What if the bearded ones bring prosperity?"

Council members huddle with Napuctan along the far rim of the sinkhole. The rival prophet gestures at the Jaguar Priest.

Chilam Balam glances up at the heavens. The dark rift of the Milky Way slices north-south across the cosmos, its black road meeting the horizon.

Midnight passes. Nothing happens.

A stone flies past Chilam Balam's ear. Another strikes his leg.

The prophet's loyal followers crowd around him, forming a protective wall. His soul mate, Blood Woman, moves to his side.

Napuctun beckons from across the cenote, silencing the crowd. "The Itza have assembled, Chilam Balam. Midnight has come and gone. Why have you led us astray?"

"Does Napuctun question our great teacher?"

"I question you! Let us see if you are a worthy channel for Kukulcan. Throw the heretic and his followers into the cenote!"

The crowd amassed on the *sacbe* surges forward, driving Balam's supporters over the edge of the sinkhole. Screams rend the night air.

The Jaguar Priest grabs his mate by her wrist and jumps!

Chilam Balam and Blood Woman plunge forty feet toward a surface already violated by hundreds of splashing bodies when time suddenly stops. The prophet stares, transfixed, at a droplet of water that hovers before his right eye. His bedazzled mind captures a snapshot of his soul mate's horrified expression, her hair blown upward, each strand frozen in the moment—

—as the cenote's waters transform into a raging falls that flow down a serpent's throat—Xibalba Be—the dark road to the underworld.

The materializing wormhole inhales Chilam Balam and his followers into a parallel universe that, until seconds ago, never existed.

5

Not only does God definitely play dice, but He sometimes confuses us by throwing them where they can't be
seen.

—STEPHEN HAWKING,

"DOES GOD PLAY DICE?"

PEKI'IN, ISRAEL

MAY 3, 2047

Ahh!"
Immanuel Gabriel's azure eyes snap open. It
takes him an unsettling moment before he realizes he is
no longer Chilam Balam, that he is himself again, buried
neck-deep in sand in front of the cave of Rabbi Shimon
bar Yochai.

The graying eastern horizon soothes his nerves, the
dim light revealing a lone figure standing by the carob tree.
Dressed in a white robe, he could be Kukulcan's twin, save
for the lack of facial hair.

"Jake?"

"I've missed you, Manny. I'm glad you finally reached out to communicate."

"How did you get here? Are you even real, or is this another vision?"

"I exist, though I am no longer part of the physical realm. What you see is the reflected light of my soul."

"Is that your way of telling me you're dead?"

"Existence as you know it is far different from the reality of the infinite world. But yes, I died on Xibalba."

Manny lays his head back, his eyes clouding with tears. "It's my fault. I should have gone with you."

"No. I was the one who was wrong. I made your life miserable. Can you see it in your heart to forgive me?"

"I forgive you, bro. I miss you."

"Our souls will always be entwined."

"I had a vision, Jake. It felt so real."

"The vision was not my doing. You channeled a prior life."

"Yeah, sure I did."

"Every human alive today has experienced at least one past life."

"Jake, no offense, but I'm still having a hard time believing we're speaking, let alone—"

"Reincarnation is not about believing. It is about understanding the very nature of the soul. The soul is eternal, a spark of the Creator that desires to exist in the Upper World. There's a lot more to this, but the physical world was created for one purpose: so that each soul has an opportunity to earn its own eternal fulfillment. The process is known as Gilgul Neshamot. A soul descends upon the physical world because it needs to make a correction, sometimes from a sin committed in a past life. If a soul lives one lifetime without fulfilling its correction, it may return three more times to complete its tikkun, its spiritual repair."

"My soul, in a prior life, was Chilam Balam?"

"Yes."

"And what is my purpose? What am I supposed to correct?"

"The destruction of the world."

"The destruction of the world? Is that all? Hell, I ought to be able to handle that, no problem."

"Manny, this is a challenge you accepted the day you refused to join me on Xibalba. By remaining behind, you altered mankind's future. In doing so, you also changed the past."

"You lost me."

"The physical universe has been caught in a time loop—a time loop created by a Doomsday device tested several years before our birth. Unbeknownst to its handlers, an anomaly was created. On December 21 in the year 2012, the anomaly appeared in the physical dimension—

"—destroying the entire planet."

The approaching dawn burns Mitchell Kurtz's eyes. From his perch on the deserted mountain highway he can see wisps of fog gathering along the treetops below, the village of Peki'in still asleep. The bodyguard yawns, then stands and stretches. He contemplates another set of push-ups, opting instead for an energy bar.

The motion sensors in his glasses alert him to the intruder a split second before he activates his pain cannon.

"Ow!"

He traces the woman's scream, surprised to find his new female acquaintance lying on the tarmac next to her road bike, the metal still sparking. "Arlene?"

"Albert?"

The name catches him off guard, Kurtz momentarily forgetting his new alias. *Albert Phaneuf . . . you're a movie producer.* "Arlene, what are you doing out here?"

"Taking my morning ride. What are *you* doing here?"

"We just finished shooting a scene, that's why they closed the road. Didn't you see all the vans?"

"No."

He helps the brunette off the ground, her well-endowed bust enhanced by her neoprene bodysuit. "Arlene, how did you get past the roadblock?"

She slips her arms around his neck, their lips inches apart. "I told them I was in your movie."

Kurtz collapses in her arms, the paralyzed bodyguard never seeing the barbed prong of the divorced woman's ring as it pricks the back of his neck.

"Jake, that makes no sense. If humanity was wiped out in 2012, how were we born? Why are we still here in 2047? And what kind of anomaly could annihilate an entire planet?"

"I cannot provide all the details, to do so could jeopardize your mission. What I can tell you is the anomaly's creation and subsequent expansion into the physical universe opened wormholes, space-time portals. They are unstable and largely rendered moot . . . unless someone enters. In that scenario, an alternate universe is created, the repercussions of which can affect all physical existence."

"I'm still lost. Who entered the wormhole?"

"You did. As Chilam Balam."

The blood rushes from Manny's face. "The cenote . . . But that happened more than five hundred years ago."

"As Einstein proved, time is not linear. While the anomaly bound the wormholes to Earth, some appeared in our past and present, others opened in the future. Ultimately, that's what offered humanity a second shot at salvation. A wormhole opened in near-Earth space on July 4, 2047, again as a result of the anomaly created by the Doomsday device. Lilith's fleet of Mars shuttles were inhaled down the time tunnel's vortex, depositing them on Earth, only Earth millions of years in the future. The planet and cosmos were so alien, the colonists had no idea they had crash-landed on their own home world."

"What happened to them?"

"Though the surface was barren, the sky harbored a magnificent domed city hovering in the clouds, possessing technologies so advanced they remained inaccessible to the Mars colonists. The cloud city had been abandoned, or so the colonists thought. Over time, consumption of the water supply genetically altered the colonists, allowing them access inside the alien structures. One of these vaults contained the physical remains of an advanced species of humanoids, possessing elongated skulls.

"The post-human society had split into two sects. One sought to explore the physical universe; the second desired to access the higher dimensions of existence. To do so, the latter group abandoned their physical forms to unleash their consciousness into the spiritual realm . . . something that violated the laws of creation.

"Lilith, my son, Devlin, and all but a few of the surviving Mars colonists discovered the post-humans' remains. Accessing their DNA, the colonists became more powerful than they already were. In doing so, these fallen ones—the Nephilim—condemned themselves to a purgatorylike existence in a spiritual realm—an eleventh dimension ruled by the negative forces of creation. They called this realm Xibalba."

"*Xibalba* is Hell? Jake, how could living beings access Hell?"

"The colonists weren't alive. The post-human DNA had killed them, they just didn't know it. The negative forces were feeding off their collective consciousness, making them believe they were still marooned on this alien world. Devlin became Satan's alter ego, torturing the colonists to absorb their light. This was the netherworld our father found himself exiled in, his being harbored within a calabash tree, his soul guarded by Lilith. Mother and I were able to release him, but I was mortally wounded in the process."

"You said existence is caught in a time loop. How—"

"Prior to injecting themselves with post-human DNA, Lilith's scientists had launched a transport ship through another wormhole. The vessel contained a biological creature capable of bridging space-time, potentially allowing the marooned colonists to return to present-day Earth. When the Nephilim transport entered the wormhole, it was pursued by the post-humans' starship, the *Balam*. Aboard this artificial intelligence were the Guardian—colonists who had refused to be corrupted by Lilith and Devlin and had fled to the far side of the moon. The *Balam*'s entry inside the wormhole altered its trajectory, sending both vessels back in time 65 million years. The transport became the object that crash-landed in the Gulf of Mexico, killing the dinosaurs.

"Lilith's scientists had stabilized the wormhole's opening in their time period; now it was just a matter of waiting until the exit point returned to Earth-space on the winter solstice of 2012. Knowing the biological creature would awaken on this date, the Guardian orbiting the Earth in the *Balam* set a plan into motion: they would remain asleep until modern man evolved, then land the *Balam* and begin cultivating civilizations to erect monoliths that would conceal the *Balam*'s array. They also seeded the Maya, Aztec, and Inca with low doses of Hunahpu DNA so that one of their own bloodlines could access the *Balam* in 2012. Our father emerged a thousand years later as One Hunahpu—their genetic messiah."

"Let me get this straight: humanity was really destroyed in 2012, only this Doomsday device opened a wormhole in 2047, creating an alternate universe that bypassed the Doomsday event?"

"Not bypassed entirely. When our father activated the *Balam* on December 21 in 2012, he not only destroyed the biological creature, he destroyed the Doomsday anomaly."

"Then we're cool, right?"

"No, Manny. By not coming with me to Xibalba, you unraveled one end of the time loop. The free end is the wormhole that will appear in two months on July 4. If Lilith's shuttles enter, then time will loop again, only to an alternate past where there is no biological creature buried in the Gulf of Mexico. The anomaly will simply appear on the 2012 winter solstice, annihilating the entire planet."

Manny closes his eyes, his mind struggling to wrap itself around these bizarre cause-and-effect scenarios. "What do you need me to do?"

"Enter the wormhole when it appears on July 4. Because Earth no longer exists in the future, the wormhole must open sometime in Earth's past, prior to the 2012 event. You must enter the wormhole and go back in time, then find a way to destroy the Doomsday device before it is activated."

"How the hell am I supposed to do that?"

"Seek Lilith's help."

"Seek Lilith's help? Jake, why do you think I've avoided accessing the Nexus these last fourteen years? Your wacky girlfriend is a psychopath. Her soul's as dark as they come."

"The soul is a spark of perfection. Lilith's darkness originates from her own tainted past. If our souls are entwined, Manny, then she is your soul mate, too."

"Oh, no. No, no, no. That crazy bitch killed my true soul mate minutes after you left Earth. Her assassin murdered Lauren!"

"Go back in time and Lauren can live again."

"Huh?" Manny's thoughts race. "Yeah . . . that's true. Wait, what about Chilam Balam and his people . . . er, my people? What happened to them?"

"When Chilam Balam and his followers fell into the sacred cenote, the sinkhole manifested into a wormhole, again created by the Doomsday device that destroys the Earth in 2012. By entering the wormhole, you and your Mayan brethren created another alternate universe, one that circumvented Doomsday but deposited you into a future where Earth was thawing from a ten-thousand-year ice age, caused by the eruption of the Yellowstone caldera."

"The caldera? Jake, Lauren had been working on a solution to the caldera, the University of Miami was funding her work."

"Lauren's death may have been necessary; it served the alternate universe created when Chilam Balam and his people entered the wormhole in the 1500s."

"Necessary? What the hell are you talking about?"

"Chilam Balam and his people arrived in a post-caldera alternative existence. His Mayan colony thrived. A thousand years later, his society—your society—succeeded in harvesting zero-point energy to colonize other planets. It was Chilam Balam's future generations that evolved into the Hunahpu—the post-human species encountered by Lilith's Mars colonists.

It was the Hunahpu who built the *Balam*. They built it for us, Manny. And they named it after you."

Manny lays his head back against the sand, feeling dizzy. "Jake, about Lilith—"

"The greatest transformation of darkness yields the greatest light. Lilith transformed on Xibalba. After I died, I cleansed her soul."

"What about our parents? Did you cleanse Mick's soul, too?"

"Our parents never died. Their collective consciousness remains trapped."

"Trapped? Where? Jake, where are they trapped?"

"On Phobos."

"Phobos? As in the Mars moon, Phobos? How the hell did they get there?"

"Our parents were taken aboard a Guardian transport before the sun went supernova. The transport entered the wormhole, followed by the *Balam*. The wormhole deposited both vessels far into the past. Phobos isn't a moon, it's all that remains of the Guardian's transport vessel. Our parents are held inside, their consciousness trapped in cryogenic stasis."

"They're still alive? Jake—"

The sun's brilliance peeks over the horizon. Jacob disperses with the golden light—

—his presence replaced by armed commandoes. Dressed in black, they aim weapons at Salt and Pepper, the two bodyguards bound in neural cuffs. The commando leader kneels to reach Manny, snapping a sensory collar around his neck.

"Immanuel Gabriel, you are under arrest for treason. This collar monitors your brain waves. Attempt to access the Nexus and the change in brain activity will activate your friends' neural cuffs, electrocuting them."

6

At every stage of understanding the universe better, the benefits to civilization have been immeasurable. None of those big leaps were made with us knowing what was going to happen.

—BRIAN COX,
CERN PHYSICIST

The Federal Democratic Republic of Nepal is a land-locked country shaped like a five-hundred-mile-long east-west bacon strip situated between China and India. While Nepal's southern lowland plains maintain a tropical climate, the two elevated regions to the north drop quickly into alpine temperatures as the geology rises into the Himalaya Mountains. Formed by the tectonic collision of the Indian subcontinent meeting Eurasia, the Himalayan arc makes up the northern part of Nepal and contains eight of the highest elevations in the world, including Sagarmatha, better known as Mount Everest.

The climbing party numbered eight. The two Americans, Shawn Eastburn and her nephew, Scott Curtis, were both from Oklahoma and the weakest climbers. Their employer, Sean Cadden, was Canadian; it was his travel company that had sponsored the trip. Jurgen Neelen and Karim Jivani had joined them in Kathmandu, the two Europeans far more experienced mountaineers. Ultimately, of course, the success of the climb relied on the three hired Sherpas, who not only led the way but bore the brunt of their belongings, each blue nylon bag weighing in excess of sixty pounds.

The five foreigners had arrived in Nepal's capital on Thursday, the climbing permits alone costing $14,000 per person. Another $16,000 was spent on equipment rental, oxygen, insurance, and Sherpa fees.

While Sean Cadden claimed his assault on the world's highest mountain was all about promoting his business ventures, deep inside he knew it was personal. The adrenaline junkie had attempted Everest three years earlier when a spot had opened on a February climb, only things had gone bad quickly. The weather had been vicious, an avalanche claiming two lives and ending the attempt at Base Camp III. Undaunted, the CEO had promised his employees that he would return to claim the mountain. Now he was back: granted, in May, when the weather was far more stable—if fifty degrees below zero and winds blowing in excess of a hundred miles an hour could be so defined.

After two days of preparation and equipment tests the team finally arrived at Lukla, making their way up to Base Camp at 17,600 feet. Shawn Eastburn, an insulin-dependent diabetic, was the first to suffer from high altitude sickness. At Sean Cadden's urging, the forty-two-year-old district manager and mother of two had valiantly continued on to scale the Khumbu Icefall at 19,500 feet. Resting at Camp I in the Valley of Silence, she declared her climb over.

The others had pushed on, ascending to Camp II at 21,300 feet. The harrowing Lhotse Face was completed by dusk, bringing the team to Camp III at 23,500 feet. There they rested, allowing their bodies to acclimatize for the nearly three-thousand-foot ascent to Camp IV, located in the "death zone."

Altitudes in the Everest death zone exceed 26,200 feet. The air is frigid, requiring every speck of flesh to be covered lest frostbite set in. Atmospheric pressure is only a third of that at sea level, forcing all non-Sherpas to use oxygen. The snow is densely frozen, the icy surface leading to a greater incident of fatalities from slips and falls. Climbers who are injured in the death zone have a high mortality rate. Those who perish here are usually left behind. Over 160 frozen corpses remain a permanent part of the Everest geology.

Scott Curtis is in his tent shivering, the howling wind abusing his shelter. The Oklahoma native wishes he had remained behind at Camp II with his aunt, or better yet, in Tulsa. Exhausted from having to gasp eighty to ninety breaths a minute in the oxygen-deprived air, he has been using his O_2 tank since Camp III. Now, as the sun rises and the wind swirls into a white haze, he knows there are no reserves left in his spent body to even contemplate the final three thousand feet.

The weather window opens an hour later. The three remaining climbers and two of their Sherpa guides begin the final assault. Down mittens clench poles, masked faces breathe oxygen behind tinted goggles.

At precisely seventeen minutes after noon beneath a cobalt-blue sky, the five men arrive at the 29,035-foot summit, the highest point on Earth.

The view is like no other. Snowcapped peaks and billowing cloud banks. Heavens that hint at the darkness of outer space.

For twenty minutes they videotape one another and snap photos, sharing the same cruising altitude as the commercial jetliner that brought them to Kathmandu. No evidence of their presence will be left behind, no trash or debris jeopardizing their $5,000 environmental deposit and the mountain's good karma.

The karma changes at 12:37 p.m.

It commences with a roll of thunder, low and deep, echoing across the valley of snow-covered peaks. Sean Cadden kneels in the snow, seven miles of mountain shaking beneath him. "Earthquake!"

The three climbers hang on to one another as the rumbling builds. Jurgen Neelen's scalp tingles, his thoughts turning to his fellow climbers at the lower base camps, their location rendering them vulnerable to an avalanche. His head continues itching. He rubs a mittened hand atop his wool ski cap, generating sparks of static electricity. The loosened hat flies off his head, caught in an upswell of frigid air.

Snow flies past his face, followed by particles of rock that glance off his goggles before raining skyward. Jurgen looks up, mystified, his gray eyes following the trail of debris as it rises into the forming tail of a white tornado! The rotating column of air soars high over Everest—a massive churning vortex that twists skyward like a monstrous snake before disappearing into the event horizon of a gelid maelstrom located hundreds of miles above the mountain.

Sean Cadden stares at the hole in the sky, dumbfounded. "What the hell is that?"

Karim Jivani shields his face against flying debris. "Hey . . . what happened to the Sherpas?"

"They're descending without us," yells Neelen. "Come on!"

The three climbers head for the ropes as the updraft's intensity increases, inhaling Karim's camera right out of his hand. Cadden's oxygen mask snaps free, flapping above his eyes. He grabs it by its hose, holding it to his face as he ducks low, following his companions down the rapidly disintegrating trail from which they ascended.

Chunks of frozen snow break loose like miniature icebergs, spinning into the air. A thirty-pound brick of ice bashes Karim in the face, shattering his goggles, which are quickly wrenched free from his head.

Jurgen reaches the ropes first. He snaps the carabiner attached to his belt around the line and begins a rapid rappel, his two companions right behind him.

The tornado's suction rips the masks and helmets from their heads. The mountain peak shudders, shaking loose a million tons of snow in a blinding whiteout that sweeps the three men away from the rock and into the air, their feet splayed over their heads, the nylon rope all that tethers them to Everest.

Through the gravity-defying ice storm Sean Cadden looks up into the three-mile-wide radius of the anomaly, its gelid-clear orifice defined by the inhaled debris, its event horizon pushing closer.

The roar is deafening—a thousand freight trains vibrating every atom in the Canadian thrill-seeker's body, swallowing his scream—

And suddenly there is silence.

The sky is clear, the anomaly gone. The three men gaze at one another, still suspended from their ropes, unsure of what just happened, or how they are still alive.

ORGANISATION EUROPÉENNE POUR LA RECHERCHE NUCLÉAIRE

EUROPEAN ORGANIZATION FOR NUCLEAR RESEARCH

CERN RESEARCH BOARD MINUTES OF THE 162nd MEETING OF
THE RESEARCH BOARD HELD ON
THURSDAY, 6 FEBRUARY 2003

STUDY OF POSSIBLY DANGEROUS EVENTS DURING HEAVY ION COLLISIONS AT LHC

J. Iliopoulos reported on the study made by a committee that he chaired, concerning the possibility of producing dangerous events during heavy ion collisions at the LHC. A previous study made for RHIC (Relativistic Heavy Ion Collider at Brookhaven National Laboratory, USA) had concluded that the candidate mechanisms for catastrophe scenarios are firmly excluded by existing empirical evidence, compelling theoretical arguments, or both. Following their investigation, the committee members concurred with this conclusion. They studied the possible production of black holes, magnetic monopoles, and strangelets. They also reviewed the astrophysical limits coming from interaction of cosmic rays with the moon (or with each other), which, under plausible assumptions, exclude the possibility of dangerous processes in heavy ion colliders. Black holes produced in theories with extra-compact dimensions, for which the fundamental scale could be as low as 1 TeV, might be copiously produced at the LHC. However, only extremely massive black holes, beyond the reach of any accelerator, would be stable. It has been speculated that magnetic monopoles might catalyze proton decay. At each catalysis event, energy is released by the decaying proton, causing the monopole to move. They estimated the number of nucleons that the monopole would destroy before escaping from the Earth and found it to be negligibly small. Most of the committee's study concerned strangelets, a hypothetical new form of matter containing roughly equal numbers of up, down, and strange quarks. They may become dangerous if they can be produced at the LHC, are sufficiently long-lived, are negatively charged so that they can attract and absorb ordinary nuclei, and finally if they can grow indefinitely without becoming unstable. The committee found that, from general principles, if negatively charged strangelets exist at all, they would not grow indefinitely: they soon become unstable. Furthermore, the committee concluded that any hadronic system with baryon number of order ten or higher is out of reach of a heavy ion collider, and the LHC will be no more efficient at producing strangelets than RHIC. To be dangerous the strangelet would need to be stable from a very low baryon number, where production is possible, all the way up toward an infinite baryon number, a possibility that has been excluded by the stability studies.

L. Maiani thanked J. Iliopoulos and his committee for their work, and the Research Board took note of the report.

END MINUTES

Note: The official position of CERN assumes the theory of black hole evaporation is correct, though it should be noted that *no empirical evidence exists to support this theory.*

Earth News & Media

May 8, 2047: Albania residents continue to dig out from yesterday's magnitude 7.7 earthquake. The quake's epicenter was located twenty-two miles E-NE of the city of Tirana. Government officials estimate casualties will exceed three thousand.

H.O.P.E. SPACE CENTER

CAPE CANAVERAL, FLORIDA

The eighteen-wheeled military transport follows its police escort east across the NASA Parkway, crossing the Banana River land bridge to Cape Canaveral. The caravan of vehicles is waved through three security checkpoints, then led to one of twelve steel and concrete structures towering over the southernmost tip of the Project H.O.P.E. Space Center.

The left bay door is open. The military transport enters the facility, proceeding over a wasteland of concrete before arriving at the ten-story infrastructure and an interior tunnel sealed by a twenty-two-foot-diameter vault door.

A dozen cyberwarriors exit the truck. Dressed hood to boots in a bulletproof, explosive-resistant lining dubbed "camouflage skin," the soldiers by their presence bespeak the importance of the three fugitives housed in the truck's portable sensory prison.

The squad leader approaches the rear doors of the transport and touches his gloved palm to the computer keypad. The encrypted security codes are relayed from the White House through neural conduits in the soldier's glove, the signal of which must match his own biorhythms before being uploaded.

The rear hatch opens, activating a ramp. The sensory prison—an eight-by-twelve-foot windowless lead-gray steel and acrylic cube set on a magnetic hover pad—is maneuvered out of the truck.

Devlin Mabus watches everything from his balcony on the sixth floor. The seven-ton steel vault door opens, its magnetic hinges whisper-quiet.

The sensory prison, escorted by the detail of cyberwarriors, is guided inside.

Though only ninety-six square feet, the interior of the holographic relocation cell appears as a vast Jamaican island beach resort. Artificial lighting coming from the ceiling panels re-creates the sun, the bulbs tinged with ultraviolet rays. Temperature-controlled fans provide a salty ocean breeze, with an occasional gust offering a saline "spritz" from the tropical sea.

Shaded by the gently swaying palm fronds of a coconut tree, Mitchell Kurtz lies back in his lounge chair, enjoying the nubile bikini-clad women walking in the ankle-deep surf before him. "If this is prison, I'll take two life sentences."

"Shut up, fool. You and your damn pharmaceutical-fed libido is what got us into this mess in the first place." Ryan Beck has his ear pressed to the cabana deck, the hotel "guests" distorting as they pass across his body. "Magnetic couplings are being shut down. Wherever we are, I'd say we just arrived. Manny, wake up."

Immanuel Gabriel slips out of his rapid eye movement trance and sits up in the holographic sand. He has spent most of the last eighteen hours in a state of hypnotic rest, preparing himself for the battle to come.

The internal lights flicker, the beach scene replaced by four porous gray walls, ceiling, and floor. A hatch opens along one wall, revealing a squad of heavily armed soldiers.

"The prisoners will exit the vehicle. Move!"

Manny climbs down out of the cell, followed by his two companions.

There are standing in Chichen Itza's ancient Mesoamerican ball court, the thousand-year-old stone baked warm beneath a cloudless blue Yucatan sky.

Kurtz looks around. "This is like a bad déjà vu."

The playing field is a good football-field-and-a-half long, though slightly narrower in width, a rectangle of grass imprisoned within four walls constructed of limestone block. Anchored to the two perpendicular walls like a giant vertical donut is a circular stone ring, its hoop twenty inches in diameter. Below the timeworn goals are slanted embankments adorned with Mayan ballgame reliefs. Situated atop the eastern wall is a twenty-six-foot-high structure—a replica of Chichen Itza's Temple of the Jaguar. Towering in the distance is the Kukulcan Pyramid.

Manny closes his eyes and inhales deeply, his senses processing their surroundings. "We're in a holographic arena, the same one Jake trained in twenty years ago."

Beck curses under his breath. "Hangar 13. Your brother spilled a lot of blood and sweat in this place."

Manny nods. He can smell his twin's lingering scent as clearly as one can detect smoke from a nearby forest fire.

The mobile prison is maneuvered out of the arena by armed cyberwarriors. One of the soldiers aims his pain cannon at Salt and Pepper. "The two of you are to come with us. Gabriel, you'll remain behind. If you're victorious in battle, then your friends will be set free. Should you lose, they will die painfully."

"Couldn't you just toss us back in that prison cell with a few six-packs?"

Facing Kurtz, the soldier fires a short burst of energy from the device secured to his forearm, causing the bodyguard to double over in agony. He turns back to Manny. "You may remove your neural collar once we exit the arena. You are no longer restricted from using the Nexus."

The military men escort Beck and Kurtz out of the training facility, leaving behind a pile of body armor, the black exoskeleton identical to the one Immanuel wore fifteen years ago when Jacob had attempted to train him for combat on Xibalba. The suit's outer layer is composed of nanofiber ceramics backed by a lightweight carbon, the fabric as strong as steel yet as light as cotton.

The weapon is a sword, its double-edged blade peppered with dime-size electrical conductors. The faster the sword is wielded, the hotter the steel will heat.

Manny takes the weapon, ignoring the body armor.

The warrior approaches from the western end of the ball court. White exoskeleton. Flowing white hair and intense black eyes, framed in thick red blood vessels. A sword carried in one hand, his headpiece in the other.

"Hello, Uncle."

"You look so much like your father it's scary."

"Put on your battle armor."

"I don't need it."

"This is a fight to the death."

"Is that why I can taste your fear?"

Devlin clenches his teeth. Tossing aside his own headpiece, he wields the heavy sword in both hands, whirling it before him in a repeating figure-eight pattern, the blade heating up until it glows red.

With a warrior's bellow, he attacks.

Manny's front thrust kick is a blur, the sole of his boot striking his nephew's chest plate like gunshot, the blow cracking Devlin's body armor while propelling the teen backward twenty feet.

Lying on his back, the stunned fourteen-year-old struggles to breathe, his sternum badly bruised.

Manny stands over him, his sword poised over his cracked chest plate. "To the death then?"

Devlin's eyes tear up. "Do it, Uncle. End my suffering."

"Oops, you said *uncle*. That means I win." Manny smiles, tossing the blade aside.

The confused adolescent sits up in agony. "Wait. This isn't over!"

"You said *uncle*. Back in my day, saying *uncle* meant you give up." He walks off, heading for the exit.

The g-force that strikes him from behind is equivalent to a locomotive slamming into a stalled pickup truck, far more powerful than Manny had expected. Had he not been waiting for the attack in the Nexus, the bone-crushing force would have been lethal.

Harbored in the gelid corridor leading to the higher dimensions, Immanuel Gabriel parries the blow, then spins his startled nephew into a headlock, securing him from behind.

And that's when he feels it, a dark force seething deep within Devlin's aura, a wellspring of energy that far surpasses his own, fueling the teen's fight despite the fact that the choke hold becomes more lethal as he resists.

It takes all of Manny's strength to bridle his bucking nephew, who finally goes limp in his arms. *Stubborn as your father . . .*

The two Hunahpu emerge from the Nexus.

Manny leaves the unconscious teen in the holographic arena, using his heightened olfactory sense to track down the boy's mother.

Evil does not exist, or at least it does not exist unto itself.
Evil is simply the absence of God. It is just like darkness
and cold, a word that man has created to describe the
absence of heat. God did not create evil. Evil is the result
of what happens when man does not have God's love
present in his heart. It's like the cold that comes when
there is no heat, or the darkness that comes when there is
no light.

—ANONYMOUS

Moving through Hangar 13, Immanuel Gabriel quickly detects the intoxicating scent of Lilith Aurelia Mabus's pheromones. The Hunahpu half-breed finds himself in a state of arousal that charges every vasomotor-driven nerve ending in his body.

Olfaction, the process of locating through smell, is a sense that varies greatly among species. Sharks can smell a drop of blood or amino acids among billions of droplets of seawater. A dog's sense of smell is a thousand times more powerful than a human's.

The evolutionary process that transformed primitive man to modern man greatly reduced the olfactory sense in the hominid nose from 80 million to 5 million receptors. Conversely, the post-human society that evolved from *Homo sapiens* on "future Earth" developed a heightened sense of smell, which was used to select a compatible mate and track him or her over great distances.

Manny finds her waiting for him in a repair terminal on the northeast side of the complex. His heart pounds in his throat as he approaches, her musk oozing beneath the skin-tight red and white H.O.P.E. jumpsuit, unzipped just enough to reveal a hint of bare cleavage. Her raven hair is long and wavy, draped over one shoulder in a tight ponytail.

Aroused by Manny's presence, Lilith leans against a forklift, panting.

Born on the same day thirty-four years ago, the two blood cousins have never met nor have they ever spoken. Suddenly brought together, they circle each other like predators in heat, inhaling each other's scent, the diminishing space between them charged with electricity. Presumed enemies, they struggle to refrain from physical contact, their act of restriction rendered meaningless by their senses, which quickly confirm a perfect genetic match. Every scent of breath intoxicates with a madness that breaches all logic and agenda, all part of a mating ritual unknown to either prior to this very moment in time, yet predestined long ago by their Hunahpu DNA.

Immanuel Gabriel and Lilith Mabus cease to exist, their angst replaced by blind animal lust. Eyes rolled upward, they attack one another in a fit of passion, their tongues entwining, their kiss so violent it crushes their lips, drawing blood. Lilith's legs wrap around Manny's hips as they moan into one another's mouths until the rush of endorphins nearly causes them to pass out.

Manny reaches for her jumpsuit, attempting to expose her lower body, only Lilith restrains him, panting as she pushes him away. "Why have you remained hidden from me?"

"You tried to kill me."

"I was confused. Your brother rejected me. An act of cruelty that spawned a thousand retaliations."

"Jacob rejected you out of fear. Our father told him you were dangerous."

"I've changed."

"Why should I believe you?"

"Because you want to. Because you were the one responsible." She backs away, gasping like a fish out of water, forcing starvation upon her overloaded pleasure centers. "Your brother and I were children when we first communicated in the Nexus; we were twenty when we met and he inseminated me with Devlin. It was an act of seduction on my part, born from a dark past that instilled in me an agenda I was compelled to pursue. That agenda has been excised, all because you defied your own destiny and remained behind. Jacob was powerful but imbalanced emotionally, easily exploited. Not you. We may lose each other to lust, but I could never seduce you, not when you're the anchor of restriction that transformed me into something I never imagined I could be."

"And what is that?"

Her eyes tear up. "Someone capable of love."

Her scent dissipates, enabling him to take her in with his eyes. Moving closer, he kisses her gently on the lips, then hugs her to his chest, their genetically driven hunger quenched by something far deeper.

They remain locked together until the late afternoon sun bleeds into dusk.

98

"Manny, I need to show you something. The reason why I brought you here."

"First, my two bodyguards."

She touches a comm link on her collar. "Gabriel's bodyguards . . . where are they?"

"The holding cell on level 2."

"Release them and feed them, I want them treated as guests. Tell them Manny will meet with them tomorrow night."

"Understood."

Manny's eyes widen. "Where are you taking me?"

For more than four decades, the space shuttle *Orbiter* remained the heart of NASA's Space Transportation System (STS). Designed in the 1970s, the bulky 122-foot-long craft was launched vertically as a rocket and landed as a space plane, its 172,000-pound girth powered by three Rocketdyne Block II engines and seventy thousand pounds of fuel. Designed as a reusable space vehicle, the *Orbiter* delivered an average payload at a cost of $1.5 billion. Despite upgrades, it remained an antiquated means of transportation until it was finally retired in 2011.

H.O.P.E.'s space plane was engineered to be far more aerodynamic and fuel efficient. Twice the length of the shuttle, with a far larger wingspan yet only half the diameter and a third of the weight, the supersonic craft looked more like a souped-up Concorde. Taking off like a commercial jet, the space plane flew to the edge of space before vertical thrusters powered it into orbit. With it designed strictly as a tourist transport, payloads ran less than half a million dollars for a twelve-hour trip, a cost easily dwarfed by the $4 million in passenger fees.

Lilith and Manny are alone in the main cabin, strapped into bucket seats designed to withstand four Gs of force. The pilot communicates with them from the flight deck using the video-comm. "Mrs. Mabus, we have clearance for takeoff. Are you all set?"

"We're good to go." Lilith squeezes Manny's hand. "You've never been in space, have you?"

"No. But I came close once."

"I've been on more than a hundred flights and it never gets old, though it's probably more impacting during a day launch."

The space plane accelerates down the deserted runway and rises smoothly into the night. The cabin lights are lowered, the Hunahpu couple's blue eyes radiating a soft gray in the darkness.

"So, is this cruise business, mythology, or pleasure?"

"Perhaps all three." Her expression turns serious. "Manny, when you faced my son in the Nexus, did you feel another presence in the void?"

"Yes. It was strange, like a malevolent force causing an internal conflict. For a moment I registered two genetic signals, different, yet symbiotically compatible. It's as if your son was being guided by a darker, far stronger spiritual energy, only the higher power—"

"—is his own consciousness."

"Yes. But how is that possible?"

"Somehow, many years from now, Devlin and I will both come to exist in another reality—an underworld described in the Popol Vuh as Xibalba. In this alternate existence, our souls will be corrupted by dark forces attributed to Satan, though in truth, my own soul was tainted long ago. I must have died on Xibalba, yet somehow Jacob managed to cleanse my soul. The effects rippled back across space-time to affect me only days after he left. Devlin was born pure, his soul darkening with the arrival of adolescence, as mine did when I was his age. What you sensed in him was the malignant adult reaching across the higher dimensions to corrupt the soul of the adolescent. Each day I lose him a little bit more."

"He's dangerous. As a pure Hunahpu, he's far stronger than either of us, he just lacks the neural development to coordinate his powers. He needs to be neutralized before that happens."

Lilith grabs his arm in a viselike grip. "He's still my son, your brother's own flesh and blood. He can be saved!"

She releases him, rubbing his biceps. "I'm sorry. And I know what you must be thinking—can I trust this crazy bitch? Is she the Delilah to my Samson? Will she corrupt me like she corrupted Jacob?"

"The thought had occurred to me."

"The answer comes down to nature versus nurture. Why does evil run rampant? Is it in our nature, our DNA? Or is it a result of the way we were raised, the values instilled in us that guide us when it comes to free will?

"I was born into violence. My father, if you can call him that, stabbed my mother to death in a fit of drunken rage minutes after I was born, all because he expected to be raising a son to ensure his legacy. The man who ended up raising me, my foster grandfather, preferred me as a girl; he began sodomizing me at the age of eight."

"Jesus . . ."

"Jesus had nothing to do with it, but I certainly never hesitated to blame him as he watched my legal guardian rape me from his perch on the crucifix mounted above our bed. As you can imagine, my mind was decimated by the abuse. Trapped, I learned to mentally hibernate during the physical abuse by escaping into the soothing light of the Nexus. One day I felt another presence sharing the void, and that's how I first came in contact with Jacob, or at least his consciousness. Your twin was my only friend; he helped me get through the torment until we were Devlin's age, when he abruptly abandoned me."

"You murdered our aunt."

"My mind was poisoned. Jacob's sudden absence left me suicidal. And then a dark presence came to me in the form of a Nagual witch, a spirit by the name of Don Rafelo. Claiming he was my great-uncle, Don Rafelo taught me how to use my physical beauty as a weapon, and from that day forward I ceased being a victim. As my Hunahpu powers grew stronger, I lost myself to temptation, the witch driving me to worship Satan. At the same time, I was also created to serve a Hunahpu agenda—in my case, the preservation of our species. You might think this would have been in direct conflict with Satan; in fact, it was the fallen angel who pushed me to succeed, for without man and his acts of negativity, Satan is nothing more than a lifeless deflated vessel."

"What made you believe humanity was in danger?"

"Sometime around my seventeenth birthday, I began experiencing intense nightmares, all detailing images of a global cataclysmic destruction. The Mayan calendar prophesied the Doomsday Event I was envisioning, but the dates made no sense. The end of the fifth cycle concluded on December 21 in 2012—nine months before our birth—yet somehow humanity had survived. Still, the threat obviously remained, and through my visions I tracked the destruction foretold in my dreams to the Yellowstone caldera. Like a modern-day Noah, I set a plan in motion to construct a fleet of space arks, first by marrying Lucien Mabus, then by using his company and wealth to revolutionize the space tourism industry. It's taken me seventeen years to ready a dozen shuttles and a colony on Mars, and now, because of you, everything has somehow changed. While the Doomsday threat is more real than ever, the cause of the cataclysm has shifted."

The pilot's voice interrupts. "Approaching fifty thousand feet. Activating rocket boosters in ten seconds. Nine . . . eight . . . seven . . ."

"What do you mean, 'the cause of the cataclysm has shifted'?"

"I'm going to show you."

Manny's body is suddenly crushed into the thick padding of his chair as the space plane's rocket boosters fire, accelerating the vessel to 2,500 miles an hour, three times the speed of sound. For twenty seconds the roar of the engines overwhelms the cabin, then silence takes the ship and his body floats off the seat.

Lilith unbuckles her harness and he follows her lead, the two of them swimming in liquid air, frolicking in zero gravity. He maneuvers to the nearest window and stares at the Earth, transfixed by the planet's beauty, moved by the emotional reality that supersedes war and hatred and greed— that this warm blue world, surrounded by the vast cold emptiness of space, is a life-harboring gift.

Lilith squeezes in beside him. She points to the planet's curvature that reveals Earth's atmosphere, a thin protective envelope of blue set against the black cosmos. "That tiny layer of atmosphere is the only thing that separates Earth from Mars."

The pilot's face appears on the cabin multiple screens. "We're moving into a near-polar orbit as you requested. Everything is ready for your space walk."

Manny glances at Lilith. "Space walk?"

*   *   *

H.O.P.E. astronaut Ryan Matson is waiting for them in the airlock hatch, located mid-deck, directly below the passenger cabin. Six space suits of varying sizes are secured to one wall. Matson takes a quick look at Manny's physique, then floats over to the largest space suit and frees it from its coupling. "You sure you want to do this, fella?"

"Why? Is it dangerous?"

"If you consider tethering in space to a ship traveling through a shooting gallery of debris at ten times the speed of a bullet dangerous, then yeah. Ever wore one of these suits?"

"Only to clean my pool."

Matson is not amused. "This suit has eleven layers, including a liquid cooling and ventilation garment and a pressurized bladder to keep your blood from boiling. There are five layers of insulation, allowing you to operate in temperatures ranging from minus 250 degrees Fahrenheit to plus 250 degrees. You'll be breathing pure oxygen, but we've been pumping it into the cabin, so you should be fairly acclimated by now. Don't panic if you hear the internal fan going on and off, it's designed to remove excess body heat to keep your helmet from fogging up and causing dehydration. The Kevlar outer skin should protect you from micrometeroids, but there are several million far more lethal objects orbiting Earth, so try to stay close to the ship."

"Okay, hypothetical situation. Let's say I accidentally puncture my space suit."

"In that case, your suit would depressurize immediately, causing anoxia and rapid death."

Manny glances at Lilith, who is already dressed. "You'll be fine."

"That's encouraging. Are space walks part of your standard package for paying customers?"

"We don't offer EVAs to our clients. Way too dangerous." Matson hands Manny a headset. "As per Lilith's orders, I set the comm links to allow you two to talk in private. There's an override switch on your belt that will open a channel with the flight deck, just in case."

The astronaut sprays the inside faceplate of Manny's polycarbonate helmet with an antifog compound, checks the internal lights, then fits it over his head. "Ready?"

They exit the cargo bay into silence. There is no wind or sound in space, nor any real clue as to how fast they are actually moving as the ship passes over the Middle East, following a near-ninety-degree orbit designed to pass over the planet's northern pole. Manny does a quick calculation in his head, dividing the Earth's circumference by their ninety-minute orbits, determining their velocity to be 4.63 miles a second. The information renders him dizzy.

"Manny, are you okay?"

"Why am I here, Lilith?"

"To answer that, we need to observe the Earth from the Nexus."

Manny feels the blood drain from his face. "That's extremely dangerous. The pressure alone . . . it'll be like swimming in lead."

"I've done it three times. It'll be a bit disorienting at first, and yes, it will be difficult to move, but it's necessary. In the end, I guess it comes down to trust. Are you willing to trust me? If the answer's no, then we have no future together, and I mean that in more ways than one."

"Why was Lauren Beckmeyer killed?"

"Who's Lauren Beckmeyer?"

"She was my fiancée, a geology major at Miami. Lauren's dad was an engineer. They were working on a plan to vent the Yellowstone caldera using a robotic device called GOPHER."

"It wouldn't have worked."

"She was assassinated, Lilith! Along with her mentor, Professor Bill Gabeheart. Recognize the name?"

For a long moment, the two astronauts hover silently in space, the Atlantic Ocean passing beneath them.

"I wasn't the one who gave the order, but I was involved in the decision to keep everything quiet. Gabeheart figured out the data coming out of Yellowstone had been doctored. I imagine he told your fiancée, so they killed her, too. It may not mean much to you, but I truly am sorry."

"You're sorry?" Tears flow from his eyes, the change in humidity causing his suit's internal fan to blow cool air on his face. "Where's the justice in this world? Who pays the price for decisions that steal the lives of the innocent?"

"We all do. At least let me show you. Afterward, if you still want revenge, you can do with me whatever you please." She loops the crook of her left arm around his right elbow before he can protest. "Together on three. One . . . two—"

Closing his eyes, Manny wills his consciousness into a higher dimension—

—his insides instantly crushed beneath several Gs of force. The pain dissipates as he opens his eyes, his mind taken by his suddenly altered perception of reality.

The Earth's rotation has slowed to a barely noticeable crawl, reflective of the increased rate of speed within the Nexus—a corridor of space-time connecting them to the nine higher dimensions. As the physical world around him slows, he can now see things that had been moving far too fast only moments ago.

Debris orbits the planet like a flowing river of garbage. Tiny glittering granules of dust, paint flakes, and droplets of coolant expelled from rocket boosters form a geosynchronous ring around the equator while larger objects, dispersed in a low earth orbit, flutter like satellites. He spots a screwdriver spinning fifty yards beneath his feet, its torn cable trailing behind like a comet's tail.

Then, as their shuttle climbs over Russia, another object comes into view, causing his blood to run cold.

Hovering ten thousand miles above the Earth's northern pole is a starless black spot, its event horizon approximately twenty percent of the circumference of the moon. Blending in with space, it is visible only by its gelidlike swirling distortion and a thin trail of gray-green debris that appears to be unraveling along its perimeter, constricting in a tight string of energy that pierces the Earth's atmosphere. Following the planetary axis, the singularity continues moving through the planet's core—

—emerging from the South Pole as a cord of fiery red molecules that coalesce around the expanding orifice of a second black hole opening in space below the Southern Hemisphere, its event horizon twice the size of its shrinking twin.

"My God . . ."

"Keep watching."

As the gravitational anomaly poised above the Northern Hemisphere empties, a new object appears over the Sea of Japan.

"A wormhole?"

The wormhole remains stable for the seven minutes and forty-two seconds it takes the remains of the northern singularity to be pulled through the planet's core and out the other side. Then the wormhole disappears.

The starless black spot of space poised over the Southern Hemisphere remains, the black hole's event horizon slightly larger than its cannibalized twin.

"Lilith?"

"It's called a strangelet, a type of black hole, most likely created by one of the Hadron Colliders. The first time I saw it was on my honeymoon on H.O.P.E.'s maiden voyage back in 2031. We were flying over the aurora borealis. Back then, the strangelet was no larger than a basketball, too small to generate a wormhole. The only reason I even noticed it was because the ship's starboard wing passed through the singularity as it exited the Earth's northern axis."

"Did it damage the ship?"

"No. It doesn't exist in the physical dimension, at least not yet, but the density of its mass is growing larger, and the larger it grows, the greater the effect on Earth's tectonic plates. It's the reason we've had so many earthquakes and tsunamis."

"What about the caldera?"

"Two weeks ago, the magma chamber collapsed. The anomaly is pushing us toward a cataclysmic eruption. As bad as that will be, it's nothing compared to what's coming. At some point the strangelet will accumulate sufficient mass to exert a gravitational pull in our physical universe. When that happens, the fully formed black hole will make one last pass through the Earth's axis before devouring the entire planet."

"Who else knows about this?"

"Just the two of us, and Devlin. Humans can't detect it yet."

Manny stares below as they pass over Greenland, his being filled with rage. Despite all the warnings, mankind had finally done it, only it was not a nuclear weapon or engineered plague that would unleash the prophesied Doomsday Event, it would be man's unbridled intellect, fed by his enormous ego.

They pass over the southernmost ice floes of the Arctic Circle. "Manny, we need to leave the Nexus."

Manny doesn't hear her, his mind too focused on the mission tasked by his brother in the holy land. *The strangelet was unleashed years ago. I need to find out which Hadron Collider did the deed, and when.*

The mere thought of the physicists responsible sickens him; while they collected their accolades and awards, their Doomsday particle's fuse had continued to burn—

Manny! Lilith's voice snaps him from his thoughts as she reaches out to him telepathically from within the Nexus. *We're passing over the polar axis. You need to leave the Nexus, it's too—*

There is neither a sound nor warning, just an eye that blinks open over the northern axis below his feet. For a harrowing split second he can see an orange-red speck that reveals the planet's violated core as the singularity bursts out of the planet, rocketing upward at them at the speed of light.

His mind leaps from the Nexus—his consciousness caught within a cosmic tsunami of proton particles that passes through his being, delivering him into its soothing white light.

106

9

I want to know how God created this world. I am not
interested in this or that phenomenon, in the spectrum
of this or that element. I want to know His thoughts; the
rest are details.

—ALBERT EINSTEIN,
LETTER TO ESTHER SALAMAN, 1920

Perhaps it was the waterfall that caused him to wake,
its mist dissipating across the azure lagoon, leaving
cool beads of precipitation on his skin. Or the birds' shrill
call in the distance, masked by the ruffle of palm fronds
obliterating his view of the sky. Regardless, Immanuel
Gabriel opens his eyes and stretches out in the pink sand
by the lagoon being fed by the waterfall in the lush garden, smiling at the thought that his soul has moved on,
relieving him of his earthly burden.

*No, Manny. Your soul has temporarily vacated its phys-
ical vessel, but you have not moved on.*

"Mom?" He springs to his feet, not through muscular
exertion but because he willed it. He never moves, instead
it is the foliage that parts around him and the landscape

that unfolds before him in a bubble of existence where time has been replaced by cause and effect.

The inverted tree is mountainous, its glory rooted in the heavens above and beyond his scope of sight, its upper three entwined trunks flowing down into a thick cluster of six branches before ending in the one.

The one, directly ahead, melds into a man and woman . . . both towering a hundred feet high.

They are standing back to back as if their vertebrae were fused like the teeth of a zipper, their nudity strategically concealed by vines that bind them further. The woman, a dark-haired Mesoamerican beauty, is on the left; the man, a youthful thirty bearing an athlete's physique, on the right.

Michael Gabriel.

Dominique Vazquez Gabriel.

Manny drops to his knees in the Garden of Eden before the tree of life that sprouts his parents and wills himself to speak, only the thought is vocalized telepathically before his voice box can engage. *How is it that I am here?*

Because we willed it. His father never moves. His blazing ebony eyes remain unblinking.

Is this real?

No, his mother communicates. *What you perceive is a manifestation of thought energy. We are bound to it by our terminal existence in the Malchut.*

Is the Malchut a prison?

The Malchut is the physical universe, answers his father. *The lowest of the ten Sefirot, the ten dimensions formed by the Tzimtzum . . . the contraction.*

The contraction?

The effect you call the Big Bang.

Manny's mind reels. *What was the cause of the Tzimtzum?*

The cause was the vessel Adam's desire to be like the Creator and share. But the vessel Adam was created only to receive endless fulfillment. And so the vessel Adam shunned the Creator's light and the Tzimtzum occurred.

The vessel Adam? They're revealing the story of creation, the real deal . . .

Mother, before the Big . . . the contraction—what was there?

Before refers to time. Time does not exist in the infinite, therefore there is no before, there is only cause and effect. In the infinite reality of existence where time does not exist, there is the Creator, there is the unknowable essence of the Creator, and there is the light that comes from the Creator. The light exists in the Endless. The light is perfection. We can never know the Creator, but at His essence is the nature of sharing. Because there was nothing upon which to share, a reciprocal energy was necessary to complete the circuitry—a vessel to receive the Creator's infinite light. And so the vessel Adam was created, and its entire purpose was to receive. The vessel Adam was the unified soul, and every soul that exists today is a spark from Adam.

His father takes over: *The vessel Adam was divided into two aspects. The female aspect, Eve, was composed of negatively charged electrons; the male aspect, Adam, was the vessel's positively charged protons. And the vessel had only the desire to receive, and the light only gave, and so there was boundless fulfillment. But as the light continued to fill the vessel, it passed along the Creator's essence—the desire to share. The vessel Adam had no way of sharing. The vessel Adam also felt shame because it had not earned the endless fulfillment it was receiving. And so the vessel Adam shunned the Creator's light. Without the light, the vessel Adam contracted into a singular point of darkness, which was the Tzimtzum.*

But Father, if the Tzimtzum was the contraction, what caused the sudden expansion that gave birth to the physical universe?

To suddenly be without fulfillment was too much for the vessel Adam. In rushing to regain the Creator's light, the vessel Adam expanded too quickly and shattered, its molecular structure exploding outward, releasing protons and electrons into a bubble of physicality, the infinite birthing the finite.

But why would the Creator allow the vessel Adam to shatter?

The vessel Adam desired to earn its own fulfillment. The Creator, who loved the vessel unconditionally, gave it the opportunity it desired.

What opportunity?

Manny, each living thing possesses a soul, a spark of the shattered vessel Adam. Life in the Malchut is an opportunity to earn the endless fulfillment. It is why we are here.

Why ten dimensions? What is their purpose?

Each Sefirot acts as a filter, concealing the Creator's light from the physical world. The upper three realms—Keter, Chochmah, and Binah—are closest to the Creator and do not exert direct influence in man's physical realm. The next six Sefirot are enfolded into one superdimension, the Ze'ir Anpin. Beneath this bundle of six lies the Malchut—the physical universe. Light from the Ze'ir Anpin is accessible to those who seek it.

But why conceal the Creator's light? If people knew—I mean, come on . . . do you know how much better life would be? No hatred, no greed—

—no transformation, interrupts his father. *Fulfillment must be earned. The Sefirot veil the Creator's light, ensuring free will. The Opponent ensures fulfillment will be earned.*

The Opponent?

The Opponent is Satan. Satan resides in the eleventh dimension, rooted in the human ego as temptation and greed, lust and violence. To resist Satan is part of the test.

Always remember, son, darkness cannot exist in the light.

Father, why have you brought me here?

Man's ego has allowed the serpent into the garden. The Creator does not wish the Malchut destroyed. You have been chosen as the cause that can change the effect.

And what is the effect I am to change?

The tree, the garden, his parents, and all their surroundings are filtered into a soothing white light, a light so intense that he cannot gaze at its infinite source.

When he opens his eyes, he is confronted by a serpent, its red eyes staring at him through enormous black pupils, its upper torso reared to the height of his chest.

Greetings from the eleventh dimension, Uncle.

Devlin?

Is that your soul I taste oozing fear? How far the other shoe has dropped since our last encounter when the boy still ruled the man.

Who are you?

I am what will come to pass. Take a glimpse, Uncle, at the future that awaits you should you pursue your holy mission. I offer you a taste of real fear . . .

"Manny, follow my voice . . ."

Lying in the pit in bone-deep cold through an eternity of emptiness and darkness, he detects the pattern of pink behind eyelids sealed in amber.

"—try to open your eyes."

He struggles against an immovable weight until he realizes he has no arms.

"Fight your way out. Create pain."

He stands amid blackness and feels for the wall, bloodying the cold stone with his face. Over and over he strikes the dungeonlike enclosure until he finds his hands tingling somewhere in the abyss. Encouraged, he bashes the pit's rounded walls harder, all the while opening and closing his long-lost appendages, the pain giving birth to arms. His fingers walk up his broken upper torso to the diseased flesh he has bashed into pulp and claw at the amber sealing his eyes until he unveils the light—

—a bright room with blue sky and curtains laced with IV tubes— interrupted by the face of a goddess, her vanilla scent infiltrating the sulfu-

rous taste still lingering in his lungs, her hands, warm and soft, caressing his whiskered face.

Unable to speak, Manny stares at Lilith, attempting to communicate telepathically.

She sees him struggling. Offers him a glass of orange juice, positioning the straw between his parched lips. "Sip this slowly. Manny, I was so scared, I thought I lost you forever. Are you in pain? Can you remember anything?"

He looks around the bedroom, bewildered, his blinking eyes swimming in confusion. "Tortured me . . . how long?"

"Tortured you? No, Manny, that must have been a dream. We were spacewalking, don't you remember? The singularity passed through you while your consciousness was still harbored in the Nexus. You've been unconscious seven weeks."

Seven weeks. The forty-nine days of Omer. Is it possible? Confusion turns to anger. Enraged at having his prison sentence reduced in Lilith's eyes he struggles to sit up, his body aching and weak. "Not seven weeks. It was longer . . . forty years of darkness. Forty years of torture!"

"Forty years, wandering in darkness? Just like the Israelites, huh? That must have been some dream."

Manny's head whips around, the blood draining from his bearded face. The familiar male voice echoes in whispers that infest his mind with a coldness that lacks all warmth—verbal tentacles of evil that wrap all rational thought in fear. Terrified beyond the ability to reason, Manny falls off the far side of the bed like a flogged animal, tearing the IV needles from his veins in his hasty retreat.

Devlin Mabus smiles from the doorway to his mother's bedroom suite. The bloodshot sclera of his eyes are now totally red, his aura cold and settled—the adolescent permanently excised. "Welcome back, Uncle. We missed you."

U.S. DISTRICT COURT
EASTERN DISTRICT OF NEW YORK
CASE NO. 00CV1672 [2000]:

WALTER L. WAGNER
(Plaintiff)

vs.

BROOKHAVEN SCIENCE ASSOCIATES
(Defendant)

SWORN AFFIDAVIT

I, H. Kimball Hansen, PhD, declare under penalty of perjury as follows:

I am a Professor, emeritus, of astronomy in the Department of Physics and Astronomy at Brigham Young University, Provo, Utah. I was a member of the faculty there between 1963 and 1993, and from 1968 through 1991. I was also associate editor of *The Publications of the Astronomical Society of the Pacific*.

I have read the First Amended Complaint, the Affidavits of Drs. Richard J. Wagner and Walter L. Wagner, the Safety Review[1] referenced therein, and the science article on strangelets by Joshua Holden, and am familiar with the issues therein with respect to operation of the RHIC [Relativistic Heavy Ion Collider at Brookhaven National Laboratory].

I concur that the so-called "supernova argument" used in the Safety Review to ostensibly show the safety of the RHIC is wholly faulty. It presupposes the stability of small strangelets, with lifetimes on the order of centuries or longer, long enough to travel great distances through space. The authors had previously asserted that to be dangerous strangelets only needed to have lifetimes on the order of a billionth of a second, just long enough to travel a few centimeters and reach normal matter outside the vacuum of the RHIC.

There are a number of theoretical arguments that show that strangelets might be dangerous, and there are faults in the arguments presented, to date, to show

[1] Review of speculative "Disaster Scenarios" at RHIC

the safety of the RHIC. I am of the opinion that it would be wise to avoid head-on collisions in the RHIC until a more thorough safety review, preferably before the physics community as a whole, has been obtained. However, the fixed-target mode of operation for the RHIC would be acceptable.

H. Kimball Hansen, PhD
May 17, 2000

10

GENEVA, SWITZERLAND

I t comes down to the how and the why. The why deals
with God and religion, the how is what particle physics is all about."

They are riding in the back of a limousine through the
French countryside, the aging physicist and the CIA-trained
assassin having arrived in Geneva an hour ago aboard Lilith
Mabus's private jet.

Dr. Dave Mohr is lost in his element.

Mitchell Kurtz is just lost. "Okay, Doc, having spent all those billions of dollars building these massive particle accelerators, maybe you could tell me what you eggheads actually know about the Big Bang?"

"We know that approximately 13.7 billion years ago our universe sprang into existence as a singularity. Singularities are entities which we still lack the knowledge to define, though we believe they exist at the core of black holes. According to astrophysicists like Stephen Hawking, the singularity that originated the physical universe didn't appear *in* space; rather, space began inside of the singularity."

"So what existed before the singularity?"

"Before the singularity nothing existed. Not space or time, matter or energy."

"Let me get this straight: the singularity that created the entire universe came from nothing? It just appeared . . . *poof!* God, that has got to be the dumbest thing a smart guy has ever said."

"Maybe God was part of that side of the equation, we don't know. What we do know is that our physical universe was and still remains inside the expanding singularity. Before the Big Bang occurred it didn't exist and neither did we. Whatever it was, it was infinitesimally small—smaller than an atom—and extremely hot. And it didn't explode, it more or less expanded outward in all directions at the speed of light.

"The Big Bang produced matter and antimatter in equal amounts. Seconds after creation, these two materials collided and destroyed one another, creating pure energy. Fortunately for us, most of the antimatter decayed or was annihilated, leaving enough matter intact to allow the physical universe as we know it to take root. As the universe expanded and cooled, quarks stuck together, forming protons and neutrons. Helium nuclei formed after one hundred seconds, but it took another hundred thousand years before the first atoms appeared. A billion years passed before helium and hydrogen massed together to form stars, all the while the universe continued cooling and expanding. It was Edwin Hubble who discovered this phenomenon in 1929, his observations, among others, tracing the expansion back to that concentrated superhot singularity."

"If you know so much, why the need to build more of these Doomsday colliders?"

"Because the puzzle of creation is missing key pieces which can only be found in the subatomic particles created a millionth of a second after the Big Bang. Isaac Newton was way ahead of his time when he first initiated the field of particle physics, introducing the world to what some scientists called his 'forbidden wisdom.' Two centuries passed before Ernest Rutherford discovered atoms are mostly empty space, their mass concentrated in a tiny fat nucleus orbited by lightweight electrons. Physicists later discovered protons and neutrons inside the nucleus. That wasn't enough, so they began probing the interior of these structures and discovered quarks. Meanwhile, Einstein's general theory of relativity introduced the fabric of space-time and the revelation that matter bends space, all of which literally added another dimension—or, more accurately, a total of ten dimensions—to the theory of existence."

"But that wasn't enough either, huh?"

"The reason it wasn't enough, Mitchell, is that theoretical physicists prefer everything neat and orderly. The Big Bang created ten dimensions, but we don't know why. We question our standard model for elements within the physical universe because it's chaotic and feels incomplete—fifty-seven particles, sixteen of which are fundamental particles, not counting antimatter or neutrinos which, as we sit here, are streaming through our bodies at the rate of trillions per second. It's too complex. Physicists desire a set of basic, simplified rules of how particles interact."

"And so you eggheads had to start smashing atoms together."

"It was the only way to test the theories of quantum physics. When I said there were missing pieces to the puzzle I was referring to a hypothetical seventeenth fundamental particle, known as the Higgs boson. Physicist Peter Higgs theorized that the void of space is not really empty, it's permeated by an invisible field that acts like cosmic mud, providing mass to particles that shouldn't have any. That cosmic mud is the Higgs boson, which has become the Holy Grail of particle physics. Some have labeled it the God particle. Particle accelerators were constructed to find it."

"Ironic that the search for the God particle may end up destroying everything God created."

"We sought knowledge of the universe. Was that so wrong?"

"Knowledge is power, Doc. Wisdom is knowing when to back off." Kurtz glances out the window as they turn down Route Schrödinger, heading for a private compound of buildings. "When was the last time you were here?"

"July of 2010. I was assigned to ATLAS, a detector that's seven stories tall. There are four detectors positioned around the LHC. The heaviest is the Compact Muon Solenoid, which weighs more than the Eiffel Tower. The detectors record the collisions and help us to analyze massive amounts of data measured in petabytes—thousands of trillions of bits. The World Wide Web was actually created by a CERN physicist as a means of sharing his data with scientists across the globe."

"So how does this particle collider work?"

"Essentially, the LHC is a large ring housed in a tunnel seventeen miles in circumference, located about one hundred feet underground. Two beams of particles race in opposite directions around the tunnel ten thousand times a second, guided by more than a thousand cylindrical, supercooled magnets. The collider accelerates protons to energies of 7 trillion electron volts and smashes them together at the four detector locations at near–light speed. The collisions transform matter into clumps of energy, creating an incredibly intense fireball smaller than the size of an atom, with a temperature about a million times hotter than the center of the sun. The singularity is so dense it's like condensing the Empire State Building down to the size of a pinhead. By colliding these particles, the LHC re-creates circumstances that existed about a millionth of a second after the Big Bang occurred, in order to discover new particles, forces, and dimensions."

"And in doing so, you create black holes?"

"Small ones, yes."

"According to the wicked witch, the one that passed through Manny wasn't so small."

Dr. Mohr gazes out his tinted window. "Everyone knew there was an inherent danger, no one believed it could actually happen. Actually, that's not true. President Chaney believed it—I think it was the twins' mother who pushed for the moratorium. And before that, a group of physicists sued Brookhaven's Collider over concerns the experiments would create microscopic black holes or possibly strangelets, either of which had the potential to destroy the entire planet. According to their theories, a microscopic black hole would bounce around, striking and absorbing other atoms before it would repeatedly pass through the Earth's magnetic core, each time growing larger. Our scientists dismissed their concerns, claiming mini black holes were too unstable to be sustained. The bigger concern was the creation of strangelets, a more stable type of singularity. If a strangelet passed through the chamber and escaped, it could theoretically convert any matter it came into contact with into a part of itself. Apparently that's what happened, only it came into being in another dimension, an unexpected variable impossible for us to measure."

"And if this unexpected variable materializes in our physical universe like Lilith fears?"

The physicist exhales a deep breath. "I don't know. If it becomes a true third-dimensional black hole, and if it acquires the right size and gravitational forces, then yes—it would present a serious threat to our entire planet."

"Marvelous."

"It's easy to play the blame game, Mitchell, and there's plenty to go around. What's important now is that we discover when the strangelet was created."

"It must have been recently. The black hole that sunk Evelyn's cruise ship—"

"That wasn't a black hole, it was a wormhole, a residual anomaly created after the singularity passed through the Earth's magnetic core."

"Manny was talking about using a wormhole to travel back in time to a period before the 2012 Doomsday Event."

"I don't see how that's possible. You can't direct a wormhole."

"Maybe he can." Kurtz glances out his window as they arrive at the gated entrance of CERN's Geneva campus. "So who's this brainiac we're here to see?"

"His name is Jack Harbach O'Sullivan. I call him the Jackson Pollock of physics. If Lilith and Manny really saw a strangelet passing through another dimension, Jack will know how to verify it."

The limo proceeds to the visitor's gate. A guard matches their biochip to the guest list, and they proceed to one of the white brick buildings ahead.

GULF OF MEXICO
JULY 2, 2047
4:37 A.M.

The jet-copter soars beneath a starry night sky five hundred feet over the dark waters of the Gulf of Mexico, its pilot maintaining a southwesterly heading toward the Yucatan Peninsula. Ryan Beck occupies the copilot's seat, the aging assassin snoring lightly. Lilith is in back, Manny's head cradled in her lap. The Hunahpu twin is heavily sedated. His eyelids flutter, his breathing restless pants that have gone on unabated since they left South Florida two hours earlier.

Whatever was infecting Immanuel Gabriel's mind had removed all rational thought. Entrenched in a state of fear, he had bolted Lilith's bedroom by smashing through a set of hurricane-resistant French glass doors, leaping from the second-story balcony to the beach below. He had sprinted nearly a mile before Lilith caught him using the Nexus. Subduing him within the ethereal corridor of space-time, she injected him with a shot of Thorazine.

If Manny's fear was worrisome, then Devlin's transformation was outright terrifying. The teen's cold, calculating demeanor had faded with the daylight, his schizophrenic behavior in full bloom by midnight. Stalking through the Mabus compound, jabbering in ancient tongues, the dangerous man-child seemed oblivious to his physical surroundings, his mind immersed in another dimension, the portals of which refused to allow him entry. Infuriated, he prostrated himself on the pool deck in the lunar light, pounding his skull against the brick pavers. It had taken enough tranquilizer to put down a horse before he had mercifully passed out.

The eastern horizon grays, revealing Ciudad del Carmen, the coastal city part of the Mexican state of Campeche. Continuing to the southwest, they fly over a green valley peppered with small lakes and sinkholes. Twenty minutes later, the Chiapas Highlands rise beneath a dense tropical jungle.

The pilot reduces his speed and altitude, then activates the jet-copter's three-blade rotor as he retracts the wings, converting the plane back into chopper mode. The airship circles the dense foliage until a series of gray-white stone temples protrude from the canopy of green. Locating a flat open field a quarter mile west of the ruins, the pilot lands.

Palenque: Ancient capital of the Mayan city-state of B'aakal, known to the indigenous Indians as Lakam Ha. Springs and small rivers flow through the jungle fortification, which dates back to AD 300. In AD 431, K'uk B'alam became the first leader to ascend to the throne. Ten kings and 144 years later, an adolescent by the name of K'inich Janaab' Pakal I (Pakal the Great) began a sixty-eight-year reign as ruler of the most important city in the classic Mayan era.

Ryan Beck tosses Immanuel Gabriel over his broad shoulder, then follows Lilith along a footpath leading into the manicured park. Waves of white mist cool the foliage in gentle waves, filtering the predawn light. The jungle slowly awakens around them in a concerto of chirps and catcalls and a thousand fluttering wings.

The path leads them through a cluster of temples known as the Cross Group. The park appears deserted, the gates not set to open to tourists for another three hours.

The old woman is waiting for them at the Temple of the Inscriptions, the five-foot Aztec Indian dwarfed by the two-hundred-foot-tall limestone monolith. A thin layer of leathery flesh hangs from her brittle bones, her cataract-ridden blue-gray eyes as cloudy as the mist. Her face is gaunt and weathered, her body wiry yet deceptively strong for a centenarian.

Lilith bends down and kisses her maternal great-aunt's knobby cheek. "Chicahua, thank you for coming on such short notice."

"We do not have much time. Awaken the Hunahpu."

Beck glances down at Lilith, unsure.

"Chicahua is a seer, her ancestors advised kings. Do as she says."

The bodyguard lowers Manny to the temple steps, then injects him with a shot of Adrenalin.

Manny's eyes snap open, wild and full of fear. He looks around, cowering as if the spirits of the dead are rising up through the earth around him.

Beck clotheslines him around his neck with his right biceps as he tries to flee, holding on for dear life. Manny twists out from the headlock, tossing the big man over his shoulder as if he were a schoolchild.

Blue-gray puffs of smoke meet the Gabriel twin's nostrils, exhaled from the old woman's herb-laced cigarette. Manny teeters back on his heels, the terror vacating his expression.

The old woman places both of her knotty hands over his eyes, pressing her right ear against his chest. "Chilam Balam . . . I recognize you. Lurking in the shadows like a wounded cat. Full of fear, Balam, your thoughts so tainted . . . filled with poison."

"What's wrong with him?" Lilith demands. "And why are you calling him Chilam Balam?"

"The Hunahpu's soul has been possessed, affecting past lives as well as the present. The spirit responsible is dark and powerful."

Lilith hovers close, whispering in Chicahua's native language. "Can you save him?"

"I can sever the connection that binds them, that is all."

"Then do it."

"There is a price." The old woman eyes Beck.

"Not him. I brought another."

Antonio Amorelli sits alone in the jet-copter cockpit, his eyes focused on the palm-size GPS in his left hand. The tiny tracking device he slipped into Immanuel Gabriel's pants pocket continues to function perfectly, the red dot slowly ascending the Temple of Inscriptions.

With his right hand he speed-dials the cell phone.

"Speak."

"Dev, it's Antonio. I flew your mother and the Gabriel twin away from the compound late last night. Thought you'd want to know, although your mother would kill me if she knew we were speaking."

"Perhaps I should tell her."

Antonio's heart beats rapidly, the sweat pouring from his face. "I called out of loyalty."

"I'm not a fool, Mr. Amorelli. You're in Palenque."

The pilot swears to himself. "I knew you knew, I mean . . . I only called to let you know that I placed a tracking device on your uncle, you know, just in case."

"Then there's hope for you yet. Sever the copter's fuel line, make it look like a malfunction. I'll be there soon. Oh, and expect a large credit transferred into your offshore account."

"That's . . . very generous."

The line goes dead.

They ascend the pyramid steps, divided into nine tiers representing the Nine Lords of the Night. The old woman is assisted by Lilith. Manny follows in a drug-induced stupor, the aging bodyguard bringing up the rear, his T-shirt drenched in sweat. Reaching the temple summit, the Aztec seer walks to the center entrance, one of three doors leading inside.

"The African will remain here." Without waiting for a response, she pushes open the door, entering a long vaulted room featuring three hieroglyphic inscriptions, one on either side of the chamber, the last on the rear center wall. Behind the central pillar is a hole in the floor where a fourth inscription has been carved into a massive stone. The tablet has been removed, revealing a secret passageway. Guided by the beam of a finger-size halogen flashlight, Lilith helps the old woman down a narrow flight of sixty-six steps, the limestone surface slick with condensation. Manny follows closely behind.

At the bottom of the steps is a tunnel, its walls set at an angle, meeting at the ceiling to form a triangular passage. They follow it as it widens and turns east, their light revealing another stairwell, this one descending twenty-two steps to a small chamber.

Another turn and they are standing before Lord Pakal's tomb.

The sarcophagus that once held the jade-masked remains of Palenque's deceased ruler is immense—twelve feet long by seven feet wide. Inscribed upon the five-ton lid are glyphs representing the sun, the moon, Venus, and various constellations of the cosmos. The centerpiece of the relief is a carving of Pakal riding on the hilt of a dagger-shaped space vessel. A cross attached to the blade symbolizes the tree of life. Adorned in the mask of the sun god, the moving vehicle represents the transition from life to death. Pakal is fleeing the jaws of a serpent, descending into the underworld of Xibalba.

The old woman instructs the two Hunahpu, "Remove the lid."

Together, Manny and Lilith brace their legs, pushing the lid with their hands, sliding the ten-thousand-pound stone just enough for someone to enter its empty claustrophobia-inducing interior.

Chicahua turns to Manny. "Climb inside."

In one fluid motion, Manny slips inside the limestone structure.

Lilith grabs Chicahua's arm. "Explain to me what you are doing before you do it!"

"Do you care for him, Lilith?"

"He is my intended soul mate. I know in my heart we were meant to be together."

"Perhaps. But not in this lifetime."

"Sorry, but I don't believe that."

"Listen to me carefully, child. This lifetime is over for you and Gabriel and every soul who dwells in the physical universe. I am a seer, and right now there is no future to see, only emptiness. If that is to change, then it can only be conceived in the past. If you were intended to be together, then you may find one another again, but Lilith Aurelia Mabus and Immanuel Gabriel are two entwined pieces of sand in a rapidly diminishing hourglass, and when you cease to exist your soul shall be remanded for Gehennom."

"You're wrong, old woman. My soul has been cleansed. Jacob cleansed it in Xibalba."

"Your soul has not been cleansed. What Jacob did on Xibalba was merely to remove the veils of darkness that were filtering the Creator's light. Yes, you may have transformed into a being capable of love, but you have also committed horrible acts of evil in this lifetime. Every soul must earn its fulfillment before returning to the higher dimensions, it cannot be bestowed upon you by either an angel or a deceased Hunahpu twin."

"How do I earn fulfillment if my soul is destined for Hell?"

"You can't. Not if humanity ceases to exist. Come here, look at the inscription on Pakal's tomb, for it was carved to depict the end of times we now face. Pakal, traveling with the tree of life, is about to enter Xibalba in his vessel. He is being chased by the same demon serpent now haunting your Hunahpu soul mate. See the bone piercing Pakal's nose? The bone is the seed of Pakal's resurrection. It means that even death carries with it the seed of rebirth. Should Immanuel exorcize himself of the serpent that now occupies his mind, then he too must travel down the dark road in order to plant a new seed of humanity—and save your soul."

The old woman shines her light inside Pakal's burial tomb at Immanuel Gabriel, who is lying on his back. "Seal the lid. Remain inside until the Lords of Xibalba have vacated your mind."

Using his powerful legs, Manny presses the lid upward, then back in place.

Lilith runs her hands over the inscription, her limbs trembling. "And if he fails?"

"Then he will suffocate, and your soul will remain trapped in Gehennom for all eternity."

The Final Papers of
Julius Gabriel, PhD

Cambridge University archives

You cannot erase time.
—ANDRÉS XILOJ PERUCH
K'ICHE DAYKEEPER

Decoding the Mayan Popol Vuh

. . . the lords who once ruled a kingdom from a place called Quiche, in the highlands of Guatemala, once had in their possession a "seeing instrument" that enabled them to know or see distant or future events. The instrument was not a telescope, not a crystal for gazing, but a book. The lords of Quiche consulted their book when they sat in council, and their name for it was Popol Vuh or *Council Book*. Because this book contained an account of how the forefathers of their own lordly lineages had exiled themselves from a faraway city called Tulan, they sometimes described it as *The Writings About Tulan*. Because a later generation of lords had obtained the book by going on a pilgrimage that took them across water on a causeway, they titled it *The Light that Came from Across the Sea*. And because the book told of events that happened before the first sunrise and of a time when the forefathers hid themselves and the stones that contained the spirit familiars of their gods in forests, they also titled it *Our Place in the Shadows*. And finally, because it told of the first rising of the morning star and the sun and moon, and of the rise and radiant splendor of the Quiche lords, they titled it *The Dawn of Life*.

—Popol Vuh: The Mayan Book of the Dawn of Life (1550)

Much like the Bible stories written in the Old Testament, the Mayan Popol Vuh is encrypted with a knowledge intended to be ambiguous to the layperson. However, when translated by a "daykeeper," an oracle of Quiche Mayan descent, the Mayan Book of Creation takes on a whole new meaning, detailing events that date back to the earliest days of existence. And yet herein lies the paradox, for what is described in <u>The Light that Came from Across the Sea</u> *is not the dawn of humanity, it is the journey of another branch of Maya, an "offshoot" that came to exist in a far different reality from the indigenous people conquered by Cortés and his invading Spanish armada.*

Let us examine a verse translated from chapter 1 of the creation story, which describes life in this alternate reality:

They were pounded down to the bones and tendons, smashed and pulverized even to the bones. Their faces were smashed because they were incompetent before their mother and their father, the Heart of Sky, named Hurricane. The earth was blackened because of this; the black rainstorm began, rain all day and rain all night. Into their houses came the animals, small and great. Their faces were crushed by things of wood and stone. Everything spoke: their water jars, their tortilla griddles, their plates, their cooking pots, their dogs, their grinding stones, each and every thing crushed their faces. Their dogs and turkeys told them: you caused us pain, you ate us, but now it is you whom we shall eat . . . Such was the scattering of the human work, the human design. The people were ground down, overthrown. The mouths and faces of all of them were destroyed and crushed.

What this passage describes is a cataclysm, an event that blackened the earth and pulverized people down to their bones and tendons. An outsider might assume these conditions were caused by the aforementioned "Hurricane" assigned by the god-name "Heart of Sky." While this simplified interpretation reflects our twenty-first-century perspective, we must dig deeper to discern the true meaning of the author.

Having spent a decade or more in the company of the Quiche Mayan daykeepers, I am now convinced the "black rainstorm" that "crushed . . . wood and stone" is indicative of volcanic ash rained from the heavens. A clue as to the extent of the damage is offered by the phrase "scattering of the human work, the human design."

"Human design" refers to DNA. That the people were "ground down, overthrown" tells us the author was providing commentary on the annihilation of an already established civilization. The phrase "Everything spoke" relates to the problems suffered by the survivors of this volcanic event and how they perished. A water jar "speaks" only when empty, thus we are to assume the black rain tainted the fresh water supplies. The references regarding the tortilla griddle, plates, cooking pots, and grindstones suggests starvation. The dog in this line refers to the family pet who "spoke" when provided nothing to eat. The next line, "Their dogs and turkeys told them: you caused us pain, you ate us, but now it is you whom we shall eat," *is easier to interpret: the animals once consumed as food by humans were now consuming human remains as food.*

The last section of this opening chapter describes the end of darkness that covered the Earth and the rise of a malevolent threat, referred to as Seven Macaw:

. . . when there was just a trace of early dawn on the face of the earth and still there was no sun, there was one who magnified himself; Seven Macaw was his name. The sky-earth was already there, but the face of the sun-moon was clouded over. Even so, it is said that his light provided a sign for the people who were flooded. He was like a person of genius in his being.

Said Seven Macaw: "I am great. My place is now higher than that of the human work, the human design. I am their sun and I am their light, and I am also their months. So be it: my light is great. I am the walkway and I am the foothold of the people, because my eyes are of metal. My teeth glitter with jewels, and turquoise as well; they stand out blue with stones like the face of the sky. And this nose of mine shines white into the distance like the moon. Since my nest is metal, it lights up the face of the earth. When I come forth before my nest, I am like the sun and moon for those who are born in the light, begotten in the light. It must be so, because my face reaches into the distance."

It is not true that he is the sun, this Seven Macaw, yet he magnifies himself, his wings, his metal. But the scope of his face lies right around his own perch; his face does not reach everywhere beneath the sky. The faces of the sun, moon, and stars are not yet visible, it has not yet dawned. And so Seven Macaw puffs himself up as the days and the months, though the light of the sun and moon has not yet clarified.

Several clues in this passage tell us more about the previously mentioned cataclysm: "there was just a trace of early dawn on the face of the earth and still there was no sun." And again later: "The faces of the sun, moon, and stars are not yet visible, it has not yet dawned." There are only two known events that could unleash a global ash cloud expansive enough to envelop the entire planet and block out the sun's rays. The first is an asteroid strike, similar to the one that struck the planet 65 million years ago; the second is the eruption of a supervolcano, more commonly known as a caldera. In either case, the results are the same—a temporary cessation of photosynthesis, followed by mass starvation and an ice age.

Whoever they were, the Mayans recording these events must have arrived in this devastated land at the tail end of the ice age: "there was just a trace of early dawn on the face of the earth," and "his light [Seven Macaw's] provided a sign for the people who were flooded." The flood, of course, is the thawing of the glacial event.

The introduction of Seven Macaw reveals his malevolent power. "there was one who magnified himself; Seven Macaw was his name." "Magnified" refers to the human ego, the ego's desire to receive for the self alone being the darker side of human existence. The word "light" ("it is said that his light provided a sign for the people who were flooded") means power, in this case an intellect ("He was like a person of genius in his being") that enabled Seven Macaw to manipulate those members of his tribe who survived the deluge.

Seven Macaw's ego is on full display in the next passage: "I am great. My place is now higher than that of the human work, the human design. I am their sun and I am their light, and I am also their months." And yet, for all his power and dominance, the people knew this malevolent force was no god: "It is not true that he is the sun, this Seven Macaw, yet he magnifies himself, his wings, his metal." The author also tells us that Seven Macaw had an Achilles' heel ("But the scope of his face lies right around his own perch; his face does not reach everywhere beneath the sky"), a revelation that will come into play in these next chapters.

In summary, the Popol Vuh describes a world void of human life, devastated by a cataclysmic event. Somehow, a tribe of Quiche Maya arrived in this world at the end of the planet's glacial cleansing, only to be met by a malevolent demigod. But as powerful as this Seven Macaw appears, he cannot see everything—most importantly, the rise of a great warrior who would challenge the demon underlord and lead his people to freedom.

11

The future doesn't exist, or if it does exist, it is the obso-
lete in reverse. The future is always going backwards.
Our future tends to be prehistoric.

—ROBERT SMITHSON,
INTERVIEW WITH PATSY NORVELL, 1969

The fear had pushed him beyond the brink of sanity.
It whispered into his brain—his torturer perpetually
lurking in the shadows of his mind. It crawled beneath his
skin and suffocated all rational thought. Held within the
bonds of a drug-induced narcosis, it twisted his childhood
into scenes designed to inject more terror into his already
damaged psyche: *Mengele in his lab in Auschwitz, performing genetic experiments on twins; a Catholic priest offering a
lingering Nosferatu-like gaze from the bowels of an empty
church.* Each dream ended with a bloodcurdling scream,
each scream unraveling another stitch in the fabric of his
existence until his identity became the terror.

Awake!

The burners extinguish in his brain, allowing his
white-hot synapses to cool. Surrounded by the soothing

quiet, his mind crawls out of its shell, exploring an existence void of his torturer's demonic coos.

He opens his eyes to a dim grayness. He lacks all knowledge of where he is, who he is, or how he came to be here. He stands, his bare feet pressing against the coarse earth, his hands palpating the rock overhead.

A cool wind whistles through his surroundings. He follows its source through a twisting, rising tunnel until a bright white light appears overhead. His eyes adjust as he continues his ascent.

The light becomes daylight and a cloudless blue sky.

He crawls out of the cave, gazing in wonderment at a horizon rippling with snowcapped mountains. The altitude is high, the air temperature a brisk forty degrees. He pulls the fur cloak hanging from his neck across his brown shoulders and discovers his Indian heritage. He winces at the pain pulsating along the right side of his throbbing skull and realizes his head is bleeding.

The memories play back in his mind's eye, settling the rising fear.

I ascended the sacred mountain to seek wisdom from the great teacher about my enemy. The stone gave way and I tumbled, striking my head.

"I am Chilam Balam, Jaguar Prophet—seed root of the Hunahpu."

The dark-haired warrior gazes below at his kingdom—a fertile valley fed by freshwater streams flowing steadily from the snowcapped mountains. Steeped terraces have been carved into every mountainside as far as the eye can see, yielding bountiful crops. The city below this agricultural potpourri ripples outward from a centrally located palace and marketplace before becoming an organized maze of aqueducts and canals, bridges and temples—all servicing the Itza commerce centers. Farther out are the populace dwellings, teeming with a new generation of followers—all originating from the loins of the 620 who awoke on the shores of the alien sea during the first hour of the creation event.

It has been thirteen tuns since the followers of Chilam Balam experienced their rebirth in the New World. While historians recount their arrival as a blessed moment, the Jaguar Prophet's account in the Council Book tells a different story.

The air had been far colder than the wind now chilling Chilam Balam's bones, churned by a raging sea specked with floating white mountains. The Jaguar Priest and his people had no concept of frozen water back then, or the vastness of the icebergs that flowed north from the glacier-impacted South Pole. Reasoning that the colder climate had birthed these white temples of the ocean gods, Balam led his people north in search of warmth and food and sanctuary.

Seven cruel months of winter claimed a third of their people. Balam's female, Blood Woman, had nearly perished from sickness and had to be dragged on a stretcher for weeks by her soul mate. At times they came upon parcels of bare earth and the remnants of a past civilization, the bones crushed under the weight of time and ice.

Believing the land cursed they had moved on, continuing their journey along the Pacific coastline of South America.

And then, out of a morning mist appeared the sign of the great teacher himself—a three-pronged spear as tall and wide as the Kukulcan Pyramid, the trident carved into the side of a mountain. Arriving at the entrance of the valley they discovered a freshwater river flowing into the sea, teeming with fish. Following the waterway to the east led them into a lush forest overgrown with fruit trees, wildlife, and edible plants. Uncountable streams wound down from the surrounding mountains, bringing with them fertile soil.

The Jaguar Prophet immediately proclaimed the land to be the site of their future kingdom.

For the next ten tuns, peace and prosperity reigned over the Itza. Sheltered from the weather by the mountains, with no worldly enemies to fear, the task of building their city remained uninterrupted—buoyed by their leader's blossoming knowledge of agriculture, architecture, and engineering.

But every Eden has its snake, every leader a rival. And so it came to pass that Chilam Balam once more ventured up the sacred mountainside to access the cave of wonders, hoping to ask the great teacher how best to deal with Seven Macaw.

It had been Blood Woman who had discovered the cave. Walking alone by the shoreline, still barren of child after two tuns in the New World, she had been praying to the creators of the trident when she noticed birds flying out from a location near the summit.

It took Chilam Balam a full day of climbing to reach the top of the engraved symbol, another hour to achieve the summit and cave entrance, which actually faced east. He remained at the holy site for three uinal cycles, drawing fresh water from a stream and sustenance from the fruit of a grove of jac trees.

The cave itself descended deep inside the mountain, bringing him into the godly dwelling of another legendary wise man.

What Kukulcan was to the Maya, Viracocha was to the Inca. Inscriptions and reliefs describe the creator-teacher as a bearded Caucasian man with silky white hair and turquoise-blue eyes set in an elongated skull. Legends of the Aymara Indians of South America tell how Viracocha rose from Lake Titicaca during the time of darkness to bring forth light. Like Kukulcan, Viracocha brought great wisdom to his people. He eventually left the Indians, crossing the Pacific Ocean by walking on water.

So close in appearance was Viracocha to Kukulcan that Chilam Balam believed he was channeling the spirit of the Mayan wise man when the pale Inca prophet first appeared to him in the cave. Viracocha explained that both teachers were Hunahpu—the future of mankind. The Jaguar Prophet had been chosen to seed their species into the New World.

After sixty days in seclusion, Chilam Balam returned to his people, claiming to have been given a secret wisdom that would ensure the Itza's survival. The people dared not question their prophet's claim, for his eyes now radiated the same turquoise-blue of the great Mayan teacher himself.

Nine months later, Blood Woman gave birth to twin boys. Balam named the fair-haired child Hunahpu, his dark-haired brother Xbalanque. Once each solar year, Balam returned to the cave with his sons to pay their respects to Viracocha.

On their last visit to the mountain they had been followed.

Not everyone who had ascended to the New World had supported Chilam Balam. Many, in fact, had merely been caught in the tide of Maya pushing the prophet's followers into the sacred cenote and were driven over the edge by the frenzied crowd.

Though Seven Macaw claimed himself a wise leader and seer, his promotion to the High Council had been secured not on merit but as part of a debt owed to his grandfather, Five Macaw, a great warrior whose Toltec ancestors had joined the Itza, Xio, and Cocom tribes at Chichen during the reign of Kukulcan.

A practitioner of black magic, Seven Macaw was convinced Chilam Balam had summoned a giant serpent to rise from the sacred cenote. The serpent's throat was Xibalba Be—the black road to the Mayan underworld. Certainly the extreme cold and alien geography, littered with the bones of the dead, indicated they were now in Xibalba.

Better to leave Chilam Balam to confront the dark underlords himself, Seven Macaw reasoned. He would observe and learn, biding his time.

What Seven Macaw observed was that the Jaguar Prophet clearly drew his wisdom and strength from the sacred cave. And so the Toltec seer followed the prophet and his sons, intent on possessing the dark magic for himself.

Three moons passed before Seven Macaw returned to the city from the cave of wonders, his transformation complete. His eyes now glittered like red rubies and his teeth were stained blue, as sharp and as fanged as a jaguar's. His body was as powerful as the strongest five warriors among them.

Standing by the palace steps, flanked by his sons, Zipacna and Earthquake, he addressed the gathering crowd: "I am Lord Seven Macaw and I am great. My place is now higher than that of the human design. I am your sun; I am the foothold of the Itza that keeps you from falling prey to the underlords of Xibalba. Worship me and I shall protect you. Follow Chilam Balam and you shall perish, for my wisdom is greater, my light is greater. This is why I have been summoned to replace him. I am Lord Seven Macaw!"

The crowd parted, allowing Chilam Balam to approach his challenger.

Seven Macaw circled the Jaguar Prophet, dancing and prancing and calling up to the gods of the sky—his right hand concealing a white powder he had prepared from the borrachero plant. Spinning around, Seven Macaw flung the white dust in Balam's face, causing the Jaguar Priest to inhale the burundanga powder.

His jaw locks. His muscles turn to stone. His vision constricts behind a white haze. He cannot move. He cannot think.

For the first time in his life, Chilam Balam is deathly afraid.

The sons of Seven Macaw bind the paralyzed prophet to a post. The new lord of the Itzas demands the wife and sons of Chilam Balam be brought to him so they may be sacrificed to the underlords of Xibalba.

A search of the city yields nothing. Blood Woman and her twins are long gone, having heeded Viracocha's warning.

Fear has pushed Chilam Balam beyond the brink of sanity. Seven Macaw whispers into his brain, his torturer lurking in the shadows of his mind. The demon crawls beneath his skin and suffocates all rational thought. Held within the bonds of the borrachero plant's drug-induced narcosis, Balam is helpless to prevent the Mayan sorcerer from injecting more terror into the Jaguar Prophet's already damaged psyche. In vivid nightmares Balam witnesses his soul mate skinned alive by Seven Macaw, his sons sodomized by the black magician's offspring. Each dream ends with a blood-curdling scream, each scream unraveling another stitch in the fabric of his existence until the terror had become his identity.

Like an autumn breeze, Viracocha moves through the mist, the great teacher's presence extinguishing the burners in his brain, allowing his white-hot synapses to cool. Surrounded by the soothing quiet, Balam's mind crawls out of its shell, exploring an existence void of his torturer's demonic coos.

He opens his eyes to darkness. He lacks all knowledge of where he is, who he is, or how he came to be here. He stands and strikes his head on stone. Lying on his back, he presses his feet to the object. With a primordial yell, he engages his powerful legs, launching the five-ton lid away from the ancient limestone coffin.

Immanuel Gabriel climbs out of Lord Pakal's burial tomb, his mind returned, his Mayan fear gone.

133

12

It shall burn on Earth; there shall be a circle in the sky. It shall burn on Earth; the very hoof shall burn in that ka-tun, in the time which is to come. Fortunate is he who shall see it when the prophecy is declared, who shall weep over his misfortunes in time to come.

—CHILAM BALAM,
BOOK OF OXKUTZCAB

Earth News & Media

July 2, 2047: An estimated one billion delighted onlookers living in the Northern Hemisphere gazed skyward with cameras last night at what may go down as the most unusual aurora borealis ever viewed. Originating approximately 150 miles over the North Pole, the lights materialized just after 9:00 p.m. EST. A brilliant bloodred halolike ringlet filtered down in ever-widening circles that changed from shades of bright green to blue, ending in a violet band that could be seen as far south as Sacramento, California. Appearing during intense sunspot activity, the aurora borealis and its southern twin, the aurora australis, are composed of fast-moving electrons and protons that reach Earth, only to become trapped in the planet's protective Van Allen radiation belts. The electrically charged particles then collide with air molecules in the planet's atmosphere to form hydrogen atoms, emitting luminous colors in the process. Though breathtaking to behold, the invisible magnetic particle waves can severely damage power grids and satellites. Dr. Kassandra Horta, an atmospheric scientist from the University of Wyoming, seemed unconcerned. "There's been no unusual sunspot activity over the last six months. Nature's simply treating us to her light show, and we should enjoy it while it lasts."

CERN LARGE HADRON COLLIDER (LHC)
GENEVA, SWITZERLAND

The seventy-six-year-old physicist paces back and forth in front of the twelve-foot-high virtual lecture hall screen like a caged tiger. Every word spoken is simultaneously translated in more than thirty languages, every outburst transmitted to more than a million personal computers across the world.

Jack Harbach O'Sullivan pauses to drain his coffee mug, reflecting before a dry-erase board filled with chaotic mathematical equations. "We scientists are an awesome company of tailors, always attempting to fit our theories into the perfect set of clothes. It never works. It didn't work for Isaac Newton, it didn't work for Einstein. And the reason it doesn't work, my little flock of moths, is that our perception of the flame is all wrong.

"While the singularity remains the prime model for just about every energy object in our observable quasi-knowable universe, string theory has distracted the scientific community from scrutinizing the monumentally nonproductive shortcomings of quantum physics—a field accorded near-religious status. Call me a heretic if you wish, but heed my advice: the answers to our existence lie in the virgin realms of the exotic—dark energy and gravion waves, and super M-brane theories that deal with ten dimensions, all but our shared parcel of physical universe void of any concept of time."

He glances at his watch. "Interesting concept, time. I used to refer to time as space-time-normal. Now I think of time as a function of our three-dimensional linear world—a nonreal concept that is simply the illusion perceived by our particular species of bioplanetary hominids so that we can keep track of our activities within our hyperbubble of nonreality.

"More heresy, you say? Not when one realizes that our perception of reality is poisoned by our own three-dimensional existence. Let's begin with a few basics: everything in our physical universe is composed of atoms, only atoms exist in the virtual world of no-time. Atoms are the reality, it is we who are the illusion. Consider space, be it the distance between objects in the micro world or the macro world of colliding galaxies. In his limited theories on gravity, our lord and savior, Albert Einstein, suggested gravity occurs as a result of the curvature of space, as if the cosmos were a giant canvas made of foam. According to Lord Albert, Earth acts like a giant revolving bowling ball, its weight causing the moon to circle our planet like a roulette wheel in the same manner the planets circle the sun. Wrong, Mr. Patent Office Clerk! Not every object in our solar system, let alone space, fits into your tailor-made two-dimensional gravitational well theory. As evidence, I submit that Uranus's moon, Oberon, orbits its planet over the poles while Charon, Pluto's moon, also refuses to conform. Despite overwhelming evidence to the contrary, quantum physicists refused to refute Brother Albert's bowling-ball-on-the-mattress theory of gravity, fearful of being labeled a heretic. Instead, they simply tailored his theory to fit our needs.

"The answer to gravity, like time, is held within the atom. As first alluded to by Sir Isaac Newton, every atom in the universe is bound to every other atom by what can be described as an electromagnetic rope. Imagine two hydrogen particles, each possessing four atoms. Imagine each of the four atoms in particle one linked to each of the four atoms in particle two by electromagnetic ropes. That's a total of sixteen ropes, for you non-mathematician-types counting at home. Now, imagine these ropes as spiderwebs. As the two particles move away from each other, the sixteen spiderwebs lengthen and superimpose, thus appearing and acting as one. As the particles move closer, the tension increases as the spiderwebs again fan out among the two sets of four atoms. This is important to gravity because proximity among atoms alters the angle of tension. Since weight is location-specific, the approaching objects actually accelerate toward one another. The closer together the hydrogen particles get, the stronger the tension and the faster the object will move to its next location. We call this increase in speed acceleration.

"Why does an object in space spin? Because its atoms are tugging on other atoms in space, causing the object to spin. Our electromagnetic rope theory continues to make even more sense when we remember that gravity penetrates all objects, which is why the space industry will never succeed in building an effective gravity shield. Can't be done. Not when every atom in the entire universe has a symbiotic relationship with every other atom in the universe.

"Let me toss another log on this exotic flame: If Nature-slash-Creation-slash-Existence-in-the-Physical-Universe relies on the electromagnetic spiderwebs linking atoms, then splitting the atom technically violates the laws of Nature-slash-Creation-slash-Existence. Think about that a second. Split the atom and we get nuclear power, which begets atomic bombs, which begets nuclear radioactive waste. Collide atoms, and we may ultimately pay an even bigger price."

With a mischievous smile, Jack O'Sullivan waves to his CERN handlers standing in the wings—shocked to see his old colleague, Dave Mohr.

"You spent a decade working on a transdimensional nano-bio starship capable of traveling at hypergravionic tachyon velocities, and you didn't call me! I hate you, Mohr. You're not Mohr to me, you're less. David Less. As in less than a friend." Jack O'Sullivan leads the physicist and his friend inside his private office and slams the door.

Dr. Mohr makes his way across a minefield of stacked books and open files strewn across the floor to a worn denim sofa. Tossing aside an empty pizza box, he sits. "You're a pig, Sully. Did you steal this sofa from our old frat house?"

"Don't change the subject. I should have been running Golden Fleece, not you."

"Stop whining. The president wanted someone not affiliated with the military industrial complex. While I was trying to find a can opener exotic enough to access the interior of the *Balam*, you were technical advisor to NASA's Advanced Propulsion Research Project, a black ops space program."

Mitchell Kurtz sidesteps a cat sleeping on an old army blanket, accidentally kicking over its litter box. "NASA was involved in a black ops space program?"

Jack shoots the bodyguard a look. "Who is this guy? He smells like Intel."

"Relax. Dr. Kurtz is a scientist."

"A scientist, huh? What's your chosen field, Dr. Kurtz? Quantum physics? Chemistry?"

"Actually, I prefer to dabble in gynecology."

"Just what we need, a comedian."

"Jack, forget him. What about this singularity my people witnessed? Is there any danger it can enter our physical universe?"

"Is there any danger? Of course there's a danger . . . if what they saw was truly the formation of a black hole originating from a strangelet. Then again, we know very little about strangelets or the higher dimensions. Even the latest M-theories shed little light on the ten dimensions we've identified, or should I say eleven dimensions, since five separate string theories required an eleventh unifying dimension to remain consistent. Is there crossover between dimensions? In my opinion, that's exactly what dark matter is—the spillover of the gravitational force of matter from a parallel universe into our own."

"Could the gravitational radiation of the forming black hole be measurable along the poles?"

"A good question." Jack O'Sullivan sits before his desk computer, clipping the thought-control mouse to the end of his right index finger. Links blink open across his monitor like flashing stars, stampeding past encoded passwords at rapid speed, the physicist's mind prying open classified sites, until he has acquired access to the desired destination.

"Sully, you have access to LISA?"

"I have access to everything, David. I could show you video of President Stuart's autopsy if you could stomach it. She didn't die of a stroke, by the way. Not that I care. Corrupt bitch."

Kurtz watches as an animated image of Earth as viewed from space moves into focus on Jack's monitor. "So who's this Lisa? Does she have a sister?"

"Mitchell, LISA is an acronym for Laser Interferometer Space Antenna, a gravitational wave detector consisting of three spacecraft in solar orbit. LISA can measure the emissions of gravitational waves originating from stars going supernova, an act that births black holes as well as the remnants of gravitational radiation created as a result of the Big Bang."

Sully focuses on the coordinates on his screen, his mind changing the target coordinates. "Okay, I'm directing LISA's lasers at the North Pole . . . getting a lot of electromagnetic interference."

"Probably from the northern lights," Kurtz states, matter-of-factly.

"What are you talking about?"

"The aurora borealis. Don't you eggheads watch the news? The images were amazing. It looked like a giant cosmic bull's-eye . . . a circular rainbow. Almost everyone north of Philadelphia could see at least part of it."

The two physicists look at one another.

"Sully, you think—"

Jack O'Sullivan's wired index finger twitches rapidly, his mind unleashing a waterfall of data that scrolls across his screen. "There's definitely a particle stream . . . it's moving through the North Pole . . . passing through the Earth's core."

Dr. Mohr hovers over O'Sullivan's left shoulder, his eyes following the fluctuating numbers. "The inner core's liquid iron, it rotates faster than the surface or atmosphere . . . acting like an electromagnetic particle vortex. Is the core being affected?"

"Give me a second, will you? I can't think." Tearing away the fingerclip linking him to the thought-mouse, he types in manual commands. "There are gravitational fluctuations emanating from the core . . . nothing substantial."

"Nothing substantial?" Kurtz scoffs. "How about all these earthquakes and tsunamis and volcanic eruptions that we've been having? Don't tell me you missed those little catastrophes?"

"Mitchell, calm down. Sully, how long until you can reposition LISA so that we can track gravitational waves emerging from the South Pole?"

"Coupla hours."

"Do it."

GULF OF MEXICO
6:23 A.M.

Daylight burns Antonio Amorelli's sleep-deprived eyes; fear keeps him awake. According to the GPS device, Immanuel Gabriel is again on the move, rising within the bowels of the Temple of Inscriptions.

Hoping to get an estimated arrival time from Devlin, he speed-dials the cell phone—unaware that his boss's mother is watching him from within the Nexus. "Who are you calling, Antonio?"

"Lilith! Geez, you startled me. I was just checking my messages."

"When will my son be here?"

"Your son? Is Dev coming?"

Lilith climbs inside the cockpit of the jet-copter, situating herself on the pilot's lap. "Antonio, if I promised to make you immortal, would you be willing to pay the price?" She nuzzles his neck, kissing his earlobe, causing his pulse to race.

He closes his eyes, his loins tingling with excitement. "Absolutely."

Immanuel moves through the jungle, his olfactory receptors locked on to Lilith's pheromones. He finds her standing by the jet-copter next to Ryan Beck, the big man's eyes wide with fear.

Lilith embraces Manny with a quick kiss. "Has the spell been broken?"

"Yes."

"Devlin's on the way, we only have a few minutes. Manny, my son no longer exists. His soul has been possessed by something evil. Something ancient. Far more powerful than either one of us. I've lost him forever."

"Lilith, this present has no future. You know it, Devlin knows it, so do I. To save Earth, we need to go back to the past."

"The wormhole?"

"Yes. It will stabilize in the physical universe when the black hole crosses into this dimension. We need to enter at that precise moment in one of your shuttles."

Beck shakes his head. "Devlin won't allow us back inside Cape Canaveral. He'll kill all of us, then lead the Mars Colony exodus himself."

"He's right." Lilith scans Manny's body with the GPS. "There's a tracking device in your back pocket. Give it to Beck. Beck, fly the chopper as far away from here as you can. We'll try to beat Devlin back to Florida."

Manny hands the tracking device to his bodyguard. "Pep, you all right?"

"No, man. I'm a long way from all right. In fact, all right ain't even on my radar."

Lilith chides him with her stare. "Go. I'll take care of Manny."

"Yeah, I bet you will." He climbs into the empty cockpit, starting the engines.

Manny leans inside. "Pep, find Salt. Once we get to the shuttle—"

"Forget about us, son. You have a job to do, so do I. I still got family out there. An ex-wife who can't stand me and two grown kids and a new grandchild who never got to know me. I'll lead this devil on a wild-goose chase, you do what you were conceived to do and give us all a second chance. Look me up in the past, before I hurt my knee playing in the Senior Bowl. Keep me outta that game. Hell, just keep me from joining the damn CIA. Don't let me down. Don't let my family down."

"I won't. Pep—"

"Love you, too, kid." Beck slams the cockpit door shut, launching the airship into a steep climb.

Manny waits until the jet-copter disappears over the jungle. Then he follows Lilith, the two of them jogging through the ancient Mayan city, heading for the tourist entrance and the parking lot.

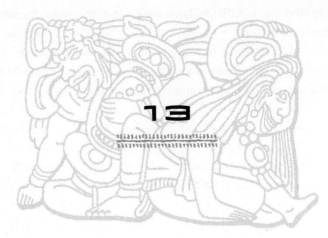

13

We know it will discover something because we have deliberately built it to journey into uncharted waters . . .

—BRIAN COX,

CERN PHYSICIST,

"IN DEFENSE OF THE LHC,"

POPSCI.COM, OCTOBER 10, 2008

Ejaculated into existence from one of a hundred thousand microscopic Big Bangs, the naked singularity had escaped the slice of space-time within the Large Hadron Collider like a sperm strangelet seeking a proton egg. Drawn into a parallel dimension of existence, it had found reproductive fuel in the atoms inhabiting an aexo–dark energy hyperspace—a successful act of conception that christened the vacuous void as its fertile cosmic womb.

The placenta of this dark energy womb was the Earth's magnetic core, an iron and nickel sphere of radioactive matter. The inner core—the very center of the planet—is 780 miles in diameter and 6,700 degrees Fahrenheit hot, yet is under so much pressure it cannot melt. It is surrounded by the outer core—1,370 miles of molten metal. As the Earth rotates, the motion of the outer core spinning against the inner core generates the planet's magnetism.

Drawn to the center of the Earth by this magnetism, the beast had grown, each pass exponentially capturing more atoms, its inertia redirected by the awaiting North or South Pole and the frozen incubator of space. Hovering above the planet after each pass, its growing atomic structure would coalesce and cool, each supercharged atom of dense gravity its own shell-encased microsingularity. Drawn together like a shoal of schooling fish, the beast—in a highly synchronized cosmic ballet of polarization—would again accelerate into a particle stream through the center of the Earth, its spinning vortex of dark energy birthing a wormhole.

Like the composite singularity, the wormhole was limited by neither dimensional boundaries nor space-time, only its umbilical cord tethered to its feeding parent. These feeding times of existence continued to expand as the beast grew larger, stabilizing the wormhole while propelling its mouth and tail across the past, present, and future membranes of the physical universe.

Just as a fertilized egg expels all intruders to its mother's womb, the presence of the growing singularity ensured that no other strangelet could conceive life from the continuously ejaculating Hadron Collider. Like an unborn child, the maturing beast occasionally kicked as it fed, each "growth spurt" causing the Earth's mantle to belch magma.

The mantle is an 1,800-mile-thick layer that surrounds the molten outer core, situated approximately six miles below the oceanic crust and nineteen miles beneath the continental crust. The crust is divided into tectonic plates, which drift slowly atop the mantle.

As the singularity's mass continued to increase, it exerted greater gravitational forces with each pass through the planet's core, unleashing a bubble of pressure that traveled across the mantle like a metal ball spinning around a roulette wheel.

The roulette wheel was rigged, the singularity's excess energy wake drawn to specific exit points in the Earth's crust—exit points lined with deposits of quartz. Like a magnet attracting the roulette wheel's metal ball, the crystal mineral contained trapped water which resonated at the same frequency as the strangelet. And everywhere there was quartz, there was also a seismic fault line.

If this wake of energy escaped beneath the fault line of two tectonic oceanic plates the result was a seaquake, sometimes leading to a tsunami; if a continental divide—an earthquake. If the bubble of pressure percolated an already volatile pocket of magma beneath a volcano, the mountain would erupt.

In the last six months, the singularity had been responsible for seven tsunamis, eleven volcanic eruptions, and more than fifty earthquakes across the globe.

"Polar shoaling" has painted its growing mass with the charged particles of the auroras. Now, as the gravitational monster approaches the moment of its birth into the physical universe, it makes one last journey through the center of the Earth, giving the planet's doomed inhabitants a taste of things to come.

LA PALMA, CANARY ISLANDS
JULY 2, 2047
3:47 P.M. (LOCAL TIME)

Located in the Atlantic Ocean seventy miles off the western coast of Africa is an archipelago known as the Canary Islands. Consisting of seven main islands and six islets that stretch west to east over three hundred miles, the chain was formed 3 million years ago by sea volcanoes.

La Palma is the farthest island to the northwest, its base situated thirteen thousand feet below the surface, its highest peak rising nearly two miles out of the ocean. The island possesses two volcanic peaks and the Caldera de Taburiente, a six-mile-wide caldera surrounded by a ring of mountains that occupy the geology to the north. A north-south ridge divides La Palma through the center of the island, the Cumbre Nueva volcano to the north, its bigger sibling, Cumbre Vieja, to the south.

On June 24, 1949, Cumbre Vieja erupted for the first time since 1712, the event lasting thirty-seven days. Lava was ejected from the stratovolcano's three vents, accompanied by two earthquakes. Left in the eruption's wake was a massive fracture over a mile and a half long, located along the volcano's western face. Geologists examining the damage discovered to their great horror that a block of rock measuring more than twelve cubic miles and weighing an estimated 500 billion tons had separated from Cumbre Vieja. Like a geological Sword of Damacles, the steeply sloped landmass remained suspended over the Atlantic Ocean, the coastal depths of which plunged almost four miles deep.

A tsunami is a large ocean wave created by a sudden displacement of water, usually caused by a seaquake, a volcanic eruption, or an underwater landslide. A megatsunami is a much bigger wave, birthed by either the ocean impact of a large asteroid, such as the object that struck Earth 65 million

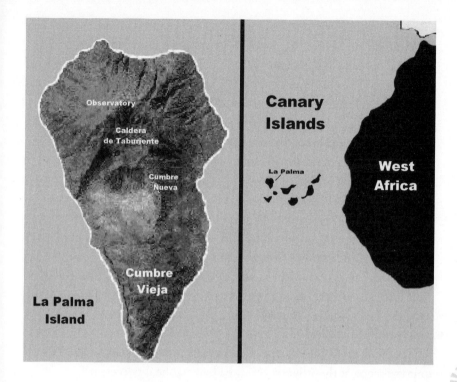

La Palma Island

Observatory

Caldera de Taburiente

Cumbre Nueva

Cumbre Vieja

Canary Islands

La Palma

West Africa

years ago, or a landslide that strikes deep water at an angle that drives the sea into a rising curl of incredible destructive force.

For decades, scientists debated whether Cumbre Vieja's western face could actually unleash a catastrophic landslide. When a 1971 eruption failed to loosen the volcano's fractured side, experts breathed a sigh of relief.

The Roque de los Muchachos Observatory is located on a remote mountain summit adjacent to the highest peaks surrounding the Caldera de Taburiente. Void of light pollution, the "Roque" operates under unusually clear, dark skies all year round, making it one of the most sought-after assignments in the field of astronomy.

Hector Javier has been working at the observatory eleven months. Exhausted from an all-night session on one of the main telescopes, the Mexican astronomer had camped out on his office floor rather than attempt the twenty-four-mile descent down the observatory's winding mountain road.

He is awakened by a deep seismic rumble and the sudden pounding of his heart. Racing to the lab, he nearly collides with Dr. Kevin Read, the facility's associate director. The Canadian's face is pale, his expression urgent. "It's

Cumbre Vieja, the volcano's erupting! Give me a hand with the seventy-inch Truss, we should be able to see something from the southwest platform."

The portable Truss telescope is locked up in storage. It takes the two astronomers fifteen minutes to carry it to the southwest platform, a concrete slab perched eight thousand feet above the Atlantic Ocean.

The ash cloud has already risen ten miles into the late afternoon sky by the time Dr. Read directs the lens at the mouth of the volcano, the scope's image partially obscured by the dense brown-gray plume of debris.

"Can you see anything?"

"Lots of smoke, no lava. It's possible the magma—"

The catastrophic eruption is as sudden as it is deafening, the terrifying explosion shaking the entire island as it launches billions of tons of ash and rock and lava fifteen miles straight into the air.

Hector Javier reaches the fallen telescope first. Resetting the tripod, he peers into the eyepiece, searching through dense smoke for the origin of the eruption. He is shocked to see Cumbre Vieja is gone, its smoldering mountaintop obliterated.

A rapid green-blue flurry of movement draws his attention. Hector aims the scope at the Atlantic, stunned by what he is witnessing.

The ocean is rising skyward in a dark, fast-curling dome of water too immense to comprehend. A thousand feet . . . two thousand feet, and still it continues to climb, ascending higher than Cumbre Vieja, approaching the height of their own observatory platform!

Kevin Read sees the deep blue mountain of water with his naked eye just before it collapses. The scientist trembles in fear, knowing all too well what he has just witnessed—a cone of water, powered by five thousand trillion joules of kinetic energy from the Cumbre Vieja landslide.

The sound reaches them twenty seconds later—a hundred thousand Niagara Fallses driving a 360-foot-high wave! The megatsunami rolls away from the southwestern tip of La Palma, racing across the Atlantic Ocean toward the eastern coastline of North and South America at five hundred miles an hour.

YELLOWSTONE PARK, WYOMING
9:47 A.M. (LOCAL TIME)

The monster had been sleeping. Six hundred forty-two thousand years. Its heart was the Earth's core and its blood the magma that heated the caldera's vacuous belly. In restless slumber it shook and quaked and bulged the lake above its gut when it stretched. It hissed and steamed and occasionally it bled, and though it was probed incessantly it did not awaken because it was old—as old as the earth.

But now the earth was beckoning again, only in a manner that irritated the beast. The quakes that rumbled its gut had grown progressively deeper and sharper, causing the magma that had long crystallized within its belly to percolate. Its insides filled with fresh lava and its blood pressure continued to rise unabated until an ancient threshold was crossed.

Angry, the monster awoke.

It would be the last time.

It was ready to explode. Any minute now.

Jon Bogner choked down the milk of magnesia, praying it would quell the hot churning sensation in his belly. His wife, Angie, had warned him to watch his diet, that the diverticulitis could not be ignored. But he needed something in his stomach before he could handle the harsh antibiotics, and his long hours at the USGS office limited his options to expensive park snacks and fast food.

Admittedly, the breakfast burrito had been a mistake.

The geophysicist chased the chalky antacid with a swig of bottled water and returned to his computer. There were forty-one permanent seismographs spread across Yellowstone Park, a dozen of which had been added over the last twenty-six months when the caldera had begun showing unusual signs of a flare-up. Jon and his seismology team concurred that the earthquakes were tectonic and not volcanic in nature, but the signs were still worrisome. Like the indigestion building in his stomach, the caldera was bulging seven miles beneath the surface, pushing the rocky basin of Yellowstone Lake upward by more than two hundred feet over a half-mile radius. Another bulge, located south of Norris Geyser Basin, had risen thirty-eight inches over the last calendar year, the protuberance spread out over thirty miles.

New mud spots were sprouting up weekly. Ground temperatures on the foot trails were approaching 240 degrees Fahrenheit. Options to deal with the caldera's threat were discussed. An elaborate system of vents and canals linked to Yellowstone Lake could potentially quell the beast, only Congress decided the $25 billion price tag was "far too excessive for a tourist attraction" and that the US Geological Survey's "scare tactics" were not appreciated.

Scare tactics? A full-scale eruption of the supervolcano carried the devastating effects of a major asteroid strike. Forget about the lava, which would spread for hundreds of square miles, or the explosion itself, which would kill hundreds if not thousands; the worst problem was the sulfur dioxide–laden ash cloud. With the equivalent impact of ten thousand Mount St. Helens volcanoes, the cloud would span the planet's upper atmosphere, reflecting the sun's life-giving solar radiation back into space. Global temperatures would plummet, crops would die, then the animals, then the people. Nuclear winter would consume the planet for years to come.

But hey, there was some good news: at least the ongoing oil wars in Venezuela and Nigeria would end, saving any surviving US taxpayers a trillion dollars a year.

The rumbling builds again. Jon Bogner stands, ready to dash to the toilet, when he realizes the disturbance is not coming from his stomach.

Caitlyn Roehmholdt is growing impatient. The twenty-four-year-old Japanese translator has blisters on her feet from walking across the hot boardwalk in sandals, and her father, Ron, refuses to leave Yellowstone until he videotapes Old Faithful.

"Dad, enough already."

"One more minute. Five, tops. Trust me, it'll be worth the wait. Here, listen to this." He reads from a brochure. " 'Geysers are hot springs with narrow constrictions near the surface that prevent water from circulating freely to allow heat to escape. Old Faithful's eruptions have increased in both duration and altitude over the last year due to an increase in earthquakes that have rocked the park. There are more than ten thousand geysers in Yellowstone—' "

"Who cares?"

"I care. Did you know that my father took me to see Old Faithful when I was seven?"

"*Baka ka*, I'm twenty-four, a bit old to care about a fubishitting dirt hole that farts steam."

"Watch your mouth."

"Sorry. Anyway, it's just stream slang."

"I meant the Japanese. You called me a stupid asshole."

Caitlyn smiles. "Asshole, dirt hole . . . what's the difference?"

The detonation from the cone geyser cuts off her father's retort as eight thousand gallons of pressurized steam and water rise nearly two hundred feet into the sky, causing hundreds of tourists to clap.

"Okay, I admit, that's pretty cool. I like the colors."

Ron looks up from behind his camera. "Colors?"

"The red mud. It reminds me of Moby Dick's bleeding spout."

"That's not mud, it's lava! Come on!" Grabbing his daughter's wrist, Ron pushes his way through the throng of onlookers, his heart racing even as he questions his own reactive behavior. *Maybe it's not a prelude to an eruption. Maybe it's nothing. No one else is running.*

"Dad, stop! I can't run in these shoes!"

He pauses at the bridge walk encircling Yellowstone Lake, out of breath. "Sorry."

"Sorry?"

"The lava . . . I thought maybe the caldera was erupting."

"Dad, it was mud."

The crack of thunder echoes across the lake. Followed by screams.

Ron steals a quick glance over his shoulder to see a panicked mob rushing away from Old Faithful, the geyser now spouting fountains of lava a thousand feet high.

"Come on!" He grabs her hand and heads south for Grant Village. Caitlyn has gone numb, her eyes watching the lake where a wall of water, sixty feet high, is sweeping up boaters and Jet Skiers as it rolls in their direction.

"Dad—"

"We can outrun it!"

"No we can't!"

"We have to in order to get to the car. Come on!"

They sprint across the length of walkway spanning the southwest tip of the lake, making it halfway across before the wave breaks upon the boat rental with the sound of pounding thunder, bashing the docks into splintering shards that are quickly engulfed in a raging tide of flipping boats and mud-laced debris.

Caitlyn feels the ground beneath her sandals rumble, a low roar filling her ears as the wave announces its arrival with stinging pellets of horizontal rain and debris before the churning wall of water swallows her sideways in its fury.

YUCATAN PENINSULA

The jet-copter pilot glances nervously from his radar screen to the white-haired man-child meditating in the copilot's seat next to him.

Devlin Mabus's hands form a pyramid in his lap. His black pupils are rolled up beneath his lids, exposing only the crimson red of his eyes. He is breathing rapidly, each breath a low growl.

"Excuse me, Dev? I've got a fix on JC-1. It's moving southeast, heading for the Atlantic coast. Should I pursue?" The pilot contemplates tapping his arm, but fears the teen might bite him.

Immersed in the Nexus, the demon that inhabits Devlin's mind has long vacated the chopper. Moving remotely through the Yucatan jungle forty miles to the south, it prowls the heavy pungent aroma of Palenque's surrounding forest, its powerful olfactory sense homing in on the scent of the womb that birthed its current physical vessel.

A second scent accompanies the first . . . a Hunahpu male.

Devlin's eyes reopen, the demon shaking itself loose from the Nexus.

"—about seventy miles away. Dev, should I follow your mother or stay on course to Palenque?"

"She's not aboard the chopper. She's with him. Set us down in Palenque."

Devlin treks through the now-familiar jungle, following a trail of scent-laden foliage until he arrives at the clearing.

The old Aztec woman is seated on a rock. Blood drips from the obsidian knife held within her knotty hands and from her whisker-laden mouth.

The teen glances at the half-eaten human heart. "My pilot?"

"He was young, filled with spirit." Chicahua smiles, her gums and the few remaining teeth in her mouth stained red with the remains of Antonio Amorelli's heart. "At least his death had meaning."

"Will yours?" He circles his great-great-aunt. "You've hidden my mother's scent trail from me. Why?"

"Because I know who you are, demon, and I know what you want. We've met before, you and I . . . a long time ago, back when I was a beauty like your mother and in love with a man who was destined to be my soul mate. His name was Don Rafelo and he was a Nagual witch—a sorcerer whom you beckoned to the dark side."

"You have it all wrong, Chicahua. It was Don Rafelo who beckoned me. Like Devlin and his mother before him, Don Rafelo sought the limitless power of the eleventh dimension. I gave him what he wanted until he became drunk with it."

"You forget, I am a seer, one who can see through your serpent lies.

Through time eternal you've plotted every action, manipulating countless thousands on your unholy quest to occupy the vessel of a Hunahpu. You sought Quetzalcoatl's bloodline, targeting my soul mate and the Aurelia clan. You used Don Rafelo to curse Madelina Aurelia and arranged her death immediately following Lilith's birth. You brought the darkness that still haunts her tainted soul, and now you possess her child, but for what end? Your actions extended the fifth cycle once. Now the Gabriel twins have ended that charade."

"Nothing has ended! The black road shall open again, only this time I shall be ready. Devlin's vessel is pure energy, able to function simultaneously in multiple dimensions. His genetics offer me immortality. Yours, however . . ."

He retrieves the obsidian knife, using her dress to wipe the blade clean.

"Kill me if you wish. My spirit shall continue to mask your sight within the Nexus."

"Now it is *you* who forget, Chicahua. As your former lover I know it is not your soul that allows you to blind me."

Flying into the Nexus he is upon her, gripping her by the scruff of her neck with one hand, stabbing the blade deep into her right eye socket with the other. Using the cavity's bony curvature as leverage, he scoops out the sight organ by its root, then pops it into his mouth before turning his attention to the remaining eye—staring at him through the ether.

ATLANTIC OCEAN
167 NAUTICAL MILES SOUTHWEST OF THE UNITED KINGDOM

The Deep-ocean Assessment and Reporting of Tsunamis buoy, more commonly known as DART, is a ten-foot-diameter flotation ring, its dorsal surface mounted with GPS antennas and a sensory mast, its belly rigged with two acoustic transducers. Tethered to the sea floor by swivel chains and a series of thousand-pound anchors, the system is designed to measure the force of an open-ocean tsunami, then transmit the data via acoustic signal to a tsunameter situated on the ocean bottom. When data is received, the tsunameter releases a glass ball flotation device, which surfaces and transmits information via Iridium satellite to NOAA, the National Oceanic and Atmospheric Administration.

The arm of the megatsunami that rushes toward the DART buoy is the northern tail of the wave unleashed by the Cumbre Vieja landslide. Having been partially deflected from open ocean by the northwestern end of

La Palma Island, the expanding ripple represents the monster's weakest appendage.

The sixty-two-foot trough of water sucks the DART buoy into its vortex with the force of a commercial jetliner landing next to a baby stroller. The monster flings the device straight into the air before churning it into an unrecognizable configuration of aluminum and plastic.

Alexis Szeifert is director of ICG/NEAMTWS, a useless acronym meant to abbreviate the Intergovernmental Coordination Group for the Tsunami Warning System overseeing the Northeastern Atlantic, the Mediterranean, and connected seas. While the Pacific and Indian Ocean divisions of the TWS command large staffs overseen by a director and three assistants, Alexis represents half of the North Atlantic group's entire work force, the other two seismologists being part-timers. While she is happy not to be busy, she has twice requested a transfer, seeking a greater use of her talents.

Seated at her desk, she rereads the garbled seismic report coming from the Canary Islands for the third time, her eyes scanning the data for the volcanic epicenter.

Cumbre Vieja. Been a while since that one erupted. No real seismic displacement to worry about. Still . . .

Noting the time of the event, she calculates the path and speed of a potential tsunami. Using her interactive screen, she clicks on the west coast of Africa, then zooms in tight on the Canary Islands. Locating La Palma, she finds the nearest DART buoy lying in the path of the ghost wave and checks for any oceanic disturbance.

DART A-114................. STATUS: OFF-LINE.

Off-line? In seven years she has never had a DART fail to respond to a command. Open-ocean tsunamis were two- to three-foot ripples at best, hardly anything powerful enough to damage a buoy or its acoustic uplink. Even in the worst of storms the system never went down. Something out of the ordinary has to have happened.

She contemplates calling the tech department when a frightening thought takes root.

Cumbre Vieja wasn't just an ordinary volcano . . .

Her heart flutters in her chest as she scans the seismic report once more, searching for any information about a possible landslide.

Nothing mentioned. Then again, if the volcano was still erupting, it could take days, even weeks to assess the damage. She recalls her supervisor's favorite saying, "Pray for the best, prepare for the worst." The worst-case scenario La Palma offered was a global nightmare.

Her fingers dance across the keyboard, hurriedly typing in her user name and password as she seeks to access the NOAA satellite array orbiting the planet.

ACCESS DENIED: SYSTEM IN USE.

Leaping onto her chair, she yells over her cubicle across the crowded chamber, "Who the hell's tying up GOES?"

A few heads turn. No one responds.

"Goddammit, whoever's using the array to sneak peeks at the nude beaches better log off now before I start tossing desks!"

"Alexis, what's the problem?"

She turns, confronted by her supervisor. Jeramie Wright is a 280-pound former mixed martial arts champion exuding a 9.7 intimidation factor on a scale of ten.

"Sir, I need access to—"

"—to GOES, yes, we all heard you. In case *you* haven't heard, every sector except yours has been in full-alert mode since six a.m. We're tracking over a hundred volcanic eruptions along the Ring of Fire alone, and have already issued seven tsunami warnings along the Western Pacific. I need you to assist a team monitoring a potential wave event in Sumatra—"

"Sir, I'm already tracking an event—Cumbre Vieja." She shows him the report. "I checked the nearest DART on the estimated event path. The buoy's off-line."

"The system's on overload. Give it half an hour and try again. Meanwhile, report to Bonnie Fleanor, she needs your help."

"Half an hour is too late. Sir, please . . . I know it's controversial, but Cumbre Vieja is still considered to be a potential megatsunami catalyst."

"The odds are too long to calculate." The intensity of her eyes softens his objection. "Where's the next closest DART on the estimated event path?"

"Way out in the mid-Atlantic. Which is why I need to access GOES. If the eruption did cause a landslide, the array would have recorded it."

Jeramie leans over her shoulder, using her keyboard to log in using his own user ID and password. "You're in. Do it fast."

The screen activates, granting her access into the Geostationary Operational Environmental Satellite network, known as GOES. She enters La Palma's latitude and longitude, the system linking her to GOES-15.

Her supervisor hovers close by as a real-time image of West Africa appears on her screen. Using her mouse, she maneuvers the screen as far west into the Atlantic as the orbiting satellite's on-board camera will allow, zooming in on the three main Canary Islands to the east, La Palma remaining too far to the west to be seen. "Sir, La Palma's in a blind spot, what should I do?"

"Forget checking the tape. Enter the coordinates of the off-line DART buoy."

She complies, the system accessing GOES-12. The new satellite image reveals parts of Spain and the Mediterranean Sea to the east. Again she pushes west, searching an endless screen of blue ocean from a zoom-lens altitude of two thousand feet. Matching the DART buoy's coordinates, she tracks to the northeast.

A thin white arcing line appears, barely noticeable over endless blue ocean.

She zooms in gradually until the line becomes a moving mass of water with no discernible backside, churning rapidly toward the coastline of Great Britain.

"Good God." Jeramie Wright stares at the object on-screen, even while his hands activate the communication device in his right ear. "This is Wright. We're tracking a megatsunami. North Atlantic, bearing . . . Szeifert?"

"—forty-seven-point-five degrees North, fourteen degrees West, 132 nautical miles southwest of Great Britain. Wave velocity 522 miles an hour, estimated height . . . sixty-three feet. At its present speed, the wave will strike the southwestern shores of Cornwall, England, in twenty-three minutes."

"Did you hear all that, Davis? Issue a tsunami warning for Cornwall, then track down Director Turzman at Homeland Security and patch him through ASAP."

The head of NOAA's Tsunami Warning Center eyeballs his pale division head. "You did good, Alexis. Unfortunately, we both know that trough is probably nothing compared to its big brother heading for the States. I want the rest of that wave tracked down and up on the main screen within the next five minutes."

"Yes, sir."

Unleashed, the monster had gone wild.

Molten silica-rich magma had been chemically evolving in the sleeping giant's belly for years, blending with water and volatile gases within the upper region of the thirteen-hundred-square-mile subterranean chamber. As these gases mixed with the magma, it expanded the sea of lava to fill the entire underground pocket until the pressure from the percolating gases and the broiling 1,800-degree Fahrenheit heat combined to exceed the force weight bottling seven miles of overlying rock that had corked the caldera for more than 600,000 years.

With the crescendo of a thousand Hiroshima-size atomic bombs, the monster had erupted.

Liquid fire exploded into the sky, scorching the air, earth, and every living thing in between for three thousand square miles. Plumes of dense mouse-brown ash clouds billowed into the stratosphere as if unleashed from Hades. Carried by the prevailing southeasterly winds, the volcanic dust quickly blanketed the states of Wyoming, Colorado, Nebraska, and Kansas with its toxic gray snow.

155

For the first hour the pyroclastic lava rolled faster than the local population could flee. Molten asphalt melted tires. Flames turned vehicles into gasoline-powered explosives. Trees and houses and buildings burned as if ignited in a blast furnace.

Terrified populations living in the Midwestern states hurriedly packed their belongings and loaded their cars and SUVs, praying and waiting for the authorities to advise them in which direction to run. Certainly not west, where earthquakes were uprooting Los Angeles and San Francisco, turning the San Andreas fault line into a separating jigsaw puzzle.

Four hours after the Yellowstone Lake basin had risen as if propelled by Poseidon, every eastbound highway west of the Mississippi was bumper to bumper in traffic. All domestic flights were canceled, the ash rendering the skies too dangerous to fly.

Americans living along the east coast shuddered at the images being broadcast over their communication screens. Fearful of things to come, many raced to grocery stores to stock up on food; others stood in long lines to purchase ammunition. All thanked their maker that they did not live out west—refusing to accept the fact that everyone was stuck on the same boat, even as the *USS Planet Earth* continued to take on water.

THE WHITE HOUSE

WASHINGTON, D.C.

Andrew Morgan Hiles has been in the Oval Office less than forty-five days, having taken over after President Heather Stuart's fatal stroke. The former vice president feels as if he is running on a river log, every global alert a precarious step threatening to toss civilization into the depths. He has asked the question "Is this the end of the world?" so many times of so many different ashen-faced aides that he has finally accepted humanity's altered course, mentally moving into survival mode.

Altered course? His press secretary had coined the phrase between tears. As if the caldera weren't enough, as if the earthquakes and "normal volcanoes" hadn't stolen enough lives, now to be told a 350-foot megatsunami was bearing down on the eastern seaboard, set to strike New York in less than an hour? The entire day, every scenario . . . it was insane. Hadn't he seen this nightmare in movie theaters a dozen times?

Playing out his role as president, he had listened to his advisors discuss the fate of 50 million Americans living along the Atlantic coast, debating whether they should risk further panicking the already panicked herd by announcing the megatsunami. Most of his advisors said no, but he had overruled them.

Besides, as horrifically frightening as the wave was, it was the caldera that was his bigger worry, with scientists forecasting seven to ten years of nuclear winter. Truckloads of canned goods and supplies were en route to Mount Weather, an underground facility where he and his family and the rest of the politically affluent would ride out the holocaust. For now, he had to remain presidential, a team player assuring the human race that life would go on, that God was with them . . . even as he was being escorted into his helicopter for the twenty-minute flight to Virginia.

His secretary of defense offers a quick salute. "Everything's being readied, Mr. President. We'll broadcast tonight's speech from inside Mount Weather."

"What about my family?"

"Already there. Everyone on the list is in the facility and accounted for, with the exception of Ken Mulder."

"Mulder's missing?"

"No, sir. The chief of staff had to rush back to Florida, apparently his wife took ill."

"His wife? I thought she lived in Illinois?"

Route 528, also known as scenic route A1A, runs east from Cocoa Beach, spanning the Indian River, Merritt Island, and the Banana River before reaching the oceanside complex of Cape Canaveral. Traffic along the six-lane highway is bumper to bumper in both directions, commuters in their westbound vehicles desperately attempting to flee the island community before it is submerged by a wave beyond their imagination, the people inching eastbound attempting to reach the H.O.P.E. Space Complex, where they will board a space shuttle and flee the planet before the same wave destroys the entire Mars Colony fleet.

Having been in the army since he was a seventeen-year-old ROTC captain, Kyle Hall has been trained to handle chaos, but what H.O.P.E.'s director of operations is dealing with is beyond any military operation he has ever faced. In less than ninety minutes he must organize and board eight hundred passengers onto twelve Mars space shuttles and successfully launch these space vehicles using personnel and security guards who know full well they are operating in the kill zone of a megatsunami. Compounding the director's problem is that his CEO, Lilith Mabus, has oversold their flight capacity by well over a thousand percent. Conveniently, neither Lilith nor her son is around to handle the blowback, forcing Kyle to deal with nine thousand of the most powerful, corrupt, egocentric, and dangerous human beings on the planet, all of whom have paid vast sums of money for themselves and their loved ones to live out their days on Mars.

Faced with a life-and-death numbers game rivaling the lack of lifeboats on the sinking *Titanic* (absent the male chivalry that allowed that captain to save the women and children first), Kyle Hall has decided on a combination of bribery and shell-game tactics to deal with his situation. To the dozen indispensable members of his flight control crew he has promised their choice of passage aboard the last shuttle or $5 million in wired funds if they remain on duty until 5:00 p.m., the wave set to strike at 5:19. To the two hundred members of his heavily armed security detail he offered a hundred thousand dollars per soldier, plus safe passage off the space complex aboard Lilith's 787 airbus, scheduled to depart at 5:05 p.m.

All but three guards have agreed to stay.

As for the shuttle passengers, Kyle has Lilith's narrowed-down list of names composed mostly of scientists, medical personnel, agriculture specialists, and engineers—all of whom have been housed in campus dormitories for weeks. These 812 men and women, the life blood of Mars Colony, have already been transported by bus to their assigned shuttle hangar. As for the politicians and bankers, Wall Street warriors and blue bloods, they will be directed to one of nine smaller utility hangars where they will be suitably "handled."

Ken Mulder is trapped in the back of the limousine, his daughter yelling at him, his son yelling at his mistress, his driver blasting the horn, threatening to turn the vehicle around if the eastbound traffic does not move within the next five minutes.

The president's chief of staff pops another Valium, staring at his watch. *Four twelve. Sixty-seven minutes until that goddamn wave hits. How the hell is Lilith going to load and launch twelve shuttles in sixty-seven minutes?*

His seventeen-year-old daughter grabs his arm, her angry eyes filled with tears. "How could you do this to Mom?"

"Do what? Is it my fault the caldera erupted? Is it my fault her flight was canceled?"

"So you brought your whore?"

"Watch it, kid." Twenty-nine-year-old Fiona Chatwin points a finger, the peroxide blonde revealing a Chinese tattoo over her right breast. "Your father arranged this trip, not me."

"Don't talk to my sister like that."

"Shut the hell up, all of you!" Mulder rubs his left eye, the migraine throbbing. "Look around. People are dying, and a lot more will end up dead very soon. For me to arrange passage to Mars Colony is an unbelievable blessing, our four tickets and living quarters are easily worth $10 billion. Yes, I know you wish your mother was here, but she's not. So here we are. Let's just be thankful—"

"I'm leaving." Amanda Mulder opens her door, stepping out onto the highway.

"Dammit." Ken climbs out in time to see the teenager disappear amid an endless road of cars. He is about to chase after her when the traffic ahead of them suddenly moves. Cursing to himself, he climbs back inside as they accelerate over the causeway.

His son stares at him, in shock. "That's it? You're just letting her go?"

"Call her on her cell. Tell her to please come back before that wave hits. I'll wait for her at the main gate."

The limo follows traffic inside a gated security area where teams of armed guards are quickly dispersing passengers to a line of transport buses.

A guard taps on Mulder's window. "I need names and identification."

"White House chief of staff Ken Mulder. I have confirmation for four, only my daughter—"

The guard speaks into his headset. "Confirming Mulder, passage for four. You'll be on Shuttle 2. Exit the vehicle and board the transport bus, it will take you to the hangar. No luggage. You'll be provided with a flight suit when you board. Let's move!"

"Wait! My daughter's on her way, we were separated."

"She's on the list, she'll be directed to your shuttle when she gets here. Now move it, you're scheduled to leave in thirty minutes."

They are hustled and prodded to the next shuttle bus in line. Climbing aboard, Mulder sees every seat is occupied by an Arab sheik. He holds on to a shoulder rail as the vehicle accelerates down the asphalt drive, his son on his left, staring at him coldly—

—a Chihuahua snarling at him from a woman's shoulder bag on his right. "We paid $275 million apiece for these tickets. Well, I told that guard that if I couldn't bring my dog, then his boss better wire me a full refund. That changed his mind."

The bus driver skids to a stop before a three-story aluminum prefabricated building. "Shuttle 1. Move quickly and watch your step."

The sheiks push their way off the vehicle.

The woman with the dog and the ten-karat diamond ring and matching necklace mumbles to her companion, "Somebody better tell the Saudis there's no oil on Mars."

The bus rolls on, stopping a half mile down the road. "Shuttle 2. Watch your step."

Mulder takes Fiona by the arm and leads her quickly off the bus, the late afternoon Florida sun beating down on them. Armed guards motion them down a path that leads inside the building.

It is dark within the barracks—a gym housing weight-training machines and a full-court basketball arena. A crowd of well over a hundred mills about while a looping instructional video broadcasts overhead, detailing the proper way to secure the shuttle seat harnesses.

Mulder checks the time: 4:27 p.m. Racked with guilt, he turns to his son. "I'm going back for your sister. Stay with Fiona." Before his mistress can protest he heads for the door—the exit locked from the outside.

The Aerion supersonic business jet soars into the overcast sky and out over the Gulf of Mexico, quickly accelerating to Mach 1.8. Shaped like a white stiletto with small wings and a tail, the $89 million, twelve-passenger plane can cross the Atlantic Ocean in two hours, has a range of 5,600 miles, and can land on most airfields.

Lilith had ordered the jet to Merida's Manuel Crescencio Rejón International Airport from the H.O.P.E. space center in Houston, Texas, while she and Manny were en route on their five-hour taxi ride from Palenque. It was not until their arrival that they had learned of the caldera's eruption and the megatsunami bearing down on the eastern seaboard of North and South America.

Manny reads the latest news report on his leather i-chair's monitor, then swivels around to gaze at the ebony-haired beauty seated next to him in the narrow aisle. Both Hunahpu are sweaty after the long trip, their perspiration—laced with pheromones—acting as a powerful aphrodisiac.

"The latest reports have the wave striking North Florida in twenty-seven minutes. We'll never make it."

"We'll make it." Unbuckling her harness, she climbs onto his lap. "I spoke with my director of operations. They'll hold the last shuttle for us." She kisses him, burying her tongue in his mouth as her fingers unbuckle his pants.

Blind with animal lust, he lifts her skirt. Palming the smooth skin of her derriere, he abruptly tears away her thong and enters her.

She grinds her pelvis into his, moaning in his ears, their minds consumed with the feast of the flesh when Lilith abruptly stops, fear in her eyes.

"What's wrong?"

"He's watching us."

"Devlin?" Manny looks around the cabin. "How?"

"Through my eyes."

It had rolled upon Britain's southwestern peninsula with the force of a four-story freight train, bashing through docks and homes, storefronts and buildings, submerging the villages and townships of Cornwall beneath a relentless wall of water that finally eased a mile from the battered shoreline.

Despite the devastation, it was merely an appetizer of things to come.

Birthed off the West African coast, the megatsunami was an expanding 270-degree wall of rushing water, thirty-three stories high, packing the energy equivalent of ten thousand twenty-five-megaton bombs, moving at the speed of a commercial airliner.

Curving around the Canary Islands, it pummeled West Africa and turned the outlying western Sahara Desert to mud.

Entering the Mediterranean, it hammered Gibraltar and sank every pleasure craft in its path.

Crossing the Atlantic, it swallowed oil tankers and cruise ships with the brutal efficiency of an eighteen-wheel truck running over a bicyclist. It chased an entire American battle carrier group into Havana's harbor, where it picked up the 150-year-old remains of the Battleship *Maine* and used its rotting steel carcass as a battering ram, sinking a naval destroyer, the *USS George W. Bush*.

Two hundred twenty miles off the northeastern coastline of the United States, the monster's forward speed was abruptly cut in half as its underlying power train met the continental shelf. Climbing the slope, the wave crested into a 470-foot-high curl, its sheer weight causing the crust of the North American plate to rumble as it thundered toward shore.

The coastal beach resorts are ghost towns. Traffic lights on the main drags still change like falling dominoes and the gulls still cull into the late afternoon, but as the sun dips gold and the hour approaches five, a pall hangs in the air.

Stephen Stocker notices something seems awry as he exits his one-story rental in Margate, New Jersey. The twenty-two-year-old quantum physics major at Atlantic City University is paying his way through college by working late shifts as a blackjack dealer at the Goldman-Sachs Riverboat Casino. Exhausted from finals week, Stephen has slept undisturbed through the incessant alarms and broadcasts that have bombarded the island residents of Atlantic City, Ventnor, Margate, and Long Port, the music coming from his sensory headpiece shielding him from the chaos.

Stephen crosses Atlantic Avenue to the beach block, feeling fortunate to miss the usual traffic. He hustles up the wood incline to the boardwalk, scares off a flock of pigeons feasting upon a turned-over trash can, then descends five steps to the beach, mentally debating whether he should run his mandatory three miles or work on his wind sprints. He has five hours of free time before he must get ready for a 12-to-8 a.m. shift. Having lost his cell phone, he has no way of knowing all businesses are closed and that the hotel casino where he works will never see the midnight hour.

The beach is gusting with wind, the sand stinging his flesh. He attributes the lack of bathers to the harsh conditions and opts to cancel his run for a swim. Tossing his towel over his backpack where dry sand meets wet, he dashes into the surf.

Stephen ducks beneath a five-foot swell, then begins swimming parallel to shore. He manages twenty strokes before the undertow spins him vertical again.

The water becomes a raging river, sweeping him out to sea. An experienced beachgoer, the college senior never panics, recognizing that he is caught in a riptide and that his best chance to escape is not to fight the fierce current but to swim parallel to shore. Launching himself into a powerful crawl stroke, he lowers his head and swims, the conveyor of eastbound shifting ocean emptying beneath him until his knee strikes sand and he's lying in an acre of mud.

"What the hell?"

The Atlantic has receded a quarter of a mile, his towel and backpack a football field away. Baffled, he stands and turns as the muck between his toes reverberates and the air grumbles a baritone roar. What he sees rolling toward him causes the hair on the back of his neck to rise and his bladder to tighten.

The wave is impossibly massive—a majestically curling monstrosity towering higher than the tallest resort hotel. It continues to climb—a looming mountain of water rapidly diminishing the blue sky. The sea floor quivers beneath its approaching girth, its stench blasting his face with an exhalation of sea life and algae and oil, its roar so frightening it paralyzes him in absolute terror.

Stephen's mind is gone, but it doesn't matter: any rational thought of escape is futile. In a last desperate grasp at self-preservation, the physics major drops to his chest and shoves both arms elbow-deep in the mud. Then he turns his head away and closes his eyes, tears flowing down his cheeks as the atheist prays to a maker he has long been convinced couldn't possibly exist.

The megatsunami plucks Stephen Stocker off the sea floor and tosses him into its raging belly, the sheer force of the dark water ripping his arms from his torso. Ocean meets concrete and steel a second later, leveling downtown Atlantic City while blasting every island residence off its foundation. The curl plunges into the bay, birthing a secondary wave, which is quickly consumed by the first.

The Atlantic never stops, it simply continues pushing inland, bashing through toll booths and car dealerships, malls and neighborhoods, before settling into a twenty-foot tide that eventually dies thirty miles west of what had once been Atlantic City's famous boardwalk.

CAPE CANAVERAL, FLORIDA

5:07 P.M.

Kyle Hall is standing on a grass-covered divide separating two immense reinforced concrete runways as an alternating procession of Mars shuttles accelerates past him in a low angled ascent—a choreographed ballet of flying metal elephants. Each airborne member of the thinning herd gradually rises to ten thousand feet before engaging its rocket boosters into a steep climb, accompanied by a sonic boom.

The control tower crackles in his earpiece. "Shuttle 7, you are a go on Runway Alpha. Shuttle 8, stand by on Runway Beta."

"Control, this is Director Hall. This is taking way too long. Screw the go–no-go bullshit and get the rest of these whales airborne in the next ninety seconds."

"Director Hall, this is Shuttle 12. We're loaded."

"Is my family on board?"

"Yes, sir."

"I'm on my way." Climbing inside a solar-powered golf cart, Kyle Hall races down the runway to one of twenty vehicle assembly buildings. Driving through the open King Kong–size doors of VAB-12, he skids to a stop, jumps out of the cart, and ascends the motorized gantry steps to the awaiting Mars shuttle, a three-story-high space plane.

He checks the time—5:13 p.m.—then hurries to the flight deck where a pilot and navigator are rushing through a series of commands while the shuttle captain starts up the space vehicle's takeoff and landing engines, preparing to taxi out of the hangar.

A copilot signals him over to the communications console. "Sir, before he abandoned the Launch Control Center, the Launch Commentator received a communication from an inbound private jet."

"Patch it through." Director Hall snatches the headphones, pressing the receiver to his ear. "Lilith? Lilith, it's Kyle Hall, can you read me?"

"—ETA in two minutes. We'll taxi straight to the hangar. Which VAB?"

The four pilots turn to Hall, all anxious, a few shaking their heads. "Sir, we need a minimum of three minutes just to taxi to the runway, another two to be airborne."

"He's right, sir. We can't wait, we need to roll out now."

The female's voice grows insistent. "Mr. Hall, which vehicle assembly building should we taxi to?"

Kyle Hall stares at the headset in his trembling hand. "Sorry, boss." Grabbing the cord, he yanks the plug free from the radio console.

Lilith slams down the radio receiver, then turns to the jet's pilot seated next to her in the tiny cockpit, her turquoise eyes seething. "Land the jet, there's still time."

The pilot looks back to Manny for help.

"I said land the damn jet!"

"No." Manny's eyes are focused out to sea where a dark brown ripple has appeared on the azure-green horizon. "Lilith, we're too late."

Wielding the fire axe, Ken Mulder swings again, tearing another sliver of daylight through the utility hangar's aluminum siding.

"Dad, stand back." His son kicks again—punching a four-foot rectangular hole through the side wall. A hundred twenty-two enraged would-be passengers rush out into the humid Florida afternoon in time to see Shuttle 12 roll out of its hangar a quarter mile to the east.

"Come on!"

Captain Brian Barker aims the nose of his space vehicle so it splits the double orange lines of Runway Beta. "This is Captain Barker in the flight deck, prepare for launch." His digital time display reads 17:16 hours as he accelerates the massive shuttle north along the five-mile stretch of concrete—only to be forced to cut the engines as the runway is suddenly swarmed upon by dozens of people, with many more making their way across the grassy expanse.

"Christ, what should I do?"

Kyle Hall's heart is pounding so hard he can barely breathe. "Don't stop! We have less than three minutes!"

Captain Barker revs the engines once more. The shuttle lurches ahead, its wingspan passing over the crowd, its front wheel rolling over an older woman and her Chihuahua. Moaning aloud, Barker veers the shuttle to the far right side of the runway, then back to the left before accelerating beyond the crowd.

17:18 . . .

"Seventy knots . . . one ninety . . . two seventy-five. Come on, girl, get your fat ass into the air!"

The shuttle lifts off, beginning a slow ascent above the rapidly diminishing northbound runway—as the towering dark wave breaks on shore half a mile to the east, blasting a thousand-foot-deep trowel of sand and sea skyward. The debris storm explodes across the space vehicle's wings and windshield, momentarily blinding the captain as the ascending space plane lumbers above two hundred feet—and is suddenly swallowed by a mountainous wall of water.

The megatsunami pile-drives Shuttle 12 sideways against the concrete runway. The portside wing snaps, the vehicle flipping over and over, its fuel tanks sparked and bursting into orange balls of fire—quickly smothered beneath the furiously moving seascape.

The supersonic jet circles two thousand feet above the invading Atlantic, which rolls westward over Cape Canaveral and the Banana River, the Merritt Island Space Center, the Indian River, and scenic Cocoa Beach, leaving devastation in its wake.

Lilith stares below, unable to breathe. Hundreds of billions of dollars' worth of facilities and technology . . . an assembly line for space planes . . . nearly two decades of space tourism and seventeen years of hard work— everything wiped out in a span of twenty seconds.

For Lilith Aurelia Mabus and her Hunahpu soul mate, there is no future.

H.O.P.E. is gone.

14

I'm in the ATLAS control room, fifteen minutes after the first high energy collisions at the Large Hadron Collider. The physicists have been waiting for this moment for more than a year and are still jumping up and down about it. It's been a long day for everyone—the journalists got here before 6 a.m.—but a lot of the scientists were here all night. A lot of delirious grins. Earlier this morning two minor glitches meant that the energy had to be ramped back down and up again twice. But everything went smoothly on the third attempt, to the excitement and relief of everyone involved. Collisions were detected in all four of the experiments at the LHC—CMS, ALICE, ATLAS, and LHCb. From where I'm at in the ATLAS control room, I can see images of the collisions being beamed in on floor-to-ceiling screens. There's just been another outbreak of clapping, following the announcement that the two beams are still circulating smoothly. This means that the inner detectors—those that will capture the most

VASTITAS BOREALIS BASIN, MARS COLONY, MARS

James Corbett grips the safety bar of the lift with one gloved hand of his space suit, the other hand twirling the palm-size sensory cane looped around his wrist—a device that feeds information from a laser pointer into a relay embedded in the engineer's brain.

James Corbett is blind, having lost his sight in a deepwater diving accident when he was thirty years old. Refusing to curb his appetite for life, he took up mountain climbing and ascended Mount Kilimanjaro and within three years was again leading deepwater descents hundreds of feet below the surface. Learning to function in his new world of darkness actually saved Corbett's life when he and a dive buddy decided to explore an inverted freighter located at the bottom of Lake Ontario. Lost in a world of silt and quickly running out of air, Corbett calmly felt his way through the ship's corridors, leading them to safety.

The descent grows bumpy, rattling the open lift's cage. Immune to claustrophobia, the chief engineer of Mars Colony has taken it upon himself to descend into the just-completed mining shaft. Seven hundred feet below the rocky Mars surface lies a mysterious mass, its potential yield weighing in at an estimated 130,000 metric tons. To find a vein of ore that can be melded into steel plates for the Colony's biodomes makes the discovery a fortuitous find; to locate it in a basin believed to be a 200-million-year-old sea has baffled his team of geologists. Using a laser-cutting tool, Corbett will cut loose a sample of the mass for analysis in their lab. Before any more exploratory shafts are dug, his team will determine the nature of the metal and whether an elaborate salvage operation is worth the cost in fuel and manpower.

The hydraulic lift slows, then stops with a clanging thud. Corbett's helmet fills with radio static, followed by a faint, "End of the line, sir."

"A simple 'You've arrived' would have sufficed, Mr. Jefferies. Which way is the targeted section?"

"Exit the lift and head west three meters, you're practically on top of it."

Corbett steps off the lift, his sensory cane determining direction and distance, the distinct reverberations leading him to the object subsumed in rock. Reaching out with his right gloved hand, he feels the shaft wall, distinguishing the rough silicate from a smooth metallic surface, its contours curved, its planed edges several inches thick, yet honed to a degree of sharpness not found in nature.

The engineer taps the mysterious object with his cutting tool, a strange sensation of déjà vu overwhelming the former salvage diver. Using a pickax, he chips away a four-foot section of rock, exposing a protrusion of the buried object.

"Sir, is everything all right? Dr. Corbett?"

"Huh? Yes, I'm . . . it's good. Actually, it's the tip of a very massive iceberg."

"Iceberg, sir?"

"It's not a vein, Jefferies, and no, it's not an iceberg. It's a buried vessel of some kind. If I didn't know any better, I'd swear it was the blade of a cruise ship's propeller."

It is located forty-six miles from Washington, D.C., a top-secret facility rivaling that of Area 51. Aboveground all seems innocuous—a dozen administration buildings set on manicured lawns, a helipad and control tower, everything surrounded by a perimeter fence. But beneath this mountain summit lies a vast underground city.

Welcome to Mount Weather, a self-contained "Doomsday Hideaway" established before the Cold War and modernized over the decades at a taxpayer cost approaching $3 trillion. Of course, Mount Weather and the more than one hundred subterranean Federal Relocation Centers spread out across Virginia, West Virginia, Pennsylvania, New York, and North Carolina were never intended to be used by taxpayers, nor was the "continuity of government" program it secretly services meant to comply with the constitution or congressional oversight. Mount Weather and its network were built with one objective in mind: surviving the apocalypse.

Built to withstand a nuclear strike on Washington and its "target areas," Mount Weather and its network of bunker facilities are literally self-contained underground cities, complete with private apartments, dormitories, streets, sidewalks, hospitals, and cafeterias, as well as a water purification system linked to underground streams and aquifers, sewage treatment plants, agricultural greenhouses, livestock, power plants, a mass transit system, and its own telecommunication system. While the world's population perishes by nuclear weapons, radiation fallout, erupting calderas, biological disasters, asteroid strikes, or nuclear winter, the inhabitants of the Mount Weather network will survive catastrophe so that humanity can go on.

That these "survivors" will most likely have been the ones to have caused the catastrophe in the first place has never seemed to bother past presidents, cabinet members, and those appointed in secrecy to man FEMA's parallel government-in-waiting. Joining this secret fraternal order of politicos are the CEOs and executives of some of the top companies in the world, along with key personnel at the Federal Reserve and the US Post Office, both private corporations.

In essence, Mount Weather is Mars Colony here on Earth, a safe haven for the rich and affluent.

President Andrew Hiles is in the Situation Room, the nerve center of Mount Weather, which is linked with Raven Rock, the Pentagon's underground facility located sixty miles north of Washington. Appearing before him is a real-time holographic image of the Earth, originating from the Defense Department's satellite array, then reconfigured. Ash clouds from over two hundred erupting volcanoes have combined with the Yellowstone caldera to cover ninety percent of the planet's atmosphere. America's breadbasket is covered in ash, its farms devastated. Photosynthesis has ceased to exist. Rolling blackouts will lead to anarchy, mass starvation, and a decade of nuclear winter. Nine billion people, save a privileged few, shall die.

Now the president must deliver a final message to the people. How does one talk of hope when none exists? How does a president prepare his constituents for death when he himself shall be spared?

With a heavy heart, Andrew Hiles is led by his trainers to his new Oval Office, where television cameras and a teleprompter awaits.

GULF OF MEXICO

The Aerion supersonic business jet ascends to five thousand feet as it banks west at Mach 1.3, soaring over the Florida Panhandle.

Manny closes the cockpit door, guiding Lilith to a chair. "Are you okay?"

"My son is possessed for an eternity by some kind of demonic force, and the only chance we had to save him—to save humanity—just got pummeled by a wave. So no, Manny, I'm far from okay, in fact, I'm about to freak out."

"Listen to me, the window hasn't closed just yet. Salvation isn't on Mars, it's through the wormhole that will appear when the singularity crosses into the physical universe. That event will happen before this day is over—I can feel the Nexus trembling beneath its gravitational weight. Lilith, we don't need a Mars shuttle to reach the wormhole, we just need a space plane. Don't you have another space port in Houston?"

Her eyes widen. "Yes."

MCMURDO RESEARCH STATION

ROSS ISLAND, ANTARCTICA

Surrounded by ocean, the continent of Antarctica covers the geographic South Pole at the bottom of the world. The landmass, fifth largest on the planet, is ninety-eight percent ice and possesses no indigenous human inhabitants. Nevertheless, each spring three thousand workers join teams of scientists that weather the extreme cold in order to staff Antarctic research stations, all part of a cooperative global effort to study conditions that serve to stabilize the planet's weather patterns.

McMurdo Station is spread out across two square miles of ice on the southern tip of Ross Island. Operated by the American branch of the National Science Foundation, the complex houses twelve hundred residents, making it the largest human habitat in Antarctica.

It may very well be its last.

Geologist T. Paul Schulte stands on the partially frozen shoreline of McMurdo Sound, staring across the waterway at the four snow-covered summits spewing ash clouds high above Ross Island. That Mount Erebus has erupted is unusual but not shocking—as part of the Ring of Fire it is one of more than 160 active volcanoes situated along the Pacific Plate. That its three usually silent sisters are also erupting is what had shaken the scientist to the core—even before he had spoken to his wife, Christine, and learned what was transpiring across the rest of the planet.

Schulte is separated from his wife and six children by an entire hemisphere. His last good-byes were cut off by atmospheric interference caused by the blanket of volcanic dust. The Mormon has prayed nonstop for the last three hours for a miracle.

Now, before his frosting gray-blue eyes, it appears as if a miracle is actually happening.

While the Earth's geographic poles are located at the center of the planet, the two magnetic poles are perpetually shifting. The phenomenon, known as polar drift, is caused by variations in the flow of molten iron in the Earth's rotating outer core, which affect the orientation of the planet's magnetic field.

As Schulte watches in terrifying fascination, the surrounding ash clouds begin slowly coalescing—rotating counterclockwise for as far as the eye can see. The center of this force is rising up from the southern magnetic pole, situated high above a patch of ocean lying to the east of the eastern-most shore of Ross Island. Drawn upward through the quickly forming eye, the swirling vortex appears to be inhaling the toxic blanket of volcanic ash into space.

GULF OF MEXICO

There is no warning; one moment they are soaring through smooth air—the next they are plunging through space at the speed of sound.

Manny lunges for Lilith, dragging both of them into the Nexus. The physical universe instantly slows around them, their bodies floating upward in the spinning cabin, gravity temporarily defied. Pushing away from the merry-go-round of furniture, they fight their way into the cockpit.

The pilot is unconscious.

Manny tosses him aside and grabs for the controls, struggling to level them out as the altimeter rolls backward from 12,800 feet to 8,900 feet to 4,400 feet—the wind shear releasing them eight hundred feet above the Gulf of Mexico into a rising torrent of wind that buffets them sideways.

Lilith takes the copilot's seat. She slips out of the Nexus, greeted by the sound of howling wind. "What happened? Did we fly into a hurricane?"

"Look at the sky."

The dense layer of brown clouds is rolling south like a raging river of mud, its airspeed in excess of a thousand miles an hour—and still climbing. Menacing gray tornadoes of ash appear over land—vertical columns of volcanic dust feeding the vacuous moving carpet of atmospheric debris.

The jet pitches from side to side, rising perilously atop a sudden updraft, only to drop again. "Lilith, it's too dangerous—we have to land."

"Do it!"

Scanning the GPS, he banks to the northwest in a steep descent when the windshield is blanketed beneath a blizzard of wet ash. Manny feels the engines seize a moment before red lights flash across his console, and suddenly they're soaring just above the Gulf, sheets of water dousing the windshield clean as he fights to keep the jet's nose up, the aircraft's belly skiing half a mile before its inertia is gripped by gravity and the cockpit settles beneath the incoming swells.

The cabin lights extinguish, and the two Hunahpu, their turquoise eyes radiating in the darkness, slip back inside the Nexus.

Manny communicates telepathically within their shared island of existence: *Pop the door, I'll grab the pilot.*

No time. Leave him!

Can't do that.

Twisting the steel handle, she yanks open the cockpit door, venting the cabin. Leaping into a maelstrom of wind and sea, she treads water, only to discover she can stand.

They are in a cornfield, the stalks submerged under five feet of water.

Remaining in the Nexus, they push through the gelid fourth dimension until they are standing on an elevated strip of concrete.

Manny releases the inert pilot, slipping out of the higher realm. A blinding wind whips at his legs, the ash clouds soaring overhead at a dizzying speed. The air is static with electricity, generating sparks of lightning that dance around upswells of wet ash, feeding the turbid heavens.

"Lilith, where are we?"

She looks to the east where waterspouts dance across an olive-green horizon, the shoreline littered with grounded oil tankers, a maze of gray battleships, and mangled pleasure craft. "I'm pretty sure that's Galveston Bay. What happened?"

"The megatsunami is what happened. It entered the bay through the Gulf and flooded the Texas coastline."

She points to a highway off-ramp. "That's the Gulf Freeway, it leads into Houston. We're about twenty miles southeast of the space port. Maybe we can find a car."

"Too dangerous. The ash cloud is moving so fast it's charging the atmosphere with electricity while popping tornadoes faster than we could avoid them. It'll be exhausting, but our best shot is to do this on foot within the Nexus. At least we can see the updrafts coming."

"What's causing the ash cloud to move so fast?"

". . . a miracle. Call it God or the Second Coming, but whatever it is, it's clearing Earth's atmosphere and jettisoning the debris into space."

172

President Hiles stares at the holographic Earth, tears in his eyes, as the gray-brown blanket of volcanic debris dissipates from the Northern Hemisphere, drawn into space hundreds of miles below the South Pole like a steadily draining hourglass. "You say it's jettisoning the debris into space—where exactly is it going? Is it orbiting our planet?"

"No, sir. Astronomers stationed at observatories in Ontario and British Columbia confirm clear views of space, at least over the Northern Hemisphere." Despite the startling developments, atmospheric scientist James Thompson appears visibly shaken. "To be perfectly honest, Mr. President, we just don't know what is happening. We're calling it a miracle simply because there's no precedent for this or scientific explanation for why any of this is happening; for that matter, we still don't know what triggered all the volcanic eruptions. We can't access our satellites for answers either; the atmosphere is so charged with electromagnetic particles that it's scrambling our communications from space."

"What happens when the atmosphere is cleared of debris? Will the process stop?"

"Again, sir, since we have no idea what's causing the phenomenon, we have no way of answering that."

"Maybe it's a do-over?"

"Sir?"

"A clean slate . . . you know, God's way of letting us know He's out there, that He's giving us a second chance."

"I'm sorry, Mr. President, I'm not what you'd call a religious person."

"Maybe that's the problem, Dr. Thompson. Maybe God wants people like you to be more religious."

Thompson fights back tears of frustration and a chuckle caused by the absurdity of the accusation. "So you think God decided to unleash a caldera and volcanoes and a megatsunami—not because of war or greed or all the hatred and killing in this world, but because people like me aren't going to church enough? With all due respect to you and your 'chosen survivors' hiding out in this bunker . . . go fuck yourself."

The atmospheric scientist pushes past the president and his political advisors, seeking the nearest elevator to the surface.

They have covered the twenty-two-mile marathon in less than an hour within the Nexus, the fourth-dimensional portal slowing time while magnifying their physical performance. But the two Hunahpu are still half-human, and the stress of moving through gelid air has drenched their muscles with lactic acid.

Lilith makes it as far as the torn steel gates of H.O.P.E.'s Houston-based space port before she collapses. Emerging from the Nexus, Manny carries her across the compound as the night sky miraculously reappears overhead—revealing a bright violet ring of charged particles from the aurora borealis.

And in that split second Immanuel Gabriel knows what is causing the ash clouds to be drawn to the south, and the fear of what is soon to come jolts his exhausted body with adrenaline.

"Lilith, the singularity's manifesting in the physical universe. Where's the space port?"

The hangar is six stories high and as long as three football fields. The space planes are lined up at their private terminals—save for one, which is parked by the sealed doors. A lone worker stands by the aluminum alloy vessel, sucking on a pacifier bong while liquid hydrogen is fed through hoses into the space plane's rocket boosters.

An auxiliary garage door is kicked open and a tall man enters, half carrying a familiar figure. "Mrs. Mabus? I wasn't sure . . . I mean, we were told you were coming—"

Lilith leaves Manny to check the fuel gauge. "Where's the pilot? Where's the launch crew I ordered?"

"Gone to be with their families. I'm the only one left. Been here thirteen years, Mrs. Mabus. I'd do anything—"

"Sober up, shut up, and listen! If I'm not airborne in the next five minutes, I'm going to erupt like that caldera. So unless you want to end up like my dead husband you'd better disconnect those hoses and get those hangar doors open—am I being clear?"

"Yes, ma'am." Shutting off the fuel pump, he begins uncoupling the hoses.

Manny looks over the space plane. "Lilith, can you fly this thing?"

"We're about to find out."

The technician tosses aside the fuel hoses, heading off to open the bay doors.

"Wait. Where's my son?"

"Devlin? Everyone assumed he was with you aboard one of the Mars shuttles. Give me a moment and I'll drive over one of the mobile gantries." The workman's mouth drops open as he witnesses two blurs of movement leap two stories onto the portside wing and enter the ship.

Unlike the flight decks of NASA's *Orbiter* space shuttles, which were organized using a g-force priority of heads-up displays, key instrument panels, and switches, the cockpit of H.O.P.E.'s space plane relies on thought control relays initiated by the pilot's and copilot's headpieces.

Strapping herself into the pilot's seat, Lilith activates her headgear and positions the eyepiece over her right eye. "Activate voice command, authorization Mabus, Lilith Alpha Tango Beta Gamma Delta."

The horseshoe-shaped onyx glass consoles activate, revealing myriad colored heads-up displays and color-oriented controls.

"Start main jet engines. Engage throttle controls."

A holographic throttle appears. Lilith grasps it, maneuvering the space plane out of the open bay doors—never noticing the twisted corpse of the technician, lying in a heap beneath several rain parkas.

The wind whips at the space plane's enormous wings, pitching the vessel as it emerges onto the deserted runway. Lilith blows Manny a kiss, then engages the jet engines, propelling them down the stretch of ash-blown concrete.

Aided by the upswell of air currents, they lift off, accelerating into the night sky. Their exhausted bodies sink against the leather seats behind three Gs of force, the space plane pitching violently as it rises into the fast-flowing current of volcanic debris.

Lilith activates the shuttle's rocket boosters, launching the space plane at a near-vertical angle through the atmospheric turbulence. The roar is overwhelming, the lateral drag threatening to unhinge every plate holding the vessel together—and then they are through, surrounded by the dark velvety silence of space.

Confronted by the monster.

It is the size of a neighborhood cul-de-sac, its event horizon as large as the moon. Brown ash swirls within its vacuous orifice, sequestered within a magnificent rainbow halo of its womblike aurora australis. The singularity rotates in space a thousand miles beneath the Earth's southern pole—a dilating black hole inhaling a stream of volcanic dust through the straw of its gravitational vortex.

As the last of the atmospheric dust is consumed, the monster begins to move.

Manny's heart pounds like a rubber mallet against his chest, the fear of what he is witnessing paralyzing his limbs as the singularity—appearing as a gelid halo—approaches Earth. Distorting the charged particles of color into spilled soup, it consumes the aurora even as it reaches for Antarctica.

There is no visible moment of contact. The monster simply consumes the icy continent in a gargantuan gelid inhalation, swallowing land and ocean within its invisible expanding orifice, exposing the fiery orange glow of the mantle as it simultaneously moves deeper and wider. Absorbing molten magma and the collapsing landmass of South America like acid on flesh, the silent killer's event horizon spreads wider into Africa and across the Atlantic Ocean, evaporating land and sea into an all-consuming vortex of nonexistence until the core itself is engulfed and there is nothing left, save a black halo of aexo—dark energy space—a temporal anomaly birthed as an innocuous proton-seeking missile of gravitational destruction, unleashed by the egocentric creators it has now consumed.

The two panting Hunahpu humans reach out to one another, entwining their fingers, neither able to speak. Finally Lilith utters, "Wormhole."

The scarlet-ringed aperture appears where the Earth had orbited the cosmos only moments before.

"Computer, take us in, sixty-second countdown. Now transferring command to copilot." Releasing her harness, she floats up from her seat, placing the controls firmly over Manny's head. "Sorry. I need to find an air sickness bag before I lose it."

"Lilith, wait—"

She's gone before he can stop her, floating through zero gravity into the next compartment.

The space plane alters course, heading straight for the wormhole.

". . . FIFTY SECONDS . . . FORTY-NINE . . . FORTY-EIGHT . . ."

"Lilith, come on! Get back here and strap in."

No reply.

The wormhole's orifice blooms into view.

". . . TWENTY-NINE . . . TWENTY-EIGHT . . . TWENTY-SEVEN . . ."

"Lilith?" Discarding the headpiece, he unbuckles his harness and launches himself out of the flight deck and through the empty ready room to the passenger deck.

The spinning object floating toward him through the ninety-foot cabin jettisons rings of scarlet bubbles as it flips over and over again until finally it becomes recognizable.

Manny bellows a wounded primordial cry as he catches the severed head of Lilith Mabus in mid-flight.

Devlin is right behind his mother's decapitated skull, wielding the bloodied blade in his right hand as he launches himself horizontally down the empty aisle.

". . . SIXTEEN . . . FIFTEEN . . . FOURTEEN . . ."

Leaping into the Nexus, Manny grabs Devlin's right wrist. Unleashing his pent-up fury, he crushes the bone into splintering fragments, at the same time twisting the knife into his nephew's abdomen—as Devlin smashes through the fourth-dimensional vortex, bludgeoning Manny's head with his elbow, the near-death blow bruising his uncle's brain, rendering him unconscious.

The demon turns to go after him—only to be confronted by the spirit of his deceased father, Jacob Gabriel.

Devlin's crimson eyes widen in disbelief. "The wormhole . . . you're controlling it?"

"As I now control you."

". . . THREE . . . TWO . . . ONE—CONTACT."

The space plane enters the wormhole's gravitational vortex, Devlin Mabus screaming in agony as the physical vessel harboring the Hunahpu abomination fragments into billions of atoms in an expulsion of matter that rivals that of the Big Bang.

Immanuel Gabriel's eyes open in slits, his being encompassed in a soothing cocoon of ethereal blue-white light, his twin brother shielding him within his aura.

PART
1

THE CAUSE

I happen to have been privileged enough to be in on the fact that we've been visited on this planet and the UFO phenomenon is real. It's been well covered up by all our governments for the last sixty years or so, but slowly it's leaked out and some of us have been privileged to have been briefed on some of it.

—DR. EDGAR MITCHELL,
APOLLO 14 ASTRONAUT

The world is made for people who aren't cursed with self-awareness.

—ANNIE SAVOY IN THE FILM *BULL DURHAM,*
WRITTEN BY RON SHELTON

Dr. Steven Greer, host: The Disclosure Project
(excerpted from opening remarks)

We are here today to disclose the truth about a subject that has been ridiculed and questioned, denied for at least fifty years. The men and women who are on this stage and the some 350 additional military and intelligence witnesses to the so-called UFO matter and extraterrestrial intelligence can prove, and will prove, that we are not alone. [. . .] I have personally briefed a sitting director of Central Intelligence, James Woolsey, President Clinton's first CIA director. I have personally briefed the head of the Defense Intelligence Agency; the head of intelligence at Joint Staff; members of the Senate Intelligence Committee; many members of Congress; members of the European leadership; the Japanese Cabinet, and others. And what I have found is that none of them are surprised that this is true, but they are uniformly horrified that they have not had access to these projects.

We can establish through these witnesses [. . .]—people who have been inside the CIA, NSA, NRO, Air Force, Navy, Marines, Army, all divisions of the intelligence and military community, as well as corporate witnesses, contractors to the government, and these are folks who have been involved in so-called black budget, or covert unacknowledged projects—these unacknowledged special access projects are taking in at least forty to eighty billion dollars per year, and they are sitting on technologies that can change the world forever. [. . .]

We can establish through this testimony that these objects of extraterrestrial origin have been tracked on radar going thousands of miles per hour, stopping and making right-hand turns; that they use antigravity propulsion systems (which we have already figured out how they work in classified projects in the United States, Great Britain, and elsewhere); that these objects have landed on terra firma, at times have been disabled, and have been retrieved—specifically by teams within the United States; that extraterrestrial life forms have been retrieved, and that their vehicles have been taken and studied thoroughly, for at least fifty years.

We can prove, through the testimony and documents that we will be presenting, that this subject has been hidden from members of Congress and at least two [. . .] presidential administrations that we are aware of, and that the Constitution of the United States has been subverted by the growing power of these classified projects and that this is a danger to the national security. There is no evidence, I wish to emphasize, that these life forms from elsewhere are hostile towards us, but there is a great deal of evidence that they are concerned with our hostility. There are times when they have neutralized, or rendered inert, the launch capabilities of intercontinental ballistic missiles. Witnesses here today will describe those events to you. They have shown clearly that they do not want us to weaponize space. And yet we are proceeding down that dangerous path [. . .].

Now, I expect people to be skeptical, but not irrationally so, because these men and women have come forward and they have their credentials. They can establish who they are, and they have been firsthand witnesses to some of the most important events in the history of the human race. As was pointed out to me by some of the men here, they were charged with handling the nuclear weapons of the United States; their word was trusted on everything of great importance for the national security. We must trust their word now. As Monsignor Balducci said at the Vatican, in an interview I had with him recently, "It is irrational not to accept the testimony of these witnesses" [. . .].

This is the end of the childhood of the human race. It is time for us to become mature adults in the cosmic civilizations out there. To do this, we must become a peaceful civilization, and we must look as we go into space with an intent of cooperating with other civilizations, not weaponizing that high frontier [. . .].

—Dr. Steven Greer
former chairman of the Department of Emergency Medicine
at Caldwell Memorial Hospital in North Carolina,
Founder and Director of CSETI and the Disclosure Project

Used by permission of the Disclosure Project

The Journal of
Julius Gabriel

DATE: JUNE 14, 1990

PLACE: NAZCA PLATEAU, PERU

AUDIO ENTRY: JG-766

I stand before the vast canvas, sharing the feeling of loneliness its creator must have surely felt thousands of years ago. Before me lie the answers to riddles—riddles that may ultimately determine whether our species is to live or die. The future of the human race—is there anything more important? Yet I stand here alone, my quest condemning me to this purgatory of rock and sand as I seek communion with the past in order to comprehend the peril that lies ahead.

The years have taken their toll. What a wretched creature I've become. Once a renowned archaeologist, now a laughingstock to my peers. A husband, a lover—these are but distant memories. A father? Scarcely. More a tortured mentor, a miserable beast of burden left to my son to lead about. Each step across the stone-laden desert causes my bones to ache, while thoughts forever shackled in my mind repeat the maddening mantra of doom over and over in my brain. What higher power has chosen my family among all others to torture? Why have we been blessed with eyes that can see the signposts of death while others stumble along as if blind?

Am I mad? The thought never leaves my mind. With each new dawn, I must force myself to reread the highlights of my chronicles, if only to remind myself that I am, first and foremost, a scientist, nay, not just a scientist, but an archaeologist—a seeker of man's past, a seeker of truth. But what good is truth if it cannot be accepted? To my peers, I no doubt resemble the village idiot, screaming warning cries of icebergs to passengers boarding the Titanic as the unsinkable vessel leaves port.

Is it my destiny to save humanity, or simply to die the fool? Is it possible that I have spent a lifetime misinterpreting the signs?

The scraping of footsteps on silica and stone gives pause to this fool's entry.

It is my son. Named for an archangel fifteen years ago by my beloved wife, Michael nods at me, momentarily warming his father's shriveled pit of a heart. Michael is the reason I persevere, the reason I do not end my miserable existence. The madness of my quest has robbed him of his childhood, but far worse was my own heinous deed, committed years earlier. It is to his future that I recommit myself, it is his destiny that I wish to change.

God, let this feeble heart last long enough to allow me to succeed.

Michael runs ahead to explore the next piece of the puzzle that has beckoned us to this desolate plateau, what I now believe is the oldest and most important inscription of these mysterious three-thousand-year-old lines and zoomorphs—a perfect series of concentric circles, known as the Spiral. The Spiral is the starting point of the artist's canvass, and yet spoiling the design is a straight line—a bold carving within the pampa, extending over rock and hill for some twenty-three miles in the direction of the Pacific Ocean.

Michael is shouting and waving at me. From this distance, it appears as if something is lying at the center of the Spiral's bull's-eye. "Michael—"

"Julius, hurry quickly!"

"I'm hurrying. What is it, kiddo? What have you found?"

"It's . . . a man."

END AUDIO ENTRY

15

The pain is a powerful impetus—forcing him from blackness into a state of conscious delirium. The reverberations in his skull cause his eyeballs to throb behind the closed lids, the heat baking the smooth surface stones beneath him, cooking his blood.

He forces his eyes open, only to be blinded by the brilliant light. He seals them again, falling back into an oven of purgatory . . . awaiting death.

He detects a presence. Someone approaching in a hurry. Trailed by a second person, the latter more cautious.

Rescuer or enemy?

A shadow passes over him. Inquisitive. "Dude, what are you doing out here?"

He searches for his voice but finds only pain. His soul slips out of his body and offers him a bird's-eye view of his death.

The teen is dark-haired and well built, his skin deeply

tanned. His father is in his fifties, a smaller, weathered version of his offspring, carefully pacing himself against the elements.

The teen shakes the body—forcing his soul back inside the vessel of pain. He finds his voice and moans.

"Michael, don't touch him."

"Chill out, Julius. I'm just trying to figure out who he is."

"You want to know who he is? Look at his jumpsuit. He's a fighter pilot. His jet must have gone down and he parachuted. If he's military, then there could be radiation."

"Project H.O.P.E.? That sound military to you?"

"Actions count, not words or titles. The military industrial complex tends to be Orwellian in naming their missions."

"What would he be doing way out here?"

"Perhaps he was chasing our friends."

"Yeah, maybe. Julius, look at the gash on his head. He's hurt bad. We need to get him to a doctor."

"He's not our problem. I'm sure his pals in the Air Force will be by to pick him up soon enough."

"And if they don't?"

"The spider glyph lies to the west of that ridge. We'll run our magnetometer tests and be back in an hour. If he's still here—"

"In this heat? He'll be dead in an hour for sure."

"Michael, listen to me—if he was chasing our friends then he's either Majestic-12 or worse, which means if we stay here then *we* could be dead in an hour. Leave him some water and let's go."

"Car keys."

"Didn't you hear me?"

"Car keys, Julius. I'm not screwing around."

"Play your game of defiance all you want, Michael. You're still not driving the Jeep over the pampa. I absolutely forbid it."

"Then I'll carry him."

"You'll carry him? You complained all morning about carrying the equipment, now you want to carry a 240-pound linebacker? Stop it. Michael, put him down. Michael, for God's sake, the Jeep's two miles away!"

"Owf . . . got him. Let's go."

"Enough already. Put him down."

"I said I got him. Whoa, he's big. Grab my bag."

"Michael, stop. Put him down and I'll let you get the Jeep."

"You're the boss."

"Easy! Careful with his head. You shouldn't jostle a head injury like that. Watch out, he's puking! Jesus, he's puking all over the Spiral! Dammit, why don't you ever listen? If Maria Reiche sees this, she'll have us banned from Nazca."

"Screw Maria Reiche. The little German dictator already hates us. Who died and left her in charge?"

"The Peruvian government. And thank God they did, or these lines would be part of the Pan-American Highway."

"They already are. Now if it was up to . . . hol-lee shit, we got company."

"Maria Reiche?"

"The E.T. Don't look up. He's hovering high overhead, sitting in the sun where we can't see him. Only I can see his shadow. Thirty yards west. Eleven o'clock."

"I see it."

"Think it's the same Fastwalker we saw Sunday night?"

"Could be."

"Maybe he's checking out the pilot?"

"That would be my guess."

"Julius, what'll we do?"

"We leave him and come back here in a few hours like I said."

"No way."

"Son, if they want him, they'll take him. There's nothing we can do about it."

"Is that what kabbalah taught you? To turn over your brother to the long skulls when they come calling?"

"He's not my brother."

"Dad, according to the Zohar, we're all souls from the same vessel."

"Don't manipulate me by using kabbalah. And stop calling me Dad whenever you want me to do something."

"Okay, Julius, let's say Mom was here sharing this little father-and-son moment. What would your soul mate tell us to do? You really think she'd leave him to die?"

"All right, enough already. Help me get him up on his feet, you shoulder one arm, I'll get the other. Watch his head!"

"I got him. What about the equipment?"

"I'll come back for it later. Ready? We have to lift him over each line. Grab his knee."

"God, he's heavy."

"He's dead weight. Pour a bottle of water over his head. It'll cool him off . . . maybe it'll revive him enough to bear some of his weight."

"Dad, what do we do if the E.T. lands?"

"Don't do anything aggressive. Don't even look at them—just keep walking."

TESTIMONIAL
May 9, 2001: National Press Club, Washington, D.C.

My name is Michael Smith. I was in the Air Force, a sergeant, from 1967 to 1973. I was an aircraft control and warning operator.

While I was assigned to Klamath Falls, Oregon, in early 1970, I arrived at the radar site and they were watching a UFO on the radar that was hovering at about eighty thousand feet. It sat there for about ten minutes, and then slowly descended until it dropped off the radar, was gone for about five to ten minutes, and then instantly reappeared at eighty thousand feet, stationary. The next sweep of the radar it was two hundred miles away, stationary. And it hovered there for about ten minutes and redid the whole cycle, twice more. When I found out what the normal—what you normally do when you see a UFO, I was told that you notify NORAD, you don't necessarily write anything down—*you don't write anything down*—and you keep it to yourself. It's a need-to-know basis only.

NORAD one night called me later in the year to let me know as a heads-up that there was a UFO coming up the California coastline. I asked them what I should do about this. They said, "Nothing, don't write it down; this is just a heads-up." And then late in 1972 while stationed at the 753rd Radar Squadron at Sault Sainte Marie, Michigan, I received a couple of panicky calls from police officers who were chasing three UFOs from Mackinaw Bridge up I-75. So I immediately checked the radar and confirmed that they were there, called NORAD, and they were concerned because they had two inbound B-52s going to Kincheloe AFB. So they diverted them because they didn't want the proximity of the two. And that night I answered many calls from the police department, sheriff's department, and stuff, and my standard response was there was nothing on radar.

I will testify to this under oath to a Congressional hearing.

—Michael Smith,
US Air Force Radar Controller

Used by permission of the Disclosure Project

16

The town of Nazca, located along the southeastern region of Peru, is nestled between the Andes Mountains and an arid plateau that runs west to the Pacific Ocean. Viewed from satellite, the isolated community appears like a patch of moss overgrown between the mountains, bleeding trickles of green across a featureless gray plateau.

A closer inspection of the plateau reveals the remnants of an ancient civilization, founded by a deity.

He arrived sometime around 400 BC, a mysterious long-skulled Caucasian with white hair and beard and deep-set turquoise eyes. The Andes Indians revered the stranger, who taught them how to construct hilltop terraces nourished by aqueducts. To protect their villages, he gave them an advanced technology to counter gravity so they could move massive thirty-ton stones and erect fortresses at Sacsayhuaman, the walls of which still stand today. To prevent a future cataclysm, he had them inscribe warnings to modern man on the Nazca plateau.

His name: Viracocha.

The geological canvas that Viracocha selected to inscribe his message was a barren desert along Peru's Pacific coast—forty miles long and six miles wide. One of the driest places on Earth, Nazca's flatland was essentially a dead zone, and yet it possessed a unique surface found nowhere else on the planet. Covered by smooth stones, the underlying soil contained high levels of gypsum, a natural adhesive. Remoistened each day by the morning dew, the gypsum kept the indigenous iron and silica stones glued to its surface. These dark pebbles retained the sun's heat, generating a protective shield of warm air that eliminated the effects of the wind.

For the artist wishing to leave his work to a future audience, the Nazca plateau was the perfect canvas, for what was carved upon its geology remained there for centuries. In fact, it was not until a pilot flew over the desert in 1947 that modern man first discovered the mysterious drawings and geometric lines carved upon this Peruvian landscape eons ago.

There are more than thirteen thousand lines crossing the Nazca Desert. A few of these markings extend for distances exceeding five miles, stretching over rough terrain while miraculously remaining perfectly straight. More bizarre are the hundreds of animals and iconic shapes. At ground level, these colossal zoomorphs appear only as random indentations made by the scraping away of tons of black volcanic pebbles to expose the yellow gypsum below. But when viewed from high in the air, the Nazca drawings come alive, representing a unified artistic vision and engineering achievement that has survived unscathed for thousands of years.

The artwork was completed at two very distinct periods. Although it seems contrary to our notion of evolution, it is the earlier drawings that are by far the superior. These include the monkey, the spider, the Spiral, and the serpent. Not only are the likenesses incredibly accurate, but the figures themselves, most larger than a football field, were each drawn using one continuous, unbroken line.

Besides the plateau drawings, there are two distinct figures carved into the slopes of the Andes Mountains. The first is a five-hundred-foot humanoid, known as the Astronaut. The second, the Trident of Paracas, is a six-hundred-by-two-hundred-foot candelabralike symbol occupying an entire mountainside facing the Bay of Paracas—a welcome post situated at the mouth of the Nazca valley.

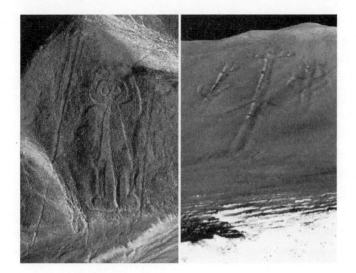

The artist responsible for the Nazca drawings?
Viracocha.

The city of Nazca is a sleepy community of twenty thousand, harbored in dense concrete neighborhoods constructed around a town square. A ten-minute drive in any direction and one arrives at a patchwork of fields that are the lifeblood of this isolated agricultural center. Founded in 1591 by the Spanish, Nazca long depended for its existence upon its ability to harvest its own food—until the discovery of its desert's artistry. Now the mysterious lines and drawings of its ancestors have offered the indigenous people a new trade: tourism.

Julius Gabriel drives the 1980 CJ7 Jeep with the rusted steel body past churches and an open bazaar, turning west on the Panamericana Sur where he follows signs to the *aeropuerto*. Nazca's airport consists of two asphalt runways and a series of hangars that store its single-prop planes. Michael calls them "puddle jumpers." To Julius—a man who has always feared flying—they are the tour buses' best friend.

The sky overhead is cloudless and blue, the late morning sun set on broil. The fifty-one-year-old archaeologist parks the Jeep outside the steel perimeter fence and waits inside the confines of his vehicle. The Jeep's air conditioner is running low on Freon, the ventilated breeze more warm than cool, but it still beats the 105-degree Fahrenheit heat rising from the earth.

After a ten-minute wait he sees the white biplane appear out of the north sky, its pilot beginning a long arcing descent to the east. Julius watches from the Jeep as the six-passenger Piper Malibu touches down, then circles back to the gate, taxiing to a stop. After five long minutes an airport employee motors across the tarmac with a portable set of steps, positioning them beneath the now-open cockpit door.

A German couple exits first, followed by a priest and two men in their forties, one carrying a camera case the size of a guitar.

She is the last one out, a pale-skinned beauty in her late twenties, wearing a red and black Manchester United football jersey and a matching baseball cap, her long brown wavy hair pulled into a ponytail that feeds out the back of the hat. Tight beige corduroy shorts reveal the muscular legs of a sprinter. She is carrying a duffel bag, her eyes concealed behind dark sunglasses.

Laura Rosen Salesa struts across the tarmac and through the gate, her shirt pressed against her sweaty flesh by the time she reaches the Jeep. Tossing her bag in back, she climbs in the passenger seat next to the driver. "God, it's hotter than hell. Hey, Jules. You look like shit."

The accent is British, tinged by a Spanish upbringing.

Julius shifts the Jeep into gear. "I look like shit because I haven't been sleeping."

"Maybe I can help ease your mind."

He glances at his sister-in-law. "That's why I called you."

"You called Evelyn first."

"Only out of respect. She is the oldest."

"Big sis refused to speak with you, huh?"

"She hates me. Your whole family hates me. They blame me for Maria's death."

"No, they blame you for her life. Michael blames you for her death." Laura removes her hiking boots and socks, resting her bare feet on the dashboard. "Speaking of which, how are things between you and Mick?"

"Pretty bad until recently. The presence of our houseguest seems to have diffused a bit of his anger. Then again, maybe it's just distracted him."

"Or maybe he just enjoys hanging out with a stranger more than he likes schlepping across desert pampas and Mayan jungles with his father."

"There's a purpose to everything I do. I don't expect you to understand."

"Oh, but I do understand. As a linguistics professor specializing in ancient languages, my father kept us constantly on the move—Hong Kong,

Moscow, Mumbai, Scotland, Kenya . . . name a country and chances are we lived there. Being the oldest, Evelyn missed most of it. Maria was in boarding school, then she went off to Cambridge. Me? I was seven years old when my parents sold our house and took to life on the road. You know how hard it is to make friends, let alone enjoy any kind of social life, when your parents uproot you every four months? I started calling my father by his first name out of anger just like Mick does with you. He's had it far worse, of course, having been home-schooled by my sister. At least my schools in Russia and China had sports teams. Who's he supposed to play American football or baseball with out on the Nazca plateau? Aliens?"

Julius shoots her a look.

"Okay, okay, lecture's over. I know Michael is 'special,' that you and Maria were convinced he has a higher calling. Tell me more about this stranger you flew me in to psychoanalyze. Does he have a name yet?"

"He still can't remember it. Michael calls him Sam."

"Why Sam?"

"It's short for Samson. The guy's built like a young Arnold Schwarzenegger, only his hair's real long, like Samson in the Bible. He's actually taken to the name, he says it feels familiar to him. What's really strange is how he looks at himself in the mirror."

"What do you mean?"

"The eyes. He stares at his eyes, sometimes for hours while he lies in bed with a hand mirror. It's as if something significant has changed."

"What color are his eyes?"

"Black. Just like Michael's." Leaving the highway, Julius heads south into the neighborhood of Vista Allegre. They pass rows of single-story homes, each dwelling no larger than a double-wide trailer, harboring families three or more generations deep, the young ones relegated to sleeping on the flat open roofs beneath a ceiling of stars, livestock inhabiting the backyard.

The Gabriel abode is located across the street from a bottling factory. A massive huangaro tree occupies the entire front lawn, with groves of saplings growing on empty parcels of land surrounding the stucco habitat.

Years earlier, a Cambridge University research group, headed by Julius and Maria Gabriel, had discovered that the huangaro tree (*Prosopis pallida*) was once the keystone species of the Nazca valley. Fifteen hundred years ago the indigenous Indians, in direct violation of Viracocha's teachings, systematically deforested the region, using the trees for food and timber while clearing more land for corn and other cultivated crops. Without the nitrogen-fixing trees the soil became less stable. In AD 500, El Niño floods struck the area, washing away the crops. Weed pollen quickly took root, collapsing the ecosystem and with it an entire civilization.

Before she had succumbed to pancreatic cancer, Maria Rosen Gabriel had spearheaded an aggressive reforestation effort. The local government had donated the land and house in her memory.

Julius parks the Jeep. Laura grabs her duffel bag and follows him inside.

The interior is an open space, more library than home. Walls are precious real estate, covered in maps. Books are simply stacked in high piles on the floor. The furnishings are limited to an old torn leather La-Z-Boy chair, several oil lamps, and a large picnic table that serves as a desk. The kitchen consists of a gas stove and refrigerator, a freestanding sink, and a warped Formica countertop littered with canned goods labeled in Spanish. A small card table sits against a yellowed stucco wall, surrounded by three folding chairs. A bedroom is cordoned off by a colorful wool blanket. Wood steps, built into the far stucco wall, lead up to the roof.

Laura shakes her head. "What is this? A home for wayward archaeologists?"

"It is what it is."

"Can't argue with that. Where's the loo?"

"If you mean the toilet, it's out back."

"Is it an outhouse, or just a shrub with a roll of toilet paper?" She looks around. "Where's the damn back door?"

"I didn't design the place. I just live here."

"Marvelous." Laura drops her hiking boots and bag on the floor, then heads outside and walks around the side of the house to the back, her bare feet burning on the hot yellow soil. Cursing, she hustles for the shade of a huangaro tree, wishing she had never left Spain.

The deflated hot air balloon occupies most of the backyard, its orange and blue envelope laid out beside the six-by-six-foot wicker basket.

And then she sees the stranger.

He is standing beyond the wood outhouse at the edge of an open flat parcel of land. Shirtless and bronze, he has muscles chiseled and oiled in sweat. His broad V-shaped back is to her as he tosses a football to her barechested nephew, who is running a deep route fifty yards away.

The pass hits Mick in stride, a perfect spiral.

Without thinking, Laura claps—revealing her presence.

The stranger turns, startled.

Oh, my . . . he is a Samson, isn't he?

He continues to stare back at her.

"Hey!" Mick jogs over, his body lathered in sweat. Passing Sam, he punches him on the shoulder, laughing as he dodges the bigger man's playful retaliatory roundhouse, the blow momentarily breaking the spell.

The two athletes approach.

Now it is Laura who stares, her scalp tingling. Though separated by twenty years, the stranger and her nephew could be father and son, their physiques and facial features eerily similar.

Mick leans in and kisses her on the cheek. "I can't believe you actually came out here. You look great. I guess being single again agrees with you."

"Yes. Wait, what did you say?"

"Your divorce?"

She breaks eye contact with the stranger. "My divorce, right. Yes, what a relief. Two years of hell, now I'm single . . . no ring, no ties. God, listen to me babble." She extends her hand. "I'm Laura, Mick's aunt. And you must be Sam."

"Lauren?" His eyes tear up. "Lauren, my God. Lauren, it's me . . . Sam!"

"Dude, she knows."

"No, Mick . . . I think your friend remembers something about his identity. Do I remind you of someone, Sam? I'm Laura Salesa. Who's Lauren?"

He says nothing, his eyes locked onto her face, his jaw hanging open as he struggles to isolate a memory.

"Okay, well, this is a bit awkward. Tell you what, while you're gathering your thoughts, I'm going to make a mad dash over to that outhouse. Now you stay right here."

She tiptoes over the hot ground, wrenches open the squeaky wooden door, and ducks inside, gagging at the stench. Bolting the lock she drops her shorts and squats over the porcelain bowl, quickly relieving herself.

Keep your head, Laura. Forget that he's gorgeous. He's lost, a mystery man clinging to a shard of memory and a woman named Lauren. Most likely his wife, probably living back in the States with their two cats and seven kids. Or maybe she's dead? Maybe he killed her?

Stop it! He didn't kill her. Isn't it obvious—he loves her. Settle him down, clean yourself up, then wait until after dinner before you begin rerouting a connection to his past. Just take it slow, he's obviously a live wire.

She fixes herself. *A gorgeous live wire.*

Laura exits the outhouse. The hot yellow soil again scorches her bare feet, forcing her to sprint back to the shade of the huangaro tree.

Mick laughs. "Where are your shoes?"

"Inside the house." She removes her sunglasses, wiping sweat from the lens. "Stupid me. I took them off on the plane, not thinking—"

The stranger drops to his knees, staring at her bright blue-turquoise eyes. "Lilith?"

She glances nervously at Mick. "What did you call me?"

"Lilith. But you're not Lilith. You're Hunahpu but you're not Lilith and you're not Lauren!"

He's losing it . . . it's coming back too fast for him to process. "Sam, stay calm—"

"Who are you? Who am I? Why am I here? How did I get here?"

"Dude, chill out."

"It's okay, Michael, I can handle—"

"Michael . . . you're Michael Gabriel. How can you be Michael Gabriel? How can he be Julius? Something's all wrong—"

"Sam, listen to me . . . I want you to take long, slow breaths, nice and easy. Mick, get us a wet towel and some water. And my shoes! Slow, deep breaths, Sam—"

"Not Sam. I am not him!"

"Okay, just keep breathing. You're not Sam, but you are someone. Who are you? Can you remember?"

"I am . . . Chilam Balam."

"Good, very good. And what brings you to Nazca, Mr. Balam?"

"I was sent here . . . to prevent the end of humanity."

TESTIMONIAL
May 9, 2001: National Press Club, Washington, D.C.

My name is Enrique Kolbeck. [. . .] I work in Mexico City as a radar controller at the International Airport of Mexico. And I am going to give an example about these sightings that we have in Mexico for several years on this issue. It happens a lot of times in my country, unfortunately. For example, on March 4, 1992, we detected fifteen objects west side of the Toluca airport. It is very close to our international airport, at fifty miles, more or less. Then, July 28, 1994, we have almost a collision, or something that we can name in that way, with a domestic flight of Aeromexico 129, commanded by the pilot Raimundo Cervantes Arruano, that has a crash with something about his main landing gear [. . .]. This occurred at night, 10:30, more or less. Then in the next week, the same year, in the same moment, the Aeromexico flight 904 has another almost collision that was reported by the pilot, Capitan Corso, at 11:30 in the morning, and we detect that object on radar, suddenly, just for a moment. Then the next week we have a lot of sightings reported by the pilots that gave us information about the weird traffic or something—bright lights, on different times, and we detect some of them in that week. But in September 15 of 1994, we have a detection of about five hours more or less on the radar, new equipment that we believed that the equipment was working in not a good way, because it's not common that you have a detection for five hours of the same object and apparently without moving. Well, we concurred with the technical persons [. . .] that the radar system was working well. And it was very exciting and we surprised when at the next day, we received information about a reporter named Jaime Maussan that is studying these cases in Mexico, about a sighting from a lot of people in the Metepec City. There is another point located southeast of the Toluca airport about a sighting of the big flying saucer apparently, of fifteen meters of diameter, by a lot of people, that lit or crash or something on the ground. Well, next November 24, 1994, we have in service officially our new radar system and after that moment we have information very exactly about these sightings at the same time with the pilots and detections. [. . .] We have a lot more cases, but I don't want to use more time on this. But it's very important that the people in the world knows this evidence and consider that it could be very dangerous for an aeronautical situation, especially in my country. I don't know why in my country that's occur frequently but the point is that it happens and we consider it dangerous. And we have only, fortunately, one crash, but we don't want to have another one. Thank you very much, and I'm sorry for my English.

—**Enrique Kolbeck,**
air traffic controller

Used by permission of the Disclosure Project

The United 737 airbus touches down with a heavy skid of rubber on concrete, its spoilers—small hinged plates situated along the top portion of the wings—flipping up into the air stream to slow the plane's forward inertia.

Pierre Robert Borgia glances again across the first-class aisle at the long-legged woman in the pleated gray business skirt and see-through blouse. It had taken the fifty-three-year-old anthropologist and son of Congressman Robert Borgia a mere three minutes to catalogue the thirty-one-year-old hazel-eyed redhead as a Tony Robbins disciple with a chip on her shoulder. Leading her easily into her favorite topic (herself) he had listened politely and nodded, all the while peppering their conversation with a few of his own superlatives—that his family were power brokers in the defense sector, that he was being groomed for a senatorial race in either 1994 or 2000, only his backers insisted he settle down first, that voters preferred their candidates married with children. "I told my father I'd rather remain a bachelor than date another former fashion model whose only aspiration as an adult was to be a millionaire's arm candy. Give me a smart, emancipated woman any day—one who's as dominant in bed as she is in the boardroom. I mean, am I right or am I right?"

By the end of the ninety-minute flight from Los Angeles, the mid-level assistant holding down a dead-end job at a second-rate insurance company was ripe for the picking, but by the time they began their descent, Pierre found himself already losing interest. To the Cambridge graduate, the final conquest in the hotel room was never as good as the game of mental masturbation, and with a "chippy" there was always the dangerous moment afterward when she realized his only interest after sex was a shower, room service, and a brief respite to catch the baseball scores on ESPN before he fell asleep. Which is why Pierre usually preferred a pro, where the outcome was predetermined and the only game was hiding his wallet before his "date" arrived.

"So, Pierre, I was thinking, if your meeting ended early, maybe we could meet somewhere for dinner."

"What's early?"

"I don't know . . . eightish?"

"Eight may be tough, but give me your phone number and we can catch a nightcap together back at my hotel . . . unless you're tired of hearing about my terminal bachelorhood."

"I'm sure we can find a cure."

"Now, don't tease me. You're way too hot for that sort of thing."

The plane's arrival at the gate triggers the usual chaotic rush of passengers fighting to claim standing room in an aisle of immovable bodies. Retrieving his bag from the overhead bin, Pierre turns back around to the redhead—

—the woman's raincoat concealing her hand at his genitals. "Call me. We'll have some fun." She slips the business card into his pants pocket and exits the plane.

Borgia's eyes remain glued to the back of her skirt. By lunch, she'll have authenticated his story; by tonight, she'll be primped and properly motivated to please.

Pierre smiles to himself. Even a pro couldn't outperform a woman with ambition.

Joseph H. Randolph, Sr., is wearing a cowboy hat and matching boots, neither accessory matching his charcoal-black business suit. The silver-haired

Texas businessman and former CIA operative greets Borgia with a wry grin and a bear hug. "Lucky Pierre, good to see you, son. How was the flight?"

"I'll let you know tonight."

"Balls deep in *poonta*, huh? Just like your old man. Of course, I could have never taken him where I'm taking you."

"Exactly how classified is this place, Uncle Joe?"

"Put it this way, Carter and Reagan couldn't have gone where you're about to go even with an act of Congress and a C-5 cargo plane loaded with subpoenas."

"What about Bush?"

"George Walker knows because he has backdoor access through Big Oil and the CIA. Even so, believe me, he don't want to know."

"And you?"

"I know because I'm the White Rabbit, and that makes you Alice. So, Alice, are you ready to go through the looking glass?"

"Hell, yes. Are we driving or flying?"

"Today we're driving, but only because it allows me time to brief you in private. In the future, you'll fly. There's a private terminal located on the north side of the airport, it's owned and operated by EG&G."

"The nuke contractors?"

"Uh-huh. Every morning they move five to six hundred ultra–high clearance suits and techs out of McCarran aboard a small fleet of unmarked Boeing 737-200s. Only thing the FAA boys in the tower know about these flights is that they all use the call sign 'Janet' and that they all fly north every hour on the hour."

They follow the baggage claim signs downstairs, then head outside into the Nevada heat and an awaiting limo.

Pierre climbs in back with the billionaire. The glass partition between the two passengers and the driver remains closed.

"Uncle Joe, you said you could never bring Dad to this place. Why not?"

"Your father was a smart man and a clever politician, but he was set in his ways, closed to new ideas . . . new realities. He lived in a world where you were either a wolf or a sheep, and being a wolf he believed he occupied the top of the food chain. What he failed to see was that being the top predator in the zoo doesn't change the fact that you're still in the zoo. You saw beyond that, you and Julius Gabriel, and your dead colleague, what was her name?"

"Maria." Mention of his former fiancée strikes a nerve. "Listen, Uncle

Joe, if you're talking about extraterrestrials, then you can drop me off on the strip."

"No, Pierre. I'm talking about existence. I'm talking about controlling the knowledge that will one day govern how this entire planet will power our civilization over the next thousand years, and just as important, who will control that power. As an anthropologist, you and your pals searched and found a dark truth about man's past. What I'm about to reveal to you are secrets that have been kept from the public for more than fifty years . . . secrets that you and your former colleagues stumbled upon but lacked the perspective to fully comprehend. My job is to bring you up to speed so your mind can accept the truth, but I can't do that until you pull your head out of your ass and see the world for how it truly is."

"I'm listening."

"Your research with Julius Gabriel focused on an epoch of alien intervention that began ten thousand years ago after the last ice age. Our work began far more recently, back in 1941 with the first crash recovery of a UFO in Cape Girardeau, Missouri. Reverse engineering of this aircraft is often credited to the success of the Manhattan Project, but that was just part of an intricate disinformation campaign, something we purposely fed to the public because it could be easily discredited. The real shit didn't hit the fan until after the first tests of the atom bomb. That's what brought the visitors to the zoo, and that's what led to the July 4th, 1947, event in New Mexico.

"The Roswell crash created a ripple effect that would lead to a series of top-secret research and development projects and the greatest technological and biological opportunity in the history of human kind. You have to understand, Roswell wasn't just physical evidence of extraterrestrial existence, it was a revelation that Earth is the zoo and we're the animals. To extricate ourselves from that subordinate reality required a massive undertaking on three different levels: First, we needed to identify the flying objects that were moving freely through our atmosphere using technologies far beyond our own. Second, we needed to reverse engineer these technologies to make them our own. Third, we needed to keep everything out of the public eye, not to mention away from the scrutiny of the Commies.

"The first three Air Force projects designated to investigate extraterrestrial sightings were Grudge, Sign, and Blue Book. Between 1948 and 1969, these three programs investigated more than twelve thousand sightings reported by military personnel, FAA air traffic controllers, and commercial pilots, as well as civilians. The programs concluded that the objects were real and described the alien vessels as elliptical and disk-shaped, capable of extreme speeds, maneuvers, and altitudes. These projects also verified that the E.T.s had the capability to shut down our nuclear missile bases and weapon systems, which they did on several occasions during flyovers."

They have been traveling on an empty stretch of Highway 375. Passing mile marker 34, the limo turns west onto an unmarked well-traveled dirt road that takes them across an empty expanse of desert, a mountain range looming thirteen miles ahead. The ride is smooth, the road surface graded to powder to reveal dust clouds that can be seen from miles away.

"Blue Book was essentially a sugar pill designed to satisfy the public's demand for an investigation while providing the government agencies involved with a disinformation paper trail that explained the unexplainable. While those investigations continued to collect data, the real work was being done by Majestic-12, a secret consortium of military leaders, avionic specialists, and scientists established back on September 24, 1947, by a special classified presidential order from Harry S. Truman. The MJ-12 geeks discovered the power source of the Roswell vessel was antigravitational in nature, allowing these objects, dubbed 'Fastwalkers,' to travel at speeds exceeding Mach 4, about eight thousand miles an hour, then suddenly stop on a dime and make a ninety-degree reverse angle turn. The boys at Lockheed Martin, Northrop, and other defense contractors began reverse engineering the designs, only they needed a place where they could secretly begin testing this alien technology. By 1955 the Air Force had opened Groom Lake, better known as Area 51. Since then, the facility has been used to test the most advanced aircraft projects in the world, including the U-2 spy plane, the SR-71 Blackbird, the F-117 stealth fighter, Northrop's B-2 stealth bomber, and a new line of aircraft, dubbed ARVs."

"ARVs?"

"Alien Reproduction Vehicles. Extraterrestrial vehicles manufactured by human military intelligence."

"Are you saying we now have access to zero-point energy?"

"Not yet, but we're making progress." Randolph points out the window as they bear right onto an extension road. "Doesn't look like it, but we just left public land and entered the Nellis Air Force Base and Area 51—a thousand square miles of restricted airspace, the entire boundary patrolled by a private security force. Locals call 'em the 'camo dudes,' seeing as they wear camouflage outfits and they don't mess around. Every road and hiking trail from here on out is mined with remote electronic sensors that can not only see and feel vibrations, but can also smell any person approaching the base. There's a surveillance installation on Bald Mountain up ahead, plus we've got a dozen Sikorsky MH-60G Pave Hawks that'll sandblast the ever-lovin' shit out of any nosey UFO hunter."

Warning signs begin appearing more frequently. The road curves into an S bend, descending into a valley. After a few minutes they arrive at a steel perimeter fence and the gated entry of the most safeguarded military base in the world.

When the CIA gave Kelly Johnson the task of choosing and building a secure test site, the U-2 spy plane designer dispatched Skunk Works foreman Dorsey Kammerer to the deserts of southern California, Nevada, and Arizona to locate a remote area near a dry lake bed, knowing the geology made the best landing field for experimental aircraft. They found what they were looking for at Groom Lake, located at grid 51 of Nevada's nuclear test site—a stretch of flatlands surrounded by mountains that had once been a World War II Army Air Corps Gunnery Range. Expanded several times since 1955, the facility featured an 18,500-foot runway, storage tanks capable of holding up to a million and a half gallons of JP-7 jet fuel, three navy surplus hangars, over a hundred administration and housing buildings, a dozen massive airship hangars located at the south end of the base, a weapons storage facility, five earth-covered igloos, and a 12,400-foot-long, 100-foot-wide runway that extended over Groom Lake, the surface of the dry bed giving it a total landing surface of nearly five miles.

Pierre Borgia and Joseph Randolph exit the car, their credentials scrutinized by two MPs. Without waiting, their limo turns around and leaves.

"Sir, your chopper's en route, it should only be a few moments."

Pierre squints into the noonday sun. The Air Force base is spread out a mile to the east. A dark object is coming in fast from the south. Within seconds it is landing, its engines whisper-quiet.

The two men climb aboard the military transport chopper, situating themselves in leather bucket seats within the otherwise empty cabin.

The airship lifts off. To Borgia's surprise, it bypasses the Air Force base, heading south. They fly fifteen miles over empty desert before another dry lake bed appears in the distance.

The billionaire smiles at his protégé. "Papoose Lake. Part of the Tonopah Test Range. Groom Lake belongs to the Air Force. Site 4 is run by Majestic-12."

The Site 4 complex is spread out over several miles across a large desert valley. Buildings are few and far between, connected by a one-lane dirt road. There are earthen bunkers and security towers specked with antennas and microwave dishes, and a few dark, cone-shaped, alien-looking towers that add a sinister appearance.

The helicopter sets down on a helipad. A Jeep and two security officers dressed in desert camouflage are waiting.

A minute later Borgia and his uncle are motoring along a dirt road leading to one of the earthen bunkers. A small sign identifies the subterranean facility as S-66. The Jeep pauses long enough to let them out.

A reinforced steel door is guarded by several security cameras and a retinal scanner.

Removing his cowboy hat, Joseph Randolph rests his chin on the high-tech security device and presses his occipital bone to the rubber scope, allowing the retinal scanner to match the blood vessel pattern of his eyeball to his identification records.

The door opens, the disturbance sending a black scorpion scurrying out from behind a rock and over Borgia's right shoe.

Randolph grins at his nephew. "Welcome to Dreamland, Pierre."

MORELOS, MEXICO

Located in south central Mexico, the state of Morelos is separated from the Mexican valley by the Sierra Ajusco mountains. The area possesses a subtropical climate, making it ideal for agriculture—a trade that began as early as 1500 BC.

The first Indian culture to inhabit Morelos was the Tlahuicas, an offshoot of the Toltec-Chichimec amalgam of Aztec tribes. Artifacts describe the Indians as being dark-skinned, with wiry large physiques and black eyes. The lords of the Aztec region were priests.

One would father a deity.

The warrior priest known as Mixcoatl was considered both a creator and a destroyer—a god of warfare and ambush. According to Aztec legend, the Sun and Mother Earth birthed four hundred stars to spread their seed across the Milky Way. When their offspring behaved selfishly, Mixcoatl was summoned to kill all his siblings. Associated with Tezcatlipoca, the dark and powerful god of the night sky, Mixcoatl's name translates as "cloud serpent," reflecting his ability to change shape. He is usually portrayed with a black mask, a red and white striped body, and long hair.

Mixcoatl married Chimalma, a mysterious turquoise-eyed beauty said to have come from Amatlán. In AD 935, Chimalma gave birth to a son—a blue-eyed, white-haired child who would become known throughout Mesoamerica as Quetzalcoatl, the Plumed Serpent. Aided by their leader's vast knowledge of astronomy and engineering, the Aztecs would come to dominate the region, erecting great cities in his honor.

Quetzalcoatl's passing left the Aztec empire in chaos. Seeking their deity's return, the Aztecs turned to human sacrifice, their festivals highlighted by the ritual killing of an Indian couple atop Mixcoatl's main temple. The woman would be slaughtered first, her head cut off and shown to the blood-thirsty crowd. The man would be sacrificed next, his still-beating heart removed from his chest by an obsidian dagger.

On April 21, 1519, the Spanish conquistador Hernán Cortés landed in the Gulf of Mexico with a force of eleven ships and 550 men. Greatly outnumbered by the Aztecs, the Spanish should have been easily defeated. What Cortés had no way of knowing was that his physical description as a bearded white man had cast him as Quetzalcoatl returning from the east. As the Spanish marched westward to engage the Aztecs, their leader, Montezuma, welcomed the bearded one and his invading army into his fortified city.

Within two years the entire region had been conquered.

Don Alejandro Rafelo was striking in appearance. Tall and lanky, the forty-eight-year-old Nagual witch possessed long graying hair that framed a face dominated by a hooked aquiline nose and eyes that were unnerving to behold. The left was a piercing azure blue, the right eye hazel and lazy, always glancing sideways, making it impossible for his enemies to maintain contact.

The turquoise eye was a genetic trait that could be traced back twenty-seven generations when a distant relative, Etienne Rafelo, arrived in Mexico from France in the fall of 1533. A practitioner of the Black Mass, Etienne eventually found his way to a small Nahuatl Indian village situated across the mountains from Morelos. Here he would meet an Aztec leader named Motecuma, whose maternal ancestors were direct descendants of Chimalma and her deity son, Quetzalcoatl. Motecuma's oldest daughter, Quetzalli, was an azure-eyed beauty who served the community as its Nagual witch. The Nagual were seers who had once counseled kings. It was said a Nagual could cause sickness by sucking the blood of his victim or by giving him the evil eye. It was believed the more powerful witches could even capture a man's soul.

Etienne and Quetzalli married. Twenty-seven generations later, Don Alejandro Rafelo was born.

The villagers of Morelos believed Don Rafelo possessed a dark *ojo*, that his *K'az-al t'an-ob* (curses) caused serious and painful diseases among his enemies. When he passed close, they looked away. When he left the area they held their tongues, knowing the witch could hear every thought cast to the wind.

Rafelo used his underlings to cultivate the superstitions. In his line of work, instilling fear among the populace was one of the keys to remaining in power.

Don Rafelo was the right arm of Los Lenones, a tightly organized cartel that ran human trafficking pipelines throughout the small towns in Southern Mexico and along the US border. The Aztec witch oversaw a slave training center in Tenancingo, a suburb located just south of Mexico City that functioned as a way station into Tijuana. It was a place where low-end local girls as young as six were kidnaped or bought into slavery, drugged and raped repeatedly until they were broken in, then sold into sex rings and smuggled across the Mexican border. Once in the States, they were transported to stash houses and apartments, some in major cities like New York, Chicago, and Los Angeles, others in smaller suburban towns—thirty thousand slaves kidnaped and sold every year.

To service America's demands, Don Rafelo and his "nephews" recruited a small army of teenaged boys from the local villages who were taught the art of hunting and entrapping local women. Tourists were always a desired target of Los Lenones, especially the tall, blond-haired women who were especially desired by the Saudis. When Don Rafelo's brigade filled these orders, they were always on the lookout for another type of woman, a far rarer breed—carrying the genome of a lost empire.

While human trafficking had made Don Rafelo a rich man, the Nagual witch knew that true power came from one's DNA. The Maya and Aztec had risen under the tutelage of two great bloodlines. The Rafelos of Mexico were part of the Quetzalcoatl family tree. What Don Rafelo sought were females whose maternal lineage traced back to Kukulcan. The desired Mesoamerican female would possess one easily identifiable feature—a pair of radiating turquoise-blue eyes.

For more than a decade, Don Rafelo had offered a $25,000 reward to anyone who brought a "Hunahpu female" to him. Up until now, the bounty had remained uncollected.

Gerardo Salazar is in his twenties, a dark, handsome youth with a strut that fits his nickname, *El Gallo*—the Rooster. El Gallo works the dusty Mexican villages, using his looks and sweet incantations of love to seduce teens and young schoolgirls. He has been trafficking juveniles for his "Uncle Don" since he dropped out of school at the age of ten.

Today he brings news that will make his uncle smile.

Don Rafelo's blue eye widens as he listens to the Rooster crow.

". . . her name is Chicahua Aurelia. She is older, in her forties, but still a beauty. I saw her when I passed through Morelos. Her eyes are turquoise just as you said, and they glowed at me just like a jungle cat. She was watching me from across the market while I was working a schoolgirl."

"Wait . . . she was watching you?"

"*Sí*. It was as if I could feel her inside my head."

"She's a seer, very powerful, very dangerous. She showed herself to you knowing you would tell me."

"You wish me to take you to her, Uncle?"

"No. I will find this one myself."

Chicahua Aurelia was born and raised in Guatemala—the surviving twin daughter and only child of Lilia Botello and Jesus Vazquez. The chromosome that gave her the ability to "slow down reality" reoccurred throughout her maternal lineage once every four generations. That her twin sister had been stillborn demonstrated the power of her unusual genetics; two Hunahpu from the same lineage could not be birthed during the same era—only the mythological male Mayan hero twins could share the same womb and survive.

Aurelia had been Chicahua's maternal grandmother's maiden name. She had begun using it after she conceived a child out of wedlock. The father had been an unknowing participant to the conception, Chicahua bedding him after intoxicating him with a powerful hallucinogen. In his eyes, she appeared to be a Russian import—a gift to be raped and exported to America.

What Don Rafelo never suspected was that he was impregnating the very genetic prize he had been seeking.

As a seer, Chicahua knew the Nagual witch was pursuing her, guided by a dark and powerful force—a demon hitched to his soul. Realizing she could not escape him forever, she had chosen to control the variables in play, knowing that once Don Rafelo's seed had taken root in her womb, his offspring's presence would actually blind the demon to Chicahua's bloodline.

What she never realized was that her daughter's conception would blanket her own abilities as well, preventing her from protecting her child from the very predator who made Don Rafelo so dangerous.

The farmhouse is located in the Sierra Ajusco mountains, a three-room structure composed of mud-brick and stone, its thatched roof generations old. A narrow mountain path is the only way up to the acre parcel, the land providing food and medicines for the owner and feed for her animals.

Don Rafelo guides his motor scooter up the trail, leaving the vehicle parked outside the wooden rail fence. The late afternoon sun casts the mountain's shadow across a front yard overgrown with herbs. He can smell a familiar aroma and follows it to the farmhouse door, entering unannounced.

The dark-haired beauty with the high Indian cheekbones is standing before a pot boiling with the offal of a goat's stomach. She looks up, her skin a dark mocha, her eyes the color of the waters off Cancun. "Tripe and onion soup. Your favorite."

"How did you know?"

Chicahua smiles. "The same way I know you have been searching for me."

"Or one like you."

"There will be none like me for another four generations."

"Why have you concealed yourself from me for so long?"

"Because a demon taints your soul."

"Our ancestors did far worse."

"And they paid a terrible price. As will you."

"The demon who taints my soul, as you call it, also protects it. I do not fear the Creator or His afterlife. I am immune." He moves closer, enamored by her beauty. "Why have you revealed yourself to me now?"

"Because I seek a mate."

"And I seek to father a child, one who will link our two bloodlines."

"My womb and my bloodline come with a price."

"Name it and it shall be yours."

"The devils of Los Lenones kidnaped a nine-year-old girl from my village several weeks ago."

"And you wish her returned to her parents."

"Her parents are dead. I wish her taken to America. She has a distant cousin living in Tampa, Florida."

"What is your interest in the child?"

"I owe a debt to the father. Locate the child, see to it that she makes it to the States safely, and I shall bear you an offspring who will share our bloodlines."

"The kidnaped child—what is her name?"

"Vazquez. Dominique Vazquez."

TESTIMONIAL
May 9, 2001: National Press Club, Washington, D.C.

My name is Daniel Sheehan. I am an attorney serving as general counsel to the Disclosure Project. I am a 1967 graduate of Harvard College in American Government Studies and Constitutional Law. I am a graduate of Harvard Law School. I served as general counsel, and one of the cocounsels for the *New York Times* in the Pentagon Papers case and was involved in briefing and arguing the case in front of the United States Supreme Court, giving permission to the *New York Times* to publish the classified documents, the forty-seven volumes of the Pentagon Papers.

Subsequent to that time, I served as special counsel to the office of F. Lee Bailey as one of the trial counsels when we represented James McCord in the Watergate burglary, and got Mr. McCord to write the letter to Judge Sirica to reveal the Watergate burglars' relationship to the plumbers unit in the White House at that time. Subsequent to my service in that case, I went back to Harvard to the divinity school to study Judeo-Christian social ethics in public policy. I did my master's and PhD work there and became general counsel for the United States Jesuit Headquarters in Washington, D.C., assigned to the National Social Ministries Office and their Public Policy Office.

It was there in 1977 that I was contacted by Miss Marsha Smith, who was the director of the Science and Technology Division of the Congressional Research Service. She [. . .] informed me that President Carter, upon taking office in January 1977, held a meeting with then director of Central Intelligence, George Bush, Sr., and demanded that the director of Central Intelligence turn over to the president the classified information about unidentified flying objects and the information that was in the possession of the United States' intelligence community concerning the existence of extraterrestrial intelligence.

This information was refused to the president of the United States by the director of Central Intelligence, George Bush, Sr. The director insisted that the president, in order to have access to this information, needed to have clearance to contact the Congressional Research Service, to contact the United States House of Representatives' Science and Technology Division, to have them undertake a process to declassify this information.

Because the DCI suspected that the president was preparing to reveal this information to the American public, the Congressional Research Service's

Science and Technology Division, under the directorship of Marsha Smith, was contacted by the House Science and Technology Committee and instructed to undertake a major investigation of the existence of extraterrestrial intelligence and the relationship of the UFO phenomenon to this.

I was contacted by Miss Smith, and asked, in my capacity as general counsel to the United States Jesuit Headquarters, National Social Ministry Office, to see if we could obtain access to the Vatican Library to obtain the information that the Vatican had with regard to extraterrestrial intelligence and the phenomenon of UFOs. I pursued that with the permission of Father William J. Davis, the director of the National Office, and we were refused access as the United States Jesuit Order, to the information in the possession of the Vatican Library.

When I reported this to Miss Smith, she then later subsequently asked me to participate [. . .] as a special consultant to the United States Library of Congress Congressional Research Service, to the classified portions of the "Blue Book Project" of the Air Force [. . .].

In May of 1977, I went to the Madison Building of the United States Library of Congress [. . .] and was directed to a basement office, where there were two guards at the door, and a third, sitting at the table, who took my identification, verified that I had been designated as a special consultant to the Congressional Research Service of the United States Library of Congress, and was admitted to the room. I thereupon found some dozen photographs of what is unquestionably an unidentified flying object on the ground that had crashed and plowed a furrow in a field of snow, and was embedded in an embankment. There were United States Air Force personnel surrounding this craft, taking photographs of the craft.

On one of the photographs I could see that there were some symbols on the side of the craft [. . .]. I had been instructed that I was to take no notes and had to leave my briefcase and all my identification outside of this room. But I had brought with me a yellow pad. And [. . .] so I opened up the yellow pad and refocused the overhead projector to the same size of the cardboard backing of the yellow pad. And I physically traced the copies of the symbols on the side of this craft, closed the yellow pad back, put the microfiche back into the canister, reclosed the box that I had, and I said, "It is time for me to leave." And I took this and proceeded to leave the office. At which point the security guards stopped me and one of them said, "What is that you have there, Mr. Sheehan?" At which point I handed the yellow pad to him and he flipped through all the yellow pages and never found the copy that I had.

And so I took that with me and brought it to the United States Jesuit Headquarters, had a meeting with the staff and Father William J. Davis, reported this to them, was authorized at that time, by the United States Jesuit Headquarters, to make a report to the National Council of Churches, and to request that the entire fifty-four major religious denominations of our country undertake a major study of extraterrestrial intelligence—which they declined to do. I was subsequently asked to deliver a three-hour, closed-door seminar to the top fifty scientists of the Jet Propulsion Laboratory of SETI—the Search for Extraterrestrial Intelligence—which I did do in 1977. I am more than happy to testify under oath to these details to the United States Congress, and would be happy to meet with any members of the press [. . .].

—Daniel Sheehan,
attorney and Disclosure Project counsel

Used by permission of the Disclosure Project

18

Laura Salesa watches her nephew tend to the stranger, adjusting his IV drip, covering the unconscious man lying on the torn leather La-Z-Boy chair with a light shawl.

She joins Julius at the picnic table, the archaeologist's attention absorbed in an ancient text. "Does Sam always pass out after one of these memory bouts? Hello? Earth to Julius?"

"Sorry. What was the question?"

"Your houseguest . . . when he gets a sudden memory rush—"

"—the blackouts, yes. The doctor called it sensory overload. It shuts everything down. He'll sleep for the rest of the day."

"What's in the IV?"

"Nutrients, mixed with a mild sedative. When these sensory overloads happen . . . well, he can get a bit excited."

"Mick's incredible with him."

"Michael? Yes." Julius returns to the text.

"What is it you are reading?"

"One of the nine books of Chilam Balam. A rare edition. It includes original photographs taken of the Mayan glyphs. At least the ones that survived." He removes his glasses, clearing the smudges with a handkerchief. "Chilam Balam was the greatest prophet in Maya history, a seer who lived during the first decades of the 1500s. He foretold the coming of Cortés and his armada and warned his people that the strangers from the east would bring violence and a powerful new god. His nine books are considered the sacred texts of the Yucatan Maya. They include passages from his dreams, the images of which he recorded in his writings. Many of them describe the 2012 Doomsday Event."

"Then you know what's going to happen?"

"Unfortunately, no. There are tremendous gaps in the codices, most of which were burned by the Spanish priests."

"And your sudden interest in this dead prophet?"

"Our friend over there didn't just sprout wings and land on Nazca, he came here seeking something. He's either an archaeologist following ancient Doomsday clues or he's Majestic-12. Either way, I intend to flush out the extent of his knowledge about the Doomsday Event."

"How are you—" Her eyes widen in recognition. "You bastard. You're going to play along with his delusion in order to pick his brain."

"It's no big deal."

"Yes, Julius, it is! By encouraging him to adapt to a false identity, your actions will not only retard his recovery, it could be detrimental to his long-term well-being."

"What about my well-being? What about four decades of research and toil? What about my son and all the people who may perish on the 2012 winter solstice because of our ignorance?"

"So your plan is to convince the poor guy he really is the incarnation of a five-hundred-year-old Mayan prophet in order to milk him of his research? You're pathetic."

"Hey, if I believed the guy could lay eggs, I'd convince him he was a chicken."

The bunker door leads into a small storage area illuminated by a single bare bulb. The walls are windowless, the floor concrete. There is nothing inside but dusty file cabinets and a pile of surplus office furniture.

Joseph Randolph moves to a pair of eight-foot-high maple bookshelves holding stacks of old Army manuals yellowed with age. He waits for the reinforced steel door to click shut behind them before he tugs on one of the Army manuals stacked on the bookshelf—triggering a toggle switch.

The bookshelves part on unseen hinges, revealing the interior of a freight elevator.

Pierre Borgia follows his uncle inside. Randolph slides his identity card into the security slot, causing the button marked LEVEL 15 to light on the interior panel. Knowing the deeper they descend, the higher the security, Borgia wonders what secrets might be tucked away on LEVEL 29, the lowest floor of the most covert underground installation on the planet.

218

The elevator drops a quarter of a mile to LEVEL 15. They exit to an antiseptic white corridor and a security checkpoint. A guard instructs them to empty their pockets, placing their possessions in an envelope.

Passing through an X-ray machine, they proceed down the hall to a set of double doors. An electromagnetic bolt clicks open, and they enter a large conference room.

Ten men and a woman are seated around an oval table—a mix of white lab coats and business suits, along with two members in military dress. Two end chairs are vacant. Randolph motions to his nephew to sit.

The woman, rail-thin in her sixties and wearing a blue lab coat, is the first to speak, her English flavored with an Italian accent. "Welcome to Majestic-12, Dr. Borgia. My name is Dr. Krissinda Rotolo, and I am in charge of personnel at S-66. Do you understand why you are here?"

"You had a vacancy, and I came highly recommended."

"The vacancy was a suicide. We average one every sixteen weeks among a staff of 170, not including security. Stephen Peterson was the fourth member of our interrogation team to kill himself in the last three years. Since you were selected to replace him, I felt it important that you should know."

"I'm very wealthy and I get laid a lot, so suicide's not on my 'to do' list,

Doctor. At the same time, you should know that hunting little green men is not a long-term gig for me either. I'm doing this because my uncle says you can assure me of winning the senate seat when I run in 2000."

"As a first step to the White House . . . provided you respect our agenda."

"I take it Stephen Peterson had a problem in those regards."

A heavyset Caucasian man in a lab coat shoots Borgia a disparaging look. "Dr. Peterson's issues were morality-based, something it appears you'll have little difficulty with."

"Listen, big fella, I didn't put up with two months of background checks and around-the-clock surveillance to be insulted. We both know I'm not the best anthropologist available; I am, however, one you can trust to maintain your secrets. The fact that I'm here in this underground tomb means you feel confident I can do the job, whatever it may be. So let's dispense with the psychological bullshit and show me what you want to show me, or else fly me back to Vegas."

"Fair enough." Dr. Rotolo touches a control box situated on the table before her.

The lights dim, revealing a holographic image of the moon, the three-dimensional sphere hovering above the center of the conference table.

"In 1961, President John F. Kennedy challenged our space program to land a man on the moon and return him safely. *Apollo 11*'s crew accomplished that feat on July 20, 1969. The last lunar mission, *Apollo 17*, landed on the moon on December 11, 1972. That was eighteen years ago, and we've never been back since.

"When President Nixon abruptly ended the Apollo program, he told the nation he did so in favor of funding the space shuttle and eventually the International Space Station. Nearly two decades, Dr. Borgia, and our manned space program remains confined to Earth's orbit. Care to venture a guess why?"

"Three Republican administrations, an oil crisis, and another war looming in the Middle East. To conservatives, exploring the moon is a waste of time and money."

"Spoken like a typically misinformed politician. In fact, the entire cost of the Apollo mission amounted to less than one percent of the annual federal budget. Unfortunately, while ignorance may be bliss in your chosen profession, in ours it cannot be tolerated. What the Apollo astronauts discovered is that they were not alone on the lunar surface, that every NASA launch and subsequent action was being observed."

Before Pierre Borgia can utter a response, the holographic moon magnifies by three hundred percent and rotates to its dark side—revealing craters concealed beneath artificial domes and small vessels moving rapidly above the surface.

"The real reason Nixon ended the Apollo program is the same reason space agencies across the world have agreed to a secret moratorium on all future lunar missions. Simply put, the far side of the moon is being used as a lunar base for extraterrestrials. The threat of a court martial or far worse has kept most of NASA's astronauts and personnel from talking. The others are dealt with on an individual basis."

"You wanted the truth, there it is." Joseph Randolph massages his nephew's shoulder. "Welcome to Wonderland, Alice."

Borgia feels the blood drain from his face. "What are they doing up there? Are they aggressive? Are they planning an invasion?"

"They're not aggressive," blurts out a scientist in a lab coat.

"That's yet to be determined," a suit responds. "We've had numerous reports of abductions—"

"Prove one! Everyone at this table knows the CIA are using mind-control techniques to foster fear about these E.T.s."

"Agreed," says another scientist. "The reality is, if they wanted to destroy us, they could have done so at any time."

"Enough." Krissinda Rotolo looks up at Borgia, concern in her weathered eyes. "As you can see, the issues are complex on our side as well as theirs. Unfortunately, when you're dealing with so many different species—"

"Wait . . . are you saying you've actually captured some of these aliens?"

"Why do you think you're here, Dr. Borgia?" She turns to Randolph, her look chastising. "You were supposed to brief him."

"Show is always better than tell. What time is today's session scheduled for?"

"We had to push it back an hour, we're short an EMT. This time make sure Dr. Borgia is properly briefed; his first session begins at fifteen hundred hours."

NAZCA PLATEAU, PERU

The hot air balloon soars a thousand feet over the desert pampa, its orange and blue nylon panels visible for miles in every direction.

Michael Gabriel operates the burners, the flames of which are fueled by several propane tanks stacked by his feet. Laura stands next to her nephew in the wicker basket, counterbalancing Julius and their mysterious friend, whom the archaeologist insists on calling Balam.

"There's the spider, Balam, definitely another one of the earlier, more sophisticated drawings. Anything look familiar to you?"

"This is not the valley of the Hunahpu. Our valley was covered by a dense rainforest, fed by many mountain streams. Our valley led to the ocean."

"The ocean's west. I want to continue east to the icon where we found you. See, there's the Panamericana Highway, we should be coming to the glyph . . . right there. See that spiral? That's where we found you. Does it jiggle any memories?"

"Jiggle?" Mick bursts out laughing. "His brain's not a toilet handle, Julius."

Laura covers her mouth.

"Ignore them, Balam. Focus on the glyph. It's a clue about the Doomsday prophecy, isn't it?"

Immanuel Gabriel stares at the Spiral, his injured brain fighting to spear an image blinking in and out of the ether now consuming his memories.

"You've seen this image before, haven't you, Chilam Balam?"

"Yes."

"Don't force it. Close your eyes and let it come to you."

He clenches his eyes shut against the sweat beads rolling down his face. In the blunted orange light behind his eyelids, the spiral glyph appears and disappears, replaced by a round object surrounded by darkness.

Laura is about to speak. Julius raises his index finger, warning her to remain silent.

Day becomes night. Night becomes space. His mind's eye latches onto a round object. Gelid. Spiraling into colors.

Laura watches as Sam's muscles begin trembling, the movement vibrating the wicker basket beneath their feet.

Night returns to day. The desert glyph reappears, only this time he finds himself focusing not on its spirals, but on the singular straight line that slices across the circular engraving to intersect with its center.

Day becomes night, the stars blotted out by a singular straight line—brown dust inhaled across space into the vacuous gelid eye . . . a hole in the physical reality, surrounded by a pattern of swirls as large as the moon, hovering a thousand miles beneath the Earth's southern pole.

His heart pounds, the blood draining from his face. He is paralyzed with fear, desperate to open his eyes, only the monster is moving, its gelid halo circling over Antarctica.

"No . . . oh God, no!"

"Balam, what do you see?"

"Julius, enough! Michael, land the balloon."

"Quiet! Balam, tell us what you see."

"I see the Earth . . . disappearing into silence—into oblivion."

"How is it disappearing? What's causing it?"

"The Spiral."

"Describe it to me."

"Cold emptiness. A hunger that cannot be quenched. It's gone."

"What's gone? The Spiral?"

"The Earth." His eyes snap open, his expression crazed. His mind consumed in fear, he grips the edge of the basket, ready to hurl himself over the side—

"—no." Laura's face is in his face, her turquoise eyes radiating a sense of calm into his being. "You are no longer Balam. You are Sam. You are Sam and you are safe. Tell me your name."

"Sam."

"Sam what?"

"Samuel Agler."

"That's correct. You are Samuel Agler. How did you get here, Sam?"

"Through the wormhole."

Julius and his son look at one another like two kids on Christmas morning.

Laura grips the back of Sam's head, keeping his face close to hers, occupying his entire field of vision with the radiance of her eyes.

A puzzled look crosses Sam's face. "Lilith?"

"Stay focused. You mentioned a wormhole. Is that what destroyed the Earth?"

"No. It was the singularity. A black hole. You saw it, too, Lilith. You were there. Only—"

"Only what? Focus on my eyes and tell me."

"He cut off your head."

"Who cut off my head? Sam, look into my eyes and tell me who cut off my head."

"Seven Macaw."

19

If suddenly there was a threat to this world from some other species from another planet, outside in the universe [. . .] we'd forget all the little local differences that we have between our countries . . .

—PRESIDENT RONALD REAGAN,
"REMARKS TO THE STUDENTS AND
FACULTY AT FALLSTON HIGH SCHOOL
IN FALLSTON, MARYLAND,"
DECEMBER 4, 1985

The phenomenon of UFOs does exist, and it must be treated seriously.

—MIKHAIL GORBACHEV,
"SOVIET YOUTH," MAY 4, 1990

W e call them EBEs—Extraterrestrial Biological Entities. You and your former pal, Julius Gabriel, would probably know better than us how long they've been coming to Earth. Maybe they consider our planet a vacation resort."

"I highly doubt that." Pierre Borgia rests his heels on his uncle's desk. "Julius, Maria, and I discovered overwhelming evidence of contact with extraterrestrials in oral traditions, as well as stone carvings, petroglyphs, and other reliefs found throughout most ancient cultures. The dominant theme of these encounters clearly focused on seeding our species with knowledge. Of course, that seeding takes on a more literal meaning if you read a passage in Genesis 6: 'There were giants in the earth in those days; the Nephilim and also after that, when the sons of God came in unto the daughters of men, and they bore children to them. These were the mighty men who were of old, the men of renown.' Nephilim translates as 'fallen ones,' as in 'fell from the sky.'"

"Sons of God . . . breeding with the daughters of men? Christ, no wonder some of them look like us. Clever bastards, using our DNA to infiltrate our world."

"The Bible isn't even the oldest message regarding extraterrestrial contact. Images of spacemen found in caves in Tanzania date back 29,000 years. A seven-thousand-year-old petroglyph discovered in Querétaro, Mexico, features four alien figures bathed in beams of light reaching up to a large flying saucer. Artifacts found in Iraq, dating back to 5000 BC, include Sumerian gods that look like reptilian space travelers, similar to the gods worshiped in ancient Egypt. An art exhibit in the British Museum includes pottery and other clay figures with lizard heads attributed to the Ubaid culture during the same period. The Nepal artist responsible for the Lolladoff plate clearly shows a disc-shaped vessel and a small gray alien next to it.

"More fascinating and harder to dismiss are the more recent artistic renderings originating from Europe. A 1350 painting called *The Crucifixion* hangs above the altar at the Visoki Decani Monastery in Kosovo; it depicts Jesus on the cross with a UFO passing across the background sky. A fourteenth-century *Madonna and Child* fresco features a similar spaceship, as does a fifteenth-century painting by Domenico Ghirlandaio entitled *The*

Madonna with Saint Giovannino. The Bayerisches National museum houses a tapestry called *Summer's Triumph* that was created in 1538 and clearly shows several disc-shaped objects along the top of the scene. A naval illustration in a volume entitled *Theatrum Orbis Terrarum* depicts a sighting by two Dutch ships in the North Sea of two disc-shaped objects moving across the sky. The French actually minted a coin in 1680 that features a hovering UFO."

"Pierre, do I look like I give a damn about some frog coin?"

"Sorry, I just thought . . . I mean, I spent fifteen years studying this stuff, and you did recruit me as an anthropologist."

"If that's why you think you're here, then you're as dumb as my brother. Wake up, son. You're here because the faction of companies that control this little venture of ours need a future liaison in the White House, not another geek with a slide rule and a degree. We're sitting on technological advances that will affect the future of this planet, including a nonpolluting power source that could replace the fossil fuel and nuclear power industries tomorrow if it fell into the wrong hands. You think we're gonna just sink the US economy by lettin' the oil companies take it on the chin? Not on my watch, and not on yours. No sir, when the time's right, the military industrial complex and Big Oil will disperse these advances as we see fit and at a substantial profit, leveraging these technologies so we can control the global economy and keep the damn Russians and Chinese under our thumbs."

"Exactly what do you want me to do while I'm here?"

"First and foremost, I need you to be a check and balance during the interview sessions with our extraterrestrial pals. There are too many big-hearted liberal tree-huggers wearing lab coats around here who believe in unicorns and think energy should be provided free to everyone. These eggheads have no idea how the real world works. Most of 'em think we're dealing with Hollywood's version of E.T. To date we've catalogued more than sixty different types of beings, most of them dead, of course. We don't know if we're dealing with friend or foe, competing species or subspecies, or beings from another dimension. Like I said, some E.T.s look so human they could easily assimilate into our society."

"If they look just like us, how do you know they're extraterrestrials?"

"Physically they're superior to us, with a heightened sense of sight, hearing, and especially smell. Their eyes are aquamarine blue, almost turquoise, and they glow like a cat's iris in the dark. They also communicate telepathically. All of these life forms do. Fortunately, we've been able to recruit some reliable human telepaths of our own to question them. Your job is to keep the interrogations focused on their technology."

"Exactly who or what am I interrogating?"

"One of the Grays. Grays come in different sizes, but they all share the same basic DNA structure—big eyes and hairless grayish bodies. We've had our boy a little more than seven months. His vehicle crash-landed in Moriches Bay in Long Island, New York, back on September 28, 1989. There were nine Grays on board, he's the only one that survived—assuming he's even a he. There's no nuts hanging from the branches, if you know what I mean. Everything's internalized with these beings . . . what fun is that? Still, they're vastly superior to us. Lockheed's rocket scientists don't last long with them; they get easily overwhelmed. For the E.T.s, it's probably like teaching algebra to their pet dog. Strike that. We're probably more like dogs with big teeth than lovable pets."

"If it's so difficult, why not stick to interrogating the more human E.T.s?"

"Try bringing one in alive. On the rare occasions a Nordic may crash and survive, they off themselves rather than face MJ-12. We've done autopsies, of course, that's how we learned about their sensory organs. And their blood type: Rh negative."

"Rh negative? You're sure about that?"

"Yeah, I'm sure. What's so important about that?"

"Uncle Joe, I know your interest is strictly on the military side and you recruit personnel based more on clearance levels than talent, but you really need to get some informed medical people inside your little coven. The Rh factor is a protein found in human blood that links our genetic heritage to primates, specifically the Rhesus monkey. About eighty-five percent of the world's population is Rh positive, meaning the evolutionary link exists. The mystery that has puzzled scientists for decades is understanding what limb of the tree the other fifteen percent of *Homo sapiens* originated from. It was actually the Rh negative factor that launched my postgraduate work out of Cambridge with Maria and Julius; it was only after Gabriel morphed our work into his nutty Doomsday prophecy that I left them."

"That, and the fact that he ran off with your fiancée."

"The hell with that. They married, she got sick and died, it's over. But if these extraterrestrials are all Rh negative like you say, then my work has real meaning. Go back to that Bible passage in Genesis. If the Nephilim bred with ancient women, then it would have formed a subspecies of advanced humans . . . perhaps as far back as thirty thousand years ago, a time period that matches those cave paintings. The injection points were regional, specifically ancient Egypt and parts of southeast Asia, with nomadic tribes following a land bridge during the last ice age into North America. There they would have crossbred with American Indian tribes, as well as the Olmec, the mother culture of Mesoamerica. Ever see one of those ten-ton Olmec heads? The facial features are clearly Asian. These genetics were rooted in the Maya, Aztec, Inca, and Egyptian cultures that succeeded where other tribes failed. Their leaders—Kukulcan, Quetzalcoatl, Viracocha, and Osiris—were clearly described as possessing Rh negative characteristics that included an extra vertebra, a superior IQ, an acute sensory system, and azure-blue eyes. Oh yes, each of these leaders also possessed an elongated skull."

"Yeah, we know about the long skulls, the Grays share that, too. Not sure I agree with the E.T. theory regarding Rh negative humans. Fifteen percent of six billion people is an awful lot of E.T.s."

"E.T. heritage, there's a difference. A purebred child or a generational hiccup would be far different."

"A hiccup?"

"A child whose maternal lineage was strongly linked to one of the injection points and whose DNA surfaced against the odds. Like when two brown-eyed parents have four kids, and one of them has blue eyes that can be traced back to great-grandparents. The Rh factor represents a separate genetic highway on-ramp from our past, and the evidence is overwhelming. For instance, did you know that when a mother with Rh negative blood is pregnant with an Rh positive child, the mingling of the two types can cause an allergic reaction called hemolytic disease, which can lead to the infant's death? The child's Rh positive blood cells attack the mother's Rh negative blood cells as if it were an alien intruder. Clearly, there was a genetic circumvention during the evolution of *Homo sapiens* that added these characteristics to our DNA pool."

"If that's the case, then I guess we ought to be grateful the reptilians didn't interbreed with us, too. Some serious anger issues with those dudes."

"Are they hostile?"

"I think the Nordics keep them in line, but they don't do well in captivity. None of them do. We're only allowed to interview the Gray twice a month and never for more than three to five hours at a time, based on how he's holding up." Randolph glances at his watch. "So, Alice, are you ready to meet the Mad Hatter?"

"Enough with the Alice in Wonderland references, Uncle Joe. This isn't child's play."

"Maybe not, Pierre, but it can be maddening."

The roof of the Gabriel abode is a flattop affair that has served as Michael Gabriel's bedroom for the last six months. A second inflatable mattress has been added to accommodate the stranger known as Sam.

Sam and Laura are alone on the roof, lying on their backs on one of the air mattresses. The midnight ceiling is a tapestry of stars, unimpeded by the pollution of light.

"Sam, what are you thinking?"

"I was thinking that the heavens look benign. And I was thinking how nice it felt not to worry."

"Such a strange yet telling statement. Perhaps you were a navigator who used the stars to pilot his vessel?"

"No."

"No? How can you be so certain? Before this afternoon you had no idea your name was Samuel Agler."

"When Michael called me Samson, the name felt right. I wasn't a navigator, I wasn't a pilot. It doesn't feel right."

"And what about this Lauren? Does she feel right?"

"There was a Lauren. Not anymore."

"Not to sound like a broken record, but again, how can you be so sure? Did you see her decapitated like Lilith?"

"I know she's gone. I can feel an emptiness in my heart."

"And Chilam Balam? You told me earlier that he too felt a similar emptiness."

Sam sits up. "Are you ridiculing me? Do you doubt my pain?"

"No."

"Then why is this so important to you?"

She stands, walking to the edge of the roof. "It's important because I feel myself being drawn to you both physically and spiritually, yet I don't know anything about you. My soul tells me you're a good person, as noble as any warrior; my survival instincts tell me to run away, that hitching my wagon to yours will take me down a path fraught with danger. Part of me likes that aspect, but as any woman would, I need to know that there isn't a Lauren Agler lying in some hospital bed out there, waiting for her Samson to return to her side; and yes, I'm also worried about a nest of Agler kiddies calling out into the night for their papa."

"Laura died. There were no children."

"And you know this because it doesn't feel right."

"If you had lost your memory, but you had given birth to children, do you think these gaps in your identity could mask your motherly instincts?"

"Probably not."

"Then don't doubt mine. Because I promise you, if my wife and child were out there needing my help, then I wouldn't be lying here beneath the stars, I'd be raging into the night trying to find them."

"Good answer." She smiles, brushing away a tear. "Bit of a romantic then, aren't you?"

"I don't know. Am I?"

"Well now, I suppose there's only one way to find out." She removes her T-shirt and shorts, returning to his side.

Julius Gabriel and his son huddle around the oil lamp, the picnic table covered with images of the Nazca Spiral.

Michael looks up, hearing his aunt moan. "Hope that roof holds up."

"Let's go for a walk."

Leaving the house, they head west past parcels of land covered in rows of huangaro tree saplings.

"Aunt Laura's falling hard for him, huh?"

"A monkey could have figured that one out. Let's train that amazing IQ of yours on something a bit more difficult. Your friend is a puzzle. Work the pieces for me."

"He believes he has lived a life as Chilam Balam, only during a period of time when Nazca was green. Since no such time period occurred in the past, he had to have experienced it in the distant future."

"Continue."

"As Samuel Agler, he witnessed the Earth consumed by a black hole. Since that also hasn't occurred, he has traveled back in time through his wormhole to our past."

"Therefore?"

"Therefore, he possesses the means to travel into the future or back into the past."

"Go on."

"To see the planet consumed required a safe vantage point in space. Which means there is a vessel, or at the very least, the remains of a vessel somewhere on the plateau in which he traveled through this wormhole back in time."

"Well done. And we shall search for this vessel tomorrow, only without him."

"I'm sure Laura can find a way to occupy him. Which is why you had her fly in from Spain, isn't it?"

"Go on."

"Laura's Rh negative, like Mom was . . . like me. Only the gene's dominant in her."

"Which means we must restrict what we tell her about Sam. Remember, son, there are no coincidences."

"Like the two of us finding Sam on the Nazca Spiral."

"Correct."

"You think he deliberately made his way to the icon from his crash landing?"

"How can you be certain it was a crash?"

"He couldn't have inflicted those wounds himself . . . unless they occurred before the landing."

"What about the Fastwalker?"

"I forgot about them. Julius, you think they were leading him across the desert to the Spiral?"

"I do."

They continue on in silence, father and son—their minds whirring in thought.

"Pop, there's something else."

"You always worry me when you call me Pop."

"Sam . . . he looks like me."

"Yes he does. What does that tell you?"

Mick stops walking. "The puzzle . . . it's a paradox of time."

"Fill in the gaps."

"Sam is a relation. A blood relative. He's returned from the Doomsday Event in an attempt to help us prevent it."

"There are no Aglers on my family tree and none that I know of on your mother's. There is no record of a Samuel Agler existing in the year 1990 that fits his approximate age."

"You ran his fingerprints?"

"The day we found him."

"Then the name is an alias, a pseudonym to protect his real identity."

"And when he discovers his true identity?"

"Then he'll fulfill his destiny."

"Which returns us to the puzzle with which we began. Who is Samuel Agler? He is an incarnate of Chilam Balam, at least he believes he is. He is a time traveler—a survivor of the Doomsday Event, returning to our past. And he is most likely a relation, A Gabriel, no doubt."

"Why not a Rosen? Oh, because of his attraction to Aunt Laura."

"Correct."

"Then this makes no sense. I have no nieces or nephews, my only living relatives are you and Aunt Laura, oh, and Aunt Evelyn—"

"—who will never bear offspring. Trust me on that."

"Then Sam was descended from me."

"A blood test has confirmed this as fact."

"Jesus, Pop, who is he? If he came from the year 2012, then the only possibility is that he's my older brother."

"I can assure you, neither your mother or I conceived of a mystery child when we were your age."

"Then I'm stumped."

"Think it through, Michael. You made one assumption in your thought process. What was it?"

"The Doomsday Event . . . it didn't happen in 2012. Somehow we managed to avert it."

"Correct, with one major point of clarification. Our time traveler speaks of wormholes, and he has entered at least one that we know of."

"Then time's been altered."

"And the events. Sam is here in 1990 for a reason. The 2012 event will occur as predicted by the Mayan calendar in the manner that he bore witness to, and now he has provided us with a vital clue."

"Pop, if it is a black hole that will consume the planet, then how can anyone stop it?"

"Think it through. Black holes occur when an object, usually a star, collapses under its own gravity. Our sun is under no such immediate threat, which means—"

"—which means man created the black hole."

"Correct. Remember, Sam first referred to it as a singularity. In researching the term I learned about a device known as a Relativistic Heavy Ion Collider, or RHIC. Apparently, physicists have built such a device in order to collide atoms and re-create the conditions following the Big Bang. Unfortunately, one of the dangers of colliding atoms is that it can form a miniature black hole, known as a strangelet. These are microscopic by nature, and the theory is that their lifetime is but a few billionths of a second. Critics, however, charge that strangelets can sustain themselves under the right—or wrong—circumstances. There is a facility in Long Island, New York—the Brookhaven National Laboratory—that conducts these types of experiments. An even larger facility is being planned in Geneva at a cost of $6 billion."

"These physicists . . . are they insane?"

"Brookhaven's scientists have won many Nobel Prizes. Like all evil, the first seemingly innocent act begins with the stroking of an ego."

Michael kneels into a squat, massaging his temples.

"Son, are you all right?"

"We've been chasing this Doomsday thing for a long time. Suddenly, the information's pouring in at light speed. It's a lot to digest."

"It is a lot to digest, but we now have a much clearer direction, guided by our mysterious new friend. Which once more returns us to the puzzle from which we've derived so much valuable information. Michael, who is Samuel Agler?"

Mick stands, tears in his eyes. "He's . . . my son?"

Julius smiles. "Emotionally, it will take years before you'll be able to accept this as fact, yet you still saw through the paradox to arrive at the truth—a truth that may very well save our species. I'm so very proud of you."

Mick smiles. "My son . . . he's a big boy, isn't he?"

"Michael, we must be very careful never to divulge this to Sam or Laura. Knowledge in the wrong hands can alter the space-time contin-uum."

"Pop, it's already been altered, a monkey could have told you that. Your grandson, who is at least twenty years older than your son, is up in the loft, banging your sister-in-law."

"Yes, but this same grandson has yet to be born. Knowing his identity could theoretically prevent you from meeting his mother and consummat-ing the act that leads to his birth. I'm not even sure he can exist in the same reality as his still-to-come infant self. All of these variables, suddenly thrown together in chaos, can affect your future, his, and that of the Earth. We must be careful to remember that we don't have enough knowledge to dare pull the strings."

They continue walking, father and son—unaware of the presence keep-ing a silent vigil high overhead.

May 9, 2001: National Press Club, Washington, D.C.

Hi, my name is George Filer III. The reason I am here is because George Filer the fifth is in the hangar and will be born on Friday. I am a retired intelligence officer and flyer, with almost five thousand hours, and I didn't believe in UFOs until London Control called us in the winter of 1962 and asked us, would we chase one? And we said, "Sure!" So we leapt down from thirty thousand feet to a thousand feet, where the UFO was hovering. And we went into a steep dive and actually exceeded the redline of the aircraft. So it's kinda dangerous chasing UFOs. And in any case, I was able to get the UFO on the aircraft radar, at about forty miles, and we could see a light on in the distance, and as we closed we kept on picking up this radar return. The point I'm mentioning is that the radar return was very distinct and solid, indicating it was some kind of metallic object. We got about a mile from the UFO, and it kinda lit up in the sky and went off into space. Very similar to what the shuttle looks like when it takes off. [. . .]

When I was in the Twenty-first Air Force, McGuire AFB, I briefed General Glau about a UFO over Tehran, Iran, in 1976. Two F-4s from the Iranian Air Force had taken off and tried to intercept the UFO, and when they turned on their fire control systems, immediately all their electric systems went out and the planes had to return to base. This was particularly significant because it was also picked up on satellites.

In 1978, on January 18, I was going into the base—every morning I did the briefing to the general's staff—and I noticed that there were some lights off in the distance at the end of the runway there. When I got into the command post, the senior master sergeant in charge said that there had been UFOs in the pattern all night, they were on radar, the tower had seen them, they had gotten aircraft reports and so on . . . and that one had landed or crashed at Fort Dix—Fort Dix and McGuire are right together. This is kinda like the "Roswell of the East." In any case, an alien had come off the craft and had been shot by a military policeman [. . .]. Our security police went out there and found him on the end of the runway, dead. And they asked me to brief the general staff, a General Tom Sadler, at the eight o'clock stand-up briefing, and I said, "I don't think I want to do this; you know, the general doesn't have a good sense of humor and I'm not sure *I* believe this." So, I did some checking, called the 438th Command Post, and everybody had pretty much the same story. At eight o'clock that morning, just before I went on, [. . .] everyone's very worried about it; they said, "Don't brief it, it's too hot," so to speak.

That's pretty much my story. I'm prepared to tell the story in front of Congress, and it is the truth. Now, because of this, I've stayed interested in UFOs. And I am the Eastern Director of the Mutual UFO Network, and between the National Reporting Center and Peter Davenport and MUFON, we get one hundred [UFO] reports a week on average of people from all over the United States that see these things regularly. And if you start checking, they're out there, and they're low, and people are seeing them all the time. And these are highly qualified people, all of whom essentially give us the reports by e-mail.

—**George Filer III,**
intelligence officer and pilot (ret.)

Used by permission of the Disclosure Project

20

The elevator descends quickly, touching down on Level 29. The security checkpoint is identical to Level 15, save for one major addition—the corridor is sealed off behind a pneumatic door that leads into a glass chamber. A warning sign is posted on the exterior wall:

Biosafety Level 2 Containment
No liquids or perishables permitted.

Pierre shoots his uncle a nervous look. "Are we dealing with contaminants?"

"*We're* the contaminants. The BSL-2 conditions are to protect our visitor's immune system."

A guard types in an access code on the security pad, waits for the bolts to release, then carefully opens the door, his effort assisted by a gust of cool air blowing outward from multiple vents.

Pierre follows Randolph into the buffer zone, then through a second door leading into a control room. The chamber is the size of a two-car garage and resembles a home theater, its three rows of six seats staggered arena style. Instead of a screen there is a thick bay window, the glass curtained from the other side.

"This is the visitors' section, we're in the bullpen." Joseph Randolph opens a side door, leading Pierre Borgia into a hallway that resembles the interior of a radio station. They pass several offices, the windows revealing recording studios filled with electronic equipment.

A pale-skinned man in his thirties exits the only double-door office in the corridor. He is dressed in physician scrubs, his red hair tucked beneath a surgical cap. "Joseph, good to see you. And you must be Pierre. I'm Dr. Robinson, but please, call me Scott, we like to keep things pretty informal. We've placed towels and fresh scrubs in your lockers. Why don't you shower and meet me in the Green Room in ten minutes. The rest of the team's already inside."

Borgia follows his uncle through the double doors into a small hallway segregating the men's and women's locker room doors. They enter the men's facility and a changing area labeled SOILED.

Borgia finds his name on a locker. Inside is a towel and pair of disposable shower shoes.

"Get undressed and leave your street clothes in the locker."

Borgia strips, slips the sandals on his bare feet, wraps the towel around his waist, and follows his uncle into the showers. The two men soap up from head to toe, rinse, dry off, and exit into another locker room labeled CLEAN. They toss their towels and shoes into a vacuum-sealed laundry basket, find their new lockers, and change into a matching set of purple scrubs and sandals.

Randolph leads his nephew into the Green Room, an antiseptic lounge equipped with a small kitchen and a dozen padded chairs. Four men dressed in scrubs are inside, two of whom are in the middle of a heated discussion.

"Gentlemen." The argument ceases as Joseph Randolph enters the room. "Pierre, allow me to introduce the members of our interview team. Dr. Steven Shapiro is our critical-care physician, Reynaldo Lopez is our telepath, and these two cackling hens we call Heckle and Jeckle, so named because they live to argue."

"Jeckle" offers Pierre a warm smile. "Dave Mohr, a pleasure to meet you. I'm the team physicist. And this is—"

"I can introduce myself, thank you. Jack Harbach O'Sullivan, engineer, resident Ping-Pong champion, and the point man during these sessions. Has your uncle explained the rules?"

"Uh, have you?"

"All verbal communication ceases once we enter the interview suite. We'll be seated in a circle, each station equipped with a keypad. If you wish Reynaldo to ask the subject a question you must type it out, then press SEND. The question will appear on Jack's monitor. Jack must approve the question before sending it on to Reynaldo's teleprompter. Reynaldo will pose the question telepathically. If and when he receives a telepathic response, he will type it out so that it appears on everyone's screen. Dr. Shapiro will limit the session to what he feels the subject can handle."

An interior door opens, revealing Scott Robinson. "We're ready in here. If you'll take your places around the horseshoe."

The interview suite is dark and cool, backlit by lime-green ceiling lights. The "horseshoe" is an oval ring of seven stations, with one end remaining open. Jack leads Pierre to a vacant post, activates the keypad and monitor, then takes his place at the master station.

Reynaldo Lopez is seated inside the horseshoe, facing what appears to be a heavily cushioned wheelchair with a built-in chest plate.

Seated upright in the chair is the extraterrestrial.

The being is frail, the size of a ten-year-old child. Its skin is hairless, more beige than gray, its skull elongated and bulbous. Its lidless black eyes are the size of baseballs and turned upward at the corners, the pupils reflecting green from the interior lighting. The E.T.'s neck is centered at the base of the skull, giving the head a top-heavy, unstable appearance. The torso is hidden behind the chest plate, its limbs protruding from arm and leg holes. The hands are thin and double-jointed, possessing three long fingers and an opposable fourth digit. The alien's legs are not visible from Pierre Borgia's vantage.

The E.T.'s movements appear disjointed, bordering on the intoxicated, its mannerisms revealing a subtle sullen state. Clearly, it does not wish to be here.

Reynaldo receives a list of prepared questions on his monitor. Closing his eyes, he enters a semi-meditative state. *How are you feeling?*

Thirty seconds pass before a response appears. *Release or terminate.*

Help us to comprehend your vessel's propulsion system and we shall release you.

Zipil na.

Reynaldo ignores the alien retort. *The tachyon carrier wave appears to be a data-encoded medium. Please communicate the energy formula.*

The E.T. grows restless within its sealed chair. "No response" appears on-screen.

Can in-flow energy be controlled in the ZPE-toroid reactor via field drag?

Release or terminate.

When the reactor is used for advanced propulsion as a point-lead hyper-gravion lobe-field power plant, how is the breach window in aexo-hyperspace achieved?

Release or terminate.

Reynaldo turns to Jack, his exasperated expression all but demanding a new topic of discussion.

Pierre hesitates, then types a question and presses SEND.

Jack reads it. Looks back at Pierre, then sends it on to the telepath.

Reynaldo reads it twice, then closes his eyes and translates. *How would you prefer to be terminated?*

The extraterrestrial cocks its head awkwardly, its black eyes, tinged green in the light, targeting the newest member of the human inquisition. *Elaborate.*

Pierre reads the response and types in his own. Reynaldo transposes it telepathically.

Is there a sacred rite of passage in your culture?

Yes.

While we would prefer to release you, we wish to respect your traditions. Will the sacred rite offer passage for your soul?

The soul must be cleansed before its journey home.

Pierre types furiously, the other members of the team having been side-lined, yet clearly fascinated by the exchange. *How can we help you cleanse your soul?*

Illogical response.

How can we arrange a sacred rite of passage?

Return me to the cell. Provide a container of soil, a candle's flame, a container of water, and an untarnished blade.

Pierre nods to himself. *Three of the four sacred elements: Earth, fire, and water, His last gasp the missing element—wind. You have something it wants, use it to barter.* He thinks, then types out a new response.

Before we can provide the elements for the sacred rite of passage, we need to know why you are here.

Harmonic convergence.

Jack glances back at Pierre Borgia, who shrugs.

Dave Mohr types: *Does the tachyon carrier wave rely on harmonic convergence?*

The extraterrestrial becomes agitated again, its head wobbling. *All things rely on harmonic convergence. Harmonic convergence is threatened. Hunab K'u will end.*

Pierre's eyes widen. He types in a question, only to see it buried behind a dozen others.

Is Hunab K'u a weapon?

What was your vessel doing when it crashed?

Are there weapons on the moon?

The alien writhes in anger, bashing its head against the chair's padded chest plate. *Zipil na! Zipil na!*

Dr. Shapiro and Dr. Robinson rush into the horseshoe-shaped pit as the E.T. foams at the mouth, one man stabilizing the flopping head, the other administering a sedative directly into the lipless crease of its orifice.

239

Scott Robinson paces through the Green Room, livid. "We had a breakthrough, it was cooperating! Why the hell would you shift back to a subject you knew would cause it to shut down?"

"You're overstepping your boundaries, Dr. Robinson," Joseph Randolph snaps. "This is a military base, not a state university. First protocol is always to calculate a potential threat. You think that Gray was just monitoring traffic over the Long Island Expressway when it crash-landed in Moriches Bay? We're dealing with superior intellects controlling superior weapon systems that have the ability to shut down our ICBMs. This creature has been uncooperative since day one. We need to put the fear of Jesus in it."

"Fear it already has, and in great abundance," Reynaldo interjects. "What I sensed was a sea-change in attitude when Pierre posed his question. This being desperately wants to die, perhaps because it cannot exist well in a theater of fear—"

"—or perhaps," states Randolph, "because it knows it's getting closer to revealing important technological information about its mangled spaceship that can lead Dr. Mohr and his team to an actual breakthrough. I'm recommending to my committee that we resume the shock therapy."

Dr. Shapiro stands, pointing a threatening finger at his superior. "Listen to me, you Nazi butcher—I'm not going to allow you to harm that being anymore!"

Randolph rolls his eyes. "Sit down, Doctor. The Jew dramatics don't impress anyone."

"Hey!" Now it is Dr. Mohr standing, hovering over the gray-haired Texan. "What'd I tell you about that stuff?"

Jack steps in to separate them.

"Let's all take a breath," Pierre says, his voice firm but rational. "I think I know of a way to get the information you seek without torturing this being."

"How?" Dr. Robinson asks.

"Those phrases it was speaking—*Hunab K'u* and *Zipil na*—I've heard them before. Believe it or not, the words are Mayan. To be specific, it's an ancient form of Nahuatl spoken by the Toltec."

Randolph grabs his nephew by the wrist. "What the hell do they mean?"

"I don't know. But I know someone who does."

NAZCA, PERU

The hot air balloon hovers one hundred feet over the Nazca Spiral, its two passengers armed with binoculars. Mick spots the tracks first—staggered slides that serpentine to the south, crossing over the Panamericana Highway.

"He must have been delirious by the time he reached the Spiral. Do you think he knew where he was headed?"

Julius steers the balloon to the south. "Like I said, there are no coincidences. He may not remember it, but Sam intended to end up at the Spiral, and we were intended to find him. Now let's see if we can find his ship."

The tracks lead them southwest past the massive glyphs of the lizard and the tree, the footprints growing progressively steadier as they near the beginning of Sam's journey. After several miles they disappear at their inception point—a Y-shaped ravine cutting between a mountain. Viewed from above, the geography of smooth rock resembles a three-leaf clover.

Adorning the southernmost face is the 104-foot-high carving of the Nazca astronaut.

Julius stares in wonder at the two-thousand-year-old rendering. "Like I said, there are no coincidences."

Mick focuses his binoculars on the ravine. "Set us down. I think I see something in the shadows."

The shuttle had come in from the west, its pilot guided by one of the straightest, longest lines on the entire plateau. Landing at the base of the mountain, the craft had entered the ravine, its wingspan barely fitting through the narrow junction.

Julius sets the balloon down just outside the jagged opening of rock, which long ago was a riverbed. The archaeologist deflates the balloon while his son gathers up the bright orange and blue envelope so that it cannot be seen from above. Armed with flashlights, the two explorers enter the ravine, approaching the tail end of a sleek red and white winged aircraft.

"This looks more like a plane than a rocket. How could he have flown this into space?"

"Look over your head, Michael. Those are afterburners." Julius climbs the ravine wall to read an insignia on the tail fin. "'PROJECT H.O.P.E. A division of Mabus Tech Industries.' This wasn't part of NASA, it was a private venture."

"Julius, over here. I found a way inside."

The elder Gabriel climbs down from his perch, then makes his way forward beneath the contoured wings of the futuristic craft to a narrow set of steps built into the open starboard hatch.

Mick reaches down, helping his father up the steep incline.

They enter the vessel, their flashlights revealing an empty cabin. Mick heads down the aisle, only to stumble on a large object lying on the floor, covered by a blanket. He retracts the covering, aiming his flashlight in the gray darkness. "Oh, God—"

It is the decapitated body of a woman, her blood-drained head a few feet away. Mick had inadvertently kicked it away from its resting place besides the severed neck.

Julius guides his son away from the gruesome sight, then kneels to inspect the name tag over the jumpsuit. "Looks like we found Lilith."

"If she's Lilith, who or what the hell was this?" Mick aims his light along the midsection of the cabin where an immense dark pattern has been splattered across the ceiling and walls like a giant Rorschach ink spot.

Julius moves down the aisle, staring in amazement at the twenty-two-foot-wide butterfly-shaped stain. "Michael, this is incredible. The flesh and blood, the bones and internal organs . . . everything was completely atomized, the energy so hot it simultaneously melted then fused the remains together. The power necessary to complete such an endeavor is beyond anything we have in our arsenal."

"You think it was human?"

"I suspect it may be all that remains of whoever killed Lilith. Let's search the rest of the ship."

The ravine is in shadows by the time they exit the space plane and return to the hot air balloon. Mick spreads the panels while Julius ignites the propane burners, filling the envelope.

Ten minutes later they are airborne, slipping out of the ravine and over the mountain's summit into the late afternoon desert sky.

Julius scans the horizon. "Looks like we're alone. Our first priority is to hide the ship."

"Camouflage netting?"

"Contact Manolo, but be discreet."

"What about tourists? If they explore the ravine—"

"—I'm more concerned about Majestic-12. If they find the ship, it won't be long before they locate Sam. Michael, it may be wiser for us to destroy the ship once we figure out how to access its computer records."

"Sam will know how. If we bring him back here, the sight of the ship could jar his memory."

"It's risky. The shock of seeing Lilith like that . . ."

"Pop, there's something I have to tell you. While you were below looking at the computers, I went back to the cabin. I placed Lilith's head near her body, then I slid open her eyes. They were blue."

"Just like your Aunt Laura's, I know."

"What the hell's happening here?"

"I don't know. I need to think it through, but I'm too exhausted. Meanwhile, don't say anything about this to Sam or your aunt. As far as they're concerned, we were out on the plateau, cataloguing zoomorphs."

The sun has set on the horizon by the time the hot air balloon is once again hovering over the city of Nazca. A few young children wave in the streets. Most people ignore the object, having grown used to its presence over the last six months.

Julius guides the craft over their backyard, then cuts the burners, setting the basket down in an open field. Mick leaps out, catching the deflating envelope by its parachute valve, spreading the panels out across the dry terrain. "Wonder where the two lovebirds are at?"

"Your aunt probably took Sam into town to do a little shopping. Apparently our taste in men's clothing wasn't to her liking."

Mick's expression darkens. "We've got company."

Julius scans the sky. "A Fastwalker?"

"Worse."

A dozen soldiers in desert camouflage race across the yard from all directions as a military jeep drives over the front lawn.

"On your knees! Now!"

Mick and his father drop down to the ground, hands held over their heads. A boot in each of their backs sends them face-first onto the cracked earth.

Julius spits out dirt, his weak heart racing. "What's the meaning of this? We're Americans. We're here legally on an archaeological grant. I demand you release us at once!"

"Same old Julius, still full of piss and vinegar, still oblivious to how the real world works."

"Pierre?" Julius wheezes as he's lifted to his feet by two soldiers to stare into the face of his former colleague and most outspoken critic. "Working for the private military sector, I see. I knew it wouldn't take long before your uncle pulled you in to the dark side."

"What you call the dark side is actually the inside. I've been given access to the most important discovery in the history of our planet, and now I'm here, against my better judgment, offering you the same access."

"Not interested. Now let us go."

"Oh, I think you'll be very interested. The pathetic truth is, you may have been right. There could be a Doomsday scenario out there, and you may be the only one knowledgeable enough to stop it."

CHAUCHILLA VALLEY

NAZCA, PERU

The orange 1980 CJ7 Jeep leaves the Panamericana Highway, its female driver veering right onto a dirt road. Laura Salesa glances at her shaken passenger as the rusted steel chassis bounces wildly beneath them.

Samuel Agler struggles to buckle his seat belt while fighting to keep from falling out of the bouncing vehicle. "If you're trying to get rid of me, there are easier ways."

"Haven't you ever gone four-wheeling?"

"Is that what we're doing? I thought we were going sightseeing."

The road continues west another seven miles, dead-ending at the two-thousand-year-old graveyard, distinguished only by a sign and a thatched roof held aloft by tree branches serving as posts. A few tourists shop at an adjacent pottery exhibit.

A guide greets them with a toothless smile. "Welcome to Chauchilla Cemetery. You are just in time for the last tour of the day. Five hundred nueva, *por favor.*"

Laura hands him ten dollars, expecting change, receiving none. "Doesn't seem like much to see."

"Treasure hunters took the gold and valuables long ago. Archaeologists removed the skulls of our leaders and sold them to museums. But their ghosts still linger, along with the remains of the commoner. Come."

He leads them beneath the roof. A dozen open graves are set in the dry earth, the walls reinforced by round stones. Situated in each tomb like ancient scarecrows wrapped in blankets are the blanched skulls and bones of the dead. Incredibly, a few of the heads still possess petrified braided hair.

"The Nazca people who were buried in Chauchilla predated the Inca," the guide explains. "The bodies were preserved using natural mummification means, no chemicals. The arid climate of the valley prevented deterioration."

Sam moves to a photo exhibit. His heart palpates, his flesh tingling.

The images are of artifacts taken from Chauchilla, held in museums across Peru. Some of the objects are elongated, others bulbous-shaped and much smaller.

Ancient human skulls. Only the beings had definitely not been human.

NAZCA, PERU

They had spoken for several hours in a military vehicle while Mick remained inside the house, guarded by a team of armed men. In the end, the archaeologist had agreed to accompany Pierre Borgia to Nevada, not because he trusted him, but because he didn't. Julius Gabriel knew his former Cambridge roommate's briefing was extensive enough to issue a death warrant should he not agree to help, and Majestic-12 was not a group to be trifled with. Like it or not, Julius was flying high above the radar; his priority now was to protect Michael and Sam.

Julius asked Borgia for a few hours alone to pack and make arrangements for his son to be taken care of in his absence. He would meet Borgia at the airport no later than 7:30 p.m.

"Pop, this is crazy. Let me go with you. If whatever Borgia wants you to see really is linked to the Doomsday prophecy, then you'll need me there with you to resolve it."

"Not this time, kiddo. I need to keep you away from Majestic-12 as long as I can."

"What am I supposed to do while you're gone?"

"Go back to Spain with Laura and Sam. Live a normal life for a change. I'll find you in Europe once I've earned Borgia's trust."

"Pop—"

"Michael, somewhere out there is your future soul mate, the mother of your child. You're not going to find her in Area 51."

TENANCINGO, MEXICO

The brothel is an island of insanity surrounded by predators. Congregating on the street outside the shanty, they leer like hungry wolves, licking their chops between swigs of whiskey.

Hiding beneath the front porch, the lamb cowers. She has no concept of what is going on inside the building behind the thirty partitions of blankets hanging from clotheslines, only that the line of men is long, and she can hear the girls inside crying.

She squeezes tighter into the shadows as she sees the car roll up the drive. A blast of horn summons the madam, who greets the man known to all as El Gallo.

The kidnaper thrusts a Polaroid photo into the woman's cherub face, his chiseled mouth spewing orders.

The woman yells into the bordello. "Dominique Vazquez! *Venga!*"

The man in the car is staring at her. He calls out to the woman.

The nine-year-old's heart flutters in her chest. In the last month she has been taken from her mother and her village, she has been beaten and starved, and now she is being tossed to the wolves as the rotund Mexican woman drags her out from beneath the porch by her feet.

But the lamb has the heart of a lion. As her hands claw at the earth, her fingers grab an object.

The madam kneels, slapping Dominique across her face, yelling at her.

The child smashes the baseball-size rock upon the bridge of the woman's nose. Blood spurts from both nostrils as the madam collapses forward in a heap.

The child wheezes several breaths, then turns to run—the Rooster scooping her up in his arms, slamming her down across the hood of his car. "You're a tough one, eh? A lucky one, too. Now listen carefully—your Uncle Don has decided to send you to America to live with a relative. You hear me? I'm taking you away from here to your family."

"You are going to kill me."

"Are you calling me a liar?" Reaching into his jacket pocket, he withdraws an airline ticket. "Can you read English? See? Dominique Vazquez. That's your name, yes?"

Dominique nods.

"Now do as I say, or I'll leave you here." El Gallo tosses her in the backseat and drives off, heading for Mexico City. "I am taking you to the airport. I will give you the ticket and identity papers when we get there. You will be taken aboard the airplane by a nice lady who works at the airline. Not many peasant girls from Guatemala ever get to fly on a real plane. You are a lucky girl."

"I want my mother."

"Your mother will meet you in Tampa," he lies. "If you try to run away, or if you tell the police about what happened, then she will not be there to greet you in America. Nod if you understand."

The child nods, tears of happiness streaking her grimy cheeks.

El Gallo smiles to himself. The plane ticket and forged papers had cost him two hundred dollars.

The girl will earn that back from his cut of her sale to the Tampa bordello in her first two weeks.

TESTIMONIAL
May 9, 2001: National Press Club, Washington, D.C.

My name is Don Phillips. I was in the United States Air Force, and I have worked with certain intelligence agencies of the United States government. Prior to joining the Air Force, I worked for the famous Lockheed Skunk Works, and I was working for them when I was attending college, and I worked for them in a capacity as a design engineer [. . .]. My main project was known later as the SR-71 [Blackbird]. [. . .]

My first field assignment for the United States Air Force was at Las Vegas Air Force Station, and that was my first experience with Las Vegas. I couldn't understand why people were so excited about going to a place such as this, but I found out about a year later.

Nellis Air Force Base is located there. Nellis is a major training center for different types of special aircraft and fighter aircraft, one of the premier training sites for pilots all around the world. [. . .] I learned that my assignment was at a radar site fifty miles out of town, up near Mt. Charleston [. . . and I] reported in, in 1965, for duty.

In 1966, early in the morning, about 1:00 to 2:00 a.m., I was sleeping—I was staying there on base, and our barracks were at about, oh, eight thousand feet. I heard a lot of commotion. You know, at that altitude sound carries, sound carries tremendously, and I thought, well, it's early in the morning, [. . .] maybe I should get up and take a look. I [. . .] walked up to the main road near my office, which was the commander's office. I was on the commander's staff—Lt. Col. Charles Evans. [. . .] Four or five people were standing there, one being the chief of security. They were looking up in the air [. . .] at the same direction. Well, I looked up to the west-northwest, and to my amazement, there were lights flashing around the sky, moving at anywhere from what seemed like 2,400 to about 3,800 miles per hour. [. . .] We continued to watch these darting lights go across the sky and stop—absolutely stop—come to a dead stop, and reverse in an acute angle their direction [. . .]. They were traveling so fast that you could almost see a pattern left by—if you are computer people, when you move a mouse real quick across the screen, you see a little bit of a tail—well, that's exactly the way these six or seven craft worked.

After five minutes of watching these things, they all seemed to group up to the west-northwest, okay? They started to come in on a circle, but what I would like to point out is that where they were putting on their display, in the north-northwest sky, just directly east of that is what is known as Area 51. Area 51 is a AEC name, okay? Atomic Energy Commission. [. . .] We knew it as the Groom Lake Flight Test Facility [. . .]. And it was where we tested our aircraft after we got the prototype made from the Skunk Works [. . .].

What they did was coalesce and started rotating in a circle, and then they disappeared. Well, I thought, gee, this is something that we have to keep quiet. That was verified by the chief of security. We waited there and talked it over for a little bit . . . it seemed like, I think it was an hour. Then came the radar people from the scopes, which were at ten thousand plus feet, came down for their dinner at two o'clock in the morning, and the first person off the bus was a good friend of mine, Anthony Kasar. He was white as a sheet, and he says, "Did you see that?"

"Yeah," we all said. "Yeah, yeah, it was a nice display. What a show."

He says, "We documented them on radar [. . .]. We didn't give 'em clearance. The standing order was, let 'em fly through the radar beam. We documented six to seven UFOs."

We don't know who was guiding those, but they were certainly intelligent. And we don't know where they landed, because they coalesced and disappeared. [. . .] I will testify under oath as to what I say is true, and I will do so before Congress.

—Don Phillips,
Lockheed Skunk Works employee and CIA contractor

Used by permission of the Disclosure Project

2 1

Eleven Years Later . . .

The Magdalena Peninsula is located along the northern coastline of Spain, bordered by the deep blue waters of the North Atlantic and the silt-tinged outflow from the Gulf of Biscay. Tucked inside this estuary is Santander, the capital of Cantabria, a city bordered by beaches and fishing villages, towering cliffs and rolling hills, its maritime streets laced with gritty taverns and five-star restaurants. More than a quarter million people inhabit the area, making it one of Spain's more densely populated centers.

Somo Beach, located by the seaside city of Ribamontán al Mar, is a thin expanse of golden sand that runs four miles to the east of the Bay of Santander. Windswept and crowded, its ocean view features an island of flat rock known as Santa Maira. With year long swells of eight to twenty feet, the area is a hotbed for surfers.

The narrow arena of seascape is no place for beginners. Waves are powerful, fueled by a heavy surf break, and the locals do not take kindly to visitors.

There are nine surfers vying for a wave—eight males ages nineteen to thirty—and the girl. Nine years old and barely sixty pounds, she is dwarfed by her fellow surfers—the runt of the litter.

To the crowd's delight, the runt is dominating her competition.

First up on every wave, balancing on surprisingly muscular legs, she attacks each curl as if it were her last, often zigzagging around any surfer in her path before going airborne, flying heels over head as she exits the dying swell as if launched from a catapult.

If her peers have any problems with the child's lack of surfer etiquette, they don't show it. Many have been watching her shred waves since she was old enough to walk. She is the pack's mascot and their identity, and they are as protective of her as is her imposing father, who is watching from his chaise lounge chair on the beach.

To the researchers and curators at the Regional Museum of Prehistory and Archaeology of Cantabria, she is known as the granddaughter of director Marcus Salesa. To the women's Olympic gymnastics team, she is coach Raul Gallon's best hope for a gold medal in the 2004 games in Athens, Greece.

To the surfers of Somo Beach, she is known simply as Sophia.

The setting sun turns the cliffs of Santa Maira to gold, the diminishing day accompanied by a noticeable chill in the air. Sophia's father signals to his daughter to come in.

Sophia pretends not to see him.

A few of her male companions chide her, knowing better than to be on Samuel Agler's bad side.

"Sophia, *regresa*! Your padre, he is growing impatient."

The girl ignores them, paddling out to greet the next series of swells rolling in on the horizon.

The first wave rises majestically before her, a wall of water far more powerful than any of the swells in the previous sets.

Her surrogate brothers warn her off.

She hesitates, then decides to ride it in, her tenacious ego refusing to back down.

The swell plucks her from the ocean and tosses her upon its back, the shoal cresting behind her at thirty-three feet. Her heart flutters in her chest as the angle suddenly steepens and she registers the wave's unbridled fury.

Fear shatters cockiness seconds before the tip of her board catches the monster's face, vaulting her head-first into the path of the roaring locomotive.

The initial blow blasts the air from her lungs even as it swallows her deep inside its churning mouth, knocking her senseless. For twelve long disorienting seconds she is a human doll in a clothes washer's spin cycle until the wave passes over her, punching her to the bottom.

The second blow is her skull meeting rock.

Samuel Agler is in the water before the crest collapses into a burst of foam. Each powerful crawl stroke sends him knifing through water that glides over his sizzling flesh like heavy motor oil. Somehow he is moving incredibly fast—

—and somehow everything around him appears to have slowed.

The sound of the ocean is a deep throttle in his ears.

The blur in his vision magnifies, allowing him to see.

The air in his lungs remains a steady source. Without another breath he surface-dives beneath the wave and torpedoes to the sea floor, plucking his unconscious child from the expanse of rock and sand.

Then, before even he realizes what is happening, he is back on the beach, hovering over her frail figure.

Sound is muted, save for the erratic timbre of Sophia's pulse beneath his fingers. Her complexion is pale, her lips blue. She is not breathing. He repositions her head and expels a breath into her collapsed lungs. Her inflating chest matches the pace of the converging mob, which moves through the gelid surroundings in slow motion.

The sea spills out from between her lips as her lungs expel the suffocating liquid.

He rolls her on her side and palms her shoulder blades with a heavy cadence.

Sophia Agler vomits up the sea. Coughs . . . and breathes.

Samuel Agler exhales—his being flung free of the bizarre corridor of time and space.

"I don't know what it was, Laura. One moment I was watching our daughter falling into a churning wall of water, then next thing I know I'm underwater, swimming like a fish, able to see as clearly as I'm looking at you now.

A blink and we're on the beach and I'm giving her mouth to mouth, only it's as if I can feel every vital sign in her body and the signals are directing me what to do. Maybe you can explain it, 'cause I sure can't."

Laura Agler watches her husband pace the open central courtyard that divides the two-story living room from the rest of the beach house. "Sam, honey, what you experienced was a rush of adrenaline. For thirty seconds you became Superman," she smiles, "or at least Aquaman."

"You think this is funny?"

"Sophie's fine."

"But I'm not. And this wasn't adrenaline. Maybe the rush of adrenaline caused it, but this was something else entirely . . . an altered state of reality where everything slowed down—everything except for me."

"Do you want me to call Ben Kucmierz?"

"I don't need a psychiatrist, Laura."

"What do you need?"

"I don't know. Maybe I just need time to think." Exiting the courtyard, he enters the primary living space of their four-thousand-square-foot dwelling. A dramatic pair of matching staircases lined with bookcases frame a corridor leading into the dining room and kitchen. Ascending the left stairwell, he bypasses the master suite and enters his office, a small chamber that looks out to a front-yard garden.

Opening a file cabinet, he pushes aside a stack of folders, fishing out the half-empty bottle of bourbon. He fills a paper cup and drains it, then pours himself a second round and sits behind his desk in the high-backed leather chair.

He is surrounded by framed photos of loved ones. Lauren and Sophia at the junior Olympics. The three of them at a ski lodge taken two Christmases ago. A shot of Julius and Michael at Chichen Itza. Laura's parents at their fiftieth wedding anniversary, the party held at their house.

A ten-year marriage. A wonderful daughter, the apple of his eye. A successful career as an architect, each beach home a unique pocket of zen and creativity tucked within Santander's urban sprawl.

Eleven years of living, the previous thirty-five sealed within a cocoon of darkness.

A man with no past is like a home built upon a foundation of sand—sooner or later, the house topples beneath its own weight.

Samuel Agler is crumbling inside a leased identity that he can never own. For the better part of a decade he has chosen to ignore this reality, preferring simply to enjoy his furlough from his true destiny, existing on borrowed time.

His daughter's near-death experience has been a sobering wake-up call, a reminder of how precious life can be. At the same time, it has also forced him to experience something from his past—an ability he had been unaware of, yet one he instinctively knows he could master over time, should he ever so desire and dare.

And that is why he is so upset; that is why he is drinking again after seven years of sobriety. Today, an eleven-year foundation has slipped, exposing the underlying bedrock of a former life and with it an underlying truth that he can no longer ignore—

—that his life is intended for far greater things.

"Your life was intended for far greater things, son. Not that working with my brother hasn't opened up channels to the private sector." Congressman Robert Borgia drains his shot of bourbon, pouring himself another. "Joseph and I have finally managed to corral Wolfowitz; he's been tied up on some secret Middle East project. Anyway, he anticipates a high-level position opening up and the job will be yours: deputy under secretary of defense. You'll be the director of the task force for business and stability operations."

Pierre Borgia exhales. "What happened to our plans to run for your seat in 2002? A future shot at the Oval Office?"

"I'm not ready to step down. Besides, your uncle and I both agree this will be a quicker route to the White House. As deputy under secretary, you'll be inside the Pentagon and among the first in line for future openings in the cabinet. Trust me, with your name and looks, a military resume, and a quarter billion in private funding, we'll have the inside track for the White House in 2008."

The hookers are gone. So are the remains of the bottle of tequila.

Pierre Borgia slumps in the suede recliner in his bedroom suite as night bleeds into day and gazes in a semiconscious stupor at his reflection in the mirror.

Your life was intended for far greater things . . .

"Huh?"

Pay attention! Open your eyes, Pierre!

The voice snaps him into sobriety. "Who said that?"

You're going to lose it all, my friend. The presidency, the power, the influence, the women—all because of him.

Pierre looks around, the graying darkness spinning in his vision, forcing him to lie back again. "I'm calling security."

We don't have much time, I need you to focus. Look at me, savant!

The image in the mirror changes, the slumped figure morphing into that of a bare-chested Mesoamerican Indian.

"I am so wasted." Pierre chokes out a laugh, which becomes a cough and gag reflex, forcing him out of the chair and into the bathroom where he vomits the liquor-doused extract into the sink.

Leaning his forearms on the porcelain, he moans as he scoops water into his mouth and rinses. Finally, he looks up at his reflection in the bathroom mirror—

—staring eyeball to eyeball with the chastising Mayan priest.

"You're not real."

Search your heart, Pierre. I am the cold lust that burns inside the vessel, the lineage of your shared soul. I was you before you were you.

"This is insane. I'm going to bed."

Fool! I am here to guide you before he destroys our legacy again.

"What are you talking about? Who's he?"

The son of your enemy. The man who stole your intended soul mate and your legacy with it.

"You mean Julius?"

Had you remained with the female Hunahpu as I intended, you would have sired kings. Instead, you allowed your enemy to best you. Then you invited him into your camp. Now his son shall destroy you, and our shared vessel in the process.

"Michael Gabriel? He's nothing. How could he possibly destroy me?"

The day you take down the father, make sure the son is not among the spectators. Heed my warning, Pierre, for I am Seven Macaw, and our shared destiny in the physical universe is at stake.

MAJESTIC-12 (S-66) SUBTERRANEAN FACILITY

15 MILES SOUTH OF GROOM LAKE AIR FORCE BASE (AREA 51)

NORTH LAS VEGAS, NEVADA

The helicopter descends quickly, causing Marvin Teperman to feel queasy.

Joseph Randolph glances at the short Canadian with the pencil-thin mustache and annoyingly warm smile. "What's wrong, Teperman? My nephew told me you two had flown together on plenty of field assignments before."

The exobiologist exhales as the chopper lands on the helipad. "Yes, but I never enjoyed them. Weak stomach for flying."

"How long have you and Pierre known each other?"

"I've only been assigned to the United Nations since January, so I guess about eight months. I understand your nephew is leaving to work at the Pentagon."

"Which is why you're here. You've reviewed Julius Gabriel's file?"

"Yes. Very impressive."

"I don't trust him. Neither did Pierre. Not since he took over as the team's primary telepath."

The two men exit the helicopter, climbing aboard an awaiting military jeep. Randolph slams the vehicle into gear and drives off, following the newly asphalted road to a series of camouflaged bunkers.

Marvin holds on to the edge of his seat, waiting until the elder silver-haired man parks before reengaging him in conversation. "Sir, according to your own report, the volume of information has increased tenfold since Dr. Gabriel took over the project. Why would—"

"Don't confuse activity with accomplishment, Teperman. We're not here to psychoanalyze these beings, we're here to comprehend and engineer their technology." Randolph pauses to key an entry code into the security pad before submitting to a retinal scan. "Pierre tells me you trained as a telepath. How good are you? Wait, I'll think of something, an inanimate object. Can you tell me what it is?"

"It doesn't quite work that way, it's sort of a rhythm thing."

"But if Gabriel was concealing information from us, you could tell, right? Our last telepath, just before he hung himself, said emotion played a big part in reading thought energy."

"Yes . . . Wait, did you just say he hung himself?"

"Unrelated. Probably an old girlfriend, or some other nonsense. Are you coming?"

Freshly showered and dressed in medical scrubs and sandals, Marvin follows Joseph Randolph down into the pit of the interview suite. The exobiologist has seen taped footage of the frail extraterrestrial with the grayish-brown bulbous skull and huge ebony eyes, but being in the same room with the alien is still startling.

Julius Gabriel looks up wearily from his computer screen as the two men enter. The archaeologist is in his mid-sixties, but he looks far older. His brown hair has grayed and receded noticeably, his posture as slumped as the E.T.'s. To the exobiologist, the two beings seem like bookends from different ends of the same gene pool.

"Julius, this is Dr. Marvin Teperman, the exobiologist I told you about."

Julius returns his attention to the list of technical questions appearing on his monitor. "Tell me, Dr. Teperman, isn't exobiology the study of life outside our planet?"

"Yes."

"And what qualifies you as an expert in these matters? A course you took as an undergrad at the University of Toronto? An encounter with an E.T. when you were a teen?"

"Well, no, but—"

"Wait, I know, you're a big fan of Steven Spielberg movies and you've always had a secret desire to be anally probed?"

Marvin glances at Randolph.

"Play nice, you two." The CEO leaves.

Julius points to a vacant terminal. "Sit down, say nothing, touch nothing."

Marvin sits.

"Computer, reduce lighting by forty percent. Play Gabriel concerto tape three, forty decibels. Continuing with interview session three-thirty-seven."

Julius closes his eyes as the soothing instrumental of Bach's Orchestral Suite No. 3 in D major, performed by the Academy of St. Martin in the Fields, plays over several surround-sound speakers. As Marvin watches, both the E.T. and its human companion begin to sway in a syncopated rhythm to the music.

Marvin closes his eyes, attempting to eavesdrop on their communication.

. . . we were discussing the Hunab K'u. On what is the existence of the cosmic consciousness based?

The extraterrestrial's thoughts are a melodic whisper, dancing on the chords of Bach's concerto. *The Hunab K'u is based upon an algorithm of measurement and movement, attributed to the mathematical structuring of the universe. The Earth functions as a living entity within this algorithm, the root seed of our existence as well as yours. The act of splitting the atom was felt across the galactic network. The colliding of two proton beams threatens all species.*

Your species is farther along than ours. Why can't you neutralize the threat?

The threat is rooted in a higher dimension. It shall remain inaccessible until it manifests in the physicality of Malchut. By then it will be too late.

But One Hunahpu has the knowledge and the means to destroy the singularity?

Yes.

The rhythm abruptly darkens. *Zipil na!*

Yes, I nearly forgot. I must give this house of sin its allotment of disinformation. Julius types rapidly on his keyboard, responding to the first series of questions pertaining to a tachyon carrier wave.

Zipil na!

It's okay, my friend.

No . . . no . . . no. The other Homo sapiens *. . . he is listening.*

The earthquake had struck in 1996 on the twelfth day of November at exactly one minute before noon, its epicenter in the sea, its devastation transforming the city of Nazca into rubble. Within a year, a major Canadian gold mining company had taken over the entire area, displacing the indigenous people whose roots traced back two thousand years but who held no legal claim to the land.

The ebony-eyed twenty-five-year-old American with the shoulder-length dark hair and athlete's physique weaves through the decimated streets of downtown Nazca on his ten-speed bike, heading for the Museum Antonini. The facility's roof collapsed during the earthquake, crushing artifacts excavated from the gravesite at Cahuachi. Mick has been helping the archaeologist-turned-curator Giuseppe Orefeci, a former colleague and close friend of Julius Gabriel, salvage as many of the damaged mummies, ceramics, and ancient weapons as possible.

Michael Gabriel carries the bicycle up the cracked granite steps and into what remains of the museum's main gallery when his eyes lock onto the woman. She is kneeling beside a wooden crate—a startling Hispanic beauty in her early thirties with alluring green eyes and a body designed to give men fantasies.

Mick is caught staring by Giuseppe Orefeci. The elder man approaches, grinning. "I see you discovered my new assistant, eh? Beware, Michael, this one, she is a heartbreaker. Come, I'll introduce you." The curator man leads him over to the Mexican female. "Adelina, this is the young man I was telling you about. Michael Gabriel, this is—"

257

"Adelina Botello, nice to finally meet you. Dr. Orefeci hasn't stopped talking about you since I arrived. He tells me you and your father have come up with some interesting theories regarding Kukulcan and Quetzalcoatl. The plumed serpent is the topic of my dissertation, perhaps we could talk over dinner?"

Dr. Orefeci nudges Mick, who is staring into her bedroom eyes. "Dinner . . . breakfast, I'm always available. You have such pretty eyes. I was just wondering . . ."

"My sign?" She smiles. "I'm a Cancer. Born on the summer solstice."

"That's cool. Actually, I was going to ask about your blood type."

22

. . . there exists a secret, "unacknowledged" operation that has used very advanced electromagnetic weapon systems to track, target, and on occasion, but with increasing accuracy, down extraterrestrial vehicles. This reckless behavior constitutes an existential threat to all of mankind and must be reined in immediately.

The so-called MJ-12 or Majestic group that controls this subject operates without the consent of the people, or the oversight of the President and Congress. It functions as a transnational government unto itself, answerable to no one. All checks and balances have been obliterated. While as a governing entity it stands outside of the rule of law, its influence reaches into many governments, corporations, agencies, media and financial interests. Its corrupting influence is profound and, indeed, it has operated as a very powerful and embedded global RICO whose power to date remains unchecked.

Upwards of $100 billion of USG funds go annually into this operation, also known as the "black budget" of the

HAARP RESEARCH STATION

GAKONA, ALASKA

Surrounded by a high-security perimeter fence, the complex occupies
thirty-three acres of isolated Alaskan wilderness eight miles north of the
town of Gakona. At first glance the site, selected because of its quiet electromagnetic location in the auroral region, appears to be some type of
hybrid electrical substation.

Welcome to HAARP, the High Frequency Active Auroral Research Program. Jointly managed by the Air Force Research Laboratory and the Office
of Naval Research, HAARP's "official" description deals with "advanc[ing]
our knowledge of the physical and electrical properties of the Earth's ionosphere which can affect our military and civilian communication and navigation systems."

HAARP's true purpose is known only to its project handlers in the
Pentagon. Situated in twelve rows are 180 antennas, each crucifix-shaped
tower rising seventy-two feet off the ground. When activated, these towers
form a high-frequency phased-array radio transmitter capable of channeling
more than 3 billion watts of power into the heavens. As the three-gigawatt
pulse corkscrews upward 125 miles above the atmosphere, the radio waves
interact with the ionized parts of atoms, causing them to circle around the
beam at the speed of light. This sudden increase in motion "heats" the particles, each becoming a little electromagnet—effectively making HAARP a
particle injector that can be used to knock out the electronic controls of anything that passes through it, be it a communication satellite, an ICBM . . . or
an extraterrestrial vehicle.

The seven limousines arrive bumper to bumper at the main gate, the dirt
and gravel access road too narrow for more than one vehicle at a time. The
VIPs concealed behind the tinted windows are expected and are waved
through.

The eighth limo arrives five minutes later.

The driver is a Caucasian man in his late twenties, carrying a slight build on his five-foot, eight-inch frame. His dark sunglasses are a constant fixture, his sensitive left retina permanently damaged from shrapnel received during his last covert mission for the CIA.

It was not the metal splinters that motivated Mitchell Kurtz to retire from the Company, nor was it the bullet that missed his spinal cord by mere inches and left him with a permanent limp. The line between good and evil had simply blurred too much, the game of spy versus spy having warped into a money grab, making yesterday's foe today's friend and tomorrow's potential killer. After five years the CIA assassin had had enough. Returning to the City of Brotherly Love, the Philadelphia native applied his combat skills to an environment where he knew they would be needed—teaching in an inner-city high school. A chance meeting with the man riding in the back of the limousine had rescued him from a life of tenured abuse.

Senator Ennis Chaney was born fifty-five years ago in the poorest black neighborhood in Jacksonville, Florida. Raised by his mother and aunt, he never knew his real father, who left home a few months after he was born. When he was two, his mother remarried, his new stepfather moving the family to New Jersey where young Ennis became a formidable high school and college athlete.

After a brief pro basketball career, Chaney would dedicate himself to civil rights issues. He would enter politics in his forties as deputy mayor of Philadelphia. A decade of service later, the maverick Republican who bucked his party's stances on social issues would run for senator of Pennsylvania and win in a rout.

Chaney looks up from his briefing as their limo approaches the gate. The dark pigment surrounding the senator's deeply set eyes creates the impression of a raccoon's mask. Chaney's eyes are mirrors to his soul, revealing his passion as a man, his wisdom as a leader. Cross him, and the eyes become unblinking daggers; his stare is known in Washington circles as the "one-eyed Jack."

Today, the one-eyed Jack is wild.

Two months earlier, a "contact" in the military industrial complex sent Chaney a secret black ops budget that showed that more than $2 trillion in unaccountable Pentagon funding had been redirected over the last fifteen years into a secret weapons and research program. As cochairman of the Senate Appropriations Committee, Chaney was livid. While the majority of these expenditures remained outside his level of security clearance, he was able to track one related expenditure—HAARP, an Alaskan facility comanaged by the Air Force and Navy.

When his inside man had learned of the August meeting at HAARP's facility, the senator from Pennsylvania decided it might be fun to crash the party.

Two heavily armed security guards approach the limo.

Kurtz rolls down the window, offering a perturbed look. "Sorry, fellas, I took a wrong turn back at the Tok Junction. Can you let us through? We're already late."

"Who's in back?"

Mitchell Kurtz removes his sunglasses, offering a sadistic grin. "Now, if I told you that, I'd have to kill you."

The MP feels his nerves buckle. "Go on up, first brick building on the left."

Kurtz proceeds through the gate, snickering his frat house laugh. "Navy boys, what a joke. I've seen better security at a whorehouse."

"Let's not do a victory dance just yet. I knew the gate would be easy; from what I hear, they hold open houses for the public. Getting me inside that meeting is the real challenge. A private security firm—Blackwater— runs things inside."

Kurtz backs the limo into a parking spot, then removes the cover of his palm-size Taser and slips it into his coat pocket. "No worries. I brought your invitation."

LAS VEGAS, NEVADA

Dusk fades the "Jewel of the Desert" into a blue hue, the diminishing day bringing new life to the city's neon trail of lights.

Julius Gabriel follows the Vegas Strip to the north, pointing out the Mandalay Bay Hotel and Casino to his passenger. "Nice place to have a drink. They've got big aquariums filled with sharks and rays, even a few crocodiles. You like wildlife, Marvin?"

Marvin Teperman gazes at the fountain show at the Bellagio. "Wildlife? Sure."

"And how do you feel about extraterrestrial life?"

The exobiologist turns to face his host. "And here I thought tonight was a social gathering."

"I know you've been eavesdropping on our conversations, Marvin."

"How can I be eavesdropping on a conversation you're supposed to be relaying to me? To all of us?"

"I need to know where you stand." Julius veers into the parking lot of a fast food restaurant, waiting in line at the drive-thru. "There are two factions holed up at S-66: the military industrial establishment that is milking Groom Lake like its own private cash cow; and the remaining few of us who still think 'humanity' is an earned attribute. Unfortunately, the morality-based scientists among us who spend prolonged hours working with the Gray end up committing suicide, or they just flat out quit after a few months. In case you get any ideas, you should know the latter still tend to end up dead. Black ops are a paranoid bunch, even with nondisclosure agreements in place."

"I didn't ask to come here, Professor. Pierre Borgia, he sort of volunteered me."

"Join the club." Julius rolls down his window. "Give me a large coffee, extra hot."

"Is this where we're eating?"

"If I wanted to kill myself, Marvin, I would have done it long ago." He drives to the first window and pays, then proceeds to the second window, where he is handed a plastic container of coffee.

He hands it back. "Son, I said I wanted it hot. Stick it back in the microwave another two minutes until it can melt steel."

The teen rolls his eyes, handing the cup to a coworker. "He wants it hotter."

"They're killing these beings, Marvin. They found a way to shoot them down, now they're stealing their technology, keeping it to themselves, then treating these E.T.s like they're collateral damage."

"How can they possibly benefit by keeping the technology to themselves?"

"They're beholden to Big Oil. Free energy for the planet would end war, end hunger, end hatred. There's no profit in peace."

"Here's your coffee, sir. I had to triple the cup, it was too hot to hold."

"You'll make a fine engineer." Holding the hot container in his right hand, Julius drives to the curb, waiting for traffic to clear before turning onto the Strip.

The white cable TV van is parked a block down the street, a driver and passenger inside.

Julius turns south, then suddenly swerves over to the driver's side of the van—

—hurtling the coffee through his open window.

"Ahhh! Ahh!"

"I warned you camo dudes not to follow me on my off-hours. Next time I see one of you in my rearview mirror will be my last day at Groom Lake, you can tell that to your boss."

Julius maneuvers his way back into one of the Strip's southbound lanes, heading for the Mandalay Bay Hotel and Casino.

"What the hell was that?"

"Gotta draw the line with these bastards, Marvin. Now, how 'bout that drink?"

"As long as you don't throw it at me." Marvin notices Julius's hands trembling, his face white as a sheet. "Are you okay?"

Julius grimaces, doubling over in pain. He slams the brakes as the traffic light turns yellow, causing the cars behind him to skid to a halt, the drivers blasting their horns.

"Are you having a heart attack? Oh, geez—"

"Glove box. Pills."

Marvin opens the glove box, searching frantically—locating a prescription bottle of nitroglycerin. "Got it! Here—"

Julius fingers a tablet, his hand trembling as he places it under his tongue.

"Let's get you to a hospital."

"No." The light turns green. Drivers swerve around them, a few saluting Julius with their middle fingers.

"Professor?"

"I'm okay now."

"At least pull over and let me drive."

Julius cuts across two lanes and parks. "We've bonded, Marvin."

"I'm flattered, eh. But it was just a pill."

"Not us. The Gray and I. It's hard to explain, but we've connected at a metaphysical level that transcends our own singular existence. His capture . . . my presence at Groom Lake, it was no coincidence. A baton's been passed from him to me, and now it's my turn to act. I'm telling you this because you're part of that plan . . . not now, but in the future. We serve a higher purpose, you and I . . . beyond anything you can imagine. For the first time in forty years I understand what the Mayan Doomsday Prophecy was all about. It wasn't about asteroids or earthquakes, it was about man's out-of-control ego. Greed, corruption, hatred, negativity . . . much of it fostered by an imbalance in society—the elite one percent continuing its dominance over the ninety-nine percent. Political leaders, Big Oil, the banks . . . the military industrial complex—entities whose only interest is to take for themselves by stifling the majority, preventing us from ascending the ladder of existence. We have to break the stranglehold, Marvin, we have to change the culture of 'me' to 'we' or we'll lose it all. There's so much out there, but the clock is ticking. If nothing changes by the end of the fifth cycle, everything within this bubble of physicality will be gone."

Marvin Teperman wipes the sweat from his pencil-thin mustache. "I don't claim to understand everything you've said, but I trust you. What do you want me to do?"

"There are diskettes in the bottom left-hand desk drawer in Randolph's office."

"Left-hand drawer . . . wait, you want me to break in?"

"Not at all. I have a passkey." Julius fishes through his shirt pocket, removing a white plastic card with a magnetic strip. "Randolph keeps it in his clean-room locker. He left this morning for a meeting in Alaska, so it won't be missed for at least twenty-four hours."

"What's in Alaska?"

"A weapon Randolph's geek squad designed to take down these E.T. vehicles. Now listen carefully—Randolph keeps the key to his desk drawer in a golf tournament mug on his bookshelf. There are several boxes in the drawer. Look for the one labeled 'Earl.' "

"Earl?"

"Earl Gray. That's what Randolph calls the E.T. It's his own sick little joke. But he's become bored with his extraterrestrial house pet, and boredom leads to sloppiness. Get me two diskettes: one that predates my arrival in 1991, when they were using truth serum on the Gray; the other something more recent. Make sure you remember to relock the drawer and return the key to the golf cup."

"What are you planning to do with the diskettes?"

Julius lays his head back, his eyes weary slits. "Trust me, you don't want to know."

HAARP RESEARCH STATION

GAKONA, ALASKA

At six feet, six inches and 285 pounds, the African American is an imposing man, possessing a sledgehammer physique honed by a four-year intercollegiate football career and extensive training in the martial arts. After a blown-out left knee crippled any chance of playing in the NFL, Ryan Beck joined the military. He spent a year as a Green Beret before the injury forced his early retirement.

He has been stationed at the Alaska facility for two weeks, having completed a "lightweight" training course at the Blackwater facility in North Carolina.

Beck restrains the reflex to reach for his sidearm as the two men hurry toward him. He does not know the small Caucasian but recognizes the middle-aged black man as Senator Ennis Chaney.

The big man scans his VIP list. "Morning, sir. My apologies, but you're not on my list."

"Exactly the way I requested it. How late am I, big fella?"

"About ten minutes. Go on in."

Kurtz opens the door—his arm snatched by Beck's viselike grip. "The senator only, little man."

"Let go of the arm, Hercules, before I fry your testicles like an omelette."

Chaney steps between them. "My apologies, my friend is a bit overprotective. Mitchell, wait out here, please."

Kurtz eyeballs the bigger man, then steps aside, allowing Senator Chaney to pass through the double doors of the small auditorium alone—just as they intended.

The periphery of the chamber is dim, the lights focused on the front of the room. Chaney finds a seat in the last row away from the other twenty to thirty onlookers, their identities shadowed in darkness.

Standing behind a lectern before a projection screen is a silver-haired civilian sporting a Texas accent and a military vernacular. ". . . during Beta arousal, human brain waves operate at fifteen to forty cycles per second, less during Alpha, Theta, and the Delta sleep cycles. By using very-low-frequency ground waves coming from our Ground Wave Emergency Network, HAARP can be used to disrupt the brain's natural biorhythm. The GWEN transmitters will be erected two hundred miles apart in targeted locations across the United States, allowing us to tailor specific frequencies based on the geomagnetic-field strength in each area. In essence, the weapon's electromagnetic waves allow us to mentally disrupt small segments of the population.

"In addition to weather-engineering and mind control, HAARP can generate focused impulses on tectonic plates, as we demonstrated back in

1996 with the earthquake in Nazca, Peru. I think you'll all agree, the Canadian gold mining operation that subsequently took over the region has yielded some nice dividends."

Light applause fills the chamber.

"Sir, would you mind stepping out into the corridor?" Chaney looks up at the flashlight's blinding beacon, rough hands dragging him from his seat and into the bright hallway.

Three security men wearing masks surround Kurtz, the bodyguard's arms behind his back, his wrists bound in a plastic restraint.

Ryan Beck seems dumbfounded by the turn of events, his eyes widening in disbelief as Chaney is placed in cuffs. "Hey, you can't do that! He's a United States senator."

"You've got a lot to learn, rookie."

"Where you taking them?"

"Sit down, shut up, and mind your post." The private militia men lead Chaney and Kurtz down the corridor and outside into the overcast morning, following a gravel path to the surrounding woods.

"Are you people insane? My entire staff knows I'm here!"

"Knows you're where, Senator? According to our records, you never arrived."

Kurtz flips his legs over his head, breaking free of his guards' grip, while kicking outward with both legs. One booted foot catches a militiaman in his face, the other strikes another in the throat—the third assailant bashing him across the top of his skull with the blunt end of his nightstick.

The former CIA assassin goes down in a heap.

The two wounded men regain their feet, one man bleeding profusely from his shattered nasal cavity. "Sonuva bitch broke my nose."

Whack! The third man crumbles, blood spurting from his head.

His wounded companions look up—their faces pummeled by Ryan Beck's fists. "Sit down and shut up, my ass." Removing his Boker knife from the clip on his belt, he runs the fixed blade across Chaney's cuffs, slicing through the plastic restraint.

"What's your name, son?"

"Ryan Beck."

"You work for me now, Mr. Beck. Pick up Mr. Kurtz, we need to get him to a doctor."

"Or we could just leave him . . . kidding."

Beck cuts through the unconscious man's restraints, then picks him up, following Senator Chaney to his limousine.

267

TESTIMONIAL
May 9, 2001: National Press Club, Washington, D.C.

My name is John Callahan. I'm a retired FAA [Federal Aviation Administration] employee. I was the division manager for the Accidents Evaluation and Investigation Division in DC. About two years before I retired, I received a call from our Alaska region, where the region wanted to know what to tell the media. When I questioned, "Tell the media what?" he says, "About the UFO." And it went downhill from there [. . .].

I had them send all that data to the FAA's tech center in Atlantic City. The next day my immediate boss, Service Director Harvey Sophia, and I went to Atlantic City [. . .]. We had them play back on the scope—you would call the scope a Plan View Display, PVD—exactly what the [. . .] controller had seen, and we tied it in with the voice tapes so we could hear exactly what the controller said and what he heard.

We taped it, and we came back the next day and briefed the administrator, Admiral Engen, on what happened. He wanted a five-minute briefing. After we started the briefing, he wanted to know if he could see the video. We put the video on; he watched the video, the whole video.

The next day he [Admiral Engen] set up a meeting [. . .]. That morning, in the FAA round room, [. . .] three men from Reagan's scientific staff, three CIA people, three FBI people, and I don't remember who the other guys were, along with all the FAA experts that I had brought with me that [. . .] could talk about the hardware and software and how it worked—we put on a "dog and pony show." We let them watch the video, we had all the data there, we had all the printouts that the computer put out. They got all excited over it. When it was all done, one of the CIA men told the people they were now sworn to secrecy, that this meeting never happened, and this event never happened, when I asked him, "Why?" I thought it was probably just the stealth bomber at the time. He said, "Well, this is the first time that we have recorded radar data on a UFO [. . .]." So I said, "Well, you're gonna tell the public about it." He said, "No. We don't tell the public about this. It would panic the public." He says, "We're gonna go back and study this."

Now, I have told this story many times, and I sometimes get funny looks from people. I have with me the voice tapes of the controllers that were involved, the FAA original tapes. You see, after we handed this stuff off to the president's staff, the FAA didn't know what to do with it—we don't separate UFOs from real traffic, so it's not our problem. [Laughter]

I have a copy of the original video that we took, which is rather interesting. And, once the thing was all over, the reports started coming into my office, but because it wasn't an FAA air traffic problem, the FAA's report ended up on a table in my office. It stayed there until I retired, when the staffers packed up all my gear and helped me move to my house. Also, in a box I found just a few days ago, with my 1992 tax returns, I have the target printouts from the computer data, and so if you want to look at every target that was up there at the time, you could now reproduce this from this piece of paper here. And it's called the UFO Incident, Japan 1648, I believe the number was. It happened on November 18th, 1986.

I am prepared to go before Congress—to swear before Congress—that everything I have told you people and that everything that is here is the truth. Thank you.

—John Callahan,
FAA Head of Accidents and Investigations

Used by permission of the Disclosure Project

23

The sanctuary is called the "War Room," a place where the forces of light engage in battle against darkness.

Kabbalist Philip S. Berg, better known as the Rav, stands before his congregation at the lectern. "This morning's Torah portion of Korach is found in Numbers 16 through 18. Back in Egypt, Korach had been a very powerful man; but in the desert he was forced to follow Moses and his brother, Aaron. This did not sit well with Korach's wife, who was constantly nagging him about how Moses had everything that Korach deserved. But blaming Korach's wife does not explain everything about Korach's fall from grace.

"Because he was rich, Korach believed he was better than everyone else, including Moses. Convinced he was the best man to lead the Israelites, he organized a rebellion, convening 250 members of the tribe of Reuben—elected men of the assembly, men of renown. Standing before these righteous men, Korach accused Moses of leading the Israelites out of Egypt, a land of milk and honey, into the hardship of wandering the desert. And Korach's followers bought into this evil tongue and threatened to overthrow Moses and his brother. In response, Moses prayed to God to reveal to him his own negativity, seeking to transform his own behavior so he could grow.

"Because of his knowledge, Korach had it in him to be a great leader. Where did he fail? A clue can be found in the first word of this portion—*vayikach,* which means, 'and he took.' For all his wealth, for all his wisdom and leadership ability, Korach was a taker, and that was his undoing, for when a person wishes only to receive, the outcome can only be negative."

Julius Gabriel glances at the dark-haired man seated next to him. Samuel Agler's black eyes are intense as he absorbs the Rav's words. Looking back over his shoulder, the archaeologist scans the back of the War Room for his son.

"Korach possessed an evil eye. The first mention of the evil eye is in Genesis and is attributed to the serpent, who was envious of Adam because he had Eve. Remember, this was no ordinary snake, it could stand up and speak. It was cunning. The evil eye covets. What did Korach covet? He coveted Moses's power, he sought recognition. Not so bad, except Korach was a taker. The lesson here is that, no matter what we have, we must transform ourselves from receivers to givers. Korach never achieved that vital inner transformation; in the end he paid for his lack of humility, as did his followers."

They are seated in the lobby—Sam, Laura, and Sophia. Julius is pacing, working his temper into a lather, when Mick finally walks in, a dark-haired Mexican beauty on his arm.

"Hey, Pop."

"You're late."

"Okay, no big deal. Adelina and I had an important errand to run. Go ahead, show them."

Adelina holds out her left hand, her fourth finger sporting a two-karat diamond ring. "Miguel asked me to marry him . . . we're engaged!"

Laura gives Adelina Botello a big hug. Sam slaps Michael across the shoulders.

Julius looks horrified. "What are you doing? What did I tell you?"

"Easy, Pop."

"She's not the one, Michael, I told you that! What's wrong with you? Are you willing to throw your entire future away—mankind's future—on this . . . this whore?"

Heads turn.

Sophia smirks.

Laura's jaw drops. "Julius—"

"Stay out of this, Laura. Michael knows I'm speaking for your family as much as anyone."

Adelina turns to Mick, tears of anger in her eyes. "Are you going to let him insult me like this?"

"No, babe. Come on, we're history." Casting a look of hatred at his father, Michael Gabriel takes his fiancée by the hand and leads her out of the Centre.

"The deputy secretary will see you now." The petite blond office manager leads Senator Ennis Chaney down a short hall to the double-door chamber of the deputy under secretary of defense.

Pierre Borgia never looks up from a stack of files spread across his oak desk. "Senator Chaney, what a pleasant surprise."

"This meeting is six months overdue, and the only reason we're speaking now is because Senator Maller owed me a favor. As chairman of the Appropriations Committee—"

"Vice chairman."

"You want to keep playing games? I can play, too. How 'bout I start with a press conference announcing the Pentagon misplaced $2.3 trillion of taxpayer dollars?"

"Secretary Rumsfeld is already investigating the matter."

"That's reassuring. Sorta like asking the fox to investigate a bunch of missing chickens at the henhouse."

"I'm sure whatever funds you're alluding to were earmarked for projects outside the jurisdiction of Congressional oversight. That's the nature of the military."

"My ass. For two trillion, you could send the entire Marine Corps to the moon. What the hell are you people up to?"

"We're safeguarding democracy, Senator. It's an expensive process."

"And how exactly is that little power plant you got zapping the atmosphere up in Alaska safeguarding democracy?"

"HAARP is nothing more than an aurora research program."

"Mind control? Earthquakes in Peru?"

Borgia grins. "You surf too many conspiracy theory Web sites."

"Save it for the Congressional hearing."

"Crawl out on that limb, Senator, and you crawl out alone. The GOP will leave you tossing in the wind."

"Been there, done that. How do you think I managed to stay in office? On my good looks?"

"There's a war going on, Senator. You may not see it or understand it, but it's a war, nonetheless."

"A war?"

"A war that will determine which nation will govern the planet in the decades to come."

"Nation or class?"

Borgia returns to his work. "This conversation is over."

"Fine by me. Guess I'll have to subpoena your Uncle Joe, seeing as he was playing the role of Grand Wizard at the Star Trek convention your black op geeks were holding up in Alaska. Funny thing about your uncle— even though he's listed as a military contractor, over a trillion dollars in Pentagon funds are quietly being funneled through his offshore companies into Skunk Works programs in the Nevada desert."

The smile on the deputy secretary's face disappears. "What is it you want?"

"Accountability, for starters. I want to hear your boss explain to the American people how $2.3 trillion somehow got 'misplaced.' Then I want the money accounted for."

"Why? You trying to be a hero? Maybe take a run for the Oval Office in 2008?"

"No, Mr. Borgia. I'm just trying to keep assholes like you from destroying the world."

273

The Final Papers of
Julius Gabriel, PhD

Cambridge University archives

Few men are willing to brave the disapproval of their fellows, the censure of their colleagues, the wrath of their society. Moral courage is a rarer commodity than bravery in battle or great intelligence. Yet it is the one essential, vital quality for those who seek to change a world which yields most painfully to change.

—ROBERT F. KENNEDY,

DAY OF AFFIRMATION ADDRESS,

UNIVERSITY OF CAPETOWN,

JUNE 6, 1966

AUGUST 23, 2001

*P*hobos: *A Greek term meaning "morbid fear."*
    Fear: A state of mind, inducing anxiety.
    On this, the eve of my symposium, my mind is consumed with anxiety, for the final piece of the Mayan Doomsday puzzle has now been laid into place, perhaps for the first time since the cursed priests of the Spanish Inquisition burned the Mayan codices

left behind by Chilam Balam. Five centuries after the Jaguar Prophet attempted to warn us of things to come I am fearful whether my own words will make a difference.

They must. Our existence depends upon it.

The Mayan calendar is composed of five great cycles, subdivided into repeating twenty-year epochs, known as katums. According to Chilam Balam, the final katum of cycle five began in 1992 and ends on December 21, 2012. During that time, Balam predicts a decade of peace and prosperity will end when a charismatic leader shall be felled by his own growing ego, his fall from grace beckoning the forces of darkness.

A great deception shall follow, designed to unite the masses behind new false prophets. War will ensue, propelled by an agenda ripe with corruption, resulting in an imbalance that uproots morality and radicalizes the king-makers.

Divided into the powerful and the oppressed, the fabric of society shall unravel. And in the melee that ensues, Nature shall cause the planet to tremble.

Five great cycles. According to the surviving codices, each of the previous four had been terminated by earthquake, wind, fire, then water—the four sacred elements. According to Balam, it is during the last cycle that a fifth element shall come into play—an element responsible for the creation of the physical universe and ultimately its destruction:

The atom.

Desiring to know the Creator, man had studied the atom.

Desiring to kill his brother, man had split the atom.

Desiring to be the Creator, man was now colliding the atom, re-creating the Big Bang, ignoring the inherent dangers. The strangelet was man's unbridled ego run amok, a fourth-dimensional cancer cell of gravity hellbent on consuming anything in its path.

It was simple cause and effect. Chilam Balam had understood it, and had painstakingly left us many clues—including one I had long ignored.

Archaeologists had unearthed more than a dozen crystal skulls over the last century, though only a few had traced back to Chilam Balam. Both Michael and I had dismissed these quartz artifacts after learning that the mineral was not unique to Mesoamerica, its shallow deposits spread beneath twelve percent of the Earth's crust.

And yet it is quartz that finally connected the dots.

Ironically, it was my own great-grandchild, Sophia, disguised by a hiccup of time as my niece, who recently forced me to reexamine the skulls. After I gave the child a quartz skull for her last birthday, she presented me with a mind-boggling theory.

"Did you know, Uncle Julius, that quartz can resonate with brain waves, that it can even affect the creative process? The skull you gave me has given me vivid dreams—nightmares of the Doomsday still to come. It is as if I have been channeling Chilam Balam himself."

"Tell me about the dreams."

"Each begins with a volcanic eruption. This is followed by an earthquake, which releases a tsunami. Fire, wind, earth, and water—the four elements tied together by the presence of quartz. I think that is the meaning of the crystal skulls, that they trigger the relationship."

"I see the relationship between fire and wind, earth and water, but nothing more. Nor do I see how quartz can trigger these violent acts of nature."

Sophia then presented me with a geological map detailing the world's known quartz deposits. "Do you recognize a pattern, Uncle Julius?"

"Nothing stands out."

"Look closely. The quartz deposits match the planet's seismic fault lines."

The child was right, they did match. The question was—what did it mean?

I consulted a geologist, who found the idea intriguing, concurring that fault lines in California, Utah, Nevada, and Idaho could be identified by the states' quartz deposits. He informed me that the mineral contained water, which when heated under pressure could indeed serve as a geological lubricant for rocks to slide and grinding tectonic plates to flow. He promised to research the theory further when he returned from a three-year field trip to Indonesia, though I wondered how Sophia's revelation would help resolve the Doomsday prophecy.

And then I thought about the strangelet.

According to physicists, these theoretical miniature black holes, created when atoms were deliberately collided at near-light speed, could escape their manmade boundaries and pass through the planet's core, seeking protons upon which to feed.

Assuming a strangelet were to be created by one of these massive colliders, would the feasting singularity somehow forge a molecular attraction to the unique properties and resonance found in quartz? If so, then these mineral deposits—shadowing geological fault lines—would serve as a beacon to this gradually enlarging black hole. With each pass through the planet's crust the strangelet would grow larger; as 2012 approached these seismic events, triggered in effect by the singularity, would grow far more destructive.

Earthquakes, volcanoes, tsunamis . . . harbingers of a far more destructive force—a force created by man—a black hole large enough to atomize and consume our entire planet.

May the Creator shed mercy on our foolhardiness.

J.G.

2 4

The sold-out crowd files into the second-floor auditorium—professors and scholars, archaeology majors and graduate students, and members of the local media—along with a bizarre cross-segment of UFOologists. Today will mark Julius Gabriel's first public appearance in more than a decade, and word has spread among the fringe elements that the aging professor intends to unveil "shocking new evidence" that supports forty years of "forbidden archaeology."

The guest speaker sits alone in his dressing room before a lighted mirror, the bright bare bulbs revealing every wrinkle and stress line that defines his weathered face. *A miniature Nazca plateau*, his internal voice comments, the thought dispersed into the ether by the knock on his door.

"Michael?"

The door opens, revealing Sam, Laura, and his "niece," Sophia.

"Laura, where's my son?"

The turquoise-eyed beauty glances at her husband for support. "Julius, we talked about this three days ago. Michael and Adelina eloped. They're scheduled to fly to Paris this morning for their honeymoon."

The words puncture his chest cavity like a dagger, the sudden stress causing the blood vessels leading to his heart to constrict.

Sam catches him as he doubles over. Laura searches his jacket pocket and retrieves the pill bottle. She quickly pops open the lid and fishes out a small white tablet, placing it under Julius's tongue.

The melting nitroglycerin pill quickly relaxes the damaged cardiac vessels, returning color to Julius Gabriel's face. He sits back in the canvas chair, exhaling phlegm-laced breaths.

Laura holds a cup of water to his lips. "Sam, I can handle this. Take Sophia out of here, I'll meet you at our seats."

"Come on, Sophie." Sam leads his daughter out of the dressing room, closing the door behind them.

"Julius, it's not too late to cancel."

"Cancel? Have you any idea what's at stake? I'm not canceling anything. Death robbed me of my soul mate, lust stole my son . . . who else is there to see this through? Go on, join your family, I'll be fine."

She shakes her head and opens the door to leave—nearly colliding with Pierre Borgia. The deputy under secretary of defense is standing in the outer hall staring at Laura, transfixed by her eyes. "Do I know you?"

"No, and let's keep it that way." She pushes past him, walking quickly down the corridor.

"Julius, who was that?"

"Laura Agler. Maria's younger sister."

"I didn't know Maria had a younger sister. Is it possible . . ."

"What is it you want, Pierre?"

"Just to wish you luck. And to remind you those military nondisclosure agreements remain in force." He picks up the prescription bottle with his right hand, reading the label. "Amazing how a man-made ingredient designed to blow things up can also be used to save one's life."

He returns it to Julius using his left hand, watching as the archaeologist slips the bottle into his jacket pocket. "We're onstage in ten. You'll enjoy my intro, it should really wet the crowd's panties."

The stage is divided by the two matching daises, the backdrop a thirty-by-forty-foot projection screen.

A female voice over the speaker system quiets the crowd. "Ladies and gentlemen, faculty and guests—Harvard University and the Kennedy School of Government welcomes you to another seminar of the sciences. Please welcome our host for this morning's event, the deputy under secretary of defense and a former Harvard undergrad, Dr. Pierre Robert Borgia."

Pierre strides to his dais, waving to an audience no longer visible beyond the bright stage lights. "Good morning. It is an honor to have been selected to introduce today's guest speaker. Professor Julius Gabriel and I studied together at Cambridge University nearly four decades ago, then spent the next three years together in the field with another colleague, the late Maria Rosen. Professor Gabriel's theories regarding the influence of extraterrestrial intelligence on ancient cultures are as legendary in the field of archaeology as they are controversial. I've more to add, but before I do, let's bring him out onstage, shall we? Ladies and gentlemen, Professor Julius Gabriel."

279

Julius hobbles out from behind a curtain, offering a half-wave as he manages his way to his podium.

Seated in the third row with his family, Samuel Agler stares at the wolfish leer on Pierre Borgia's face, the hairs on the back of his neck standing on end.

"Well, Julius, here we are, together again after our tumultuous breakup. You once taught me that the pursuit of truth remains its own cause. With that in mind, I'd like to expand my introduction just a few moments longer, before you engage the audience in your romantic theories of extraterrestrial intervention."

A rush of anxiety; Julius feels his left arm begin to throb.

"Ladies and gentlemen, last week an independent filmmaker in Hollywood sent me this short video clip—a behind-the-scenes account of a longer reel—a reel Professor Gabriel financed and developed in order to substantiate the inane theories he's about to feed you. Roll the footage."

An image illuminates the big screen, revealing Julius Gabriel seated in a horseshoe-shaped chamber surrounded by recording equipment—facing a small gray-skinned alien. There is no audio, the only sound provided by the hushed tones of the crowd.

"What you are witnessing is an alleged interview that Professor Gabriel will swear took place in a subterranean location somewhere near Area 51. In fact, the footage was filmed in a small sound stage in Nevada, and the supposed 'E.T.' was this little guy—"

From the podium cabinet Borgia removes a five-foot puppet identical to the extraterrestrial on the screen.

Julius grips the edge of his dais, his body trembling. "You lying bastard. You set me up!"

"You set us all up, Professor. The Mayan Doomsday prophecy is nonsense, your extraterrestrial theories regarding the evolution of modern man are ridiculous, and your presence here is an embarrassment to this university."

Unsure how to react, some members of the audience boo, others stand and toss their programs onstage. Borgia plays up to the crowd's angst, exhorting them on.

Julius gasps for air like a fish out of water, his chest constricting, his heart squeezed behind death's vise. He staggers away from the podium—

—Sam bounding over two rows, leaping onstage, catching him as he tumbles behind the curtain's edge. Kneeling, he holds the elder man to his chest with one arm while his free hand searches his jacket pocket, retrieving the prescription bottle. Popping the lid with his teeth, Sam dumps the pills onto his pant leg and examines one of the small white tablets.

"What the hell? These aren't your pills, they're breath mints!"

Julius gazes up at him wearily. "Borgia."

Sam turns, only Julius squeezes his hand. "My time's up, this is as far as I go. It's up to you now, Manny."

"Manny?" A rush of adrenaline jolts Sam's being like an electrical charge.

"I know who you are, I know why you are here. Our time together . . . a gift from the Upper Realm. Chaos is upon us, unleashing ripples of hatred and destruction. The monster who chased you from your time shall emerge as it was intended to in mine. Only One Hunahpu can save humanity. And you are not he."

"One Hunahpu? Julius, who is he? Who am I? Tell me, please!"

"I can't." The old man smiles with tear-filled eyes. "These are uncharted waters, son. Mind the helm."

The weight on his chest grows heavy as Julius Gabriel's soul abandons its physical vessel.

Sam cradles the lifeless body for a long moment. When he looks up, his wife and daughter are hovering over him—ushering in the sound of the auditorium and the heckling jousts of Pierre Borgia.

A torrent of hot blood rushes through Samuel Agler's being. "Wait here."

Borgia never sees him coming. One moment he is exhorting the crowd into a feverish frenzy—the next he is writhing on his back, the *craaack* of his occipital bone terminating in darkness.

Adelina Botello-Gabriel applies a fresh coat of lipstick, purposely nudging her husband awake with her elbow.

Michael Gabriel opens his eyes. "Are we boarding?"

"Not yet, darling. Why don't you get us each another coffee?"

"Yeah, sure." Standing, Mick weaves his way through rows of seats crowded with passengers and their carry-on bags. Leaving gate C-47, he scans the overseas terminal for the nearest snack bar—his ears perking at the sound of his last name.

"... Professor Gabriel was pronounced dead at the scene. No word yet on the extent of the under secretary's injury or the identity of his assailant."

Michael Gabriel stares at the televised news report, his limbs trembling. He waits until the story changes, then dashes back to Adelina.

"My father's dead! He died of a heart attack."

"Michael, calm yourself—"

"I just saw it on TV. Adelina, we can't go to Paris, we need to get to Boston."

Her pager buzzes in her purse. She glances at the text message.

"Who is it? Is it about my father?"

"As a matter of fact, it is."

"Well? What did it say?"

"It said the marriage is over. I'm sorry." She stands, gathering her belongings. "Not that it wasn't fun. What you lack in social skills you more than made up for in bed. I was going to tell you in Paris—"

"What are you talking about?"

"The priest was an actor, Michael. We were never married. Our meeting—this entire relationship—it was a sham. My job was to get close—"

He grabs her arm, his grip cutting off her circulation. "Who hired you?"

"I don't know . . . you're hurting me! Help! Officer!"

281

Two airport security men hear her pleas, approaching from the next gate. Mick pulls her in close so that their lips are nearly touching. "We'll meet again. Until then, I'd be very afraid."

He releases her, then grabs his carry-on bag and disappears in the crowd.

25

On September 10, Secretary of Defense Donald Rumsfeld
declared war. Not on foreign terrorists, "the adversary's
closer to home. It's the Pentagon bureaucracy." [. . .]
Rumsfeld promised change but the next day—September
11—the world changed and in the rush to fund the war on
terrorism, the war on waste seems to have been forgotten.
"According to some estimates we cannot track $2.3 trillion
in transactions," Rumsfeld admitted.

—VINCE GONZALES,

CBS NEWS CORRESPONDENT

MIDDLESEX JAIL

CAMBRIDGE, MASSACHUSETTS

NOVEMBER 21, 2001

Built in 1971, the Middlesex Jail is a maximum-security
facility occupying the upper floors of the same high-
rise building that holds the Cambridge Superior Court-
house. Detainees housed in these cells are awaiting trial or
sentencing.

The man being held in solitary has already been

pronounced guilty by Justice James Thompson, a judge who owes his appointment on the bench to Republican Congressman Robert Borgia.

The deputy escorts the VIP with the heavy bandages over his right eye through a short corridor leading to the isolation cell. A folding chair and a bottled water are situated ten feet from the iron bars. The prisoner sits on the edge of his mattress, waiting.

"Thank you, deputy. Again, the video camera has been disabled?"

"Yes, sir, just as you requested. Press the buzzer by the door when you're ready to leave."

Pierre Borgia waits until his police escort has left before settling himself uncomfortably in the cheap metal folding chair. "Samuel Agler. No registered fingerprints, no birth certificate, no country of origin. According to Intel, prior to 1990 you didn't exist. And please, let's forgo that 'third world orphan' story your court-appointed attorney spewed to the judge. I want to know who you really are."

The athletic man filling out the orange jumpsuit remains emotionless, his black eyes scanning the unbandaged half of his interrogator's face. "That looks painful. Does it bother you much not having a right eye?"

Borgia's mouth twitches into a forced smile. "Push my buttons all you want, my friend, but know this: I have your wife and I have your daughter."

Samuel remains seated, his jaw muscles flexing as he grinds his teeth.

"A most amazing child. A most amazing wife. To think that Maria Rosen's little sister was a Nordic . . . I mean, speaking of small worlds . . . or should I say, extraterrestrial worlds. I only wish Julius was still alive so I could tell him."

"My wife is from Britain, she was raised in Spain. Whatever game you're playing—"

"I assure you, this isn't a game. My team is going to learn all we can from your wife and daughter while they're still alive, then after we see how much torture they can endure we'll carve up their remains and analyze their internal organs. You, however, won't be so lucky. On my family's suggestion, Judge Thompson has decided to send you to a mental asylum where you'll spend the rest of your days in solitary confinement. Alone, you can think about all the nasty little things I'll be doing to your family while the staff periodically amuses themselves with your wretched existence."

Borgia stands to leave.

"You want to know who I am? You *know* who I am . . . Seven Macaw."

Borgia freezes, his head cocked to one side. After a long moment he turns to speak, his one bloodshot eye blazing red, his voice a throaty rasp. "Chilam Balam?"

Sam stands, gripping the bars. "The prophet's in my consciousness. He sees you hiding in that sickening bag of flesh. He smells your sulphurous essence. Only he won't tell me who I am or why I'm here."

The soul inhabiting Pierre Borgia's vessel paces slowly before the cell. "You are here because I am here. With each incarnation it seems our paths must cross, as if our own unfinished business is what loops the cosmos. And yet with each intersection darkness trumps the light. Do you understand the inherent meaning behind these circumstances, prophet? It means the Creator desires the darkness to inhabit the physical realm. It means He no longer cares about His creation. His indifference fuels Satan's resolve—before you die, you'll bear witness to his glorious resurrection."

285

Large Hadron Collider to Resume Operations at CERN

February 22, 2010

This month marks the resumption of operations at the Large Hadron Collider (LHC), the huge new experimental device operated by the European Organization for Nuclear Research (CERN) in Switzerland. The largest and costliest apparatus ever built to conduct physical research, the LHC was shut down for repairs for a year after an accident.

The LHC is to resume low-power operation early this week (February 22-24), and is scheduled to run at half-power sometime in March. CERN engineers decided last month at a meeting in Chamonix, France, to limit the collider to half power, about 3.5 trillion electron volts (TeV) for the next 18 to 24 months.

The LHC operated for less than a month last year, from November 23 to December 20, as part of the process of recovery from the accident that occurred September 19, 2008. A slightly misaligned magnet caused the LHC beam to vaporize six tons of liquid helium coolant, causing an explosion inside the detector.

During the experimental re-start, the two beams of the LHC were centered and stable. Each beam was operating at 900 gigaelectronvolts (GeV), or about 13% of the full energy. At these energies, the first confirmed collisions of the LHC were found.

—Bryan Dyne - wsws.org

Widespread Destruction from Japan Earthquake, Tsunamis

March 11, 2011

Japan was struck by the most powerful earthquake to hit the island nation in recorded history. The 9.0 magnitude temblor, which was centered near the east coast of Japan, killed hundreds of people and caused the formation of 30-foot walls of water that swept across rice fields, engulfed entire towns, dragged houses onto highways, and tossed cars and boats like toys. Some waves reached six miles (10 kilometers) inland in Miyagi Prefecture on Japan's east coast.

The devastating earthquake and tsunami actually moved the island closer to the United States and shifted the planet's axis. The quake caused a rift 15 miles below the sea floor that stretched 186 miles long and 93 miles wide. The areas closest to the epicenter of the quake jumped a full 13 feet closer to the United States, according to geophysicist Ross Stein at the United States Geological Survey. The 9.0 magnitude quake was caused when the Pacific tectonic plate dove under the North American plate, which shifted Eastern Japan towards North America by about 13 feet. The quake also shifted the earth's axis by 6.5 inches, shortened the day by 1.6 microseconds, and sank Japan downward by about two feet. As Japan's eastern coastline sunk, the tsunami's waves rolled in.

Why did the quake shorten the day? The earth's mass shifted towards the center, spurring the planet to spin a bit faster. Last year's massive 8.8 magnitude earthquake in Chile also shortened the day, but by an even smaller fraction of a second. The 2004 Sumatra quake knocked a whopping 6.8 micro-seconds off the day.

Note: The Shinmoedake volcano, located on Japan's southern island of Kyushu, 950 miles from the earthquake's epicenter, erupted on January 19. It spewed ash and rocks two days after the 9.0 event.

26

Eleven Years Later . . .

CHICHEN ITZA
YUCATAN PENINSULA
MARCH 21, 2012 (SPRING EQUINOX)

The pilgrims have been arriving steadily throughout the day, the parking lot filled with tour buses and rental cars, the gates of the state-owned park clogged with long lines. The entering masses follow a worn earthen path—a time portal that leads them a thousand years into the past.

In Mayan, Chichen Itza translates as "mouth of the well of the water wizard," a reference to Kukulcan and the city's sacred cenote. Surrounded by dense tropical jungle, the ancient capital's layout remains virtually unchanged—an oasis of flat open expanses and limestone structures interconnected by earthen-paved roads called *sacbe*. Chichen Itza is divided into several subsections, and its main attraction is the Great North Platform, a massive public gathering place featuring the Temple of the Warriors, the Great Ball Court, and the most magnificent structure in the Yucatan—the Kukulcan Pyramid.

The crowd gathers around the Kukulcan's northern balustrade, the first day of spring igniting a carnival atmosphere. Drums beat to traditional music as anticipation of the approaching vernal event builds. According to legend, twice each year when the day and night are equal, Kukulcan's spirit returns to his worshipers, the great teacher's arrival precipitated by the appearance of the shadow of a feathered serpent along the northern balustrade. As the sun rises in the sky, the snake's seven segments elongate, until it gradually slithers down the steps and reconnects with its disembodied head at the bottom of the pyramid.

The crowd cheers the mid-afternoon sun as the first of the creature's triangles darkens a section of the limestone facade—the shadow created by the architecture's precise alignment to the natural rotation of the Earth and sun.

Twenty feet below ancient stone that has borne witness to the conception and demise of an entire nation lies a second temple. Smaller and older, it remains concealed within the Kukulcan like an infant inhabiting its mother's womb. Follow an excavated tunnel along the northern side of the larger structure and one enters a claustrophobic access sealed in block, the limestone slick and sweating. A narrow claustrophobia-inducing flight of steps leads to a small chamber guarded by a stone *chacmool*—a gem-laced carving of a jaguar.

Seated alone before the idol beneath 100,000 tons of pyramid is Michael Gabriel. The thirty-seven-year-old son of the late Julius and Maria Gabriel suffers an existence of loneliness, anger, and angst. He is a man chained to and isolated by a mission, his only contact with other humans defined by the acquaintances reconnoitered on his annual migrations between Nazca and Chichen Itza.

Excised from his routine are the once-frequent trips to Cambridge, Massachusetts, where his appeals regarding the sentencing and imprisonment of his yet-to-be-born biological son, Samuel Agler, have been stonewalled for years. The only spark of daylight—a recent disclosure that the antiquated mental asylum was closing and that all patients would be relocated to facilities located throughout the country.

Samuel Agler has been transferred to the South Florida Evaluation and Treatment Center in Miami, Florida.

One way or another, Michael Gabriel intends to get him out . . . and the clock is ticking.

With the arrival of the 2012 vernal equinox, the Doomsday Event is now a mere nine months away. Despite exhaustive field work, Mick is no closer to resolving the Mayan mystery than his parents had been. It was as if his son's mysterious appearance had reshuffled the deck on forty years of research. Compounding the problem was the government's refusal to discuss the disappearance of his Aunt Laura and his niece, Sophia, and the more he inquired, the closer he came to being "disappeared" himself.

That translated to a Majestic-12 threat, which meant Laura and Sophia were being held somewhere in Area 51, assuming they were still alive.

The muffled acoustics of the crowd's cheers cause him to look up at the jaguar figure. Chilam Balam had known all the pieces of the Doomsday puzzle. Samuel Agler was convinced he was an incarnation of the Jaguar Prophet. After Sam's eleven years in solitary confinement, Mick prays there is a lucid stream left to mine in his son's consciousness.

He glances at his watch. The charter plane from Merida landed twenty minutes ago, the passenger having arrived from her foster parents' home in Tampa, Florida.

Mick makes his way down the slippery limestone steps, then out the excavated tunnel's sealed door into daylight.

Beginning at the two serpent heads located at the base of the Kukulcan Pyramid, the *sacbe* runs north through the dense jungle for nearly a mile before ending at the sacred cenote. The elevated earthen walkway is lined with Mayan men and women selling their wares, the "authentic" pottery and blankets, statues and obsidian daggers all supplied by the same Mexican manufacturer.

The feisty Mayan woman is in her sixties, her turquoise-blue eyes accentuated by her high cheekbones. She is seated in a canvas folding chair, smoking a hand-rolled cigarette, shaking her head at an American couple bartering over a figure of a Mayan warrior shooting an arrow into the air.

Mick waits until they leave before approaching the old woman, dropping a thick wad of twenty-dollar bills onto her lap.

Chicahua Aurelia glances up at the tall, dark American, his eyes concealed behind sunglasses. "What do you wish to buy?"

"A conversation. With your niece."

"My niece?"

"Dominique Vazquez. She arrived on the commuter flight from Merida. I need to speak with her about something important."

"My *niece* speaks her own mind. She does not need an old woman to barter her conversations."

"She refuses to speak with me. Believe me, I've tried."

"What is it you need to discuss?"

"Dominique was recently awarded an internship to work in a mental asylum in Florida. My connections inform me she was selected for a particular patient. The patient is a relative of mine . . . an older half brother. I need to get word to him . . . to communicate with him."

"Why not simply arrange a visit?"

"He's been denied all visitation rights. Eleven years ago he attacked a very powerful man . . . a dark soul. As my brother suffers, humanity suffers."

"How so?"

"My older brother possesses knowledge that could prevent the calendar's prophecy—"

"You again? I don't believe it." The thirty-one-year-old Guatemalan beauty with the high cheekbones and waist-length, jet-black hair approaches Mick like an angry tiger. Before he can expel a word, she drives her right leg into a vicious front thrust kick, the martial-arts expert's sandaled foot striking the archaeologist in his sternum, launching him backward into the jungle thicket.

"Dominique!"

"Chicahua, this man's been stalking me for three weeks." Dominique grabs an obsidian dagger from the old woman's display table.

Mick quickly springs to his feet, taking refuge behind an Acai tree. "I'm not stalking you! I just need to talk—"

Wielding the blade like an expert, she slices the air in tight figure eights, carving up an entanglement of leaves.

"Dominique, put that knife away. Now!"

She hesitates, then backs away, tossing the blade back on the table.

The old woman turns to Mick. "What is your name?"

"Michael Gabriel. I'm an archaeologist, not a stalker."

"You're an asshole."

"Enough." Chicahua waves for him to come closer. "Give me your hand."

Mick allows the old woman to examine his right palm. Chicahua closes her eyes, her fingers palpating his life line and pulse.

Her eyes reopen. For a long uncomfortable moment she simply stares into Mick's black irises, then, tearing a piece of paper from her receipt book, she scrawls something in pen.

The old woman hands him the information, returning his money. "This is my address in Pisté. You will join us tonight for dinner. Arrive at eight o'clock."

"Thank you." He nods to Dominique, then leaves.

The dark-haired beauty shakes her head. "Why?"

Chicahua Aurelia kisses her daughter's hand. "When I reconnected with you three years ago, you asked me the same question. You may not like the answer, nor will you understand it, but the reason I sent you away, only to reunite twenty years later, is so your journey would cross paths with that man."

THE WHITE HOUSE
WASHINGTON, D.C.

Secretary of State Pierre Robert Borgia stares at his reflection in the washroom mirror. He adjusts the patch over his right eye socket, then pats down the short graying tufts of hair along both sides of his otherwise balding head. The black suit and matching tie are immaculate as always.

Borgia exits the executive washroom and turns right, nodding to staff members as he makes his way down the corridor to the Oval Office.

Patsy Goodman looks up from her keyboard. "Go on in. He's waiting."

Mark Maller's gaunt, pale face shows the wear of having served as president for nearly four years. The jet-black hair has grayed around the temples, the eyes, piercing blue, are now more wrinkled around the edges. The former intercollegiate basketball player's physique, noticeably thinner, is still taut.

Borgia tells him he looks like he's lost weight.

Maller grimaces. "It's called stress. It's over between Heidi and me. Fortunately, she's agreed to keep everything quiet until after the November election."

"Sorry to hear that. I would have guessed Viktor Grozny."

"Yes, well, the Russian president has certainly contributed to my bleeding ulcer. Selling the Iranians those SS-27 mobile ICBMs was a deft move entering next week's G-20 summit."

"Sir, you can't shut down HAARP. There's only innuendo, no proof—"

"Pierre, I didn't call you in to discuss covert missile shields. Joe's decided to step down as vice president. Don't ask. Call it personal reasons. I've already held an unofficial meeting with the powers that be. It's between you and Ennis Chaney."

Borgia's heart skips a beat. "Have you spoken with him yet?"

"No. I wanted to brief you first."

"Senator Chaney is divisive to the party. He publicly challenges our presence in Afghanistan, he's been outspoken against Big Oil—"

"As have most Americans."

"Sir, we both know Chaney can't hold a candle to me when it comes to foreign affairs. And my family still wields plenty of influence—"

"Not as much as you think. Look, if it were strictly up to me, your name would be on the ticket, but the election's going to be tight. Chaney would give us a much needed toehold in both Pennsylvania and the South. Relax, Pierre. No decision's going to be made for at least another two weeks. But I need to know, are there any skeletons in your closet we need to be concerned with? Something the media will run with?"

"I'm clean."

"What about the incident back in 2001?"

"I was the victim, Mark. I lost an eye, for God's sake."

"You know how things will get spun. I'm only asking because my sources tell me your assailant is due for his annual medical evaluation, only this time he's in an institution that actually will evaluate his mental state. In other words, I wouldn't want him appearing on talk shows or attack ads come November."

"Mr. President, trust me—the lunatic who did this to me will never see the light of day."

PISTÉ, YUCATAN

Pisté is a small Yucatec town located a mile from Chichen Itza on Mexico's Route 180, its brightly painted stucco stores shelved with Mayan memorabilia. Beyond a block of shops sandwiched around a local inn lies a sleepy residential area, its indigenous populace entrenched in a simple life that rarely exceeds the city limits.

Day has stretched into dusk by the time Michael Gabriel maneuvers his motor scooter off the main drag through dirt streets inhabited by brown-skinned natives, barefoot children, and stray dogs. Locating the address,

Mick parks his ride close to the sitting porch of the one-story stucco dwelling and knocks on the screen. The interior door is open, releasing the scent of homemade cornbread.

Dominique greets him, wearing a one-piece ivory-colored frock and an attitude of indifference.

"For you." He hands her the bouquet of wildflowers.

"Whose garden did you steal these from?"

"I'm fine, thank you. Though my chest is bruised from your last greeting. Where'd you learn to kick like that?"

"You're the one doing the snooping, you tell me."

"I'm guessing cheerleader camp?"

He's rewarded with a quick flash of a smile that accentuates her cheekbones, lightening his heart. "You can come in, Mr. Gabriel, just keep in mind I know six different ways to kill a man."

"Hopefully cooking's not one of them." He follows her past a small sitting room to a kitchen where Chicahua is portioning food onto three colorful serving dishes.

"Come in, Mr. Gabriel. Doesn't my niece look beautiful this evening?"

"She does."

The old woman motions for him to sit at the dining room table. "I made some inquiries about you since our last meeting. Your father was Julius Gabriel, your mother was Maria Rosen. You spent many winters of your childhood living in this area while your parents continued their research. Your family has many allies among my people. What you don't have, Mr. Gabriel, is an older brother."

Mick's eyes water as beads of perspiration trickle down his armpit. "He's more of a half brother, I told you. Julius apparently sowed his wild oats before meeting my mother. Kind of embarrassing."

"Your mother's ancestry hails from South America?"

"Peru. But only on her maternal side."

"Dominique's maternal lineage traces back to the Itza. My great-grandmother claimed our family tree was rooted by Kukulcan himself."

"That's . . . impressive."

"I noticed you staring at my eyes earlier in the park. The shade is unusual, yes?"

"Mayan blue."

"You've seen this color before? Perhaps your half brother?"

"My aunt. My mother's younger sister."

"And where is your aunt now?"

Mick fights not to look away, wondering if the old woman can read his mind. "She's gone. She and her daughter went missing eleven years ago."

"And this older half brother of yours—the one locked up in the asylum—he may know where they are?"

"It's possible, yes. But he may also know what's going to happen in nine months."

"Nothing's going to happen in nine months," Dominique snaps. "This whole 2012 thing is just mythological nonsense—a morbid interpretation of the end of the calendar's natural cycle. A new cycle will begin the day after the winter solstice and life will go on."

Mick smirks. "Spoken by the woman whose bloodline traces back to the tall Caucasian whose knowledge of the cosmos caused a serpent's shadow to appear this afternoon on his pyramid."

"I wasn't raised in a Third World country like my aunt."

"You mean your mother, don't you? Or your biological father, a slave runner named Don Rafelo."

Chicahua's startled expression matches the girl's. "Who revealed this information?"

"Like you said, my family was close to your people, including members of the Sh'Tol brethren. The sacred society knows everything that goes on in their land."

Dominique turns to Chicahua. "You told me my father died long ago."

"He did. The day he turned to the dark side for his sorcery."

"Yet you chose to be with him? Why?"

"This is not for Mr. Gabriel's ears."

"You invited him into your home, let him hear it. Unless he already knows. Do you?"

Mick hesitates, feeling the old woman's eyes upon him. "Your father's bloodline belonged to Quetzalcoatl. I suspect he wanted to cross-pollinate the two lines."

"Cross-pollinate? What am I, a bee?"

"Actually, you'd be the flower."

"Shut up. In fact, I think it's time you left."

"I'll leave, but know this: before he died, my father spent decades investigating the origins of a superior race of humans whose Rh negative blood type traces back to the great teachers. I'm Rh negative, so are you, so is the man in the Miami asylum you'll be assigned to when you begin your graduate internship this summer. Is this man my brother? Not exactly. But if I told you any more, you'd probably cancel your internship, and then . . ." Mick pinches tears from his eyes, shaking his head as he chokes out a laugh. "God, this is crazy. Or maybe I'm the one who's crazy. I've been chasing ghosts for so long I don't know anymore."

"As a soon-to-be psychologist, I can probably get you committed."

The two of them share a laugh.

The old woman smiles.

Dinner is served.

MAJESTIC-12 (S-66) SUBTERRANEAN FACILITY

15 MILES SOUTH OF GROOM LAKE AIR FORCE BASE (AREA 51)

NORTH LAS VEGAS, NEVADA

As the late Julius Gabriel often said, there are basically two ways to boil a frog. The hard way was to toss him in a pot of boiling water and battle him until he croaked. The easier way was to leave him in a pot of cool water and gradually increase the temperature until he comfortably cooked to death.

It had taken Project Blue Eyes for Dr. Dave Mohr to realize that Majestic-12 had slowly cooked his morality in their crock pot of cynicism and greed. And though he was program director, he had also been around long enough to know titles at the S-66 facility were window dressing—that the real power came from an unseen board of directors whose objectives were based on profit, not science.

Mohr's assistant, Marvin Teperman, had finally forced the rocket scientist to "cowboy up" when the Canadian exobiologist and his staff flatly refused to subject Laura Agler and her daughter to any more medical procedures. Mohr's subsequent meeting with Joseph Randolph resolved the matter when the scientist convinced the MJ-12 supervisor that Laura's Hunahpu DNA had not yet "evolved." As such it was better to wait until after she had acquired her powers before beginning any invasive procedures.

For years the results from Laura Agler's bloodwork had remained stable. Then, six months ago, the thirty-nine-year-old's white cell count began rising steadily, driving her bone marrow to release higher numbers of stem cells into her blood vessels. At first Mohr suspected an infection, but further testing indicated the stem cells were targeting the woman's brain, causing the number of her neural synapses to increase.

Within weeks, Laura's sudden "evolution" progressed to her muscles and tendons, the fibers increasing in density, making her stronger, faster, and more flexible—all of which were very discreetly noted, lest MJ-12 be alerted.

296

Easier to disguise were the magnification and acuity of Laura's senses—especially her olfactory cells.

Laura Rosen Agler was evolving into a post-human, forcing Dave Mohr and Marvin Teperman into a decision: report the test results and condemn their subject to death, or risk their lives by altering the data and pray no one noticed.

For the two scientists, there was no debating the choice. Both had watched the Gray's life signs flatline on August 24, 2001—the E.T.'s death coinciding precisely with Julius Gabriel's own final breath. The experience had been devastating, compounded by sixteen months of postmortem work, after which the two men were debriefed on Project Blue Eyes.

By then, Laura and Sophia had been properly "indoctrinated" to their new existence in their Bio-2 habitat. Mohr and Teperman were incensed: to keep a mother and daughter locked up because they were suspected of possessing extraterrestrial DNA was barbaric, reminding Marvin of the Nazi reels he had seen of Joseph Mengele completing his gruesome experiments on Jewish children during the Holocaust. In the end the two scientists had agreed to run Blue Eyes for one reason—had they not, Joseph Randolph would have appointed two hardened military commanders to do the job, condemning the Agler women to quick lobotomies.

December 21, 2003—the day Dr. Dave Mohr had effectively climbed into his own pot of cold water.

Laura Agler's blood is simmering, her sweat-soaked body trembling as she stalks the common area of her "habitat." Eleven years have passed since Borgia's men stole her and Sophie from the real world—eleven years of mental anguish, of not knowing whether her husband, Sam, is alive or dead . . . or worse. Like a caged tigress she fought her captors and guarded her cub until she was finally felled by exhaustion—only her daughter's wry wit has kept her sane over the years. Having given in, her brainwaves gradually shifted from her aroused low-amplitude, faster Beta phase into the higher-frequency, far slower Delta waves.

And that's when she discovered the Nexus.

She had slipped inside the corridor one night just before dozing off, the sensation similar to an out-of-body experience. Entering this alternate realm of existence soothed her frayed nerves and brought a sense of warmth and calm, and with practice and patience she eventually learned to control the sessions. So as not to arouse her keepers, who kept her under round-the-clock observation, she requested a yoga DVD and used it as an excuse to meditate for hours at a time, pushing her mind deeper within her new cerebral domain.

Two days ago, she had heard the voice.

It happened on the vernal equinox, and instinctively she knew the nonsensical rants were coming from Sam. Was he dead? Or was he like her, able to enter the higher corridor of consciousness? She called out to him in the void, and the reply made her shudder.

"I am not Sam! Now leave me alone, witch. Disturb me again and I shall cast your Sam into the depths of Xibalba where the Underlords shall feast upon his eyes."

"If you are not my husband, then who are you?"

"Deceiver! Is it not enough that you have vanquished me to darkness and endless suffering? Must you toss your excrement at me? Shine a spotlight on my nakedness? Why has my existence attracted your wrath? No, witch, I shall perform for you no further. I am satiated with pain, your threats of torture are laughable. Go ahead! Bleed me until my wretched vessel drains, I don't care anymore. I don't care! I don't care! I don't care!"

The schizophrenic response, such overwhelming evidence of her husband's agonized existence, was too much for Laura to handle. Feeling utterly helpless, she had stormed into the exercise room, grabbed a ninety-pound dumbbell from a rack, and flung the weight into the hurricane glass, shattering the barrier into a million-piece jigsaw puzzle—

—the Herculean effort recorded on videotape, which would soon be watched by a dozen Majestic-12 eyes.

27

No problem can be solved from the same level of consciousness that created it.

—ATTRIBUTED TO ALBERT EINSTEIN

The South Florida Evaluation and Treatment Center is a seven-story white concrete building with
evergreen trim, located in a run-down ethnic neighborhood just west of the city of Miami. Like most businesses in the area, the rooftops are rimmed in coils of
barbed-wire fencing. Unlike other establishments, the
barbed wire is not meant to keep the public out, but its
residents in.

Dominique Vazquez weaves through morning rush
hour traffic, cursing aloud as she races south on Route
441. The first day of her internship and she is already
late. Swerving around a teenager riding the wrong way
on motorized skates, she pulls into the visitors parking

lot, squeezes into the first open space, and exits the car, jogging toward the entrance.

She is greeted by an air-conditioned lobby and a Hispanic woman seated behind the information desk, the receptionist absorbed in reading the morning news from her iPad. Without looking up, she asks, "Can I help you?"

"Yes. I have an appointment with Margaret Reinke."

"Not today you don't. Dr. Reinke no longer works here." The woman fingers the page-down button, advancing the news monitor to another article.

"I don't understand. I spoke with Dr. Reinke two weeks ago."

"And you are?"

"Dominique Vazquez. I'm here on a postgraduate internship from Florida State. Dr. Reinke's supposed to be my advisor."

She watches the woman pick up the phone and press an extension. "Dr. Foletta, a young woman by the name of Domino Vass—"

"Vazquez. Dominique Vazquez."

"Sorry. Dominique Vazquez. . . . No, sir, she's down here in the lobby. She says she's Dr. Reinke's intern. . . . Yes, sir." The receptionist hangs up. "You can have a seat over there. Dr. Foletta will be with you in a few minutes." Her job requirement fulfilled, the receptionist returns to her iPad.

Dominique sits, her mind racing. *Mick was right: Borgia replaced Reinke with Foletta.*

Ten minutes pass before a large man in his late fifties makes his way down a corridor.

Dr. Anthony Foletta looks like he belongs on a football field coaching defensive linemen, not walking the halls of a facility housing the criminally insane. A mane of thick gray hair rolls back over an enormous head, which appears to be attached directly to the shoulders. Blue-gray eyes twinkle between sleepy lids and puffy cheeks. Though overweight, the upper body is firm, the stomach protruding slightly from the open white lab coat.

A forced smile, and a thick hand is extended. "Anthony Foletta, chief of psychology." The voice is deep and grainy, like an old lawn mower.

"What happened to Dr. Reinke?"

"Personal situation. Rumor has it her husband was diagnosed with terminal cancer. Guess she decided to take an early retirement. Reinke told me to expect you. Unless you have any objections, I'll be supervising your internship."

"No objections."

"Good." He turns and heads back down the hall, Dominique hustling to keep pace.

They approach a security checkpoint. "Give the guard your driver's license."

Dominique searches her purse, then hands the man the laminated card, swapping it for the visitor's pass. "Use this for now," Foletta says. "Turn it in when you leave at the end of the day. We'll get you an encoded intern's badge before the week's out."

She clips the pass to her blouse, then follows him into the awaiting elevator.

Foletta holds three fingers up to a camera mounted above his head. The doors close. "Have you been here before? Are you familiar with the layout?"

"No. Dr. Reinke and I only spoke by phone."

"There are seven floors. Administration and central security's on the first floor. The main station we just passed through controls both the staff and resident elevators. Level 2 houses a small medical unit for the elderly and terminally ill. Level 3 is where you'll find our administrative offices, as well as our dining area and the mezzanine to access the yard. Levels 4, 5, 6, and 7 house residents." Foletta chuckles. "Dr. Blackwell refers to them as 'customers.' An interesting euphemism, don't you think, considering we haul them in here wearing handcuffs." They exit the elevator. A guard buzzes open the security gate, allowing them to enter the third floor and a short corridor to Dr. Foletta's office. Cardboard boxes are piled everywhere, stuffed with files, framed diplomas, and personal items.

"Excuse the mess, I'm still getting situated." Foletta removes a computer printer from a chair, motioning for Dominique to sit. Squeezing uncomfortably behind his own desk, he leans back in his leather chair to afford his belly ample room.

He opens Dominique's folder. "Good test scores, some nice references. There are several other mental facilities closer to FSU than ours. What brings you down here?"

Dominique clears her throat. "My parents live over in Sanibel. It's only a two-hour ride from Miami. They're getting up there in age and I don't get home very often."

Foletta guides a thick index finger across her bio. "Says here you're originally from Guatemala."

"Yes."

"How'd you end up in Florida?"

"My parents—my real parents died when I was six. I was sent to live with a cousin in Tampa."

"But that didn't last?"

"Is this important?"

Foletta looks up. The eyes are no longer sleepy. "I'm not much for surprises, Intern Vazquez. Before assigning a patient, I like to know a staff member's psyche. Most residents don't give us much of a problem, but it's important to remember that we're still dealing with some violent individuals. Safety's a priority with me. What happened in Tampa? Says here you ended up in a foster home."

"Suffice it to say that things didn't exactly work out with my cousin."

"Did he rape you?"

Dominique is taken back by his directness. "If you must know—yes. I was only ten . . . the first time."

"You were under the care of a psychiatrist?"

"Eventually." She returns his stare. *Stay cool, he's testing you.*

"Does it bother you to talk about it?"

"It happened. It's over. I'm sure it influenced my choice of career, if that's where this is leading."

"Your interests too. Says here you have a second-degree black belt in tae kwon do. Ever use it?"

"Only in tournaments." She smiles. "Recently in the Yucatan. I was on vacation. This guy, he pissed me off."

The cherub face breaks into a smile. "Nice." Foletta closes the file. "I have you in mind for a special assignment, but I need to be absolutely certain that you're up to the task."

Here it comes. "Sir, I can handle him."

"Him?" The blue-gray eyes become alert.

"Or her. It. Try me. I mean, I'm here to work, sir."

Foletta removes a thick brown file from his top desk drawer. "As you know, this facility believes in a multidisciplinary team approach. Each resident is assigned a psychiatrist, a clinical psychologist, social worker, psychiatric nurse, and a rehab therapist. My initial reaction when I first got here was that it's a bit overkill, but I can't argue with the results, especially when dealing with substance-abuse patients and preparing individuals to participate in their forthcoming trials."

"But not in this case?"

"No. The resident I want you to oversee is a patient of mine, an inmate from the asylum in Massachusetts where I served as managing director."

"I don't understand. You brought him with you?"

"Our facility was shut down for budgetary reasons. This particular patient is certainly not fit for society, and he had to be transferred somewhere.

Since I'm more familiar with his case history than anyone else, I thought it would be less traumatic for all concerned if he remained under my care."

"Who is he?"

"Officially, his name is Samuel Agler, though he hasn't responded to this name in eleven years. Unofficially, he's a complete mystery. No birth certificate, no past, at least none that we can find. But he's psychotic, and he's violent."

Dominique swallows hard. "What did he do?"

"He assaulted Secretary of State Pierre Borgia during a 2001 Harvard lecture. Claims his wife and daughter were stolen by 'men in black' and that a government conspiracy has kept him locked up all these years. In the Mule's mind—that's his nickname, the Mule, as in stubborn-as-a-mule. Samuel—he's the ultimate victim, an innocent man attempting to save the world, caught up in the immoral ambitions of a self-centered politician."

"I'm sorry, you lost me on that last bit. How is he trying to save the world?"

"Actually, the answer to that question is right up your family tree. Agler is a Mayan calendar fanatic. Our mystery man claims he was sent here to save humanity from destruction on December 21."

The top four floors of the asylum each house forty-eight residents in units divided into north and south wings, each wing containing three pods. A pod consisted of a small rec room with sofas and a television, centered around eight private dorm rooms. The center's most dangerous patients were housed on the seventh floor—the only floor that maintained its own security station.

Fifty-seven-year-old Paul Jones ran security on Level 7 the way he ran his prison block in Pulaski County, Arkansas. Dr. Foletta calls the guard over. "Paul Jones, this is my new intern, Dominique Vazquez. Is Mr. Agler ready for his interview?"

Jones looks uncomfortable. "He's in the seclusion room, as you requested, but frankly, sir, I wasn't expecting an unseasoned intern. If you ask me, there are far more stable candidates on Level 4—"

"No, I have my reasons. Take her in, I'll watch from behind the glass."

Jones mumbles something beneath his breath, then leads Dominique past the security gate and to a steel door marked "Seclusion room."

"Listen carefully: this guy may seem quiet, but he's a live wire, so no sudden movements." Jones holds up a cigar-shaped metal device, his thumb over a red button. "Remote transponder. All Level 7 patients are rigged with an ankle cuff, so if he tries anything I'll put him down fast. He may attempt to grab you first, so be leery or you'll wake up on the floor next to him with a new hairdo."

Dominique says nothing, her heart pounding too hard in her throat to speak.

Jones retracts a steel plate from the door, peering inside the holding cell. "Looks okay. Ready?"

"It's my first time."

"Congrats. Remember, no sudden movements. He's a tiger, but I have the whip."

"Why don't you give me the whip? And a chair."

"Trust me, you're safer with me holding it. Try to get him to speak, he hasn't done that since he arrived from Cambridge. Okay, in you go." Jones opens the steel door, allowing her to enter.

Samuel Agler is seated on the floor, leaning back against the far wall. He is wearing a white T-shirt and matching slacks, his physique lean and very muscular. He is tall—nearly six feet, six inches. His black hair is oily and long, running down his back. If not for his pale complexion, Dominique would have assumed he was part American Indian.

He's a big one. Knees, throat, and testicles. She winces as the door is bolted closed.

The seclusion room is ten by twelve feet long. No furniture. A smoked panel of glass on the wall to her right is the undisguised viewing window. The room smells of antiseptic.

Samuel Agler remains motionless, his head slightly bowed so she cannot see his eyes.

"I'm Dominique Vazquez. I'm just a grad student, so go easy."

Sam looks up, revealing animal eyes so intensely black that it is impossible to determine where the pupils end and the irises begin. But it is not his gaze that causes Dominique to shudder, it is the reality that he is sniffing the air—smelling her.

In one slowly uncoiled motion he is on his feet, leaning forward, inhaling her scent.

She backs away, her heart pounding furiously. "It's a new perfume, do you like it?"

"Blood." The word is rasped, forced up his esophagus like a dying gasp. He moves closer.

She sets herself, her muscles quivering. *Screw Mick Gabriel. If this lunatic crosses into my personal space, I'll snap his knee like kindling.*

Sam closes his eyes, his nostrils flaring. "Two bloodlines. Kukulcan . . . and Quetzalcoatl." His eyes reopen. "Your blood flows through my veins. How can this be?"

Her mind races. *Indulge him. Keep him talking.* "Good question. I'm going to tell you, but before I do I need to ask *you* a few questions . . . like, what is your name?"

"I am Chilam Balam."

"Do you know why you are here?"

"I was sent back to save the Earth."

Christ, he's the poster child for schizophrenia.

"What is schizophrenia?"

A chill jolts her spine, her flesh breaking out in goose bumps. "How did you—"

Careful, we are being watched. Seven Macaw has vassals everywhere.

Dominique grabs her head, the flow of thought energy buzzing her brain like a tuning fork.

He moves closer, the fluorescent bulbs performing a moonlight dance in his eyes. *We need to work quickly. The equinox is coming, another strike is imminent. How soon can you free me? I cannot keep the voices at bay much longer.*

The walls spin, the blood draining from her face.

The door swings open.

Shoving Paul Jones aside, she flees the seclusion room, the inmate's voice gradually fading from her head.

Dominique exits the treatment facility's lobby six hours later, the late afternoon heat blasting her in the face. A distant bolt of lightning streaks across an ominous afternoon sky as she presses her thumb to the keyless entry, unlocking the driver's-side door of the brand-new, black Pronto Spyder convertible, an early graduation gift from her foster parents.

Rain splatters heavy across her windshield as she exits the parking lot, her nerves still jumpy from the morning session with her new patient.

Thirty minutes later, she turns into the parking garage of the Hollywood Beach high-rise. Exiting the car, she takes the antiquated elevator up to the fifth floor, holding the door open so Mrs. Jenkins and her white miniature poodle can enter.

The one-bedroom apartment is the last door on the right. She keys in, greeted by the pungent aroma of fresh vegetables, garlic, and teriyaki sauce—Michael Gabriel mixing the stir-fry ingredients in a wok.

"What are you doing here? How did you get in? This is a high-security building!"

"I told them you were my fiancée. They practically gave me the key."

"You just can't break into my apartment whenever you want and . . . and start cooking. What are you cooking?"

"Stir fry."

"Yeah? Well, serve it up, then you can leave."

"I was right about Foletta, wasn't I?"

"You didn't tell me Agler was such a wack-job."

"He's been locked up in solitary confinement for eleven years. Imagine how you'd be after eleven years of hearing your own inner voice speaking at you."

"No no no, this is way beyond sensory deprivation. He practically sniffed me like a dog, somehow distinguishing my two bloodlines. Then he spoke to me telepathically! Who is this guy? A vampire?"

"Don't be ridiculous. What did he say?"

"He wanted to know how I was going to free him, presumably so he could save the Earth."

"The Earth? Not humanity? You're sure?"

"Don't be more annoying than you already are. Yes, the Earth. The whole thing sounded like bad dialogue from a B movie. He also said something about another strike coming on the equinox. Oh yeah, when I asked him his name, he called himself Chilam Balam."

Mick pauses. Turning off the stove's burner, he moves to a worn leather sofa and lies down, closing his eyes.

Dominique stares at him, growing agitated. "Well, sure—go on and make yourself comfortable. Can I get you anything?"

"I'm thinking."

"I'm eating." Grabbing a ladle, she scoops some of the simmering chicken and vegetables into a bowl, then grabs a beer from the refrigerator and sits down at the kitchen table to eat. "This is actually edible. Do you clean bathrooms as well?"

"Shh."

"You know, you'd make a nice catch if you weren't so weird. Why don't you forget about this whole Mayan calendar thing and get a real job?"

"Chilam Balam was a seer—the most revered prophet among the Maya. Maybe Sam really is channeling a past life?"

"You're easy on the eyes, and you seem pretty smart. Ever think about applying to medical school?"

"Assuming Balam also shares Sam's knowledge, then whatever happens on the equinox might also clue us in about how we can prevent Earth's demise on the winter solstice. When's your next session with Sam?"

"Not for two weeks. I have to go through their staff orientation program."

"Learn all you can about this equinox strike. I'll get back when I can."

"Where are you going?"

"Chichen Itza. Somewhere in the ancient city may be Chilam Balam's starship. If it's there, I need to find it."

Huge $10 Billion Collider Resumes Hunt for "God Particle"

Is the Large Hadron Collider being sabotaged from the Future? Or merely by birds?

The LHC, the world's largest particle accelerator, has been under repair for more than a year because of an electrical failure in September 2008.

Now, excitement and mysticism are building again around the $10 billion machine as the European Organization for Nuclear Research (CERN) gears up to circulate a high-energy proton beam around the collider's 17-mile tunnel. The event should take place this month, said Steve Myers, CERN's Director for Accelerators and Technology.

The collider made headlines last week when a bird apparently dropped a "bit of baguette" into the accelerator, making the machine shut down. The incident was similar in effect to a standard power cut, said spokeswoman Katie Yurkewicz. Had the machine been going, there would have been no damage, but beams would have been stopped until the machine could be cooled back down to operating temperatures, she said.

—CNN, November 11, 2009

28

Dominique parks her roadster in the staff lot, exhausted from having barely slept. After two weeks of orientation she is finally scheduled to begin her first session with Samuel Agler, and the thought of confronting the patient the staff refers to as "the Man from Mars" is giving her much trepidation. *At least it's Friday; you have the entire weekend to recover.*

She enters the facility, heading for the first-floor security checkpoint, wincing as she is greeted by Raymond Hughes.

"Good morning, Sunshine." The barrel-chested weightlifter with the short-cropped red hair and matching goatee flashes a yellowed smile from the other side of the steel security gate. "Guess what you're doing this weekend?"

"I don't have to guess. I'm spending the weekend in Sanibel Island."

"Skip it. I'm competing this weekend at the South Beach strongman contest, and you're my special guest."

"Yeah, that is tempting, Ray, but—"

"What's wrong? I'm not good enough for you?"

"Ray, I have plans, I'm seeing my parents this weekend. Maybe another time, okay?"

"I'm gonna hold you to that." He buzzes her in, the gate unbolting. "I saw on the docket you're working with the Man from Mars. If he gets out of hand, you just say the word, and your old pal Raymond here will arrange a midnight run."

"What's that?"

"Just a little after-hours lesson in civility."

"Thanks, but I don't believe in that sort of thing. Neither does Director Foletta."

The yellowed teeth reappear. "Sure he doesn't."

The elevator deposits her on the seventh floor. Paul Jones escorts her through security and down the main corridor to the patients' quarters.

"Remember, Dominique, this time you're entering his turf. Don't touch anything, don't become distracted. I'll be watching everything from my monitor, but if you feel threatened in any way you just double-click this device." He hands her the transponder. "You want the whip, it's yours. One double-click and you'll light him up with fifty thousand volts."

"He's a pretty big guy. Are you sure that will be enough to stop him?"

"Put it this way, if it doesn't, there won't be much left in him to accost you."

"Not quite the answer I was hoping for, Mr. Jones." Transponder in hand, she follows the guard through a short hall, entering the middle pod of three located in the northern wing. The lounge area is empty.

Jones stops at room 714 and speaks into the hall intercom. "Resident, your new intern is here to see you. Remain seated on the floor where I can see you." Using a magnetic key, he unlocks the door.

"Any last words of advice?"

"Just like before, don't allow him to get too close."

"The cell's ten feet long. What's your definition of close? His hands wrapped around my neck?"

She enters the cell, its dimensions matching her master bath. Daylight streams in from a three-inch sliver of plastic running vertically along one wall. The bed is iron, bolted to the floor. A desk and set of cubbies are fastened next to it. A sink and steel toilet are anchored by the wall to her right, angled to give its occupant some privacy from the steel door's peephole.

The bed has been stripped. Samuel Agler is seated on the floor on a magazine-thin mattress and pile of bedclothes. His head is tilted down, as if he is sleeping.

Wary, Dominique remains close to the door. "Good morning, Mr. Balam. It's nice to see you again. Am I disturbing you?"

No response, either verbally or telepathically.

She gazes at the wall above his head, dominated by a hand-drawn map of the world. Dime-size colored dots appear seemingly randomly across the globe. Framing the map are mathematical equations that continue along the other three walls like Einsteinian graffiti.

Inscribed above the bed is a second drawing—a trident, the strange icon resembling a three-pronged pitchfork.

"In case you forgot, my name is Dominique Vazquez. I'm pleased to tell you that I'll be working with you over the next six months—"

Thought energy flows from Samuel Agler's mind like a rippling creek, carrying with it a sorrow so deep its emptiness brings tears to her eyes. *Why do you make me suffer? Free me so I may again feel the warmth of Kinich Ahau on my face. Let me breathe with the galaxy . . . to feel my soul mate's touch one last time before the fifth sunlit Kinich Ahau ends and I am vanquished to Hell.*

She hesitates, then focuses her response inward. *Where is your soul mate?*

Imprisoned somewhere in the darkness. Anchored by my transgressions in the eleventh dimension. First Mother, please—you have the power to bring us back into the light. Free me before evil stains our divided soul for all eternity. Reopen my vessel so that I may die fulfilling my destiny and not in this cage. Please, First Mother, I beg of you—

"Enough!" Her head snaps back, severing the voice. "I mean, enough silence. I'm here to help you. I can only do that if you communicate with me . . . you know, by talking. Out loud."

He looks up at her with hollowed sunken eyes—black pools drowning in eleven years of sensory deprivation and a loneliness that shakes her being. And in that single moment of clarity a higher instinct welled deep within her DNA gushes to the surface, its warmth cleansing all prejudices and fears. Moving to him, she kneels by his side and wraps her arms around his head and neck, hugging him tightly to her chest.

The touch of flesh to flesh elicits a jolt of electricity as sudden and as startling as connecting a positively charged battery cable to a negatively charged pole, causing Sam's neural synapses to snap open at the speed of light. So powerful is the electrical discharge that it momentarily short-circuits the cell's video feed and causes Dominique's hair to stand on end.

Like a starving child given sustenance, Samuel Agler embraces the woman from whose womb he was birthed fifty years ago—though he has yet to be conceived. Dominique's flame reignites his psyche's internal wick, the light emitted doubled between them. They remain locked together for several minutes, their connection flowing with energy until the generated body heat becomes too much to handle.

Samuel pulls away. For the briefest of moments his eyes radiate a turquoise hue.

Dominique never notices, her thoughts lost in the chaos of the severed connection. *Who are you?*

I don't know anymore. So many voices . . . so many memories from past lives I cannot remember, but whose losses I feel every waking moment.

Who am I to you?

Again, I don't know. But I've been anticipating your arrival, I felt your aura during the arrival of the spring equinox. Whoever you are, somehow you've managed to pull me up from the depths of the underworld.

It wasn't my doing. Michael Gabriel sent me.

Michael? Eyes widening in recognition, he backs away on all fours, his mind racing to catch up with this abrupt new clue of his ever-changing reality.

"Samuel Agler. Lauren and Sam. Laura and Sam, but not Sam. Not Sam. Who am I?" Anxiety washes over his sudden awareness like a breaking dam. "Sam and Laura . . . and Sophie! They have my family!" He rushes to the narrow slit of plastic and smashes his fist through the tinted shield, screaming at the daylight. "Laura! Sophie! I'm coming!" Like a crazed bull he charges the door, ramming the steel barrier over and over with his 240-pound frame until the hinges begin to buckle—

Zap!

The electrical shock courses through his body, stunning him rigid.

He shakes it off and is struck again.

Sam sways. His muscles abandon him. Saliva drips from his jabbering mouth.

Like a falling timber his knees buckle and he collapses upon the wafer-thin mattress in a twisted heap of twitching limbs and sweat-laced flesh.

29

If nature is kind to us and the lightest supersymmetric
particle, or the Higgs boson, is within reach of the LHC's
current energy, the data we expect to collect by the end
of 2012 will put them within our grasp.
            —SERGIO BERTOLUCCI,
        RESEARCH DIRECTOR, CERN
    CERN PRESS RELEASE, JANUARY 31, 2011

SANIBEL ISLAND, FLORIDA
SEPTEMBER 22, 2012 (FALL EQUINOX)

Dominique slows the black Pronto Spyder convertible, keeping the roadster just under fifty as she
passes over the causeway to Sanibel, a residential and resort area nestled on a small island on the Gulf Coast of
Florida. She drives along East Gulf Drive, winding her way
west past several large hotels before entering a residential
neighborhood.

Edith and Isadore Axler live in a two-story beach
home situated on a half-acre corner lot facing the Gulf of
Mexico. At first glance the exterior redwood slats enclosing

the home give it the look of an enormous party lantern, especially at night. This layer of scrim protects the structure from hurricanes, creating, in effect, a house within a house.

The south wing of the Axler home has been renovated to accommodate a sophisticated acoustics lab, one of only three on the Gulf Coast interfaced with SOSUS, the United States Navy's underwater Sound Surveillance System. The sixteen-billion-dollar network of undersea microphones, originally built by the federal government during the Cold War to spy on enemy submarines, is now a tool used by marine biologists to track sea life in the Gulf, especially in the wake of the BP oil rig disaster that left large segments of the waterway a dead zone.

Dominique turns left down the cul-de-sac, then right into the last driveway, comforted by the familiar sound of pebbles crunching beneath the weight of her roadster.

Edith Axler greets her as the convertible top snaps shut into place. Dominique's foster mother is an astute, gray-haired woman in her early seventies, with brown eyes that exude a teacher's wisdom and a warm smile that projects a parent's unconditional love.

"Hi, doll. How was your drive?"

"Fine." Dominique hugs the elder woman, squeezing her tight.

"Something's wrong?" Edith pulls back, noticing the tears. "What is it?"

"Nothing. I'm just glad to be home."

"Don't play me for senile. It's that patient of yours, isn't it? What's his name . . . Sam? Come on, we'll talk before Iz knows you're here."

Dominique follows her to a wooden park bench facing the beach, the Gulf as serene as a lake. "I remember when I was young—whenever I had a bad day, you always used to sit with me on this bench and we'd watch the sea. You used to say, 'How bad can things be, if you can still enjoy such a beautiful view?'"

Edie squeezes her daughter's hand. "Tell me why you're so upset."

Dominique wipes away a tear. "You remember when Chicahua showed up at our door, how Iz questioned her motives?"

"I did, too. What kind of mother sends her only child to another country—convincing her she's an orphan, only to attempt to reconnect twenty years later? This woman has a screw loose, if you ask me."

"Or maybe she really is a seer. Edie, she knew Mick Gabriel was coming to find me, just like she knew there'd be a connection with Sam."

"What sort of connection?"

"It's hard to explain. It's like we know each other from a past life."

314

"Okay, so there's a connection. Use it to help your patient get better, then move on."

"That's just it: the only way to help him get better is to free him."

"Slow down. When's Sam due to be released?"

"His evaluation's coming up, but according to Mick, Borgia means to keep Sam incarcerated for the rest of his life. During his trial, Sam told Mick that Borgia had swapped out Julius's heart medication before the lecture—that he purposely incited Julius so he'd become overly stressed. The judge refused to allow any of that evidence to be admissible. Mick said that what should have been a case of simple assault resulted in a never-ending sentence in a mental ward."

"Mick said? Dominique, from everything you've told me about Mick, I wouldn't be so quick to trust what he says either. Secretary Borgia is one of the most powerful people in the world. Why would he risk his entire future over an archaeologist? Forget Mr. Gabriel, forget all these ridiculous Doomsday prophecies and conspiracies, and just focus on completing your internship so you can finish school and get on with your life."

Dominique squeezes Edith's hand. "You're right. Between Chicahua and Mick, and this crazy patient of mine, I've completely lost my internal compass. Come Monday, I'm going to ask Dr. Foletta to assign me to a different patient. After spending eleven years in solitary confinement, Samuel Agler's haunted by demons Sigmund Freud couldn't begin to address."

"Don't misunderstand, I'm not telling you to give up. Sometimes we cross paths with people in need of our assistance, only we don't know how to help them. While their immediate problem may seem important, the root cause of most situations is the absence of the light from a person's life."

"By light, you mean God?"

Edith nods. "By helping others reconnect to God, we're actually removing the darkness from our own lives while helping the other person to heal the root cause of their problem."

"Sam's convinced he's been sent here to save the planet."

"We all need to do our part. Between the carbon emissions and the oil spills, Earth's becoming a toxic wasteland."

"No, Ead, I mean he literally thinks he's here to save the planet from the Mayan Doomsday—you know, December 21, 2012. He told me there'd be another prelude to the end sometime today."

"Okay, so he's a few cards short of a full deck, who cares?" She pauses. "Do you really enjoy working in an asylum? You know, you did get into law school. It's not too late—"

Dominique hugs her—as Isadore Axler comes running out of the house, the aging biologist frantic. "Ead? Ead!"

"I'm over here. What in God's name—"

"Seaquake . . . a big one! Campeche Shelf . . . southwest of the Alacran Reef." He bends over, struggling to catch his breath. "The entire sea floor just collapsed . . . *whoosh*! SOSUS is tracking a series of tsunamis that are rippling across the Gulf." He glances at Dom. "Hey, kiddo."

"Did you alert the Coast Guard?"

"And FEMA. And the Sanibel sheriff's office." He looks up as sirens blast in the distance. "Whatever you want to save, grab it fast and get in the car before we hit a major traffic jam. The first wave will reach us in twenty-three minutes. I want to be across the causeway in five."

CHICHEN ITZA

The ancient Mayan capital swelters beneath a cloud-covered sky, the lack of a serpent's shadow dampening the spirits of 78,000 visitors, most of whom are gathered around the Kukulcan Pyramid.

Abandoning the esplanade, Michael Gabriel falls in line among a moving conveyor of tourists, all heading north through the jungle to see the sacred cenote. The watering hole and hundreds like it are the primary source of fresh water in the Yucatan, created 65 million years ago when a seven-mile-in-diameter asteroid struck the Earth, crushing the sea floor and fracturing the Gulf's submerged limestone basin. When the Yucatan landmass eventually rose from the sea, these fractures became the freshwater sinkholes destined to nourish the future Mesoamerican Indians.

The clearing is up ahead, the sacred cenote an enormous round chalky-white limestone pit. Mick waits his turn behind a procession of perspiring tourists, the crowd gradually moving to a vantage along the edge of the sinkhole. After ten minutes the group ahead of him parts, allowing him to stand before the pit that, according to Chilam Balam and the Mayan Popol Vuh, served as the gateway to the underworld.

The thirty-seven-year-old archaeologist stares at the cenote for what is easily the thousandth time. The pit drops sixty feet straight down to its stagnant olive-green water, its curved walls matted in thick vegetation.

A tremor causes his skin to tingle. The reverberation migrates into his bones. For a moment he assumes the rumbling is coming from the weight of the moving mass of people, the sensation similar to standing near a railroad track occupied by an approaching locomotive.

Then he notices the surface of the cenote is bubbling.

An earthquake? He looks around, confused yet excited.

Women scream. Men point.

Michael Gabriel looks down in time to see the percolating waters of the sacred cenote suddenly flush down the sinkhole as if it were a toilet.

The maître d' switches on his smile as the fourth-most-powerful person in the United States enters the posh French restaurant. *"Bon soir, Monsieur Borgia."*

"Bonsoir, Felipe. I believe I'm expected."

"Oui, certainement. Follow me, please." The maître d' leads him past candlelit tables to a private room next to the bar. He knocks twice on the outer double doors, then turns to Borgia. "Your party is waiting inside."

"Merci." Borgia slips the twenty into the gloved palm as the door swings open from the inside.

"Pierre, come in." Republican party cochairman Charlie Myers shakes Borgia's hand and slaps him affectionately on the shoulder. "Late as usual. We're already two rounds ahead of you. Bloody Mary, right?"

"Yes, fine." The private meeting room is paneled in deep walnut like the rest of the restaurant. A half-dozen white clothed tables fill the sound-proof room—all empty, save for one.

Joseph Randolph embraces his nephew with a one-armed hug, the other used to balance on his cane. "Lucky Pierre, or should I say Mr. Secretary of State. Washington must be good to you, looks like y'all put on a few pounds."

Borgia blushes. "Maybe a few."

"Join the club." The heavyset man seated at the table stands, extending a thick palm. "Pete Mabus, Mabus Enterprises, out of Mobile, Alabama."

Borgia recognizes the defense contractor's name. "Nice to meet you."

"Pleasure's all mine. Sit down and take a load off."

Charlie Myers brings Borgia his drink. "Gentlemen, if you'll excuse me, I need to use the little boys' room."

Randolph waits until Myers has left the room. "Pierre, I saw your father last week up in Rehoboth. All of us are real upset 'bout you not getting the vice presidency. Maller's doing a real disservice to the entire party."

Borgia grimaces. "The president's watching the polls. His campaign manager thinks Chaney gives him the support the party needs in the South."

"Maller ain't thinking down the road." Mabus points a chubby finger.

"What this country needs now is strong leadership, not another dove like Chaney as second-in-command."

"I couldn't agree more. Unfortunately, I have no say in the matter."

Randolph leans closer. "Don't be so quick to assume this cake is fully baked. The senator has a lot of enemies who lurk in the shadows, the president as well. Should a tragedy happen after the November election, you'd be tapped to serve."

"Jesus, Uncle Joe." Borgia uses his linen napkin to wipe sweat beads from his upper lip.

Peter Mabus leans forward. "This upcoming Iranian-Russian-Chinese military exercise has pissed a lot of people off. Wholesale changes will have to be made in the joint chiefs and the Pentagon."

"Pete's right, son. You need to prepare now. A rising tide raises all boats. You're the tide, Pierre."

The vibration of the cell phone in his pants pocket causes Borgia to jump. He verifies the White House code and clicks on the text message. "My God."

SANIBEL ISLAND, FLORIDA

The tsunami is twenty-seven feet high when it rolls in from the Gulf—a tide of frothy water that moves inland with the speed and power of a locomotive. The wave bludgeons everything in its path, flipping beach chairs and patio furniture, flooding pools and the first three stories of every home, hotel, and street on the island. By the time the force of nature crosses the island it has quieted into a relentless eight-foot swell, depositing its wares into Pine Island Sound and Tarpon Bay before slamming sideways into the section of tsunami taking dead aim at Fort Myers.

Dominique's roadster, the Jeep Grand Cherokee transporting the Axlers, and thousands of other vehicles fleeing the Gulf Coast inch forward along McGregor Boulevard in bumper-to-bumper traffic, all eyes focused on the mound of water racing across San Carlos Bay.

Isadore Axler climbs halfway out his window, waving at his adopted daughter in the tiny vehicle behind him. "Get in our car! Quickly!"

Dominique tries opening her car door, only to find herself jammed in against the passenger side of the Lexus in the lane next to her.

The tsunami strikes the beach a hundred yards away, pile-driving sand fifty feet into the air as it charges up manicured lawns and asphalt.

Flipping open the roadster's convertible top, Dominique climbs over the windshield and onto the hood of her car before leaping onto the Chero-kee's roof. She manages to grab onto the luggage rack, her body dangling across the rear window—as a river of fish-scented sea bashes sideways into the clogged lanes of vehicles. The unstoppable rush of water rises beneath her roadster, flipping it onto the Lexus with a devastating crunch of glass, the tide sweeping small and mid-size vehicles across the four-lane highway.

The Cherokee rocks but never budges, its two occupants watching in horror as their daughter is submerged by the mud-brown wave. A full min-ute passes before daylight reappears—Dominique gone.

Edith bursts out in tears.

"Stay here." Isadore exits the Jeep in a knee-deep current, gazing dumbfounded at the pile of cars tossed like beer cans into a flooded canal.

"That was too close."

Iz looks up, overjoyed to find Dominique splayed out on the roof of the Cherokee.

"Did you see what that damn wave did to my car?"

"That damn wave was only the first in a series of damn waves. Get inside, kiddo, we need to move!"

Dominique jumps down, climbing in the backseat as a second wall of water appears on the horizon.

30

The countdown to "D-day" has started. Our group has
been preparing for LHC data for many years now and we
are all truly excited about the prospect of finally getting a
glimpse of whatever surprises Nature has in store for us.

—DR. PEDRO TEIXEIRA-DIAS

LEADER OF THE ATLAS GROUP

AT ROYAL HOLLOWAY,

UNIVERSITY OF LONDON

SOUTH FLORIDA EVALUATION AND

TREATMENT CENTER

MIAMI, FLORIDA

NOVEMBER 6, 2012

It is 10:57 at night by the time Dominique enters her
apartment, greeted by the scent of fresh apple pie on
the stove and the uneven duet of snores coming from her
bedroom. Careful not to wake her parents, she pulls the
door closed and turns on the television, catching *The Daily
Show*'s take on the presidential election.

As expected, the Maller-Chaney ticket has won,

largely based on the way the administration handled the tragedy in the Gulf. Thanks to post-Katrina evacuation plans and the SOSUS early warning system, less than five hundred lives were lost. But the devastation to the Gulf Coast and its barrier islands was immense, and President Maller had wasted no time in placing his new vice president in charge of organizing the aid.

With threats to imprison any FEMA administrator or insurance representative responsible for creating red tape, Ennis Chaney had the homeless fed and sheltered before the end of day 1, families in trailers soon thereafter. Global satellite images taken before and after the disaster were used to settle insurance claims so as not to delay the clearing of debris. By mid-October all coastal roads had reopened, reconstruction under way.

Seismologists reported the seaquake had occurred beneath the Chicxulub impact crater, site of the asteroid collision 65 million years ago. The forces responsible for collapsing this long-fractured section of sea floor were still being investigated.

Dominique had wasted no time confronting Sam about the disaster. His response was to show her his hand-drawn wall map, the colored dots listing every major earthquake, tsunami, and volcanic eruption that had occurred since 2010, beginning with the magnitude 7.0 seismic event that had devastated Haiti on January 12, followed by the Icelandic volcano that erupted on April 15, three months later. For nearly an hour he attempted to explain his quantum equations, his calculations based on everything from the angle of the planet's tilt on its axis to the gravitational pull generated by the massive black hole located at the center of the Milky Way—a force that caused the Earth and every object in the galaxy to travel through space at an incredible 135 miles per second, a cosmic merry-go-round charted by the Mayan calendar.

"I can't tell you what caused these earthquakes and eruptions, Dominique, but using these mathematical equations I can tell you when the next event will occur."

"And when would that be . . . wait, don't tell me—December 21, 2012."

"Yes, only the magnitude of the winter solstice event will be far greater than the last."

"Okay, let's say I buy into your Doomsday equation—how do we stop this from happening?"

"I don't know. According to the Mayan Popol Vuh, only One Hunahpu can prevent the end of the fifth cycle."

"Great. More Mayan mythology." Moving to the wall behind his bed, she pointed to the drawing of the trident. "What is this supposed to be? Is this devil worship?"

"I don't know what it is. The icon comes to me in my dreams, along with the faces of people I'm sure I've met but I just can't seem to remember. Maybe Michael would know?"

"Forget about him. Your pal, Michael, is about as helpful as One Hunahpu. He left town before the fall equinox. I haven't heard from him since."

The annoying sound draws her from REM sleep. Her eyes search for the digital clock on the television's cable box—3:22 a.m.

She sits up on the sofabed as she hears the soft knock on the door.

Dressed in a Florida State football jersey barely concealing her underpants, she makes her way to the apartment door and looks out the peephole. "Unbelievable."

Dominique unbolts the lock and opens the door, staring at Michael Gabriel. "Where the hell have you been? Six weeks you've been gone . . . do you know I was almost killed?"

"Nice legs. But your breath stinks. Can I come in?"

She waves him in, checking her breath behind his back. "It's three in the morning."

"Three thirty. I didn't want to wake your foster parents. Sorry I didn't call, but your phones are being tapped."

"Tapped? By who?"

"The only people who tap phones, Dominique. You made Borgia's shit list the day you began working with Sam. You're now what they call a person of interest."

"No more games, Mick. I'm not helping you another minute until I know who Sam really is."

"That's why I'm here. Pack a bag, we'll be gone two days."

"Two days? I can't leave for two days."

"You're off tomorrow and Thursday, what's the problem?"

"The problem—" She lowers her voice. "The problem is, I don't trust you."

"Do you trust Sam?"

"Yes."

"Then trust me, because what I do now I do for the two of you."

*   *   *

The commuter airport is located thirty minutes away in Boca Raton. The private jet—a Hawker 900XP—sits on the tarmac, fueled, its pilot awaiting his two passengers.

Mick pays the taxi driver, leading Dominique toward the security gate.

"A private jet? How the hell did you arrange a private jet? You have a rich uncle I don't know about?"

"I called in a favor from a friend."

"What friend?"

"Ennis Chaney."

Dominique stops walking. "The vice president of the United States is lending you his private jet?"

"This is Ennis Chaney, not Dick Cheney. The current VP has no interest in private jets. He simply arranged transportation for us."

"Why would he do that?"

"My father spent the last ten years of his life working for a black ops military program. One day he hacked into his director's computer and found a secret Pentagon budget that had diverted about $2 trillion from the US treasury. My father sent the file to Senator Chaney. He sort of owes us."

"And where exactly are we going?"

"No worries, someplace close."

The burst of brilliant sun bleeds red through Dominique's closed eyelids, causing her to roll over. She nearly falls off the sofa as the cabin tilts beneath her, the jet dipping its starboard wing as it circles to land.

Minutes later they are standing on empty tarmac, the sunrise obscured behind a mountain range.

Dominique rubs her eyes, exhausted. "Where are we? Arizona?"

"Try Nazca, Peru." He starts walking toward an aluminum hangar, Dominique hustling to keep up.

"Peru? Are you shitting me? You told me we were going someplace close."

"Peru is close. Certainly closer than Australia."

"Why the hell are we in Nazca?"

"I'm going to show you."

They enter the hangar. Inside, an American in his sixties, dressed in Navy overalls, is working on the engine of a World War II naval fighter. The mechanic acknowledges Mick with a quick glance, his greasy hands occupied by a crescent wrench.

"BT-13 Valiant. The Navy retired them after the war. With a bit of work, I think I can get this old girl back in the air. This her?"

"Lew Jack, Dominique Vazquez. Lew's ex-Navy, a former pilot. According to my father, he was also a decent shortstop way back when they were in high school."

"Second baseman, and quit buttering me up. So you're Dominique Vazquez? Nice to see Mick interested in women again, especially a looker like you. Of course, the last Mexican beauty yanked his pecker so hard I'm surprised he has any teeth left."

Mick shoots Lew a look. "It was a long time ago."

"Yeah, it was. Dominique, are you a US citizen?"

"Yes. Why? Was this former pecker yanker of Mick's an illegal alien?"

"All right, enough."

Lew grins. "She's got some kick in her. I like that."

"You have no idea."

"Your ride's out back ready to go; there's sandwiches and water in the cooler." He glances at Dominique, pointing to a rusted steel door next to a ransacked office. "Bathroom. I suggest you use it, it's a long ride. I ran out of toilet paper, but there's some paper towels."

"Thanks anyway, but I peed in the twenty-million-dollar jet."

"Feisty, I like that in a woman. If Mick disappoints you, make sure you come back here, I'll take you for a ride in my Piper."

Dominique chases Mick across the hangar and out the back door. Anchored out back is Julius Gabriel's hot air balloon, ready to launch.

Dominique backs away. "This is your ride?"

"It's perfectly safe."

"Are you kidding? There's more patches on this thing than my foster mother's quilt."

Mick swings one leg over the basket. "Trust me."

"Forget it. And the whole trust thing—it's getting old. Now call a cab or something, it's hot out here."

"Dominique, we're crossing the Nazca plateau, the place with all the cool lines and animals. You can't drive on the desert, and it's too hot and way too far to walk."

"And I'm afraid of heights. Seriously. I get real panicky."

"You were fine on the jet."

"That was a jet. This is more like a bad carnival ride."

"Fine. Stay here with Lew. Maybe he'll show you his tattoo."

"Wait!"

The balloon soars effortlessly over the pampa, the late morning sun baking the desert's flat round stones to its yellow geology.

Dominique remains seated in the basket, her limbs trembling.

"We're about to pass over the Nazca whale. Come on, Dom, take a look, it's not so bad."

"I'm fine, thanks."

Mick pulls her up by her elbows, dragging her onto her feet.

She punches him hard on his deltoid, nearly dislocating his shoulder. "Don't manhandle me. Ever."

"Sorry." Mick rubs his throbbing arm. "I just wanted you to see the drawings. At least take a look."

She steals a quick glance below, her eyes widening. "Wow. Is that a fish? Who made it? And those lines. I've seen photos before, but they're so perfect. How old are they?"

"The more sophisticated images are several thousand years old. They trace back to Viracocha, an ancient wise man who taught the Inca astronomy and agriculture. Viracocha preceded Kukulcan and Quetzalcoatl. It's his blood that runs through my maternal ancestors' veins."

"Why are the drawings here? What's their purpose?"

"There are many theories, but my father believed they were part of an ancient message intended for extraterrestrials."

"Extraterrestrials? Like in little green men?"

"Gray, actually."

She shakes her head. "You know, every time I begin to feel comfortable around you, you have to go and ruin it by saying something stupid."

"Sorry. I didn't realize you knew everything there was to know about human existence and the cosmos."

"Here I thought you were this amazingly intelligent guy, not someone who believed in aliens. Oh wait, Lew said something about your last girlfriend being an alien."

"Cute. Very cute. For the record, my last girlfriend worked for Pierre Borgia. She was paid to occupy me—occupy being defined as sex, love, and a fake wedding ceremony, all so I wouldn't be around to help my father. As for your opinions about man's existence, like most blissfully ignorant people your knee-jerk reaction is based on fear—an emotion that retards all rational thought and prevents any new knowledge from seeping into your brain."

"Hey, I'm not some wetback who just snuck over the border to pick strawberries. I'm six months away from earning my doctorate!"

"And we're six weeks away from being annihilated. But hey, you know better, so just keep relaxing in that warm bath, Mr. Frog, while the heat simmers your flesh into soup."

"Whatever the hell that means." She turns away in anger, questioning for the hundredth time why she has allowed herself to be manipulated by this man. *Forget about him, forget about Sam and your crazy biological mother. The moment you get home, call your advisor and request a transfer to another facility. Who cares if you graduate late. I need to get away from all of these Doomsday wackos.*

After several minutes of mutual silence she realizes they are descending to land.

The mountain blemishes the flat desert plateau like a mole on flesh, its Y-shaped ravine dividing the smooth mass of rock into three sections. Carved into the southern face is the ten-story image of the Nazca astronaut.

Mick lands the balloon at the entrance to the widest ravine. Within minutes he has deflated the bright orange and blue envelope so that it cannot be seen from above.

"Why did you bring me here?"

"You wanted to know who Sam is—I'm about to show you." He leads her into the ravine, a shadowed avenue of desert slicing between rock walls.

The object is as large as her freshman dormitory—a red and white winged aircraft concealed from above by camouflage netting. An enormous pair of afterburners in the tail section leads to the rest of the hull and an insignia.

"Project H.O.P.E.? What is this? An old airplane? Are you saying Sam's a pilot?"

"The ship is old, only it's not an airplane, it's a space plane. Its technology is far more advanced than any space shuttle that was in NASA's fleet."

"Meaning what?"

"Meaning, it's a paradox, a statement of fact that conflicts with the universe as we know it. Project H.O.P.E. built this ship. Project H.O.P.E. doesn't exist. Samuel Agler piloted this ship. Samuel Agler doesn't exist."

"Of course he exists. We may not know where he comes from, but—"

"I know where he comes from. Come with me and I'll show you."

He leads her up a narrow set of steps built into the open starboard hatch, the two of them entering the dark confines of the vessel's main cabin. They work their way forward to the command center cockpit.

"It took me four years to figure out these controls. Not sure I could pilot this thing, but I know how to access the ship's video log. You'd better sit down."

She occupies the copilot's seat, watching as he removes a helmet from a hidden storage space. "Everything's based on thought control, the relays are in this headpiece. It's similar to an Apache chopper's fighter pilot controls, only far more sophisticated. The difficult part was hacking into the mainframe to create a new password."

Strapping himself into the pilot's seat, Mick dons the headgear. "Activate voice command, authorization Gabriel, Immanuel, Beta Alpha Gamma Delta Tango."

"Did you say Immanuel?"

The console lights up like a Christmas tree.

Dominique smiles. "Very cool."

"Prepare yourself. What you're about to see isn't easy to watch." He closes his eyes, focusing his thoughts.

A small rectangular flat screen blinks to life on the center console.

"This is the ship's last recorded log entry." The screen darkens. A date and time code appear:

JULY 04, 2047—19 HRS. 06 MIN.

"July 2047? How is that possible?"

"Keep watching."

The nose of the shuttle appears in the lower left corner of the screen, the ship suddenly accelerating down a runway through a blistering gray haze. Mick mentally advances the playback until the dust clouds are replaced by velvety-black space, a billion stars . . . and the Earth, rotating like a giant blue beach ball.

The small, clear, marblelike object hovers beneath its southern pole . . . moving closer.

As Dominique watches in horror, it begins consuming the planet.

"Oh God . . . oh my God. What the hell is that thing?"

"It's a type of juvenile black hole, called a strangelet. Sort of an unwanted afterbirth created by a bunch of physicists who decided it was worth $10 billion and the future of our planet to collide atoms, just so they could win a Nobel Prize. Keep watching, this next scene is important."

A wormhole materializes, appearing in the void of space occupied by

Earth only moments earlier. The space plane alters course, heading straight for the open portal.

The screen goes blank.

Dominique shakes her head, unnerved. "Sam comes from our future?"

"Correct."

"He came to warn us about the strangelet."

"Correct again."

"But this is a good thing. Thanks to Sam, we have thirty-five years to prevent the problem from ever happening."

"Incorrect. The strangelet has already been conceived, its due date is December 21 of this year."

"Wait . . . what? How is that possible?"

"This may be hard to grasp, but try to imagine your life traveling down a highway linked to countless intersections. Every path is fully charted, your future is simply based on whichever path you choose to engage. Some paths dead-end in tragedy, others lead to fame and fortune, and everything in between.

"Human existence travels along a similar path. The Mayan calendar predicted the highway would dead-end on December 21, 2012. That dead end was somehow averted in the 2012 that belonged to the occupants in Sam's world. The off-ramp wasn't perfect—it dead-ended from the same cause that now threatens us, annihilating the planet in 2047."

"Then how are we alive?"

"We're alive because the wormhole deposited Sam back in time to the pre-2012 highway, only the variables have changed."

"How do you know all this?"

"I've spent months in this shuttle, poring over historical accounts. In Sam's version of 2012, a cosmic rift opened between Earth and the underworld of Xibalba. What saved the planet was a weapon fired from an even larger spacecraft buried beneath the Kukulcan Pyramid. Six weeks ago I was in Chichen Itza when the Gulf floor collapsed. The quake caused the sacred cenote to drain. I was part of an excavation team that explored the pit—searching for an entrance to an aquifer that runs beneath the pyramid. In Sam's 2012, that aquifer led to the spacecraft buried beneath the Kukulcan Pyramid—a starship referred to in these historical records as the *Balam*."

"*Balam*? As in Chilam Balam?"

"Yes. Only the ship isn't here in our 2012."

"Why not?"

"Because time shifted down a different exit ramp in Sam's 2012—an exit ramp that looped time back to our own 2012 after Earth was destroyed in 2047. Only our 2012 is the 2012 where the strangelet appears. The sea-quake in the Gulf was actually caused by the strangelet passing through the planet's core. I know it's confusing, but we're in some serious trouble here, Dominique."

She sits back, numb. "This is unbelievable."

"Unbelievable? That train hasn't even left the station yet. According to the ship's historical records, two people entered the *Balam* in December of Sam's 2012 and activated the starship's weapon. One was a female graduate student from Florida State who was working at a Miami mental asylum."

"What?"

"The other was the mental patient she helped to escape."

"Sam?"

"There was no Sam back then. The guy who piloted this ship through a wormhole in 2047—the same guy my father and I found on this desert in 1990 who is currently sitting in a cell in a Miami asylum—wasn't born in 2012. I was the mental patient!"

Dominique smiles, then breaks into bouts of hysterical laughter, the sheer absurdity of the situation too much to handle. "This is a joke, right? I'm on one of those new reality shows that sees how far they can screw with your mind. Because none of this can possibly be real."

Mick closes his eyes.

A new image appears on-screen—a newspaper headline. Beneath the *New York Times* ledger is the date: September 22, 2013, followed by the lead story:

Vazquez-Gabriel Gives Birth to Twin Sons
DNA confirms Jacob and Immanuel's father as Michael Gabriel

The photo reveals a smiling Dominique in a hospital nightgown, cradling her two newborn sons.

"Oh my God . . ."

"See the dark-haired one? That's our son, Sam, only his name is really Immanuel. Look at Jacob's eyes, see how blue they are. Same color as your biological mother, Chicahua, and my Aunt Laura. Just by his appearance, you can tell Jake's farther along in his development. According to the article, I disappeared on the 2012 winter solstice . . . Dominique? Hey!"

He grabs her as she falls forward, unconscious.

31

This truly is a new age of physics and the understanding of our universe—we've never before seen these unprecedented energies that the collisions will be at the Large Hadron Collider. The idea is that it accelerates particles to close to the speed of light and then it smashes them together. Now this doesn't sound necessarily very interesting but actually if we go to Einstein's equation, E=mc squared, if we've got loads of energy we can make really massive particles—particles that might not have been around since the very beginnings of time. So we can create these massive particles and we can actually study them, and this gives us our whole plethora of information about the early universe and how it began and how nature really works on a fundamental scale.

—CLAIRE TIMLIN

CMS PHYSICIST, IMPERIAL COLLEGE, LONDON

Located in the West Wing of the White House, the command center known as the Situation Room is a five-thousand-square-foot complex designed to link the president and his cabinet with key personnel and sectors throughout the world. Born out of President Kennedy's frustration after the lack of reliable intelligence that led to the failed Bay of Pigs invasion, the Situation Room fuses communication among Homeland Security, the intelligence sector, and the military. There are three conference rooms designed to accommodate national security meetings, acrylic privacy booths for secure international phone calls, five secure video rooms, and two tiers of curved computer terminals that handle incoming data from around the world.

Vice President Ennis Chaney makes his way through the complex, pausing as the privacy fog lifts on a sealed booth, revealing a physician removing a blood pressure cuff from President Maller's arm. Pretending not to notice, Chaney continues on to the main conference room, the high-tech chamber a rectangle of smart walls adorned with flat screens set around a large mahogany table.

The new VP takes his place in the empty gray leather chair opposite Secretary of State Pierre Borgia. The uncomfortable silence is broken by President Maller, who hustles inside, sitting at the head of the table before a video control center.

"Before we discuss Iran, there's an important item in this morning's daily briefing that we need to go over. If you're not familiar with the situation in Yellowstone Park, there's a summary waiting in your e-mail, make sure you read it. For those of you not familiar, in essence nature deposited a ticking time bomb beneath Yellowstone in the form of a supervolcano, called a caldera. To define this as a Doomsday scenario would not be exaggerating—should the caldera ever erupt, we're looking at devastation that would equal ten thousand Mount St. Helenses. The USGS monitors the situation around the clock, and though there've been a few concerns over the years, overall the situation has remained reasonably stable . . . until now."

The president presses a switch on his control panel, broadcasting a live feed from Yellowstone Park over the conference room's six flat-screen plasma TVs. A man in his forties appears on-screen, wearing a black USGS collared shirt and matching baseball cap. "Dr. Mark Beckmeyer is the associate director of the United States Geological Survey–Earthquakes Hazard Program and the man in charge at Yellowstone. Dr. Beckmeyer and I have been speaking since late last night. Doctor, if you can give my staff a brief summary of what we discussed?"

"Yes, sir. I'm not going to get into defining the caldera or Yellowstone's substructure as I've included all that in the e-mail. Our biggest concern is an earthquake triggering an eruption. Earthquakes come in swarms at Yellowstone, most of the clustering due to the size and shape of the caldera's ring fracture. For instance, during the month of July we recorded 152 earthquakes in the Yellowstone region, seventeen more than in 2011. Fortunately these events tend to be benign, and in fact our ground deformation data shows that uplift of the caldera beneath Yellowstone Lake has ceased. That's the good news. The bad news is that the September 22 seismic event not only affected the Gulf of Mexico but Yellowstone's geology as well, triggering the collapse of the caldera's three volcanic chambers, in essence creating one massive magma pocket. Pressure within the pocket continues to rise. Our geologists have been working with the Army Corps of Engineers in an attempt to design ways to vent the chamber, but should another earthquake event occur like the one on the fall equinox, then an eruption would be imminent."

"Dr. Beckmeyer, paint us the worst-case scenario."

"Simply put, an eruption of a major caldera like Yellowstone is a planet-changing event. The last one occurred around seventy thousand years ago at Lake Toba in Sumatra and nearly wiped out every air-breathing life form on Earth. Yellowstone's caldera is far larger than Toba. Should the caldera blow, the explosion would instantly wipe out the surrounding population, with lava flowing over thousands of square miles. The Midwestern states would become ground zero, devastating our crops. As bad as all that sounds, the far worse problem is atmospheric debris, which will blanket Earth's atmosphere and blot out the sun. We're looking at a volcanic winter, with global temperatures plunging as much as a hundred degrees. Power grids will fail, populations isolated, the economy lurching to a standstill. Millions will perish during the first few weeks just from the cold. Roads will be impassable. Within a month or two, those who haven't frozen to death will starve."

The vice president loosens his collar, struggling to breathe. "There must be something our scientists can do?"

"We have teams working on it," Beckmeyer replies. "So far, nothing looks promising."

"Thank you, Dr. Beckmeyer, I'll see you in Washington." The president disconnects the line. "I know many of you are shocked, and of course we're all praying to avoid another seismic disturbance like we experienced back in September, but the truth is that our experts have been analyzing this threat with the same thoroughness as the Pentagon rehearses war game scenarios, and contingency plans are under way. Mr. Secretary?"

Pierre Borgia turns to face the cabinet members seated on his left. "Yellowstone is an issue of survival. Survival means making difficult choices. It means accepting the harsh reality that, should Yellowstone erupt, then six billion people—save a handful of the prepared and protected—are going to die . . . painfully."

Using his laptop, Borgia uploads a series of graphs that are displayed on the surrounding plasma screens. "Our objective is to stockpile food, water, livestock, and seed vaults in the 106 subterranean emergency facilities located outside the ground-zero states. Early estimates suggest we can house upward of twenty-seven thousand people for five years, eleven thousand over a decade, five thousand for twenty years. These numbers reflect a five-to-three birth rate versus death rate per colony."

Chaney shakes his head. "What about the residents in the kill zone—are we going to warn them ahead of time so they can leave?"

Borgia looks hard at the VP with his one good eye. "Alert the masses and panic will ensue. There will be anarchy, rendering the highways and rail systems useless. It may seem cruel, Mr. Chaney, but being incinerated is probably far more humane than starvation."

"Why don't you try both and let us know?"

President Maller slaps the tabletop with both palms. "Ennis, this isn't political, it's about the survival of our species."

"You mean, the survival of the elite. Anyone not a politician or billionaire gonna be invited into these underground shelters of yours? Five thousand worthless chiefs and no Indians. If that's the gene pool that represents the future of this planet, then I'm glad I won't be around to see it."

The vice president stands, heading for the door.

"Was that your official resignation?" Borgia calls out. "Because we accept!"

Chaney flips him the middle finger and leaves.

President Maller catches up to him in the corridor. "Privacy room. Now, Mr. Chaney."

The vice president glares at his commander-in-chief, then follows him into one of the soundproof privacy booths.

Maller fogs the windows. "What's with you? Since when do you allow Borgia to bait you over a hypothetical catastrophe? You're smarter than that."

"Maybe I'm tired of dealing with stupid people, Mark. See, the problem with stupid is it's forever. You can't change stupid. Believe me, I've tried."

"I need you to try harder." The president looks him in the eye. "I have my own ticking time bomb to deal with. December first will be my last day in office."

Chaney's eyes tear up. "How long have you known?"

"About seven months."

"Yet you still ran?"

"I ran so we'd get elected, so you'd be there to take the baton."

"Why me?"

"For all the reasons you just demonstrated in that meeting. Because you put the people first. Because you care about what's really important. Now, it's your show. You want to change stupid, you'll have your chance. Clean house. Do what's necessary."

"And the caldera?"

"Pray it doesn't happen. Warn the people if you feel it's best. Most won't leave anyway, but do it if you feel it's the right thing. Meanwhile, quietly prep the facilities, just in case. Just remember, it's a lot easier to object to who goes in than to actually select who gets saved."

SOUTH FLORIDA EVALUATION AND TREATMENT CENTER
MIAMI, FLORIDA

"Out of the question." Dr. Foletta continues moving down the corridor, Dominique giving chase. "The Mule's been in solitary for a long time, suddenly forcing him outside, even for only an hour a day, would potentially be a danger to the other residents."

"I thought about that, sir. The yard's clear from 2:15 to 3:15 every day."

"We'd have to post more guards, deviate from the inmate's routine. Today's my first day back from vacation, give me a week to settle in."

"With all due respect, sir, Samuel Agler's been in solitary for eleven years. Maybe that goes over in Massachusetts, but it'll never fly at this facility. Now you either allow me to arrange yard time for my patient, or you can explain to the board of regents why he's the exception to the rule."

Foletta turns on her, his cherub face flushing red. "Who the hell do you think you are, Intern? I've been running asylums since before you were born."

"Then you know I speak the truth. One hour a day, that's all I'm asking for."

"And if I agree?"

"Then I'll cosign his evaluation as you requested."

Foletta's gray eyes scrutinize her, sweat beads dripping down the side of his face. "One hour. Nothing more. And you'll sign his evaluation before lunch."

The yard at the South Florida Evaluation and Treatment Center is a rectangular stretch of lawn surrounded on all four sides. The L-shape of the main building encloses the perimeter to the east and south, the north and western borders walled off by a twenty-foot stark white concrete barrier topped with coils of barbed wire.

There are no doors in the yard. To exit the grass-covered atrium, one must ascend three flights of cement steps, which lead to an open mezzanine running the length of the southern side of the facility.

Samuel Agler walks across the expanse of lawn, enjoying each blade of grass squeezed between his bare toes, luxuriating in every breath of fresh, unfiltered air. Tilting his head back, he allows the sun's rays to beat down upon his face, causing his flesh to tingle and his blood vessels to vasodilate.

Dominique watches him, feeling the eyes of every guard upon them. "How do you feel?"

"Reborn."

Mick and I finally have everything ready, we're getting you out tonight. How?

I've been staying late, pretending to be studying for my certification. Paul Jones makes his last round at eight fifteen, then the night guy takes over—Luis Lopez. This is Lopez's second job, and his wife just had a baby, so he usually dozes off by eleven in one of the pods. I'll spike his coffee just to be sure.

First-floor security is wired in to every video camera, how do we manage to bypass the system?

Raymond works the night shift this week. I'm going to bait him into paying you a late-night visit. He'll shock you before he attacks. Mick gave me a device that will interfere with the transponder receiver on your ankle cuff. Slip it inside your shoe before you leave the yard, then once you're alone in your cell adhere it to the ankle bracelet so it covers the wireless antenna. Mick will be waiting outside for you in a white van.

They stroll past the concrete wall, Sam's eyes casually inspecting every crack and fissure. *What about you? You'll be a fugitive.*

When Raymond wakes up, I'll be lying next to him, unconscious. You'll erase the master tapes before you leave to protect my cover story. We'll rendez-vous when we can.

You mean in Nazca?

How did you know that?

Mick took you there weeks ago. Whatever you saw—it made you afraid.

Let's stay focused on tonight. She checks her watch. *Stop walking and put on your shoes, I need to give you the device.*

He stops and kneels in the grass, slipping on his shoes.

From her pocket she removes a metal wafer the size of a stamp and casually drops it on the ground.

Sam slips it inside his shoe.

One last detail—we need to get into a fight. I'm going to ask you to leave. Walk the other way. That will alert the guards. I'll stop them from Tasering you and insist that I handle the situation. When I approach I want you to back-hand me across the face. Hard.

I can't do that.

Yes you can. Think about Laura and Sophie. This is your only shot at saving them.

Dominique checks her watch again. "Quit stalling, Sam. It's time to return to your cell."

Sam hesitates, then walks the other way.

Anthony Foletta watches the yard from his third-floor office, his eyes focused on Samuel Agler, his mind on the voice on the other end of his cell phone. ". . . he'll be in to replace your regular night-shift guy, who will have car trouble. Pull the master fuse on the seventh-floor security cameras at ten fifteen and leave it out for twenty minutes. That's all the time he needs to take care of our friend."

"What about the autopsy?"

"The autopsy will indicate Agler died of heart failure."

"Understood . . . Jesus!" Foletta jumps out of his chair as he witnesses his intern backhanded in the face.

"What's wrong?"

"Your boy just flipped out in the yard. I better get out there before he ends up in the infirmary!" Foletta hangs up, charging out of his office.

A thousand miles to the north, Pierre Borgia hangs up the receiver inside one of the Situation Room's acrylic privacy booths, the secretary of state smiling to himself.

32

The magnet failure last week at the Large Hadron Collider (LHC) means that the accelerator will not be up and running again until early spring 2009, say officials at CERN.

The LHC has lost up to a tonne of liquid helium after some of its superconducting magnets inadvertently heated up. [. . .] The collider is designed to accelerate the subatomic particles known as protons to energies of seven trillion electron volts, far surpassing any other accelerator on Earth, and smash them together in search of new particles, forces and dimensions. To keep the project on schedule, the team running the accelerator near Geneva have decided to skip a planned test run at an intermediate energy level and re-start the LHC in 2009 at the full beam energy of 7 TeV.

—PHYSICSWORLD.COM

SEPTEMBER 24, 2008

Paul Jones finishes his rounds, returning to his security station to collect his lunch pail and car keys. He finds Dominique sprawled out on the vinyl couch, studying.

"Either you've suddenly become studious, or you and Lopez have something going."

"Please. He's married with a new kid. I'm just cramming for my written exams, and it's a lot more quiet here than at my place with my parents."

"How much longer are they staying with you?"

"At least another month."

"How's your face?"

"Still swollen. Guess I learned never to let my guard down."

"You should have shocked him the moment he walked away from you. Don't hesitate. Second chances are rare with these hardcore crazies."

"Understood. Good night." She waits until Jones leaves, then makes a fresh pot of coffee, adding a dozen sedatives to the brew.

An hour passes, still no Luis. Anxious, she takes the elevator down to the first floor, unbuttoning the top three buttons of her blouse.

Raymond has his feet propped up on his desk, the security guard engrossed in a college football game on a palm-size TV. "Going home, Sunshine?"

"Not yet. What happened to Luis Lopez?"

"Called in with car trouble. The agency has a sub on the way. Why? You hot for that little Mexican dude?"

"Actually, I prefer barrel-chested redheads."

Raymond turns to her, flashing a yellowed grin. "About time you came around." He approaches, his eyes glued to her cleavage. "You have no idea how many times I thought about this."

She backs up as he's suddenly pressed against her, his thick calloused fingers caressing her buttocks. "Ray, slow down. Can we just talk a second? Ray . . . look at my face, did you even notice my swollen cheek? Do you know who did this to me? It was my patient, the guy I risked my internship trying to help out. He hit me so hard I saw stars."

"Don't worry. When I finish with him he'll be in a body cast."

"You'd do that for me?"

"After we're through."

"Ray, stop. Ray, someone's coming!"

The man is in his late thirties, his shaved head and dark eyes hidden beneath a New York Mets baseball cap. The security uniform remains taut over a wiry muscular frame. "The agency sent me. Open up."

Raymond looks him over. "Got any ID?"

The man holds up a security card, his mannerisms far too professional for this line of work. Dominique shudders. *A hired assassin?*

"You're on the seventh floor." Raymond buzzes him through, then hands him a transponder and magnetic passkey on a chain. "I assume you know how to use this?"

"No problem, big fella."

Raymond scowls. He waits until the man steps onto the elevator before returning his attention to Dominique. "Now, where were we?"

Samuel Agler hears the elevator ring. He listens intently for the guard's footsteps, but there is no noise.

The CIA assassin slides in stocking feet down the hall, moving silently toward cell 714. His orders are to subdue the target, then inject him with the drug. Pausing outside the pod, he checks his watch: 9:58 p.m.

Too soon. Slowing his breathing, he examines the transponder, waiting . . .

Anthony Foletta dons rubber gloves as he keys into the third-floor electrical closet. He quickly locates the rectangular metal fuse box labeled "Level 7" and opens it. Aided by a flashlight, he scans the rows of three-inch fuses until he finds the one corresponding to "Vid Cam." Using a flathead screwdriver, he pries the fuse free from its slot, then returns to his office to wait.

Raymond is all over her, tearing at her clothing, his bulk too large and close to fend off—just like her cousin so many years ago.

Dominique's heart pounds in her chest, the anxiety making it impossible to breathe. The more she pushes his groping hands away, the more incensed he becomes, driving her panic to a frenzy. She tries to scream, but his garlic-laced tongue muffles her words. She bites down, tasting blood as her mind screams:

Sam! Help!

The cell door opens. The assassin aims the transponder.

Sam flops onto his back on the floor, his mouth frothing with the mixture of water and toothpaste, his mind focused on the turn of events. *New guard. He wants me subdued.*

The guard moves in quickly, the hypodermic needle concealed in his right hand.

Wham! Sam's heel catches him in the chest, the powerful kick crushing his sternum while causing the bundle of nerves in his solar plexus to spasm. He writhes on the ground by the open door, wheezing air.

Sam contemplates taking the guard's uniform when he hears the desperate cry from the void:

Sam! Help!

"Uhh!" He looks down in disbelief, the spent hypodermic needle protruding from his calf muscle, the guard lying on his side, grinning.

"Trick or treat."

Sam kicks the smile off his face before stumbling backward, the cell spinning in his head, his heart pounding, his mind tracking the icelike presence in his vein as the foreign substance circulates methodically through his bloodstream—

—slowing to a crawl as Sam slips inside a strangely familiar corridor of existence, the air gelid, his movements propelling him out of the cell and into the awaiting elevator.

Steroids have shortened Raymond's fuse, turning lust into an act of aggression. He spits out blood, then balls his fist and punches Dominique in the face, breaking her nose.

She goes limp beneath him.

The elevator rings, causing him to look up. The doors open.

Turquoise-blue eyes race toward him behind a blur of white, striking him with the force of a tank. His rib cage crushes his internal organs and squeezes his heart muscle so hard his aorta bursts a second before his spine shatters against the cinder-block wall.

Dominique awakens to flesh so hot it scalds. She is moving impossibly fast through the reception area on a gurney, only somehow it is not a gurney. Before she can fathom who is carrying her she is outside, looking up at a blurred night sky.

The heavens are replaced with the back of a van. Mick's voice echoes in her brain, the sound shaping into words—escorted by the explosive pain in her face.

". . . he's been drugged. Dom, I need you to drive the van. Dominique!"

"Okay!" She climbs behind the wheel and accelerates away from the asylum, using her sleeve to wipe blood and tears from her swollen face.

341

33

We are born with the schizophrenia of good and evil within us, so that each generation must persevere in self-recognition and in self-control. In ceding to the automatic reassurance of our logic, we have abandoned once more those powers of recognition and of control. Darkness seems scarcely different from light, with the web of structure and logic woven thick across both. We must therefore cut away these layers of false protection if we wish to regain control of our common sense and morality.

—JOHN RALSTON SAUL

VOLTAIRE'S BASTARDS, 1992

I am great. My place is now higher than that of the human work, the human design. I am their sun and I am their light, and I am also their months. So be it: my light is great. I am the walkway and I am the foothold of the people . . . I am the vanquisher."

Seven Macaw dances before Chilam Balam and his followers in the shadow of the great temple, the evil one's eyes red and serpentlike, his fanged teeth stained blue.

Every inch of his skin is tattooed, his fingertips ending in sharp clawed nails.

The scent of burundanga powder is heavy in Chilam Balam's nose. He can feel the toxin moving through his bloodstream, delivering its icy wave of paralyzing rigidity to his muscles. Terror turns to panic as he loses the capacity to breathe, the air wheezing from his mouth like a downed deer succumbing to the arrow.

I am Chilam Balam who led you across frigid wasteland and shoreline blackened with death. I am the Jaguar Prophet who guided you to this fertile land. Will no one come to my aid?

A warm light, soothing in its brilliance, appears above his head. The voice of Viracocha reaches out to him from the void: *You gave them everything, and still it was not enough. Greed has led them to the dark side, where chaos abounds. And yet they could have had it all—happiness and eternal fulfillment beyond any riches.*

How, Lord? How could they have had it all?

Simply by understanding the true test of existence—that we were created to love one another, that our own fulfillment comes when we treat others with dignity.

And what of Seven Macaw?

Evil is the necessary test that determines whether your nation is worthy of the gift of immortality. This generation is not. The people are laden with selfishness and want, the seed of evil passed on to their children. Their hands are stained by the blood of their enemies, their altars soiled from human sacrifices. Do you believe this is what the Creator desires? Do you believe the Holy One seeded man so that He could watch his children destroy one another through the self-validation of hatred and intolerance? Prayer is nothing more than a burden when the assembly tramples flowers in the Creator's garden. Justice washes clean the soul only when the oppressed are aided, the powerful rebuked, the fatherless cared for.

Chilam Balam's heart goes silent, the air still, save for Seven Macaw's blade severing his head from his neck.

His body slips away, the warm light catching his soul, embracing it. He gazes upon his decapitated vessel and his fallen nation—the people crying out in horror as their holiest of temples buckles with their dead prophet, the pyramid's base collapsing beneath an avalanche of greed and negativity, envy and hatred.

* * *

—try to open your eyes.

The female voice startles him into action. He struggles against an immovable weight until he realizes he has no arms.

Fight your way out. Create pain.

He stands amid blackness and feels for the wall, bloodying the cold stone with his face. Over and over he strikes the dungeonlike enclosure until he finds his hands tingling somewhere in the abyss. Encouraged, he bashes the pit's rounded walls harder, all the while opening and closing his long-lost appendages, the pain giving birth to arms. His fingers walk up his broken upper torso to the diseased flesh he has bashed into pulp and claw at the amber sealing his eyes until he unveils the light—

—a narrow slit of geography teasing him from above—a torturous crevice of rock situated between daylight and the rat-infested hovel he now occupies. He looks around, his mind, fighting to awaken from its forced hibernation, still too numb to comprehend his surroundings.

He reaches high along the cracked ceiling into the crevice, managing a precarious grip of rock. Pressing his bare feet along the ceiling for leverage, he pulls himself into the fissure and begins climbing, working his way up the narrow shaft. Shards of limestone slice apart his flesh, tree roots force him into binding contortions that pin him so tightly to the earth he can barely draw a breath.

Finally he emerges to daylight, his effort rewarded with a rush of briny air.

His perch resides at the summit of a mountain. A fine white mist conceals the sea to the west—he can hear the waves as they batter the rocky shoreline below. Looking down, he can make out a symbol, glistening with sun-doused moisture on the mountain's western face—a massive trident, carved deep into the rock.

Then he sees the man.

Tall and pale as the mist, with matching silky-white hair and beard and piercing Mayan-blue eyes, he is standing by the summit's edge, waiting.

"Are you my guide? The one who will take me to *Hunab K'u?*"

"You have not earned the right to see the Creator."

"Who are you to speak to me in this manner? I am Chilam Balam, the greatest prophet in history."

"If you were such a great prophet, Chilam Balam, then how were you defeated in battle? You should have foreseen the evil of Seven Macaw and struck him down. Instead, you continued to feed upon the tree of knowledge until it satiated your ego and blinded you to your quest."

"Quest? What quest?"

"You were tasked with advancing the evolution of the Hunahpu. Your desire to bathe in the light of *Hunab K'u* for yourself alone has brought darkness to your people."

The mist clears to the east, unveiling a city situated in a mountain valley. Once-fertile land has dried to near-desert conditions, the surrounding hillsides plundered for their minerals.

A bloodred pyramid towers above the city, its surface sparkling with encrusted gemstones. Thousands of worshipers have gathered below. A dozen wait to be sacrificed.

Seven Macaw emerges atop the summit platform, his voice booming across the city's decimated remains: "I am great. My place is now higher than that of the human work, the human design. I am their sun and I am their light, and I am also their months. So be it: my light is great. I am the walkway and I am the foothold of the people . . . I am the vanquisher. Bring forth the soul mate of Chilam Balam."

A woman, naked and painted blue, is led up the temple steps, her presence ushering the onlookers to silence. Four priests escort her to an idol where she is laid faceup over the convex stone, her arms and legs held in place, the men's eyes wandering.

Seven Macaw stares lustfully at Blood Woman, then, with a bone-chilling screech, he plunges the ebony blade of the obsidian dagger just below the woman's left breast. Quickly reaching inside the wound, the *nacom* priest withdraws the victim's still-beating heart from her gushing chest cavity and passes it to one of the four clerics, who smears the blood onto the stone idol.

Returning to the butchered corpse, Seven Macaw kicks the remains of Blood Woman down the steep pyramid steps, the lifeless body cracking and twisting and contorting its way to the bottom where it is collected by lower-ranking priests. The barbarians quickly skin the remains, leaving the hands and feet attached to the human hide.

Seven Macaw's son, Earthquake, is presented the flayed suit of flesh. Securing it to his own limbs, he dances among the solemn spectators, re-animating the dead woman.

"Search the mountains and coast. Bring me Hunaphu and Xbalanque. The sons of Chilam Balam shall honor my greatness with their blood before the next full moon."

The mist returns, once more cloaking the valley.

Chilam Balam kneels, tears blurring his vision. "Am I dead?"

The pale warrior with the white hair and beard turns to face him. "Chilam Balam is dead, but the spirit that commands you shall be reborn. Are you ready to continue your journey?"

"And my soul mate?"

"She too shall be reborn."

"Will our paths cross again?"

"If you are so deserving."

"Then take me to her, but first, tell me your name."

"My name is Jacob. I am your brother."

Languishing in a feverish delirium, Immanuel Gabriel opens his eyes, his heart beating rapidly in his chest, a tube down his throat, incubating his chest. Through a slit of vision blurred with hot tears he sees a man resembling a youthful Mitchell Kurtz hovering over him, hurriedly connecting an intravenous bag to his veins.

Drips of soothing warm relief drift slowly into his bloodstream, thawing the ice, pushing his mind toward blessed unconsciousness.

346

34

God places the heaviest burden on those who can carry its weight.

**—REGGIE WHITE,
NFL HALL OF FAME DEFENSIVE LINEMAN
AND ORDAINED MINISTER**

And so it is with a heavy heart but unwavering confidence that I relinquish the office of the presidency to Vice President Ennis William Chaney. May God bless our new president, his family, administration, and the people of the United States of America."

The plastic case containing a Ted Williams autographed baseball smashes the fifty-two-inch HD television with such force it knocks the flat screen off its stand, sending it crashing onto the marble floor.

Pierre Borgia searches his desk top for something else to throw. He reaches for the near-empty bottle of Jack Daniel's, drains the remains of the copper-colored whiskey, then heaves the object at a framed black and white Ansel Adams photograph of Yosemite National Park, denting the wall instead.

The cell phone rings again. Borgia glances at the number. Groans, then answers it. "What?"

"This changes nothing, son. Trust me."

"Trust you, Uncle Joe? Marion Rallo's been tapped for VP, Chaney's already asked for my resignation. As for the war—expect him to announce the complete withdrawal of troops in January's State of the Union speech."

"It'll be handled. The bigger problem is all the loose ends from your little bugaboo in Miami."

"There are no loose ends. Whoever drove off with Agler probably dumped his corpse in the Everglades. As for the girl, there's a massive manhunt going on across the state, though she's most likely dead, too."

"And the security guard?"

"The sheriff's office is blaming Raymond's death on Agler. I made a statement . . . what else do you want from me?"

"You still haven't watched the tape, have you?"

"What tape?"

"Pierre, don't you get my phone messages and e-mail? I sent you an excerpt pulled from the first-floor surveillance camera."

"I saw the original footage, Uncle Joe. There was nothing to see."

"There was a blur that appeared on tape a second after the elevator door opened. That blur, slowed down frame by frame, was Samuel Agler."

Pierre sobers. "My guy swears he injected Agler with the cardiac inhibitor, there's no way—"

"His eyes were Nordic blue; he was moving through a higher plane of existence when he struck that moron, Raymond. Your guard didn't just die of internal bleeding, Pierre; his organs burst."

"Assuming Agler's still alive, he'll try to find his wife and daughter."

"Agreed. I want you back here at Groom Lake. There's a private jet waiting for you at Dulles."

"I can't just up and leave. If something's going to happen with Chaney, I need to be available."

"Wrong, for two reasons. First, in your present state of mind I don't want you anywhere near the television cameras. Two, Agler doesn't know where his wife and kid are. That means he'll be coming after you."

"Ahhhhhh!"

Immanuel Gabriel shoots up in bed to a roar in his ears and a stabbing pain coming from the left side of his chest cavity.

Mitchell Kurtz yanks the spent hypodermic needle from his heart. "Sorry, pal. My orders were to wake you. A shot of Adrenalin seemed like the best option."

Manny gasps air, the clamor in his ears reduced to an annoying siren. His extremities are tingling, his throat too parched to speak.

As if reading his mind, Kurtz places a bottle of water to his lips.

He drinks, chokes, and drinks some more—his eyes widening as a youthful Ryan Beck enters the room.

"Man, you ain't gonna believe the shit that's happening. He's awake?"

"He's still coming out of it. Where's Dom and Mick?"

"On their way."

"Get him on his feet. See if you can help him find his legs." Kurtz turns to Manny. "Someone hired a trained assassin to kill you. He injected you with a very fast-acting agent designed to stop the heart. You've been in a coma for four weeks; by all logic, you should be dead. Somehow you were able to slow your heart down to the point that the poison stagnated in your femoral artery. Lucky for you, Mick called me, I'm familiar with the drug that was used and was able to advise the ER physician how to treat you. We got you out of Dodge two hours later. You're in Nazca, Peru. This morning all hell started breaking loose, and we decided to take a chance and wake you."

"What day . . . is it?"

"Friday."

"He means the date," says Beck, who is shouldering Manny, helping him to his feet. "Today's December 21. By the way, I'm Beck; he's Kurtz. We work for President Chaney."

"I know who you are. I've known the two of you since the day I hope to be born."

Kurtz makes the crazy sign to Beck behind Manny's back.

"Salt and Pepper, that's what my brother and I used to call you. Mitch, the last time I saw you, your hair was the color of salt and you were telling women you were a movie producer just to get laid. Pep here was a grandfather, still a big man at sixty-five."

The two bodyguards look at one another, unsure.

The front door of the Gabriel home bursts open; the entering Mick and Dominique find themselves confronted by the barrels of the two bodyguards' assault weapons.

"Whoa, easy, fellas."

Kurtz holsters his gun. "I gave you a knock, Mick. You either use it or get shot; it's your choice."

"He's awake?" Dominique rushes over to Manny, looking into his eyes. "They're black again. Last time I saw them they were Mayan blue. Sam, can you remember anything?"

"I'm not Sam. Sam was never my name, just an alias I used when I was a teen . . . when I refused to accept who I really am. My name is Immanuel Gabriel. You and Michael are my parents."

Dominique stares at him, her lower lip quivering. "Mick told me, I didn't want to believe it."

Kurtz shakes his head. "I'm living in an episode of *The Twilight Zone.*"

"We don't have time to rehash this," Mick says. "Manny, today's the last day of the fifth cycle. The Yellowstone caldera exploded an hour ago. Volcanoes are erupting everywhere."

"The same thing happened in 2047. The strangelet's making its final pass through the Earth's core."

"Please tell me you know how to stop this thing."

"No, but I know who does."

An ominous brown haze has spread quickly across the distant northern sky by the time the hot air balloon lands on the Nazca plateau. Beck and Kurtz secure the basket to the ground, Mick and Dominique escorting Immanuel to the center of the Nazca Spiral.

"Manny, you sure my father said only One Hunahpu can stop the strangelet?"

"They were Julius's last words."

"I don't understand," Dominique says. "Who is One Hunahpu?"

"It's best I don't say."

Brown ash falls from the heavens like snow flurries as they reach the center of the Spiral.

Mick pulls his T-shirt over his mouth to speak, his eyes searching the darkening heavens. "You know, Manny, my whole life Julius was in my head, preparing me for this day. I have to confess, I didn't fully believe it could happen until I saw the video records aboard your shuttle. Even then . . . But now that it's here—this is seriously bad."

"My brother, Jacob, was on me the same way. 'Gotta train harder, Manny, the Underlords want us dead.' He drove me crazy. Then the day arrived and the *Balam* appeared out of the heavens and suddenly it was time to go. And I refused. All I wanted was to play pro ball and live in a big mansion and be a star. Instead, I spent the next fourteen years in hiding."

Dominique rubs his back. "Edie used to tell me, 'God only gives us the burdens He knows we can handle.' "

"No offense to God, but I think our family's had more than our share." Manny's eyes widen. "Dominique, are your foster parents still living in your high-rise?"

"Yes. What's wrong?"

"There's a tsunami headed their way. A big one—higher than your building."

"Oh my God." She powers on her cell phone to text Edie, no longer worried about the FBI tracing her location.

Mick's eyes catch movement overhead—a glimmer of metal descending from the volcanic ash clouds. "Dom, we need to go."

"I'm not done texting—"

"Text back in the balloon, our friends have arrived." He turns to Manny. "Julius was right, there are no coincidences. Whatever happens, I'm glad we had a chance to meet."

Manny pinches away tears. "Me, too."

Father and son embrace, then Michael Gabriel takes Dominique by her hand and the two of them make a hasty retreat back to the balloon—as a white light bathes Manny in its soothing brilliance, the twinkling aura of energy levitating him away from the Nazca pampa into the awaiting aperture of the bulbous-shaped extraterrestrial ship.

For a long moment the Fastwalker simply remains poised above the desert carving. Then it shoots into the heavens at the speed of light, joined in space by hundreds more, their designs representing dozens of different subspecies—all emerging from the far side of the moon to escort their long-lost prophet to the destiny that awaits.

35

The white haze filters into a cool mist that dissipates across the garden's azure lagoon.

Immanuel Gabriel opens his eyes. He walks along the pink sand past the pristine waterfall to the mountain-size inverted tree, its upper three limbs beyond his scope of view, the cluster of six branches that follow spread out majestically overhead as far and wide as his consciousness can perceive. Ahead, the trunk melds into the naked man and woman standing back to back—hundred-foot giants fused at the vertebrae.

Manny approaches the illusion projected across the cosmos by the unified thoughts of his parents. "The last time I was here was because you willed it. This time the choice is mine. Tell me what I must do to save the Earth."

His father's voice speaks to him telepathically. *You think yourself worthy of such a task?*

Manny stands before the tree of life, his being trembling. "Am I worthy? I've suffered the loss of two soul mates. I've spent an eternity tortured by Seven Macaw. I haven't seen my wife and daughter for eleven years. What more do you want?"

Transformation. You continue to see yourself as a victim of existence. Salvation requires a connection with the higher realms, a connection with the Creator's light. Victims cannot access this energy, they remain consumed by the ego.

"I'm not here as a victim. Give me the opportunity and I'll prove to you I'm worthy. Let me rid your garden of its serpent."

What you fail to see, Immanuel, is that you are the serpent.

"What? How am I—"

The hero twins were conceived with a symbiotic relationship. Your brother, Jacob, cleaved to the tree of life that you see before you, which is why his soul remained pure. You were bound to the tree of knowledge, a dark side that cleaves to the human ego. Lacking restriction, you consumed the tree's forbidden fruit until you became a slave to it. As Chilam Balam, your soul sought the dark gift to become a powerful sorcerer and seer, yet you never challenged the Maya to end its savage violence, fearful of angering the Council and losing your power. As Immanuel Gabriel, you refused to accompany Jacob to Xibalba, seeking only to live out your days for yourself alone.

"I was afraid. And yes, it's true, I was selfish. I didn't want to lose everything I had worked so hard for just to appease Jacob. It was his mission, not mine. He was more advanced than I, far stronger."

And yet, as powerful as Jacob was, he could not succeed in the eleventh dimension of Hell without your ability to adapt to the dark side. You were the yin to his yang. Through cause and effect, you lost everything. Through cause and effect, it was you who brought the singularity to the winter solstice of 2012.

"I brought it? That's insane! Jacob instructed me to return to this time."

And because you lacked a connection with the light, your journey through the wormhole served as a conduit for the strangelet. Now it is too late. Earth, and humanity with it, shall perish.

"That's it? I don't believe you! Where is the Fastwalker taking me? To Xibalba?"

The white haze rises from the soil, concealing his parents and the tree of life. When the mist clears, Immanuel finds himself in the extraterrestrial craft, staring out a vast portal into deep space.

The ship is orbiting Mars, soaring just above another object in space—an immense eighteen-mile-long, twelve-mile-wide mouse-gray spherical object, its surface identified by an enormous crater.

Immanuel Gabriel's pulse quickens as he stares at the moonlike mass racing along the starboard portal.

Phobos . . .

SITUATION ROOM, WHITE HOUSE

The chamber has gone quiet, every man and woman focused on the nearest flat-screen television as the images from Camp Borneo display on-screen.

The dense clouds poised over the North Pole are engaged in a powerful clockwise dance, the swirling vortex drawing the toxic blanket of volcanic ash into space as if inhaled by a heavenly maelstrom.

"Sir, NASA is receiving images from the Hubble. They confirm the funnel cloud is jettisoning the atmospheric debris into space."

"It's a miracle," an aide cries out, her outburst effecting an avalanche of applause.

"Quiet!" A harried President Chaney stares at the rushing gray-brown river of atmospheric debris, as baffled as the dozen scientists in the room. "You say it's jettisoning the debris into space—where exactly is it going? Is it orbiting our planet?"

"No, sir. NASA says it's streaming into space and dissipating, at least as far as they can tell. There's a lot of atmospheric interference. Maybe it really is a miracle?"

Nods of agreement.

"Now listen up," Chaney bellows. "I don't want to hear about miracles or Second Comings or any such nonsense. I want answers, and I want them fast. Where the hell's that damn megawave?"

"It just struck Jacksonville, now it's bearing down on the coast of Miami."

SOUTH FLORIDA EVALUATION AND TREATMENT CENTER
MIAMI, FLORIDA

Anthony Foletta continues moving down the empty seventh-floor corridor, hounded by his new head of security.

"Sir, the bus is loaded and waiting," Paul Jones pleads. "All that's left is the Level 7 patients—"

"—who will remain incarcerated, Mr. Jones. Why I allowed you to talk me into this course of action in the first place . . . I should have my head examined. No wave is going to reach this far inland, I don't care how big it is."

"Sir—"

"Get on the bus and leave. Now, Mr. Jones, before I change my mind and order all inmates returned to their cells."

Jones shakes his head and races to the elevator.

Foletta sits in the security lounge, returning to his laptop and his application for the directorship vacancy in Ontario, Canada. The salary is far less than he's earning in Miami, but the cost of living in Ontario is lower, and severing his ties with Pierre Borgia is necessary for his own mental health.

He continues working on the application another fifteen minutes, when he hears the rumble.

Foletta saves the file, then walks to the alcove and the fire ladder leading up to the roof. He contemplates the climb, then pulls himself up one rung at a time as the rumbling grows louder.

The painful impact of his right shoulder against the metal hatch forces open the exit. He climbs onto the roof, gazing east.

The seven-story building is far too low and inland to view the Atlantic Ocean, but something large is definitely approaching. His eyes lock onto a high-rise blocking his sightline, his pulse pounding, the reverberations registering in his bones.

He winces as the high-rise collapses surreally before him, revealing a horizon of surging ocean. He refuses to move, not even when the first concrete-laced droplets of sea strike him in the face, nor when the mega-tsunami bashes through the streets, foaming as it reaches the asylum, searching for a way in.

It finds nothing.

Foletta smiles as the five-story surge makes an island of his rooftop sanctuary, affording him the best view in Miami.

And then, like a slowly bursting dam, the aged cinder-block structure crumbles along its eastern face and the rooftop fragments, the Atlantic Ocean swallowing the facility beneath him.

The dense brown volcanic cloud blanketing the once-cobalt-blue sky has turned into a raging river of mud, sweeping the hot air balloon and its four frightened occupants to the northeast at a terrifying 125 knots.

"It's the Rapture," Beck yells, crossing himself.

"It's the caldera," Kurtz counters. "No trumpets, no Jesus riding on a white steed, just a lot of snow and ice and mass starvation."

"Ain't no caldera causing this wind! This is Revelation!"

The Pacific Ocean beckons beyond the plateau, offering certain death. Spotting the mountaintop, Mick shuts off the flame, collapsing the envelope. Dominique cries out as the balloon drops into a steep descent. The basket skims the mountain's western face, bounces across the summit, then abruptly smashes into the side of a boulder with a bone-jarring jolt, flinging its startled occupants across the jagged crest.

Within seconds, hurricane winds sweep the partially deflated balloon high into the air. For several minutes it spirals out of control, until the wind shear snatches it, driving it into the raging Pacific whitecaps.

Dominique is on her knees. She is battered and bruised, but her attention is focused on a monolithic carving etched into the western face of the mountain.

Mick crawls over, shouting to be heard over the gale. "You okay?"

"What is that?"

"Trident of Paracas. Traces back to Viracocha. Come on, I saw a cave to the east, we can take shelter!" He drags her to her feet, leading Dominique and the two guards to the dark void, partially concealed behind boulders.

Kurtz shakes his head. "You three go on in, I'm a bit claustrophobic."

Beck nods. "I'll stay out here with the little guy."

Kurtz waits until Dominique and Mick are inside the cave before conversing. "I was able to reach the Situation Room," he yells above the atmospheric roar. "There's some kind of vortex poised over the North Pole, drawing all this ash into space."

"You think it's HAARP?"

"Let's hope so. I sent POTUS a photo I took of that alien spacecraft."

"Think he'll believe it?"

"Hell, I don't believe it and I saw the damn thing. But he needs to be aware, just in case the object sucking up the atmosphere isn't one of ours."

Mick and Dominique enter the cave—a seven-foot-high tunnel of rock that twists and disappears into darkness.

"Mick, that trident . . . I've seen it before. Sam drew it on his cell wall. What do you think it means?"

"I don't know, but as my father used to say, there are no coincidences. Let's see where this cave leads."

They follow the tunnel of rock into the darkness, the cave becoming a twisting, rapidly descending cavern, its geology lit by a soft blue hue coming from somewhere below.

"Mick, where's that light coming from?"

"Let's find out. Take my hand, it gets pretty steep."

He takes the lead, the thirty-degree slope forcing him to crouch into deep side-steps, the rock beneath his boots offering a natural traction.

"Dom, listen! Do you hear that?"

"The rush of air?"

"No. Something deeper . . . like a generator switching on."

The cavern continues spiraling downward, funneling them deeper into the mountain until the path abruptly levels out and they are standing before an immense object—a twelve-foot-high rectangular frame of highly polished metal.

Centering the object, glowing in neon-blue light, is the symbol of the Trident of Paracas.

"Mick?"

"I can't be sure, but I think . . . it's the *Balam*."

"How can that be? You told me Jacob and I left on the *Balam* back in 2032."

"Manny looped time, maybe the *Balam* did, too?"

"How do we get inside?"

"We possess the twins' genetics; let's try telepathy. Hold my hand, then close your eyes. On three, imagine the passage opening. One . . . two—"

The portal slides open, beckoning them inside.

Dominique shrugs. "Sorry. Jumped the gun."

They enter a dimly lit corridor, the floor, walls, and thirty-foot arched ceiling composed of a highly polished, translucent-black polymer. The confines are warm, the only light coming from the obsidian panels' luminescent blue glow.

Mick pauses to press his face against the dark glass, attempting to peer inside. "I think something is behind these walls, but the glass is so tinted, I can't see a damn thing." He turns to Dominique, who gives him a terrified look. "You okay?"

"Okay?" She grins nervously, her lower lip quivering. "No, I don't think I've been *okay* since the day I met you."

He takes her hand. "Don't be scared. This vessel belongs to our son."

"Mick, we don't have a son. Another Michael and Dominique in another lifetime had twin sons. You and me? Never happened. Nor will it ever happen. Not because I don't like you," she wipes back tears, "but because I don't think we're going to survive the day."

He moves in close, hugging her to his chest. "We'll survive."

"How do you know?"

"I know because I'm standing in a starship that's probably more powerful than anything else in the galaxy. I know because the bloodlines of a superior race of humans run through our veins. Most of all, I know because I have faith."

She holds him tightly. Then she looks up into his ebony eyes, leans in, and kisses him.

3 6

We know nothing at all. All our knowledge is but the knowledge of schoolchildren. The real nature of things we shall never know.

Reality is merely an illusion, albeit a very persistent one.

—ATTRIBUTED TO ALBERT EINSTEIN

PHOBOS

Discovered in 1877, the celestial object dubbed Phobos is seven times larger than the Red Planet's other moon, Deimos, and revolves so close to Mars that it actually orbits faster than the planet can rotate. This unusual characteristic, combined with its unique surface density, led astrophysicists to postulate that Phobos was neither a moon nor asteroid but a hollow iron sphere.

A white haze obscures Immanuel Gabriel's vision, and then it absorbs him, its particles dancing across his flesh and deep into his muscles and bone marrow. His body trembles; as if the mist has penetrated every cell in his body, stretching the spaces between every proton, neutron, and electron in his body—

—the effect culminating in the sudden sensation of gravity literally pulling his collection of molecules *through* the atomic structure of the extraterrestrial vessel—his atoms having separated just enough to allow him to slip into the cold vastness of space, only he cannot feel the cold, merely the rush of vertigo as he is squeezed inside the rocky metallic surface of Phobos.

Immanuel doubles over in agony as the microscopic gaps between his cells shrink back to their original size, the bizarre feeling causing him to tingle and itch.

Then he realizes it is not his flesh that is itching, it is a thin luminescent dermal film encasing his entire body like a second skin, warming and protecting him while allowing him to breathe.

He looks around, his suit's light revealing a metal interior scorched long ago from what appears to have been a flash fire.

Immanuel recalls his brother's words, delivered outside the cave of Rabbi Shimon bar Yochai. *"Our parents never died. Their collective consciousness remains trapped."*

"Trapped? Where? Jake, where are they trapped?"

"On Phobos . . . Our parents were taken aboard a Guardian transport before the sun went supernova. The transport entered the wormhole, followed by the Balam. The wormhole deposited both vessels far into the past. Phobos isn't a moon, it's all that remains of the Guardian's transport vessel. Our parents are held inside, their consciousness trapped in cryogenic stasis."

Guided by the glow coming from his protective second skin, Immanuel Gabriel moves through an access corridor where he comes across evidence of a mortal breach in the ship's hull. The craterlike indentation, as large as a three-story building, has been sealed, but not before the asteroid impact caused a tremendous explosion, venting the interior of the transport ship.

The corridor leads to the top section of a massive acrylic dome, covered in dust. Brushing away debris, Manny peers through the top of the glass—a vast particle chamber, one of dozens that service a photonic reactor—an antimatter power plant generating hundreds of trillions of photons, each traveling at the speed of light. These avalanches of potential energy remain separated from their matter counterparts by collection chambers made up of powerful electromagnetic rotational fields.

For several minutes Manny simply stares, mesmerized by the swirling emerald-green vortices of antimatter, the power hub of the ship.

Continuing on, he enters a massive cathedral-like chamber as large as three Superdomes. Set in countless levels and rows like alien dominoes are eight-foot-high pods—tens of thousands of them. Most of the containers are shattered and empty, their contents having been sucked out into space by the breach in the ship's hull.

Manny approaches a row of containers that appear intact. He rubs at the frosted glass of one pod, revealing the lifeless remains of a tall being, its body naked and frozen, its skull hairless and elongated.

Post-humans. The genetic donors of the Hunahpu.

The thought is projected into his mind so quickly it startles him.

Mick?

He follows the perceived direction of the buzzing sensation in his skull, crossing a walkway to an immense vaultlike door. The panel lights are glowing with power.

He drags open the vault door and enters a small lab, his senses bombarded by "ghosts" of thought-energy being projected from the spherical chamber's walls.

He listens as his mother asks, *What is this place?* He is about to respond when he hears a second female voice, the two engaged in a conversation that had occurred eons ago in this very chamber.

Dominique, this vault is a secured sensory pod, its power source and life-support systems independent of the rest of the ship. Its walls create white noise which serves to shield its occupants from telepathic communication—in essence, rendering it a quiet zone.

Manny looks around. At the center of the chamber are two cryogenic pods. Myriad hoses and wires run from each machine into the floor, linking the pods to one another.

The power source blinks ACTIVE. Manny rubs the frosted glass of the pod on the right, revealing a body inside. "My God."

Michael Gabriel is unconscious and naked, sealed in an amberlike wax. Star-shaped electrodes are melded to points along his scalp, crown, forehead, solar plexus, heart, sacrum, and feet.

His mother is sealed in an identical pod on the left.

More ghostlike thoughts are purged from the chamber.

Why is Mick in there? What are you doing to him?

The experience of fighting off the Abomination for so long has damaged One Hunahpu's mind. The only way to restore his sanity is to rebuild his memories. The post-human's technology gives us the ability to manipulate Michael's mind, to place him into soothing, safe, virtual environments that will allow us to nurture him back to sanity. But the therapy requires a hands-on guide, someone who knows One Hunahpu intimately . . . someone he trusts. The therapy will not only heal his damaged mind, it will allow the two of you to be together. Once inside the pod, you will not be able to distinguish your shared virtual existence from the real world.

Manny stares at the two pods holding his parents. "Lying bastards. They sealed you up in their cryogenic goo and left you for God knows how long."

One hundred twenty-seven million years.

"Dad? How—?"

Your mother and I were joined in a virtual never-ending reality, our consciousness programming its own immortality and fulfillment. Like the Balam, this starship is controlled by an artificial intelligence designed to serve our bloodline. Over the eons, our fused consciousness was able to effect repairs and maintain the vessel's antimatter chamber to prevent the ship's orbit from decaying. Unable to perish, our souls remain anchored to our bodies, which can never be revived. Allow us to move on, Immanuel. Release us from this purgatory.

"How?"

Shut down the power source to our pods. End our existence in the physical world so our souls can move on.

"I will. I'll do it. But first I need your help. Julius told me that only One Hunahpu could prevent the strangelet from consuming the Earth."

The black hole that threatens Earth is a conduit to the eleventh dimension— Xibalba Be, the dark road descending into Xibalba . . . Hell. The passage can only be sealed from within the Underworld itself. Julius suspected I was One Hunahpu, believing I could seal the strangelet from Xibalba based on his interpretation of the Mayan Popol Vuh's creation story. When I entered the serpent's wormhole in my time, I became One Hunahpu, and was trapped in Xibalba by Lilith's son. In that cause-and-effect off-ramp of existence, your brother, Jacob, freed me. Trapped in this endless state of bridled consciousness, I can no longer access the eleventh dimension. I am no longer One Hunahpu.

"Then Earth is doomed. As you said, I'm not worthy enough to save it."

Immanuel, the test of existence is not a test of perfection, it is a test of transformation.

"You were imprisoned in Xibalba; Jake was defeated. If the two of you failed in Hell, what chance do I have? Hello? Dammit, answer me!"

Filled with rage, Manny grabs hold of the power couplings linked to his parents' chambers and violently rips the hoses from the control panels— severing the connection.

The panel lights go dark.

The chamber shudders.

Manny's hair stands on end, the room suddenly charged with electro-magnetic particles as the unleashed souls of his mother and father encircle him, causing the flesh beneath his false skin to spark.

His mother's voice lingers in his ear. *You were chosen for this mission, Manny. Figure out why.*

Gravity tugs on his being with the force of several Gs, expanding his atomic structure even as it yanks him through space and back inside the extraterrestrial vessel. Doubled over in pain, he never feels the light-speed acceleration until the Fastwalker reenters Earth's atmosphere. Charged with electricity, the high-speed conveyor of volcanic ash short circuits the E.T.'s engines.

Spinning out of control, the vessel plunges toward a flat desert terrain before regaining enough of its antigravity propulsion to pull out of the dive. The belly of the extraterrestrial ship skims sand and rock before crash-landing upon its intended landing zone—

—Area 51.

37

I, at any rate, am convinced that He [God] does not
play dice.

—ALBERT EINSTEIN,
LETTER TO MAX BORN,
DECEMBER 4, 1926

ABOARD THE *BALAM*
NAZCA, PERU

In the corridor of a starship that predates their own existence, a naked man and woman caught in a loop of space-time join as one, doing their part to conceive the first generation of an advanced race who may one day build the very starship they now inhabit.

The act of copulation over, Mick rests his weight on his elbows, staring into the eyes of his predestined soul mate. "So beautiful . . ."

Her eyes closed in a state of bliss, Dominique smiles, clenching her legs tighter around the small of his back. "Admit it—this whole Doomsday thing . . . it was just an excuse to get me in bed."

"The first time I saw you . . . I knew you were the one—the one I'd spend eternity with."

She opens her eyes and notices his irises radiating azure blue. "Mick, your eyes!"

"Yours too." He rolls off of her, his mind racing.

"What's happening to us?"

"Our Hunahpu genes are active." He pulls on his pants.

"Where are you going?"

"To the command center. If I'm right, we now have control of the ship."

She dresses quickly, following him into an onion-shaped control room, its domed ceiling three stories high. Mick stands in the center of the chamber. Closes his eyes . . .

A neon-blue beam illuminates the top of his skull. Seconds later, the onyx glass panels light up like a Christmas tree, the floor reverberating beneath their feet as the *Balam*'s power plant activates for the first time since dinosaurs roamed the Earth.

"Mick, what are you doing?"

"I need to see that black hole. I'm going to fly her into space."

"Her?"

"It. Does artificial intelligence have a gender?"

"What about Beck and Kurtz? Break free of this mountain and you'll bury them in rubble."

"Yeah, you're right. Stay here, I'll get them, just don't touch anything while I'm gone. Don't even think. Think about baseball."

"I hate baseball."

"Then think about the fertilized egg growing inside your womb."

"Michael, shut up and go!"

Lying on his back on the coarse desert sand, Immanuel Gabriel gazes up at the turbulent brown sky, the seemingly endless heavens of volcanic ash racing north at more than five times the velocity of a commercial jet. Exceeding supersonic speed, the generated forces cause the atmosphere to crackle and growl, the earth to rumble.

Turning to his left, he sees the simmering remains of the extraterrestrial vessel. The electricity generated from the fast-moving debris clouds has short-circuited his unknown "hosts'" transport ship. He has no idea whether the craft had been remotely piloted or if there are life forms inside.

Turning to his right, he sees the heavily armed MPs. Emerging from the bunker, they duck low, wary of tornadoes spontaneously blossoming across the open terrain. Grabbing him by his arms and legs, they carry him roughly inside the bunker.

ABOARD THE *BALAM*

NAZCA, PERU

The earth trembles. The trident marking the mountain's western face slides into the sea as the fractures deepen, rending the dispersing geology into an avalanche of rock and soil that collapses upon the Paracas shoreline—revealing the starship *Balam*.

The 722-foot dagger-shaped star cruiser rises into the heavens. Inside the command center, Michael Gabriel grins like a teen given the keys to a new sports car. Thought control has revealed a 360-degree viewport, offering the four passengers a view of the diminishing Peruvian coast.

Dominique squeezes Mick's hand as they pass through the churning volcanic ash, the atmospheric tsunami polishing the *Balam*'s soiled hull to its original golden luster as it rocks the ship.

And then they are through, the sky darkening into space. A billion stars greet them, along with the aurora borealis. Below, the planet's Western Hemisphere is visible, its lower latitudes, from the South Pole to the line of soot just north of the equator, now clear of volcanic ash. The rest of the Earth's clogged heavens continues to drain into space like the sand from an inverted hourglass. The charged atoms of this cosmic rainbow bleed away from the North Pole into a twisting particle stream that rises ten thousand miles above the Earth—where it swirls into the gushing mouth of the strangelet's event horizon.

Kurtz stares at the ominous aperture, the eye of the galactic storm as large as the diameter of the moon. "What the hell is that thing?"

Michael Gabriel is no longer smiling. "It's called a strangelet. Believe it or not, it's a man-made black hole."

"Man created that?" Beck rasps. "Why?"

"Forget the why," Kurtz snaps. "Will it harm the Earth?"

Mick points to the trail of debris being inhaled into the black hole's event horizon. "All that ash is feeding the monster positively charged atomic particles. The particles have given the strangelet size and mass—enough to stabilize it inside the physical universe. When the remains of the volcanic ash are swept into space, the strangelet will be drawn to the planet in order to continue to feed. This time, when it passes through the core, it will consume the entire Earth."

"How do we stop it?"

"I have absolutely no idea."

MAJESTIC-12 (S-66) SUBTERRANEAN FACILITY

The elevator plunges down the subterranean shaft, stopping at Level 29. Secured in shackles, Immanuel Gabriel is dragged down a bright empty corridor and through a security checkpoint.

The prisoner offers no resistance. Manny's mind's eye is absorbed in a bizarre slide show of subliminal images—*Chilam Balam's journey through the sacred cenote's wormhole . . . his capture by Seven Macaw . . . Blood Woman's execution . . . Lilith's decapitated body . . . his journey through the 2047 wormhole*—the images repeating over and over, accompanied by the double pulsating beat of two synchronized hearts.

The pain is sudden—a thousand nails hammered into his flesh, driven deep through his bones. He cries out, instinctively knowing the source. *The heartbeats . . . Jake and I have been conceived. The same soul cannot exist in the same dimension within two separate vessels. I'm being torn apart by the presence of my own fetus!*

Squeezing his eyes shut, he slips inside the Nexus.

Relief is immediate, the gravitational forces easing. He looks around, realizing the corridor of existence bridging the physical universe and the upper realms has changed. Below the soothing ether is a dark hole, its mass latching onto him, attempting to drag him into its swirling orifice.

The strangelet . . . it's crossed through the Nexus.

Rising from the eleventh dimension's portal is Seven Macaw.

The blue-fanged abomination circles Manny, its icy presence terrifying.

Chilam Balam . . . I've waited all eternity for this moment. Enter the dark road and I shall serve as your personal escort into Xibalba.

The surgical suite has three operating tables. Laura Agler is strapped to the first, her twenty-year-old daughter, Sophia, to the second. Pierre Borgia stands next to the gorgeous younger woman, his right hand smoothing her hair back as if she were a pet, his left holding the scalpel.

Leaning on his cane, Joseph Randolph instructs the MPs to handcuff their barely conscious prisoner to the third table. Then he dismisses them.

The white-haired director leans over Manny. "Wake up, Mr. Agler." He slaps his face. No response. "What's wrong with him, Pierre?"

"He's taken refuge in the Nexus."

"Draw him out."

"How?"

Randolph motions to Sophia. "Cut her."

Laura closes her eyes, slipping inside the Nexus. She finds the light of her husband's soul caught in a tug-of-war with the gravitational forces of a black hole, his being circled by a malevolent force of nature, the presence of which curdles her blood cold.

Seven Macaw's red eyes appear from within the vapor, paralyzing Laura in fear. *Blood Woman! How I've missed the taste of your soul. I have the sun, and now I have the moon. And soon I shall possess the souls of every spark of the shattered vessel of creation. And the serpent in the garden shall be the Creator!*

Serpent in the garden . . .

Serpent in the garden.

A surge of adrenaline jolts Manny's being as the words, encoded into his subconscious by his father during their last encounter, reveal their true meaning.

Jacob cleaved to the tree of life that you see before you, which is why his soul remained pure. You were bound to the tree of knowledge, a dark side that cleaves to the human ego . . . As powerful as Jacob was, he could not succeed in the eleventh dimension of Hell without your ability to adapt to the dark side . . .

What you fail to see, Immanuel, is that you are the serpent.

Manny flees the Nexus and opens his eyes, his thoughts focused despite the wave of agony that greets him, his soul's divided presence in the physical universe threatening to unleash every cell in his body like a miniature Big Bang.

The pain is necessary; to free Laura's consciousness from Seven Macaw he must draw the devil out of the Nexus.

Raising his head from the surgical table, he stares at Pierre Borgia. "I can smell you, Seven Macaw. I can smell the sulphurous rubbish of your soul. Face me like a true deity; stop hiding within the flesh of this pathetic human. You call yourself the sun and the moon; you consider yourself a creator? Ha! You are nothing. Show yourself, coward, and I'll descend through Xibalba Be into the eleventh dimension. Continue to hide, and all shall know of your weakness."

Pierre Borgia freezes, his head cocked to one side. After a long moment he turns to speak, his one bloodshot eye blazing red, his voice a throaty rasp. "Chilam Balam?"

Laura's inert form reanimates as she expels a deep gasp, freeing herself from the Nexus.

Laura, can you hear me?

Yes, Sam.

Whatever happens, do not follow me into the Nexus.

Joseph Randolph turns to his nephew. "What's going on? Explain!"

"Answer your master, Seven Macaw. Prostrate yourself like the dog you've become. Lick his hand in obedience."

"Pierre, enough games. Question the Nordic. If he doesn't answer, begin working on his daughter."

"You heard your human master. He gave the sun a direct order; he demanded the moon do his dirty work. Obey, you pathetic bag of bones. Obey your master!"

Tightening his grip on the scalpel, Pierre Borgia whips the blade through the air—slicing open Joseph Randolph's throat. Immanuel Gabriel leaps back inside the Nexus, beckoning his unborn twin, Jacob, from within his mother's shared womb . . .

Dominique's face goes blank, her body rigid, her turquoise eyes widening as her Hunahpu mind receives instructions from her unborn son. Pushing Mick's consciousness aside, she takes command of the *Balam*.

Through the void of space, the starship locates the island of antimatter orbiting Mars.

The *Balam's* artificial intelligence communicates with the post-humans' vessel, activating its propulsion system as Dominique has commanded.

The seed of thought had been planted in Immanuel by his father, nourished by a single troubling thought: after 127 million years, why were his parents still alive?

Michael and Dominique's fused consciousness was controlling the transport ship. Had they truly desired to release their trapped souls through their own physical deaths, they could have simply allowed the vessel's orbit to decay eons ago, sending Phobos hurtling into the surface of Mars.

Only they hadn't. They had maintained control.

Why?

The answer was as simple as it was selfless—they knew Manny would need the vessel on the last day of the fifth cycle.

Now, as Phobos races at light speed toward Earth, Manny releases himself from the Nexus, his consciousness falling into the black depths below—

—his soul entering Hell.

 370

38

Hell is a place, a time, a consciousness . . . in which there is no love.

—RICHARD BACH,
THE BRIDGE ACROSS FOREVER

XIBALBA

ELEVENTH DIMENSION—HELL

The sky is a molten vermillion red, obscured by choking charcoal-gray clouds, like smoke from a petroleum inferno. As his watering eyes adjust to the tremendous heat, Chilam Balam realizes it is not a true sky he is observing, but a simmering subterranean ceiling, located high over a mountainous terrain.

The Jaguar Prophet gazes at what was once a fertile Nazca valley. The landscape is covered in lead-gray volcanic ash, the mountain streams degenerated into swampy cesspools of silvery-brown ooze, stagnant with feces, bones, and the smoldering remains of ashen flesh. Twenty-inch scarab beetles feast upon the offering by the tens of thousands, their sharp mandibles creating a nerve-wracking crunching sound as they feed.

The Mayan city that had been alive with greenery, farmlands, and irrigation canals is a dead zone—a shantytown of soot-covered abodes and ash-laden streets. The fallen temple of Chilam Balam has been replaced by a ten-level pyramid, topped by a summit structure adorned in jade.

The Jaguar Prophet stands between the temple's two main pillars, his arms stretched high and wide, strapped to each support. The stone beneath his bare feet is stained black from the ash, save for a crimson creek of dried blood that originates from the massive *chacmool* situated before him, running down the narrow southern steps to the base below.

The woman is laid out on the *chacmool*'s back, her naked form secured by her four limbs to the stone idol. Blood Woman turns her head to face him, her turquoise eyes filled with terror. "Balam? How is it we are alive?"

"We are not alive, my love. I have entered Xibalba, and because you are my soul mate, you have been cast into Hell with me. Fear not—"

His response is cut off by the thundering metal reverberations of a gong, its sound summoning the people to the base of the temple. A procession of grunting, moaning, mutilated transhumans exit their shanties, making their way through the streets. Some of the beings lack legs, others arms. They are dressed in heavy soot-covered robes, their elongated skulls tucked inside hoods. Exposed flesh has long disappeared beneath adhering layers of mouse-gray silicon, giving their faces a heavily pruned appearance. Neanderthal-like brows protect dark, deeply set eyes. Noses and surrounding cartilage are missing, leaving behind only open nasal passages from which they expel a fine ebony mist with each excruciating exhalation. Lipless mouths remain slack-jawed, exposing teeth caked with atmospheric dust and film.

Like cattle, these tortured souls push and prod each other, inching their way closer to the pyramid to receive a morsel of sustaining light from their oppressor.

Seven Macaw exits the jade temple to greet his followers, raising his tattooed arms triumphantly to the gathered flock. "I am great. My place is now higher than that of the human work, the human design. I am the sun and the moon, I am the light, and I am also the months. I am the walkway and I am the foothold of the people. And now I am the vanquisher of man, my power as great as that of the Creator."

Seven Macaw faces his prisoner, his red upturned eyes dancing from the glow of a dozen torches, his fanged grin stained blue. "Chilam Balam . . .

at last. I have chased your soul since the vessel Adam rejected the Creator's light. Our fates have remained connected throughout existence, every new rebirth of your physicality spawning my own, each reincarnation ending in your death by my hand, along with that of your soul mate. The souls of your deceased followers have kept me nourished these last six hundred years; now, with the end of the fifth cycle I shall finally drink from your light. Welcome to Xibalba, Chilam Balam. Your soul is mine for all eternity."

Balam smiles at the Mayan death god. "No, Seven Macaw, it is you who are mine."

The subterranean ceiling fractures and crumbles, exposing the transdimensional portal to the underworld—an emerald-green vortex. The stranglet's eye opens to the stars, revealing a brilliant orange speck streaking across the dark cosmos. Guided by the hero twin's consciousness, it soars toward the funneled opening, growing larger with each passing second.

A suddenly panic-stricken Seven Macaw grabs Chilam Balam by his long dark hair, his fanged mouth pressed against the prophet's right ear. "How are you doing this? As a spark of the Creator you have no power in the eleventh dimension!"

"I share a soul with my twin. His half was nourished by the tree of life, mine by the tree of knowledge. I was conceived for this very moment. I am Chilam Balam—the dark prophet. I am the serpent in *your* garden!"

The celestial object fills the entire eye of the stranglet's event horizon, its light cleansing the lost souls of Xibalba. Gray silicon melts away, yielding to revitalized flesh and limbs. Chilam Balam's followers ascend the pyramid steps, drawn to the light of the Jaguar Prophet.

Seven Macaw's face morphs into the angelic appearance of Devlin Mabus. The Seraph sprouts a pair of massive wings, keeping the people at bay. "You cannot win, Uncle."

"It's not about winning. The end of the fifth cycle is about man transforming his negative behavior, recognizing—finally—that we are all sparks of the collective soul. Love, Devlin, can transform the darkest depths of Hell into the brightest heaven."

Born from energy dispersed during the near-light-speed collision of matter, the monster had nursed in a parallel dimension. Feeding from the Earth's core, it had outgrown its womb, its coalescing gravitational forces crushing a path into the physical universe. Inhaling a mass-stabilizing meal of volcanic ash, it had breached adolescence into adulthood to become a fully formed black hole, its infinite orifice consuming everything venturing near its event horizon, from gaseous debris to stellar light.

The monster registers the Earth's gravitational forces. Unable to move the massive planet, the strangelet latches onto the watery world like a magnet drawn to steel. Though smaller than the Earth, the black hole's mass equals that of a dozen suns. In the physical universe the rules are simple: size yields to density, atomic structure to gravity.

The monster will consume the planet and nest in its cosmic vacancy. Over time it will continue to grow, until it replaces the sun as the gravitational center of the solar system. Eventually it will consume every planet and asteroid and moon caught within its vortex until it inhales the sun itself—extinguishing the light.

The monster never detects the moon-size object until the ship plunges unannounced through its gullet and detonates. Like acid on flesh, the particle wave of escaping antimatter from the transport ship's engines burns through the strangelet's atomic structure, disrupting the sweeping tide of its gravitational vortex.

The event horizon ceases spinning. The eye of the beast flutters and closes.

Birthed in an instant, the strangelet dies in an instant, choking on a belch of antimatter.

Mick squeezes Dominique's hand as a streaking bolt of orange light soars past the *Balam* and disappears into the black hole as if guided by the hand of God.

For a split second nothing happens. Then a soft white ethereal light bursts silently in space and is gone—sealing the black hole with it.

The four passengers exhale. Then they smile and cry and hug one another, their bodies trembling with adrenaline and fatigue.

Embracing his soul mate, Michael Gabriel gazes through the *Balam*'s massive portal at the Earth. The planet's atmosphere appears blue and clear, their preserved home world offering humanity a second chance.

39

Destiny is no matter of chance. It is a matter of choice: it
is not a thing to be waited for, it is a thing to be achieved.

—WILLIAM JENNINGS BRYAN

M anny, follow my voice . . ."
    *Lying in the pit in bone-deep cold through an
eternity of emptiness and darkness, he detects the pattern of
pink behind eyelids sealed in amber.*

"—try to open your eyes."

*He struggles against an immovable weight until he
realizes he has no arms.*

"Fight your way out. Create pain."

*He stands amid blackness and feels for the wall, bloody-
ing the cold stone with his face. Over and over he strikes the
dungeonlike enclosure until he finds his hands tingling somewhere in the abyss. Encouraged, he bashes the pit's rounded
walls harder, all the while opening and closing his long-lost
appendages, the pain giving birth to arms. His fingers walk
up his broken upper torso to the diseased flesh he has bashed
into pulp and claw at the amber sealing his eyes until he
unveils the light—*

—an onion-shaped chamber, its curved onyx walls illuminated in multicolored controls, encircled by a 360-degree viewport of the Earth, as seen from space.

His soul mate leans over and kisses him. "Welcome back."

"Laura?" He sits up and hugs his wife, his energy spent. "I missed you terribly. What happened? Where are we? Where's Sophia?"

"I'm here, Dad."

Immanuel turns toward the hologram, the image of a Las Vegas hotel suite appearing in the center of the command post. His daughter is standing between Mick and Dominique. Kurtz and Beck are seated in the background, the two bodyguards eating room service on a balcony facing the Strip.

"I don't understand? Laura, where are we? Where's Sophia?"

"She's safe, back on Earth. We're aboard the *Balam* . . . inside the Nexus."

"The *Balam*? How? Why?"

"You're aboard the *Balam* because I'm pregnant," Dominique answers, offering a wry grin. "We had no choice. You were dying, Manny. Apparently, the same soul can't exist simultaneously in two different vessels during the same time."

"We landed after the Mars moon sealed the strangelet," Mick explains. "The starship protected you by moving into the Nexus. The dimensional corridor will keep the cruiser hidden from radar and telescopes."

"But what happens when I'm born . . . again?"

Laura helps him to his feet. "It'll be okay. Come, I want to show you something." She escorts him to the viewport.

"My God . . ." Swirling out in space is a wormhole, its event horizon stable and beckoning. Hovering close to the entrance are several hundred extraterrestrial vessels of varying sizes and shapes.

"What are they doing out there?"

She squeezes his hand. "They're waiting for you."

"The wormhole . . . where do you think it leads?"

"I don't know, baby. How about we find out together?"

"Laura, no . . . I can't let you do that."

"I'm coming with you, Sam . . . er, Manny. Sorry, that's going to take some getting used to. But we were meant to be together, I know that for sure. So just dismiss any thoughts of leaving me behind. I waited eleven years to be with you, now you're stuck with me. Besides, I'm Hunahpu, too."

He leans in and kisses her. "What about Sophia?"

"I'm going to stay behind," his daughter replies. "Mick and Dom said I can stay with them. It's going to be hard to be normal again, but I have to try. Besides, they'll need help with the twins." She smiles. "How many people can say they babysat their own father?"

"The child won't be your father," Mick says. "The time loop has been unraveled, your father's lifespan is a loose end, not a repeating circuit of space-time. Whatever happens from this point forward can't be prophesied. Maybe that's a good thing."

Kurtz joins them. "The president knows what you did, Manny. He's keeping it quiet, but your family will be well taken care of. Mick used the *Balam* to destroy the underground complex at Groom Lake. Majestic-12 is history."

"What about Borgia?"

"Borgia's in jail for murdering Randolph. They should both rot in Hell."

"Mitch, there's something I need you and Beck to do for me. It's very important."

"Name it."

The *Balam* leaves Earth's orbit, gliding silently toward the entrance to the wormhole. Immanuel Gabriel hugs his wife and soul mate, his heart full—

—a new destiny awaiting.

With a sudden surge, the golden starship enters the conduit, the extra-terrestrial ships following in its wake.

Seconds later, the wormhole disappears, transporting its passengers across time and space.

40

Once more unto the breach, dear friends . . .
—**WILLIAM SHAKESPEARE,** *HENRY V*

BELLE GLADE, FLORIDA
SEPTEMBER 22, 2013
12:21 A.M.

Seventeen-year-old Madelina Aurelia thrashes naked beneath a sweat-soaked bedsheet as she cries out to her foster father, "Get this goddamn baby outta me!"

Quenton Morehead, an ordained minister and struggling alcoholic, squeezes the teenaged girl's hand, his dark eyes lingering on her exposed pelvis. "Don't blaspheme, child, the midwife's on her way."

"Where's Virgil?"

"I don't know."

"Find him!"

The minister cringes as the girl's high-pitched screech penetrates his brain like a tuning fork. He hears the front door open and sighs a quick *Amen.*

"Virge?" Madelina stops thrashing. "Virgil, honey? That you . . . you cheatin', whorin' sonuva bitch!"

A heavyset black woman enters. "Calm down, baby, everthin' gonna be just fine."

Madelina tears at the mattress as another contraction grips her torso. "Vir . . . gil!"

The midwife turns to the minister. "Go on and find him. I can handle things here."

Quenton backs out of the bedroom, then hurries out the front door of the sweltering stucco home and into the night.

Reverend Morehead enters the strip club fifteen minutes later, his senses immediately seized by the smell of alcohol and smoke and sex. He heads for the bar, then sees his son-in-law in a back room, receiving a lap dance.

"Virgil! Get your heathen butt home, your son's on the way."

"Aww shit, Quenton, give me two more minutes."

"Now, boy!"

"Sum'bitch." Virgil climbs out from beneath the stripper, squeezes an exposed breast, whispers, "I'll be back soon," then follows Quenton into the parking lot.

TEMPLE UNIVERSITY HOSPITAL

PHILADELPHIA, PENNSYLVANIA

12:43 A.M.

Dominique Gabriel gazes through feverish eyes at her foster mother, Edith Axler, as another contraction begins. The wave of pain crests higher, the pain excruciating. "Edie, get me drugs!"

"Hang in there, doll. Mick went to get the doctor."

"I need drugs, now!"

"Okay, okay." Edith rushes out of the birthing room to find the nurse.

"You do not need drugs," says Chicahua. "The uterus is a woman's center. If the uterus is not in proper position during birth, nothing in the child's life will be right." Placing her hands on Dominique's pelvis, she begins to massage the exterior of her daughter's swollen abdomen and lower back, softening the muscles while repositioning the uterus.

Mick enters the room a moment later, in time to see the old woman extracting a red-faced newborn from his wife's birth canal. "What the hell are you doing?"

"What I have done since before you were born." She spanks the blood-streaked, fair-haired child lightly on its rump, encouraging an air-breathing gasp. "Hold your son while I fetch his brother."

Michael Gabriel stares teary-eyed at his offspring, the child's eyes wide and azure blue. "Hey, Jake. Daddy's here for you this time, pal."

Moments later, Jacob Gabriel's dark-haired brother is born, announcing his arrival with a healthy wail.

BELLE GLADE, FLORIDA

12:57 A.M.

Reverend Morehead hears the sounds of a baby crying as he reenters the sweltering stucco home. "Madelina?"

The rotund midwife is in the kitchen, an infant in her arms. "Look. There's your grandpa. Say hi, Grandpa!"

"My Lord, will you look at his eyes, I've never seen eyes so blue."

"Silly, it's not a he, she's a little girl."

"A girl?" Quenton feels the hairs raise along the back of his neck. "Where's the father?"

"Puking his guts up outside. Quickly, take the child and—"

The screen door slams open and Virgil approaches, a line of spittle running from his lower lip to his stained T-shirt, a ring of white powder visible in his left nostril. "Okay, le' me see my boy."

Quenton and the midwife exchange frightened looks. "Now, Virgil, take it easy. We need to talk." The minister steps in front of the wailing infant.

"Outta my way, Quenton, I said I wanna see my son."

"Virgil, the Lord . . . the Lord has blessed you with a child. A daughter."

Virgil stops. Facial muscles contort into a mask of rage. "A girl?"

"Easy, son—"

"A girl ain't shit! A girl's nuthin' but another goddamn mouth to feed and clothe and listen to her whining." He points at the screaming infant. "Give her to me!"

"No." Quenton holds his ground. The nurse stands, preparing to flee with the child.

"I want you to sober up, Virgil. I want you to go to my home and—"

Virgil punches the minister in the gut, dropping him to his knees.

The midwife tucks the infant under one arm, brandishing a kitchen knife in the other. "Y'all git outta here, Virgil. Go on!"

Virgil stares at the blade quivering in the fat woman's fist. In one motion he grabs her wrist, wrenching the knife free.

The midwife screams, backing away.

Virgil stares at the infant, then hears someone moaning from inside the bedroom. "Madelina? You're dead . . ." Wielding the knife, he ducks inside the bedroom, locking the door behind him—

—surprised to find a massive black man inside, seated in a folding chair.

Ryan Beck looks up from reading the newspaper. "Evening, Virgil."

"Who the hell are you? Where's my wife?"

"Someplace safe. You'll be happy to know her Uncle Sam is going to take care of her from now on, along with your daughter, Lilith. Your little girl will be raised in a safe, loving environment away from you and her pedophile grandfather."

"That so?" He brandishes the knife. "What's in it for me?"

"For you? A hearty congratulations." Beck smiles. "You've won a Darwin award."

"Darwin award? What the hell's that?"

"It's an award given to those who remove themselves from the human gene pool in order to improve it."

Beck joins Kurtz in the van ten minutes later. The former CIA assassin is cradling the turquoise-eyed newborn. Madelina is sedated in back.

"She's a cutie, isn't she?"

"Yeah."

"How'd her old man die?"

"He accidentally stuck a butcher knife up his own ass."

"Hey, it happens." Handing Lilith Eve Aurelia to his friend, Kurtz drives the van, heading for the commuter airport.

EPILOGUE

*When the power of love overcomes the love of power,
the world will know peace.*

—ATTRIBUTED TO SRI CHINMOY GHOSE

Evelyn Mohr opens her eyes. The world is spinning in vertigo, her flesh tingling. For a moment she fears she has been struck by lightning, then she remembers.

The cruise ship . . . the hole in the Atlantic!

She is lying on her side in a darkness so complete she cannot see her hand in front of her face. She can hear grunts and groans, but she has no idea where she is. Feeling around the carpet, she manages to locate her i-glasses. Tries to contact her husband, Dave, but gets only static.

Adjusting the smart glasses' setting, she changes the lenses from tint to night vision. The impenetrable blackness becomes an olive-green corridor, harboring several dozen bathing suit–clad passengers, sprawled out in clusters. Most remain unconscious; a few are sitting up, disoriented, their eyes glowing a nocturnal silver.

Searching the corridor, Evelyn locates the steel hatch leading outside. Standing on wobbly legs, she pushes open the watertight door and ventures out onto one of the ship's privacy sun decks.

"Oh my . . ."

The sun is long gone, the night sky sparkling with constellations and nebulae and distant spiral galaxies as vivid as images taken from the newest Earth-orbiting telescopes. To the north she sees Jupiter, as big as the moon, its moons twinkling like diamond dust. To the east is Saturn; beyond, Neptune—a neon-blue dot partially eclipsed by its sister planet's rings of ice.

Her eyes catch movement in the heavens—two small moons. One orbits directly overhead, the other is moving unusually fast, rapidly dipping toward the inky ocean horizon.

"Where the hell are we?"

"A different time, a different place."

She sees him standing by the guardrail, a lanky Adonis with long dark hair and a bodybuilder's physique. His eyes appear azure blue in the lunar light.

Evelyn approaches. "You're Anna's friend, the one who saved me."

"Julian. And you're Evelyn, Dave Mohr's wife."

Her heart races. "Did Lilith send you?"

"My mother sent me. You can trust me, I'm a friend."

"What happened to us?"

"The cruise ship was dragged down a wormhole. Our presence in the portal created an alternative universe of space-time."

"You sound like my husband."

"Your husband no longer exists; he won't be born for another 127 million years."

"What?" Her throat constricts as other passengers join them. "How is that possible?"

"Look around you. This isn't Earth, Evelyn. It's Mars—back when the Red Planet was green and possessed an atmosphere . . . just before the great cataclysm." He suddenly pauses, his eyes darting to focus on the water. "They found us. Everyone back inside the ship!"

The gathering crowd shoves its way back inside the corridor.

Evelyn grabs onto Julian to keep from being dragged away, her eyes catching a glimpse of the terrifying lizardlike creatures surfacing off the starboard bow. "Who are you? The truth!"

"My name is Julian Agler Gabriel. My friends call me Jag. Like my mother, Sophia, I'm full-blooded Hunahpu."

"Why are you here?"

"I'm here to ensure humanity's future."

He drags her inside, securing the hatch behind them as the predatory reptilian Martian race begins its assault on the *Paradise Lost*—Phobos reappearing on the western horizon, glowing orange in the alien night sky.

To be continued . . .

Visit www.SteveAlten.com
for a sneak peek.

 384